PSION BETA

PSION BETA

BY

JACOB GOWANS

Published by Jacob Gowans 2010

For Kat, my Gefjon

Acknowledgments

Thank you for picking up this novel. This small segment can't adequately express my excitement to share my story with you in print, nor can it properly describe how appreciative I am to you, first of all, for reading it, and also to several others whose aid in this work has allowed me to conquer the insurmountable task of writing, editing, and publishing my first novel. Please allow me to take a moment and acknowledge some of them by name.

For those who read early or late drafts and edited them to varying degrees of completion, thank you: James Nelson, Bret Wright, Kerry Dunn, Megan Bostic, Tracy Walshaw, the members of The Writing Bridge, Braden Atkins, Lewis Gunter, Jimmy Dunn, Scott Peterson, Thomas (The Cheat) Barber, Adam (The Sneak) Morris, Shannon Wilkinson, Adam Gowans, Floyd Gowans, Carol Crosby, Matt Crosby, and anyone else whom I may have missed over the 4+ years of work. For inexhaustible enthusiasm: David Collette.

Worthy of special mention is Lacy Chaffee, who prepared the manuscript, edited and formatted with a scrutinizing eye, and made insightful suggestions; and also Britta Peterson who prepared the cover art and fonts for the book. Both helped me visualize and realize my dream.

Two more people I must mention whose assistance has been immeasurable. The first is Kirk Anderson. Kirk came on board early in the game and never let me lose hope. His unfaltering encouragement for *Psion Beta* bolstered me in times of rejection and made me believe in myself. His words of wisdom kindled my spirit many times. The second is my wife, Kathryn. Without her sacrifice of time that could have been spent with her, I would still be writing my early manuscripts. She has lifted me and voiced her confidence when times were the best and the worst.

Psion Beta

1 | **Brains**

THE STREET LIGHTS of downtown Johannesburg cast long shadows through the dirty front windows of an abandoned grocery store. Sammy stayed in the shadows as he darted from one hiding place to another. The air around him felt cool, but sweat rolled down his forehead to the end of his stubby brown nose. He crouched behind the customer service desk at the front of the store and listened for signs of someone approaching.

As he listened, he blew the perspiration off the end of his nose with a puff. It was quiet enough to hear the tiny splash as it hit the floor. Not far away, where the shopping carts stood, someone's shoe scuffed the floor. Sammy jerked his head in that direction, banged his cheek on the corner of the desk, and bit his tongue. The taste of blood reminded him how long it had been since his last meal.

I need to go some place they won't think of, he decided. He thought of the stock room behind him. He paused to listen again, fingering the weapon stowed in his pocket. An ambulance siren wailed as it passed the store. Sammy took advantage of the moment and eased open the stock room door just enough to worm his long body through the crack.

The room became almost pitch black when the door closed. Sammy walked with his hands outstretched, waiting to bump into the ladder he already knew was attached to the back wall. When he reached the ladder, he smiled.

No way they'll look for me up here, he thought as he climbed.

At the top, he steadied himself with one hand and used the other to push on the foam tile above him. The square gave way, but a shower of dust fell on him—his first shower in weeks. Struggling not to cough, he poked his head into the ceiling space. It was much brighter than in the room below him. Cracks in the ceiling tiles allowed dim shafts of light to stream in. It was enough illumination for Sammy to see a service walkway suspended from the roof.

He pulled himself all the way up, slowly putting his weight on the walkway. It held firm without creaking. Once he stood at his full height, he gave the platform a test bounce.

"Good," Sammy whispered. "I don't want to die."

Using the cracks in the ceiling as spy holes into the main store, he went on the hunt. In less than a minute, he spotted someone creeping around in one of the aisles. The person below was tall and wore faded fatigues; his left forearm sported over a dozen watches, each face reflecting a tiny point of light. In his right hand, he held a weapon similar to Sammy's. Sammy knelt down on the walkway and lifted the nearest tile. His eyes never left the target as he took the weapon out of his pocket, put it in his mouth, and blew.

The only sound was a tiny whistle as the projectile flew out of the end of the tube, followed by a dull thump as it connected with its target. The camouflaged shoulders arched backward as it struck right between his shoulder blades. Sammy noted his good aim with satisfaction. His enemy motionless on the floor, he replaced the tile and moved on.

The next two targets he found together, working in sync, systematically moving from aisle to aisle at opposite ends. They probably hoped they could trap Sammy inside one of them. Reloading his tube as he walked down the platform, Sammy positioned himself at the end of the next aisle and waited for the one directly beneath him to leave his partner's line of sight.

This shot was even easier than the last. Sammy hit him on the side of the neck and dropped him. The third target, however, got spooked when his partner did not appear, and took cover in one of the broken freezers at the end of an aisle.

The target seemed to have no intention of coming out of hiding. Sammy tried to get a decent shot while still standing on the platform, but could not do it. In a bold move, he lay across the platform and a foam square, keeping as much of his weight on the walkway as possible. His hands shook more than before as he imagined himself falling through the brittle squares onto the metal shelves below him. With one hand holding up the tile, and the other steadying the weapon in his mouth, he took careful aim. He leaned . . . leaned . . . fired.

He heard a thump.

A perfect shot to the ribs! Sammy shook his hand in a fist of triumph. *One left.*

At that same instant, movement in the corner of his eye caught his attention. Sammy tried to adjust his body to face the source, but it was too late. A sharp pain stabbed his chest just below his collar bone, and the foam crumpled beneath him. His fingers scrambled to find something to clutch on to, anything to slow the fall, but they tore through the foam as his legs slipped off the walkway.

He screamed as he tumbled headfirst toward the shelves. His mind whirled in the panic of certain death as his arms and legs flailed uselessly around him. Then, just before he hit the metal shelf, something happened: for a fraction of a second, he slowed in mid-air. He felt it, though only barely—like hitting a thick pocket of warm air and bouncing off it. As he slowed, the weight of his legs flipped him over just in time, and he landed on his back instead of his head.

With a thundering crash, his body slammed into the top shelf. The impact forced the air out of his lungs. A second smaller crash rang out as his shelf collapsed into the one below. He stopped there, motionless and eyes closed. "I'm alive," he said, swallowing air in an attempt to regain his wind. *I'm alive. I'm alive. I'm really alive.*

Sammy heard the sound of his shooter running toward him, swearing under his breath.

"Brains!" Sammy's friend, Feet, hollered as he ran. Feet was breathing almost as hard as Sammy. "Brains, you all right?"

Sammy opened his eyes and saw his friend's pale shocked face. "Yeah—yeah, I'm fine. My back's going to be bruised, but I'm fine."

"I had no idea," Feet gasped for air, "you'd fall like that."

Sammy accepted his friend's hand and let himself be pulled off the shelf. "Did you see what happened?"

"Yeah, man. Scary!" He stared at the wreckage of the shelves. "Sure you're okay?"

"No—yes. I slowed down in mid-air!" Sammy said. His voice cracked with excitement. "I slowed down!"

Feet grinned, then laughed. "Whatever."

"No, I'm serious."

The grin stayed on Feet's face. The giddiness of getting away with doing something very, very stupid was settling into Sammy, too. "Well, at least you're not dead. Sure you didn't just land right?"

Sammy replayed the fall in his mind from beginning to end. "I'm sure. I felt it."

But Feet just shrugged his shoulders. "You saying you flew? That's nutty, man."

Sammy tried very hard not to sound as crazy as Feet thought he was. "I didn't fly. I slowed down."

"Then you landed right," Feet insisted.

Sammy considered arguing again, but decided against it.

"I think we should make the ceiling off limits," Feet continued, "just to be safe."

Sammy nodded, but was still thinking about the fall. *I didn't imagine it*, he told himself. Feet gave him a playful shove, driving those thoughts temporarily out of his mind.

"Hear me, Brains?"

The others were approaching now.

"No, I didn't."

"I said you should've been quicker."

"I can't believe you were behind those pallets." His face now mirrored the wicked grin his friend wore. "I looked everywhere for you."

"Obviously not everywhere," Feet shot back, "or you'd have seen me. Nice thinking, though—going up in the ceiling."

"That was the whole point. Catch you off guard."

"How'd you do it? Fly?"

"Ha ha." Sammy returned Feet's shove. "There's a ladder in one of the storage rooms in the front of the store."

"Yeah . . . never thought of that."

"Three months here and you've never thought about doing that?"

"Who lost? Who lost?" said short and plump Chuckles from behind Sammy, poking him in the back repeatedly. "Brains lost! Brains lost!"

Sammy made a rude gesture to Chuckles. "Shove it up your hole. I took you out. You didn't even come close to touching me."

"You still lost."

"That puts me—uh—three wins in the lead, Brains?" Feet asked. He had an innocent expression on his face that Sammy saw right through.

He pushed Feet again. "Don't give me that crap. Like you really lost track of your wins."

"Maybe if you stopped trying to be a one-man show you'd win more games," Chuckles said. "Right, Feet?"

"What do you mean?" Sammy asked.

Fro-yo's voice came from several aisles over, swearing repeatedly. "Who's got my peashooter?"

"Crap," Chuckles muttered, looking at the peashooter in his pudgy hand. "I'm pretty sure this one's mine, but I don't really know 'cuz I dropped mine after you hit me. Stupid thing must have rolled halfway across the store."

Chuckles wandered off in the direction of Fro-yo's voice.

"That a welt?" Feet asked, pointing to the spot where his marble had hit Sammy.

Sammy pulled down the neck of his hoodie and showed his friend. Feet grimaced when he saw the large bruise forming on Sammy's chest. "And," Sammy reminded him, "I'll probably have more just like that all over my back."

"What hurts more?" Feet asked. "The bruises or me being three games up on you?" He snickered at his own joke.

"Oh please, just shut it." Then Sammy lowered his voice as he asked, "What was Chuck talking about? Does everyone think that about me? That I'm a one-man show? "

Feet's answer did not come immediately. "No, Brains. But . . . you should probably start relying on your team, you know, maybe a little more."

"What's that supposed to mean?"

"Nothing." Feet's answer came too quickly.

"No, what did you mean?"

Feet kicked at one of the bottom shelves still intact and shrugged. "C'mon, man, you know what I mean."

Sammy responded with a grunt and vigorously rubbed the spot on his shoulder where he had been hit. He liked Chuckles the least anyway. Who cared what he thought? He cursed again as he looked at the spot on his chest. The thick hoodie had done little to cushion the shot. He would indeed have a full-blown welt within the hour.

"That's got to hurt nasty," Feet said as he inspected the bruise closer.

"I'll just add it to my collection. Remember the one on my butt? That only just went away."

Just then, Watch showed up, complaining about a large purple and blue bump on his back and how three of his watches were no longer ticking the time. Sammy had to admit to himself that maybe he'd gotten off lucky—but it was Feet who had won. That always burned.

That's all right, Sammy told himself. *I'll get him in the next game.*

Feet was Sammy's greatest adversary and best friend. They looked absolutely nothing alike but had everything in common. Sammy was tall with chalky brown skin and a powerful build for his age; Feet stood a good ten centimeters shorter, pale skinned with jet black hair and blue eyes that shined with much more intelligence than he let on. Because they were acknowledged by the gang as the best army players out of the seven, they were never allowed to play on the same team. The rule only fueled their competition.

Watch piped up, "So what's next on the evening's agenda?"

"Where's Honk and Gunner?" Sammy asked.

"Oh, good question. Where's Honk and Gunner?"

Gunner called out far down the aisle, another tall kid but paler and with thick glasses that always seemed on the verge of slipping from his nose. He and Honk carried about a dozen pizzas between the two of them.

Feet turned to Sammy with a raised eyebrow, silently asking what he was thinking.

"Where did the food come from?" Sammy asked them.

Honk and Gunner exchanged smirks. "Pizza Pop's down the street—like you needed to ask. Ain't eaten nothing since yesterday morning. My stomach's been screaming like a son of a—"

Sammy swore and spat a piece of dust out of his mouth. "What if you'd been caught? They catch you and we all go straight back to the Grinder! You know how lucky it is we even found this place?"

"Don't be a hypocrite!" Gunner shouted, but then Feet stepped between Sammy and the boys with pizzas. "No, Feet. For real. Whenever Sammy's the one who's starving, it's fine to steal, but—"

"Chill," Feet interrupted. He turned to Sammy. "Brains, come on, we need the food. Honk, Gunner, you really should have run it by all of us before you did it. Don't be nutty, man."

"Chuckles told us to go get it after he took us out of the game," Gunner complained.

Sammy could not ignore the rumblings in his stomach. This was not the first time he had eaten something he should have paid for; it likely wouldn't be the last, either. Besides, how could he ask for more than a piping hot pizza when his last four meals had come from cold, smelly dumpsters?

The fresh food raised everyone's spirits, Sammy's especially. The night was cool and young, and his belly was almost filled. All thoughts of the falling incident were forgotten when Gunner challenged Chuckles to see who could eat more slices. When Chuckles won on the ninth slice, the boys needed something else to do. That was the problem with life as fugitives: getting bored happened too often, and sooner or later one or more of the boys left to steal whatever they could get their hands on.

"Now what?" Fro-yo asked.

"Manhunt?" Sammy said. He loved playing games. It was easy to lose himself in the competition. The bad memories went away.

"Come on, we just played a game," Honker said, wiping his large, chronically dripping nose.

"I'm down with a run of flags," Gunner said.

"Sure, flags," Sammy said, finalizing the decision.

"How long will the game be?" Watch asked as he set the timer on his favorite digital watch. "There's a late movie tonight me and Honk are gonna sneak into. It sounds like there's a lot of boobies."

"Two— two and half hours?" Sammy suggested. Anything to keep his friends off the street for a little longer.

"That's too long," Chuckles said. "Last time we played for only an hour and a half, and both teams stole the flag almost a dozen times each."

"Just because you have trouble counting above ten with your shoes on," Sammy said, and several others laughed.

"Very funny," Chuckles said, taking a meaty swipe at Sammy's arm, but missing badly. "Me, Brains, Honk, and Gunner against Fro-yo, Watch, and Feet," he said, counting off. "Two hour time limit. Watch, make sure you're honest on the time. Everyone has to go to the customer service counter and touch—did you hear that Fro?—*touch* the register before you can throw a ball after you've been hit."

"Sounds great," Sammy said. "Who's got my balls?"

They all laughed again.

"I do," Honk said, swaggering. Gunner gave Honk a push, and Honk handed green-glowing tennis balls to Sammy, Chuckles, and Gunner, and blue-glowing racquet balls to the others.

Sammy led his three teammates to their side of the store where they set up their first flag. The store was so dark now that the flag could not be seen from a distance of more than a few meters. Sammy turned to his teammates and asked quietly, "Who's guarding the base?"

Honk whispered, "I'm on that."

"All right, just don't get ambushed. And make sure you muffle your sneezes. Remember the last time you had sneezing fits? You sounded like a flock of peahens."

"A flock of what?" Honk asked.

Sammy ignored his question. "Everyone else just play offense, got it?"

"Don't you think we should have some kind of a team strategy this time, Brains?" Chuckles muttered.

"Hmm, yeah, let's think." Sammy tapped his chin in a mocking gesture. "Strategy . . . strategy . . . how about get more flags than the other team?"

Chuckles blew a raspberry and muttered something that sounded like "one-man show." A retort was on the tip of Sammy's tongue when a shrill whistle sounded.

"They're coming," Gunner said.

"We're gonna get slaughtered," Chuckles said as he crept away.

Sammy repressed the urge to throw his ball into the back of Chuckles' head. Instead, he snuck off in the opposite direction, jamming the green-glowing tennis ball into the pocket of his sweatshirt. He stalked up the main row, looking for a blue light and listening for the sound of footsteps.

He heard the double doors in the back of the store swing open and shut again.

"Hey! Out of bounds," Sammy called. "That's a point for the other team."

As soon as he shouted, footsteps came toward him. He dashed into an aisle and hid on the floor under a low shelf. He waited there until the footsteps moved past him. More came, but this time he heard them in the aisle just ahead.

Chuckles's voice taunted in the same vicinity, "I see you."

Then Sammy heard something unexpected: the sound of compressed air being discharged from the standard-issue electroshock weapon only police were allowed to carry.

Chuckles gasped, and Sammy heard his friend's heavy body hit the floor hard.

More footsteps. Footsteps all around!

He knew what was going on: the pizzas.

"Shocks!" he screamed. "The Shocks! RUN! Get out!"

Two beams of light pierced the dark. Combined with Sammy's adrenaline rush, the store now seemed much brighter. His ears picked up every noise as he ran down the aisle to find Feet, and hoping the Shocks wouldn't find him first.

Another voice rang out, this time an older man's: "Attention children. You are all under arrest for theft and trespassing. Officers have surrounded the vicinity. You are ordered to give yourselves up."

Sammy snickered despite his situation. None of them would "give themselves up." The weight of the pact the gang had made before escaping the Grinder was stronger than their fear of the Shocks. Even still, his desperation grew as he hurried into another aisle to find his friend. He turned the corner and ran straight into him. Sammy's jaw smacked Feet's forehead, and both friends hit the ground.

Feet got up first and helped Sammy, asking in a whisper, "Do you know where anyone else is?"

"No."

"Do the Shocks know where we are?"

"I don't think so."

They heard footsteps approaching quietly from behind. It was only Fro-yo and Gunner.

"They got Honk and Watch," Fro said.

"And Chuckles," Sammy added.

Feet swore under his breath. "Get us out of here, Brains."

Sammy's brain gathered and assembled the data like a machine. *Six to twelve Shocks. All armed. Four of us—unarmed. Need cover, weapons. Two Shocks came in from back door. Front doors, side doors still being watched. Best chance … what's our best chance?*

"We're agreed that we're not going down without a fight?" he asked in a whisper.

All three gave him affirmative answers. His friends upheld the oath. That was what he wanted to hear. Sammy calculated more factors into consideration. *The shopping carts are only six—no, seven meters away. Need to distract Shocks.*

He took out the ball in his pocket and threw it as far from the carts as he could. It bounced on the top of a shelf. "Over here," a Shock said.

Sammy heard them running to the noise. "Okay, quiet. Follow me."

Sammy led them to the front of the store and motioned for them to each grab a shopping cart. "Go," he whispered to them. "Go and don't stop."

The wheels of the cart squealed loudly on the floor as the four boys sprinted to the back of the store through the narrow rows. Sammy was slow next to Feet, but by no means a turtle. A bright light shined down their aisle, right into Sammy's eyes.

"Stop right there!" a voice ordered them ahead. But instead of obeying, they ran harder and tilted the front of the carts up to shield themselves.

The Shocks fired at them, but the puffs of air were followed by the sound of metal bouncing off metal. Jolts ricocheted off the carts and electric blue sparks created tiny fireworks in all directions. The heat of the sparks on Sammy's face made him giddy with fear and the insanity of the moment. The Shocks shouted again for them to stop, realizing too late that they could not intimidate the boys.

Sammy and Feet rammed them, sending them sprawling out onto the dusty floor. Sammy picked up the shocker that clattered on the ground. Fro-yo and Gunner were first to reach the double doors in the back of the store and pushed through them with their carts. Feet continued pushing his cart while Sammy ran behind, holding the weapon ready to fire.

"Give it to Gunner," Feet said, reaching for the weapon.

Sammy pulled it out of his friend's reach and asked, "Why?"

"He shoots better."

"No, he doesn't."

They ran for the main exit in the rear of the store that loomed ahead. A Shock stepped out from behind a garbage compressor. His beam pointed square at Sammy's chest. "Drop it! NOW!"

Sammy threw himself behind the cover of Feet's cart and fired at the Shock first. His hands trembled so badly that he missed all three shots. The Shock stood his ground and returned fire. Feet snatched the weapon from Sammy, let go of the cart, and fired off three more jolts.

A shiny triangle formed by three metal darts hit the Shock in his neck. Just as the man reached up to pull the jolt out of his skin, it activated, dropping him to his knees in convulsions and finally rendering him unconscious.

Feet cursed badly, then crossed himself and said, "I've just nailed a Shock. I'm so dead if we get caught."

Fro-yo and Gunner abandoned their carts while Feet picked up the second shocker and tossed it to Gunner. They burst through the back door into the cool night, still running.

The back of the store opened into an alley with two exits. They went left. Halfway to the main street, they heard the door behind them slam open again. Sammy turned to see the other two Shocks coming out of the store, one yelling into his com as he ran, "Four juveniles, two black, two Caucasian, headed west through the alley onto Market Street. Armed and dangerous, shoot on sight."

Sammy released a long stream of curses and checked behind them again.

"Where to now?" Fro-yo asked as he followed Sammy at a run.

"Joubert Park."

"Regroup?" Feet said. "No, that's nutty."

"There's always the chance," Sammy insisted between breaths.

"There's no chance," Gunner said.

"Look at us. We got out," Sammy said finding it more and more difficult to speak while running. "How long does a jolt take a person out for, Gunner?"

"Just a few minutes," was the answer, "but I don't think--"

"Then we go," Sammy decided. "We picked the park as a group."

The others stopped arguing, probably to save their breath. As they headed north in the direction of the park, a black car with flashing lights turned onto the same road about a hundred meters behind them.

"Do they see us?" Fro-yo asked.

"Does it matter?" Sammy shot back. "Just run!"

They crossed the length of another building and turned a corner, out of view of any Shocks or passing patrols. Sammy glanced back and spotted a car with flashing lights pulling to a stop in front of the alley they had just left.

"Now what?" Fro-yo asked.

"Still going to the park," Sammy said.

"C'mon, Brains," said Gunner. "We got to go and not look back. I'm tired."

"Hey, who busted us out of the Grinder?" Sammy yelled. "Me. They didn't find us because we were in the store, Gunner. They found us because you were stupid and ripped off those pizzas. You brought them to us. You did."

"This is different, Brains," Fro-yo said. "We get caught now—after busting out once, we're going away for a long time. When they realize who we are—"

Sammy did not bother letting Fro-yo finish. He started running again. Someone cursed at him, but they all followed. Sammy led them under the shadows of buildings until they emerged three blocks east of the black car. He stopped behind a dumpster to make sure they would not be seen when they went into the open.

"Is it clear?" he asked Fro-yo.

"Brains," Feet started to say, but Sammy ignored him. "Brains, this is bad trouble—they'll get us."

"So what would you do?" Sammy asked, but Feet did not have time to answer. Fro-yo, whose head had been poking around the side of the dumpster, fell straight back into Feet. Sammy saw the jolt protruding from his friend's thin black tee shirt.

"You dirty mother—!" Gunner shouted, but his voice was cut off with a jolt to the right shoulder.

Sammy and Feet ducked behind the dumpster, scattering three rats eating a rotted apple core. "They got a heat lock on us," Sammy hissed. They had no chance of helping their friends now. "We need to shake it. This way." They ran down another alley, leaving Gunner and Fro-yo. Dense walls were their best shot at getting rid of a heat lock besides running into a large crowd of people.

Feet stopped abruptly and clutched his sides in pain. "I can't keep running like this!" he exclaimed, gasping for air. "I don't think we can get away."

"We keep going as long as we have to," Sammy said, leaning against the brick wall.

"But how long till they catch us?"

"Never if we keep running."

"We can't outrun them forever. They're Shocks. We're nothing! Sooner or later they'll catch up to us. It's just a matter of time."

Sammy shoved Feet against the wall and got in his face to snap him out of it. "Hey! We swore we'd never go back to the Grinder. I can't go back there, Feet. Never."

"I don't know what to do anymore," Feet cried. His voice cracked. "I don't want to run forever. I just want a life. I just want a freaking normal life!"

Sammy had to say something. If not, Feet was going to lose it for good.

He calmed himself first and tried to hitch a smile on his face. His mouth felt all wrong, and he wondered how nutty it made him look. "Let's leave the city for good," he suggested. "If we make it to another territory and turn ourselves in as runaways, maybe we could ask to be put in with fosters again. Maybe they'll even keep us together."

The stupid, probably impossible suggestion worked. Feet now had some hope. Most of the wild-eyed fear left his eyes and he asked, "You really think so?"

"Yeah," Sammy lied. "It's worth a shot, right?"

"Where—where would you want to go?" Feet asked, his voice still shaky and tight.

"I don't know yet," Sammy said as he turned to walk, "let's think about it."

The longer they talked, the more Feet calmed; the panicky edge in his voice gradually disappeared. Occasionally, a vehicle passed. The cars made very little noise, and Sammy often did not hear them approach until too late. Each time one passed they hid behind trash bins or parked cars. It became easy for Sammy to think they had lost the Shocks for good.

Even if he knew the idea was stupid.

An unmarked armored truck painted all black turned onto the street, silently driving toward them. Sammy had a bad feeling about it the moment he saw it. If it was a Shockbox, more than a dozen Shocks would be inside it. Then red lights began to flash as it picked up speed.

Sammy groaned, alerting Feet to the new danger. They sprinted forward to the next alleyway. Sammy could hardly see a thing. The voices and footsteps of Shocks were not far behind. As they ran farther into the network of alleys, the nauseating odor of garbage and decaying animals grew thicker. Sammy felt trapped. At any moment they might hit a dead end.

And then what?

Frantically, he led Feet through one blind turn after another, praying that each corner would not be the last. They came to a fork in the alley and Sammy went right, hoping it would take them out of the maze.

The darkness prevented him from seeing more than a couple meters ahead, and all he could make out was the blood-red brick of an old building on one side and the metal siding of a warehouse on the other. Without warning, everything in front of him went completely black, and he heard a loud BANG.

Pain shot through his skull as his head smacked into a thick metal door, sending Sammy tumbling backward. Bright spots like little bombs splashed his vision. When he looked up, hope abandoned him. The only routes left were through the metal door or past the approaching Shocks. He and Feet pulled, pushed, and pounded on the door. It was firmly locked.

How can this happen? he asked himself

The Shocks were very close; Sammy turned to meet them. Rage boiled inside him as he saw their beams of lights draw closer. The irony of it all. They had chased so long and hard after him and his friends for stealing food, but where had the worthless Shocks been when his life had fallen apart?

Where were you a year ago when my life was normal? When I was still good? It's not fair! He wanted to scream all this at them, but he was too terrified.

A reflection from the ground caught his eye. It was a pipe. Reason fled from him. He picked it up, brandishing it like a club. "Remember your promise," he told Feet, who pulled the shocker out of the back of his pants. "Don't let them get us."

The Shocks were close enough now that Sammy heard their labored breathing. Sammy hated them. He hated the world. He hated his friends for allowing themselves to get caught. And he felt real fear now. The lights on their guns bounced off the brick wall before the Shocks even turned the corner into the narrow space where Feet and Sammy were trapped.

Six Shocks stopped only two meters away from where the boys held their ground; they formed a line to barricade the only escape route. Three shockers were pointed at each boy. One of men in the middle yelled, "Put down the weapons and get on the ground. Put down your weapons!"

Feet immediately got down onto the ground, but Sammy had no intention of obeying. How could Feet give up so easily? The boiling rage inside reached a critical point. He held the pipe higher in the air and defiantly screamed, "*NO!*"

Three of them fired at Sammy. The instant he heard the sound, he closed his eyes and threw his hands out to brace himself. A powerful surge flowed from his head, down his neck, and through his arms. It spread out of his hands and fingertips. He waited for what felt like an eternity for one of the jolts to hit him—to send him down to the ground in uncontrollable spasms.

It never came.

2 | Elite

"BRAINS, WHAT—How did you do that?" Feet got up and brushed the dirt from his pants.

Sammy opened his eyes. All six Shocks lay on the ground. Their scattered guns cast points of light in all directions.

He looked at his hands and back to the motionless Shocks. "What happened?"

Feet did not answer. He was too busy crawling around, examining the pavement. When Feet found what he wanted, he stood up and exclaimed, "Here, look at this!"

He opened his hand. By the light of one of the Shocks' guns, Sammy saw a three-pronged jolt reflecting the dim light off its metal tips.

"So?"

"So? You stopped all the jolts in midair! They flew back. I saw it. How'd you do that?"

"I didn't do anything," Sammy insisted.

Two of the Shocks stirred and another moaned incoherently.

"We've got to go," Sammy said.

He and Feet grabbed two shockers apiece and ran. After retracing their path, they took another route and left the alleyway. Sammy pushed them as fast as he felt they could go, and when they were too tired to run, they stopped to rest only as long as they dared. During these rests, Feet tried to explain to Sammy what he had seen.

"You stuck out your hands." Feet said, mimicking the motion. "All six of those guys just flew back like they were hit by an invisible . . . something. Honestly, it—it was like magic."

"That's not possible," Sammy said, but the more he thought about it, the more confused he became. "No, there has to be some kind of logical explanation." It sounded like something his father would have said.

Sammy wanted to talk more, but necessity forced them to keep moving. When he became too exhausted to run, they slowed to a walk on a quiet street in the wealthier suburbs. He feared his legs would cramp up, and he wouldn't be able to move at all. He had been fighting stitches in his sides for over an hour.

But where are we going to go? he kept asking himself. With no money and no one to help them, they had no options. Feet might have been thinking the same thing, because he asked, "Should we try one of these houses? I did houses a little before the Grinder."

All the residences in the neighborhood had perfect lawns and big windows. Probably expensive alarm systems, too. They reminded Sammy of his old home. He decided they should just keep going. They traveled to the edge of the city, always hugging the roadside, staying near trees and bushes so that when a car passed, they could duck out of sight.

"You must be some kind of a . . . what do you call it?" Feet persisted, "Psycho? Psychic? You know what I mean, where you can move crap with your head. You ever get hit by radiation or something nutty like that? That's how it starts. Gotta have radiation. Everyone knows that."

Sammy rolled his eyes. "You mean telekinesis? You realize how stupid that sounds? It was probably a shocker gone haywire."

"Yeah, right!" Feet snorted. "Was the jolt you stopped mid-air part of the malfunction, too? And don't forget about what you said after you fell."

"Okay—you've got a point. But don't you think I would know if I had telekinetic powers?"

"Course not. Most don't develop tele—super powers until they're in high school. Gotta be a teenager. Everyone knows that, too."

A bell tolled nearby, cutting off Sammy's sarcastic remark. Two solemn chimes announced the time to be 02:00.

"A church," Feet said. "Let's see if it's open."

They crossed three more blocks until they stopped at the walkway leading to the building. Sammy gaped at it. He couldn't remember seeing anything so magnificent.

The "church" was an impressive stone cathedral adorned with a giant cross and dozens of angels and symbols carved into the stone. Ornate wooden double doors stood at the top of the stairs, beckoning them to venture inside.

They climbed the stairs and pushed open the doors, walking into a richly decorated lobby. The lobby split into a vestibule that surrounded the chapel. The atmosphere was serene, the lobby illuminated by natural moonlight through the windows. Sammy couldn't remember when he'd last felt safe, but he did here.

Inside, twelve ornamental stained glasses high up on the wall provided very little lighting, but dozens of candles surrounding the altars cast a mystic glow over the vast room. Sammy liked the way the polish of the wooden pews reflected thousands of points of light. He and Feet walked inside tentatively, checking to see if there was anyone worshipping. It looked empty.

The sound of shuffling shoes across the room to their right alerted them. Feet jumped back against Sammy with a shout that echoed twice, then faded. The feet belonged to an old man with thick, white hair tousled from sleep. His face looked as if it had not seen a razor in several days. Two large, but empty blue eyes stared at them for what seemed like several minutes. Finally he cocked his head at them and said in an odd accent Sammy had never heard, "Hello!"

The two young fugitives stared back with fear and wonder. Sammy had no idea what to say. It was an awkward silence. Finally the old man spoke again.

"Which one broughtcha here?"

Sammy looked at Feet to see if his friend had any idea what the man meant. Judging from the empty expression on Feet's face, he did not.

"Which—which one what?" Sammy asked the old man.

"Don'tcha know? The Holy Saints? Which one o' them led ya here? I was led here by the Holy Saint Benedict Joseph Labre."

They watched the strange man cock his head like a curious bird, and it dawned on Sammy that the man might be a little off his rocker. He felt a mixture of pity and humor.

"Er . . . we were . . . brought here by the Saint . . ." Sammy stole a glance at Feet for some help.

"Dismas," Feet interjected. "Saint Dismas."

The old man's eyes got very big. "Oh, I see. Saint Dismas," he repeated, mulling over the name silently. "In trouble, are ya? Well, you've come to the right place I should think. It's like me father always said, 'Ain't no one like the good Lord to help ya out a spot o' trouble.' "

"Ya see," the man continued, "sometimes ya think everything's coming to an end. Ya can't see no way out o' your problems, but truthfully, sometimes, that's when things really are just beginnin'."

The man looked at Sammy for a moment, waiting for a reaction. In that instant, his eyes no longer seemed vacant and lost, and then he went back to moving his head side to side, as though confused as ever.

"What's your name?" Sammy said, moving a step forward.

"Oh, I'm Amos, don'tcha know? Did I forget to introduce myself again?" Amos said to himself more than anyone else. He scratched his head, as if picking at his brain for the answers to his own questions. "Yes, yes I did. But, well, the name's Amos."

He offered his hand to shake. Feet took it first. Then Sammy took another step forward, and shook Amos's hand as well. The man's grip was surprisingly firm. Sammy remembered his own father's words: "A strong handshake usually means strong character."

"Well, you'll probably be wanting a place for a kipper, eh?" Amos grinned toothily and cocked his head again. "Tell ya what, I will, some of these pews are fer older people like myself. Ya just lie yourself right down on them and ya'll be asleep before ya've finished saying yer prayers. Try over by that wall."

The chapel pews split into three groups, the widest of the three in the middle. Amos pointed to the far left wall, though he had been sleeping in the middle aisle. Just as Amos said, some of the pews were cushioned, while others were bare wood. Sammy imagined the worshippers arriving early each Sunday morning to make sure they got a cushioned seat.

"Thanks, Amos," they both said.

"Much obliged, much obliged," he muttered in reply, "Very much obliged."

Feet and Sammy walked over to the far side of the chapel and chose two different pews, one behind the other, directly underneath a magnificent stained glass window of Jesus being baptized by his cousin John with the Holy Spirit descending in the form of a dove. Sammy stretched his body over the cushioned pew and spread out as much as the space would allow. As though a floodgate had been opened into his body, all the fatigue from the hours of running caught up to him, his mind clouded over, and the last thing he heard was Feet's soft breathing.

He had barely fallen asleep when sounds of heavy stomping woke him. At first he thought it was the Shocks. Then he realized the old man —*what was his name? Amos?* —must be sleepwalking. He wasn't sure because the chapel had grown much darker, all but a few of the candles now extinguished. But he could hear the old man walking away from his pew and muttering quietly. Amos' voice didn't sound so crazy now. A shrinking sliver of moonlight through the space between the chapel doors told Sammy that Amos had just left. Hearing the old man brought back the events of the rest of the evening, and a strong sense of danger settled on Sammy.

The door closed with a gentle thud. The remaining candle flames flickered from the movement and the shadows on the walls jumped. Then the chapel was deathly still. Feet's steady breathing was the only sound. It was deeper now than when Sammy had fallen asleep. Through the lobby doors, Sammy heard the sound of heavy boots coming up the stairs.

Sammy's eyes widened as he remembered that Amos had hobbled out of the room wearing old shoes. Amos' hobbling sounded nothing like the heavy footsteps coming now. A loud electronic hum echoed through the sanctuary as the lobby doors flew open.

"Wake up," he hissed at his friend. "Wake up." But Feet still slumbered.

Sammy ducked under Feet's pew just as the doors slammed into the stone wall. His eyes squeezed shut as he waited for Feet to wake up and make some kind of noise, but Feet still slept. He knew he had to choose: run or wake Feet?

As he tried to decide, he recalled a memory from eight years ago: He had been shopping at the mall with his mother for school clothes. There had been a bomb threat, and people all around him were saying the word "leet." He and his mom went into the parking lot and saw several large armored vans parked outside. The same electronic hums were at the mall that day. Sammy craned his head around to find the source, but his mom pulled him quickly to the car. It was one of the only times in his life he had seen her genuinely afraid. Later that night, his dad had tried to explain what had been going on . . . and what "leet" meant.

There was no mistaking the humming sound. Elite were in the cathedral.

Sammy felt real terror now. What had he done to bring on himself the wrath of the Elite? Even falling from the ceiling in a grocery store did not compare to the fright he felt now. The fear felt like icicles grinding into his heart and brain. He wanted to wake up Feet. The Elite were here for *them*.

He knew it. Sammy made a decision. If Feet woke now, neither of them had a chance.

He slipped back under the pews and crawled frantically toward the front of the chapel. The shockers weighed heavy in his pockets, and he struggled to keep his breathing quiet. At the front of the chapel was a large stage with a pulpit and seating for clergy and a choir.

Five small stairs connected the floor of the chapel and stage. Sammy paused at the foot of them, keeping his body as low as possible and hoping that somewhere on the stage he could get out of the chapel undetected. Cautiously, he put some of his weight on the first stair.

Please don't let it creak, he begged an unseen power as he started forward. *Please don't let it creak. Please . . .*

They did not creak. The slow, heavy footsteps stopped near where Feet slept. Low voices muttered.

"It's not him," he heard one say, a voice mean and guttural. "Candles are messing up my night vision."

"So blow 'em out."

Another hum and Sammy felt the air all around him move like he was in a wind tunnel. Then the chapel went completely black.

He could not see more than a half meter ahead of him. He crept around the stage, his stomach nearly dragging on the carpet, straining his eyes for some exit. He could just make out the outline of chairs and an altar now. Off to the side of the stage, Sammy saw a door.

He headed toward it, but halfway there, he stopped. It would be impossible for him to open anything without giving himself away. If the Elite were using night vision, any movement he made in their line of sight would be detected. He crawled around to the other side of the stage, growing more desperate as the sounds drew closer. On his left was a row of seats and on his right was a small wooden railing. As he put his hand down to support his weight, the carpet—no, the floor itself—disappeared, and he nearly fell through a hole almost a meter square.

Had his situation not been so dire, Sammy might have laughed out loud. A staircase went straight up to the stage from the level below. Going down head first, he used his hands for support as he half-crawled and half-slid down the stairs. As soon as his hands touched the cold concrete of the floor below, he stood up and peered around the tiny room.

By searching and feeling his way around the room, he guessed that he was in the winery. He found a door and cracked it open to listen. The dim light shining through momentarily blinded him.

When he felt safe enough to leave the room, he pulled out his shockers and pointed them in front of himself. The shockers felt heavy and awkward in his hands; his inexperience at weapon-handling was painfully obvious. He saw himself as he was: a stupid kid delaying the inevitable. It was the Elite looking for him, not his friends, not the Shocks. He navigated through the hall, passing doors both marked and unmarked. *Where is an exit?* Behind him a door opened and closed, and he broke into a half run.

Sounds from somewhere ahead told him to hide. He spotted a niche in the wall for a drinking fountain. He slipped into the niche to the left of the fountain and pressed himself against the wall. Then he ducked his knees beneath the fountain to lower his body and prayed he would not be seen by whoever was about to pass. Though he held his breath, his chest heaved and his heart pounded.

In almost unnatural silence, a dark figure passed Sammy, giving him enough time to see the high black combat boots and black pants with red skull markings. Sammy's father had told him how those red skulls put despair in the minds of terrorists during the earliest days of the New World Government.

The Elite, the NWG's most feared operatives, had earned their distinction with merciless efficiency. The presence of the symbol of the red flaming skull, not only worn on their suits, but burned into their vehicles and weapons, was usually more than enough to end negotiations or hostage crises. The Elite were the very best. And everyone knew it.

Without warning, the Elite turned and with a gloved hand, snatched Sammy by his hair, yanking on him so brutally that his scalp burned. Sammy tried to reach up and dislodge the man's grip, but he had shockers in both hands. One of them fired and caught the exposed wrist of the Elite. The Elite swore at Sammy in a stammering grunt and fell back hard. The shockers in Sammy's hands trembled as he watched the Elite soldier hit the wall and slide to the floor. He wanted to just scream and scream, but forced himself to let out a long slow breath. It had a slightly calming effect.

I can find a way out, he told himself several times to regain his composure. He squeezed out of the niche and went the opposite direction of the Elite until he found a flight of stairs. Like a heavenly message, the green, glowing letters of an exit sign hovered above a door.

The door opened with hardly a noise, and he looked out onto the east grounds of the cathedral. As his shoes touched the grass, hope kindled inside his chest. He could hide in a tree until the Elite left. Since they hadn't seemed to be looking for Feet, maybe they would leave him there. It was a good plan; the best he had at the moment.

He was not more than a few meters onto the grass when the door slammed open behind him. Sammy turned to see two Elite coming out of the church. "Target in sight," one of them said with an annoyed scowl.

"Don't move, you little bastard," the other called out.

Sammy stopped running. His heart thundered in his chest and his stomach sank. Tears formed in his eyes. He did not dare try to run yet. The Elite had their boomguns trained on him as they walked carefully down the stairs. Their eyes never left him.

Nothing made sense to him. *Why would the Elite make all this effort to come after me?*

Then one of them glanced down to check his footing on the last stair, and Sammy took his last chance. It was a stupid thing to do, but he had no options left. He raised his shockers and fired one jolt at each of them. Then he ran. From one Elite, he heard, "Target is running on the east side of the cathedral."

"Set to disable!" yelled a third, older voice within earshot, but this one carried a tone of concern.

"Firing booms on disable."

Two electric hums followed the words as the boomguns fired. An incredible force hit Sammy from behind, lifting him off his feet before he even realized he had been hit. And somewhere between the terrifying realization that he had been shot and the unforgiving impact with the cold dirt, everything went very black.

"Target is down."

3 | Conversations

SAMMY AWOKE feeling very cold. He did not have the energy to open his eyes, but the hairs on his arms and legs stood straight up. Over time he became aware that his naked backside rested on something hard and flat, but also just as frigid as the air. A sound very similar to a mosquito buzzed in his ear. The buzzing noise gradually transformed into voices. Every so often, the room lurched and shook, jostling Sammy on the table.

At first, while he was still groggy, he thought the voices belonged to his parents.

"Nasty storm to fly through," a deep male voice commented. "He smells better."

"One of the nurses washed him before putting him on the cruiser," a younger male voice replied, this one with a slight Indian accent. "I wouldn't want to put up with a stench like that for the whole trip, would you? You should have seen what he had in his hair ... disgusting." He cleared his throat. "Regardless, we got confirmation with both DNA genotyping and a high-res CAT scan. He meets all the NWG anomaly qualifications."

"Probably why he gave us so much trouble."

"I am lucky to have gotten there before he did . . . and before the Elite."

"How did you know he'd go to the church?"

"Middle of the night. Only place offering refuge for several kilos in the direction they were last seen. What would you do?"

"Brave kid firing on the Elite like that," the second man said. "But you didn't have to dress up like the crazy old man, did you?"

"For now he needs to believe Amos was real."

"We love our anonymity, don't we?"

"His name and age?" the deeper voice asked.

"That just came through the system," the voice with the accent informed the first man. "Samuel Harris Berhane, Junior. He's fourteen years, three months, two days."

Sammy's blurry mind stirred at the mention of his name. *They're talking about me?*

"Very funny, Maad."

"Just being thorough."

"Kid looks more like sixteen. Date of birth is what? November eighteenth?"

"In the year of our Lord twenty-seventy."

"You are on a roll today. Is today the seventeenth?"

Sammy did not hear the younger man's reply.

"That sounds right," the deeper voice said. "And his history?"

For a moment Sammy could only hear muffled voices as one person shuffled through paper. " . . . but his record says he was caught stealing six weeks after running away from . . . sent to a juvenile reform center for nine months—escaped after six—then spent the last three months living in an abandoned supermarket."

The older man whistled appreciatively. "Rough. No extended family?"

"None discovered. Grandparents died in the Scourge. Parents have no siblings."

"Good," the older man said, indicating he was finished.

Sammy shifted on his back so he could hear better. There was more movement nearby him.

"I put a tube into his stomach—somewhat malnourished. Probably eating nothing but junk for months."

"All right, thanks."

"Uh, oh . . . Commander," the younger man said only centimeters away from Sammy's ear. "He's waking up."

"What? Oh—sedate him again. No sense risking any problems on the flight to headquarters."

"A minor dose is all I can give. Don't want any risks."

Sammy was only vaguely aware of the conversation, as though it had been a dream, and no sooner had the words "risks" registered in his brain then he felt a tingling cold invade his elbow and creep up his arm. Had he just been given a little more time, he might have been able to piece the bits of conversation together—he might even have felt some alarm at what was said, but the sedative took its effect and he passed back into a deep sleep.

🌀 🌀 🌀

"Explain what you mean when you tell me they are not certain about recruiting him?" a familiar voice spoke. The man was clearly trying to refrain from shouting. "Why were these concerns not addressed by Command before I brought him to Reykjavik?"

There was a pause. Then the same man's voice continued: "I understand his history is suspect—that's highly unlikely—no—but he is still trainable!"

Sammy realized that this time he was hearing only half of a conversation. It was the same voice he had heard in the cold room, only now the man sounded very upset. Although unable to move his body, the unsteadiness of the room told Sammy they were flying.

"Victor, did Command even look over his file?"

Pause.

"Good. Then you know the circumstances surrounding his parents. Such a situation warrants some type of irregular behavior—No, he's too young—he's too young."

Sammy took interest in the man's words. Somewhere in the back of his semi-drugged mind, he knew this man's conversation revolved around him. Comprehending everything, however, was still too difficult with such a thick haze over his mind.

"Yes, even attacking police. The boy also has fourteen and eleven. I am not throwing him away because of one man's theory."

Another pause.

"Trust me, had that been the case we would have seen far more damage."

What are you talking about? What's going on? He tried to say these things but his jaw felt like gelatin.

"Put me on with the general."

A longer pause.

"Good evening, sir. I am fine, thank you."

This time the pause was interjected with "uh-huhs" and "good."

"Will you please talk it over with the committee and get back to me as soon as possible? Thank you, sir. Good day."

The man muttered something angrily under his breath. Sammy heard several small beeps near his head and he tried to turn to the sound, but the only response his neck gave was a tight jerk. Someone cursed gruffly on his right.

"Kid's awake again, Commander."

"Again? Maad said to only give him minimal doses until we get there."

"Yes, sir," the gruff man's voice replied accompanied by movement. Sammy felt the same cold sensation starting up his arm and all went black again.

⑨ ⑨ ⑨

Sammy awoke with a throbbing headache. As he lay in a daze, his limbs ached as feeling crawled back into them. As the drugs wore off, he became more aware of the pain lingering in his whole body.

How long have I been asleep? He vaguely recalled snatches of conversations about . . . something. He could not remember what they were about.

Where is Feet?

Memories flooded him in a rush: the game, the Shocks, the church, the Elite. *I was shot!*

With a start, he tried to sit up only to find himself pinned down by metal restraints clamped over his wrists, ankles, legs, chest, and head. *Where am I?* He knew the processing center for juvies in Johannesburg pretty well. They didn't have this much security. *Maybe they're trying me as an adult this time.*

His head could not move side to side, and so he saw nothing in the room but the brilliant white ceiling. He spoke aloud, "Hello? HELLO? I'm awake now. Can anyone hear me?"

If he was heard, no one acknowledged him. His voice died on the walls of the room, and he felt even lonelier. "Feet?" he asked tentatively.

He felt incredibly small, even for being a larger-than-average kid. *What are they going to do to me? Send me back to the Grinder?* Perhaps worse. They'd warned him he could be sent to an adult prison for multiple offenses. After all, he'd shot at Shocks and Elite. Is that what they planned to do? He wanted answers. Anything was better than being restrained on a hard table, not knowing his fate. But no one came. Over and over he thought about the events that had brought him here. He dwelt longest on what could have happened to Feet and the others. Where were they? Then he heard a hiss.

Someone had entered the room.

"Hello, Samuel." The voice was deep, rich, and familiar.

"Who are you?" Sammy asked in reply more sharply than he meant to sound. It had been a long time since he had spoken to an adult he liked or respected. "My new counselor? Are you trying me as an adult?"

"Hello, Samuel," the man repeated in exactly the same tone as before.

"Where have I heard your voice before?" Sammy pressed. "Where am I?"

"I said 'hello.'" The tone in the man's voice became disapproving.

"I don't care what you said," Sammy continued. "I want to know what's going on!"

His chest rose and fell rapidly. The outburst left him winded. He had sworn not to get caught again, and now he lay helpless and bound on a table like a wacko in a white room.

I'm so stupid.

"I think I will give you some time to learn proper etiquette," the man said politely.

The same hiss sounded as the door opened.

"Wait!" Sammy called out blindly. "Where am I?"

"Close."

A hiss again.

Sammy screamed every curse word he knew at the closed door.

Above him, a square of the ceiling turned from brilliant white to transparent. Words appeared on the screen:

Psion Training Positive Reinforcement
Session 7: Etiquette

Psion?

The movie was ridiculously old-fashioned. The female narrator sounded about a hundred years old and spoke in a too-happy, delusional sort of way. The film ran at least twenty minutes, each minute laden with cheesy catch phrases and odd-looking people acting out scenarios. To Sammy's horror, when the film ended, the same words from the introduction appeared on the screen. When the same corny piano music began, he realized he had to watch it again. The third time it started, he thought he might die.

He wondered fleetingly if showing this movie over and over might be a tactic to drive him crazy because during the third showing, he caught himself repeating a couple of the phrases along with the film.

"If you want the peas, you must say please," and, "Remember, nothing tells a person that you care more than verbal gratitude."

When it ended for the third time, he stared at the screen, daring it to play just one more time.

The square on the ceiling where the film had appeared became opaque once again, matching the rest of the ceiling so well Sammy would never have guessed a screen was there. The room became very quiet again. He heard no ticking of a clock, no sound of people in a hallway outside.

It must be soundproofed. He yelled as loud as he could for no reason. Nothing happened except his throat hurt a little now. *Where are the others?* he wondered again. *In other rooms like this one?* He missed them already. He hoped they had escaped, even if it meant never seeing them again, Feet included. He berated himself for not waking Feet in the church—so many decisions he could have made differently. Thinking about them all made his headache worse until he felt very tired. He closed his eyes to ignore the punk drummer pounding away inside his skull, and almost fell asleep when he heard the hiss of the door once more.

"Hello, Samuel," the same man said, his voice pleasant again.

"Why, hello, sir," Sammy replied in his most faux-happy voice. "How are you? I trust you have had a wonderful day ... or night. Whatever time it is."

The man gave a genuine chuckle and responded, "Very pleasant indeed. Because I have the privilege of meeting you."

"Meeting me?" Sammy asked, dropping the stupid voice.

"You know why you are here in this room, Samuel? Here, and not in Johannesburg being brought up on charges of—let me see—" The man paused and then began to read something. "—theft, breaking and entering, resisting arrest, assault with a weapon on thirteen law enforcement officers, trespassing on private property, and assault with a weapon on Elite soldiers? The last one, I should add, is enough to put you in prison for a very long time."

"Where am I?"

"Seventy-five kilometers east of Reykjavik."

Sammy jerked in surprise and knocked his head into his restraint. He swore in both pain and surprise. "I'm on—I'm on . . . Capitol Island?" he stammered. This mess was deeper than he thought. "Why—why did you bring me here?"

"I can give you some answers. How much I can give depends on you. Would you like to be released from your restraints?"

"Yes . . . please," Sammy said. The politeness came easily now.

With a small click, Sammy was free. He sat up, but his entire body ached again. Blood rushed from his head, and he nearly passed out. The grimace on his face must have been easy to read because the man commented, "You took quite a blow from those Elite back in Johannesburg. If you do not mind my saying so, firing a weapon at them was extraordinarily foolish."

Sammy got his first good look at the man speaking to him: a middle-aged man with very white hair and powerfully built chest and arms. He wore a plain gray jumpsuit adorned only with a curious golden alpha symbol attached to his chest. His sharp face made him seem very serious, but his clear blue eyes relieved the tension from his face. They were bright with discernment.

Sammy thought he could like this man if he'd stop reminding him of his mistakes. "Why am I here?" Sammy repeated.

"You are an anomaly."

Sammy shot the man an incredulous look and words flew out of his mouth. "You're an idiot. I'm not an anomaly. There's nothing wrong with me."

The man did not change his matter-of-fact expression. "I will ask you one time to show me the same respect I show you, and if you insist on doing otherwise our conversation will be over. I will not tolerate the kind of behavior you have displayed over the last several months of your life. Anarchy is appropriate for the playground. Not here." They stared at each other hard. Sammy saw a toughness in this man that he hadn't seen in anyone since his dad. "Now, let me rephrase my statement; you have an anomaly. Well, anomalies, really."

He really thinks I'm some kind of freak. He tried to explain this to the man with some sense of etiquette: "This must be some kind of—I'm not sick. You've made a mistake. I don't have whatever you're talking about."

"I am not making a mistake," the man said, and his smile returned. "Your anomalies were caused by the Scourge."

"Okay, well, I wasn't alive back then." He instantly regretted his tone and apologized to the man. Talking to an adult civilly was going to take some getting used to.

"Your parents were. They were probably very young. The vaccine caused some changes in people. This resulted in the rise of genetic anomalies in offspring. Two days ago we received intelligence from South African Territory police that a tall, black young man—you—displayed some kind of 'powers.' Or as they described it, 'a force field that attacked several officers.' So we sent the Elite to secure the situation, track down the criminal in question, and bring him to us."

"You sent—but I don't—that could have been anything that happened in that alley," Sammy cried. Even in his anger, he remembered Feet's absurd reasoning. "I don't have any super powers!"

"Of course not," the man said calmly, almost dismissively. "I never said anything about you having super powers." He turned very serious. "What I mean is that you have certain abilities that the government is interested in employing. These are not supernatural. You are not in a superhero story. This is explainable science."

Sammy rolled his eyes, but did not insult the man as he had been warned. "I would know if I had used *special abilities*," he said, using his fingers as quotes to emphasize his point, "against the Shocks."

"I have met many people with your anomaly. Almost everyone is ecstatic. You seem upset. Why?" His penetrating blue eyes stared into Sammy's, and Sammy felt as though the man could read into him.

"Because I don't have any powers!"

"Then you explain what happened."

Sammy shifted in his chair. To stall for time, he looked around the room. It was small and abnormally clean, like it wasn't used very often. A toilet stood in one corner and a sink in the other. The restraining table that had held Sammy consumed a large portion of the other side of the room. It felt like his cell in the Grinder, only nicer. The white-haired man continued to wait quietly for an answer. Sammy gave him a feeble shrug and muttered, "I don't know."

"We ran DNA tests and scans. All of them confirmed your anomaly. We know you express Anomaly Eleven and Fourteen," he said with an air of what Sammy thought sounded like excitement in his voice.

"When did you do that? Test me, I mean?"

"On the way here."

"And what does that mean to you? An anomaly?"

"Many types of anomalies exist. The government ranks them with stars. One star means someone is born with a mild birth defect. Two stars is much more severe. Three stars always is a lethality in the fetus. One to three stars are only used to class someone during fetal development."

The man paused as if to allow Sammy time to process the information. It sounded like a speech he had given many times before, and that annoyed Sammy.

"Four and five stars are a completely different scenario. They do not express themselves until puberty. An increase in sex hormones triggers the production of unique enzymes that react differently with certain parts of the body. I can explain the science of it later. For now, it is enough to know that the government wants people who have them." He gestured to Sammy, "Like in your case."

"Why would the government care about stuff like that?" Sammy questioned.

"To protect citizens from dangerous—or unpredictable—elements in the general population," the man answered. "You can appreciate the concern the government has—and the public would have—knowing citizens are out and about with uncontrollable abilities at their disposal. People get hurt. I have seen it happen several times. To use you as an example: you injured half a dozen officers in that alleyway without knowing what or how anything happened."

"Except that I am not one of your anomalies," Sammy said.

"But for now, why not pretend? Especially since you are. The government is interested in you."

"You mean the government wants to lock me up?" Sammy asked, getting to his feet. "I'll fight you, and I'll escape."

The man chuckled. "Honestly, Samuel, I do not doubt you, but the reality is quite the opposite. The government wants to employ you." Again the man displayed his ability to become very serious very fast.

Sammy walked to the sink. He looked at himself in the mirror above, and saw his brown eyes staring back at him. *Is this real? Am I some sort of freak?*

The man looked at Sammy gravely in the mirror. "Your talents can be put to great use. Here, and I mean where you are right now, we train Anomaly Fourteens in a state-of-the-art facility to prepare to enter into the employ of the New World Government."

"What if someone says no? What if they don't want to work for the government?"

Sammy saw the man's deep concern that Sammy might not accept the offer. As the man spoke, he seemed to weigh each word.

"If you choose that, no one will stop you or force you to do otherwise. However, as I said earlier, the government does not want to run the risk of having a free radical running about society unchecked. You will be given a drug, harmless of course, that informs us of your whereabouts and nullifies the enzyme that causes your anomaly. You will receive a visit from the Elite every other month for the rest of your life to ensure that you take this drug."

Sammy didn't have a response. Perhaps the man had taken Sammy too seriously. The truth was, Sammy didn't know what to think. He felt like ice water had been dumped on him.

"On the other hand," the man continued, "you will not be running about society since you will lose the clemency granted to you in order to become an agent of the NWG."

"My what?"

"I had your crimes overturned on the supposition that you would accept my offer," the man spoke as if this should have been obvious to

Sammy. "If you reject it, you will be handed back over to the South African Territorial Government so they can deal with you."

The conversation came to the point the man had warned him it would. Sammy's decision would determine how the remainder would go. Go back to the Grinder or work for the government he hated? The choices seemed awfully similar.

Except I swore I'd never go back to the Grinder. And with this man, he would be free. "Where are my friends?"

"I don't know," the man told him. "What is your choice?"

They sat in silence for several seconds. Sammy needed to know what he was getting himself into. It was too surreal. He had so many questions. Did he actually have these powers? Finally he just blurted out the next thought that came to him.

"What's your name?"

"My name is only known to those that work for me."

Fair enough. "What—uh—what are the negatives of working for you?" he asked next.

The man gazed at Sammy, impressed. "Good question. I must tell you that I can only inform you of so much until you give consent to enlist with NWG. So I will say this: The plusses far outweigh the minuses. The minuses include very real and extreme danger, a significant part of your life dedicated to loyal service to the government, agreeing to follow a strict code of guidelines in your lifestyle. I think that might be very difficult for you given your current lifestyle. You'll also have to live with anonymity for your hard work, and, again, there is extreme danger."

"Sounds dangerous."

"Good. You get the idea," the man said, no longer smiling. In fact, he almost looked sad, and his hand trembled for a second or two. "I cannot exaggerate the gravity of the duties you will acquire. I have lost people very close to me in this work. But as I said, it is worth it."

"And you're sure I'm an anomaly whatever number you said?"

"One hundred percent," the man answered.

A week ago, Sammy would have ridiculed anyone who had told him he would join the government. And now he was here sitting across from this man, a man whose name he did not even know. There was something about this man . . . Sammy liked him, and he had not met an adult he liked in a while. In the back of his mind he knew that no matter what dangers he faced, this man wouldn't let him go unprepared. Sammy took a deep breath and blew it out.

"Okay, I'm in."

"Excellent. The pay may not be great, but you cannot beat the benefits package we offer." He paused as if he had told a joke and waited for Sammy to laugh.

Sammy did not get the humor. With deep sincerity, the man put a hand on Sammy's shoulder and told him, "You made the right choice." He offered his hand to Sammy, who took it. He had a firm grip. "By the way, my name is Commander Walter Byron. You can call me 'Sir' or 'Commander.'"

"Commander of what?" Sammy asked.

"Psion Beta."

"What's that?"

"Come with me and find out."

4 | ⊙rientation

COMMANDER BYRON SHOWED Sammy out of the room and into a brightly lit hallway with white walls, ceilings, and a white foamy floor. Doors lined one side of the hallway, but the other side had none. Nothing Sammy could see satisfied his growing curiosity. They climbed two flights of stairs and came to an almost identical floor.

Silver numbers adorned each door here. The commander stopped in front of the door marked #1. Like all the doors Sammy had seen, only an eye scan would open it. Commander Byron showed Sammy inside and then said, "We have a meeting in about ..." he looked at his watch, "... fifteen minutes. Four other recruits are waiting for me on the roof. Do you mind if I go get them?"

"No problem." Sammy looked forward to having a few moments alone.

Room 1 was very large but plain, furnished only with five straight-backed chairs and a simple podium. On the seat of each chair was a small box made of black wood. Each box had a name engraved into the lid. Sammy scanned the names. Samuel Berhane, Jr. had been branded into the box on the chair farthest from the door. He opened his box. Inside, he found a sleek new com, much more impressive than even the newest models Sammy had seen kids at the mall drooling over. He had never owned one.

He held it delicately. It had been over a year since he had gotten anything new without stealing it. He took it from the box and sat down in the chair. Despite the chair's stiff appearance, Sammy thought it was comfortable. He tucked the com neatly around his ear and activated it. A holographic screen appeared over his eye showing a menu with several different options:

1. Schedule
2. Text Message
3. Personalize
4. Personal Statistics
5. Emergency

Maybe it had something to do with the fact that these were government coms, but the options seemed much more basic than his mom's and dad's had been. He chose option three, and a program came up asking him to enter his voice into the computer. It told him to pronounce several words and sounds so the computer could memorize his vocal nuances. It only lasted a few minutes, but it was fun. The rest of the time he spent browsing through the other menu options: the Schedule option came up blank, as did the Text Message and Personal Statistics. He didn't dare mess with Emergency.

The door opened and Byron led a boy and three girls inside. They followed Byron closely, looking around the room with anxious faces and toting various amounts of luggage. The commander gave each of them reassuring smiles as he gestured them to sit.

The other boy was several centimeters shorter than Sammy, and appeared to be the most scared out of the bunch. He had a pale face with brown hair and blue eyes, almost like a younger version of Feet except this boy walked with his head down and shoulders slumped. The boy read all of the names on the boxes until he came to the one resting on the chair next to Sammy. The boy caught Sammy's eye and then looked at the chair as if he needed permission to seat himself. Sammy offered a weak smile, and the boy sat down quickly.

Actually, Sammy wanted a better look at the three girls. Only boys got sent to the Grinder, and Sammy hadn't seen one up close in weeks. One was black, much darker than him, with a nice face and pronounced cheekbones. She wore a dozen wooden bracelets on each wrist, and her hair was done up in different colored ribbons with feathers sticking straight up, making her look pretty in an exotic way, but also weird.

The next girl was shorter than the black girl. Her skin had a light olive color; she had bright, poison-green hair and big brown eyes that roamed constantly, never staying one place for too long. She examined everything in the room, from the chairs to Sammy's face. This did not bother him as much as that she stood blocking the third girl from his view. When the door closed, Byron asked the girls to sit down. The green-haired girl did so, and the last girl came to view. The air left his lungs, maybe even the whole room.

Her features were so soft that Sammy had no other explanation than that the hand of a Creator had sculpted her face to perfection. She had fair skin, colored only by a dust of red on her cheeks, framed with a gentle pronouncement of her cheekbones and jaw line. Her vivid green eyes danced with an intelligent light enhanced by her dark blonde eyebrows. Even her red lips curved perfectly.

"Samuel?" Byron asked. "Samuel, are you all right?"

"Huh?" Sammy jerked out of his trance and looked at the commander.

Everyone in the room looked at him, even the blonde girl. *Oh no. How long was I staring?* Hot blood rushed to his face, burning his ears.

"Sorry, Commander."

"Are you all right?" he repeated.

"Yeah, I'm fine," Sammy quickly replied, though his voice cracked again. This forced his face to grow even hotter.

He stole a glance at the girl again to make sure she was not looking at him. Luckily, she was talking to the green-haired girl and didn't seem to notice. He needed to get her attention again somehow, get her to look at him, but everything that came to mind seemed stupid.

Commander Byron spoke, pulling Sammy's thoughts away from her: "Will each of you introduce yourselves? You will all be on the same footing as far as training goes, so you can lean on one another more than the students who have been here longer. Just stand and say your name, your age, and where you come from."

Sammy waited to see if the blonde girl would stand up first, but she watched him, as did everyone else. When he stood up, he realized he was the only person in the room besides Commander Byron wearing a com. Not wanting to stand out, he hastily took it off, and returned it to its box. In his nervousness, he shut the box too hard, and it tumbled off the chair and onto the floor. Awkwardly, he bent down to retrieve the box and replaced it on the chair. He looked down at his hooded sweater, the same one he had been wearing for weeks, and realized how much filth and stain had collected on it.

I must smell terrible. All of the things that had not seemed important with his friends, like personal hygiene and grooming, now mattered a great deal.

He wondered if he'd become immune to his own stench after spending so much time in the abandoned store.

"Er—I'm Samuel Berhane." He glanced at the blonde girl who looked back at him indifferently, almost impatiently. "My parents—well, just call me Sammy. I'm fourteen and I grew up in South African Territory. Is that all?" he asked Byron.

Byron nodded.

The small boy next to him stood up, looking not nervous, but mortified. "My name is Brickert Plack."

He sat down immediately.

"Anything else you want to say about yourself, Brickert?" the commander asked him.

Red spots formed on Brickert's cheeks as he realized he had forgotten to finish his introduction. He stood again and said, "I'm from Ireland, er, the Territory of Ireland, and I'm twelve, almost thirteen."

Without missing a beat, he dropped back into his chair.

"Yes, Brickert is the youngest Psion we have ever trained in this facility," Byron added, beaming down on Brickert, whose red spots grew and flushed to an even deeper red.

The first two girls introduced themselves as Kawai Nujola and Natalia Ivanovich. Kawai was almost sixteen and came from a smaller west African territory Sammy vaguely remembered from school geography, and green-haired Natalia had been recruited from Samara, a Russian territory.

The blonde girl stood up. Sammy couldn't help but notice her perfect posture. "My name is Jeffie Tvedt. I just turned fourteen, and I'm from Oslo in the Territory of Norway."

Sammy experienced a sudden strong connection with the Territory of Norway. *I've always liked that place. Very beautiful. Jeffie . . . Nice name.*

"Thank you," Byron said. "I hope you all become fast friends and help each other whenever needed." He cleared his throat as if to begin a speech. He surveyed the new recruits with a look of satisfaction.

"I think what you are all about to experience can be likened to putting your mouth over a fire hydrant to take a drink of water. I hope you can handle the deluge of information. Anytime you have questions, please feel free to ask."

Sammy understood this to mean "get comfortable, we'll be here for a while."

"Life at the headquarters of Psion Beta will be different than anything you have experienced. I briefed all—well—most of you about the daily routine here." Brickert glanced over, no doubt guessing that Commander Byron was referring to Sammy. "You will be trained for four to seven years to prepare to join a Psion Alpha squadron. Alphas are the most specialized task force under the NWG and consist solely of persons with Anomaly Fourteen. I want to elaborate on this anomaly so you understand precisely what you can and will be able to do with it."

Byron paused briefly to stress his next point.

"But first I wish to begin by saying this, because I feel it is most important. As a government operative you are above most laws by which civilians must abide, similar to police breaking speed laws while in pursuit. This is not because we are privileged or chosen, but because of the work we do. It is easy to slip into the pitfall of thinking we are above everyone else, or even detached from them. While you will have little contact with the outside world, make no mistake, we are servants. We never use our abilities to put ourselves above others even though, ultimately, you will never receive thanks from the people you serve and protect."

Protect from what? thought Sammy.

"How about a history lesson?" Byron said, as if he had read Sammy's thoughts.

A transparent square appeared in the wall exactly like the one Sammy had seen on the ceiling in the white room. As Byron spoke, pictures appeared.

"Late in 2054, the first Psion was discovered in the Mid-American Territory. Like all new anomalies, the government brought him to a NWG research center for study. Doctors found he had a unique enzyme that interacted with carrier proteins in the mitochondrial matrix throughout the cells in his nervous system."

Sammy recalled learning about mitochondria in school, and he recognized the one in the picture that appeared on the screen. The picture looked like a green jelly bean with a section removed to see several internal membranes sandwiched and folded against each other.

"The mutation in these organelles acted as super-catalysts in energy production, manufacturing thousands of times more energy than a normal mitochondrion. But the spontaneous adaptation of energy emitting channels in eleidin found in the stratum lucidum of the dermis . . . scientists called it a wonder of evolution."

The stratum whatsidum? Sammy wondered. The others around him all looked equally confused.

A picture of a section of human skin divided into layers appeared on the wall. Highlighted in red were certain cells in a particular layer of the skin.

"Stratum lucidum is a layer of the skin found only on the palms of hands and soles of feet, so these are the only places on the body where energy blasts can be emitted."

"What happened to the boy?" The question came from Natalia, whose eyes were wide as her finger twirled knots in her poison-green hair.

"He trained with the Elite in Siberia. Over the years, as the government discovered other Anomaly Fourteens, the boy suggested employing them as a second operative group independent of the Elite. The little group grew and named themselves 'PSIONS.' In 2060, they founded the Psion Corps. This building used to be the original headquarters until Psion Alpha and Beta formed in 2070. Now it is used only for training the Betas."

"Is the boy still training Psions?" Sammy asked and glanced over to see if Jeffie was looking at him now. *Dang.*

The screen behind the commander went dark and Commander Byron smiled. "Yes, he is. In the beginning, the Psions worked mainly as a special task force, taking on missions too dangerous for the Elite."

The screen behind Byron flashed images and clips of both peaceful and violent protests, debates in the World Congress, and ended with a world map. He spoke for several minutes about the Scourge's impact on social politics and how human life became more precious after over forty percent of the world's population died from the supervirus. Bombs, abortions, guns, and even armies became deeply unpopular as the world moved toward global peace. Byron's lecture so far reminded Sammy of the classes he had been forced to attend in the Grinder—classes about not only math and reading, but also making the world a better place through service to humanity.

The videos changed to show news cuttings during the Second Scare. Some were famous clips Sammy recognized from history in junior high. Most of the shots contained mob violence and protests at government offices around the world.

"None of you were alive during the Second Scare," Byron continued. "Scare is really too small a word to describe the terror people felt at the idea of a second, deadlier virus wiping out the rest of humanity. Every day we heard about riots and mayhem. People wanted to protect their homes, pharmaceutical companies wanted to protect their factories. But no one legally owned guns because of the weapons ban. So in 2058 several northern and southern American territories passed laws allowing their citizens the right to bear and manufacture arms. Superior Court challenged the laws and ruled them unconstitutional, and levied heavy sanctions against the territories."

"Wasn't that a little harsh?" Jeffie asked. Natalia stopped twirling her hair and stared at Jeffie, whose question sounded a little confrontational.

Commander Byron's smile seemed to invite the challenge. "What do you think?" he asked her.

"My dad says people should be allowed to have guns." Her tart tone made it clear her dad's opinion was the final word on the matter.

Byron nodded noncommittally. "It depends how you look at it. Regardless of how anyone felt about the issue, being a government means working together to solve problems, not just promoting the interests of one group. Whether or not weapons should have been allowed is less important than knowing the majority of people did not want them. As part of a larger community, or team, they should have together worked for a solution. Do you agree, Gefjon?"

Sammy used this as an opportunity to steal another glance at her. *Gefjon? Her name is Gefjon?*

"I guess so, but call me Jeffie."

The tension diffused; Jeffie seemed supplicated, and Byron resumed.

"Americans have always had a superiority complex, just like almost every other culture," Byron continued, wearing his little smile again. "I know, I grew up there. You guys probably know most of this stuff from history classes. After the Berkeley Weapon Debates in 2062 and 2063, all but five of the North American Territories shocked the world and seceded from the NWG. Then every Central and South American Territory, but two, followed. Leading to the formation of . . . ?"

"The Continental American Government," Kawai answered. She spoke it like a dirty word. It reminded Sammy of kids in school calling each other a variety of names that all had "cag" in them: cagger, cag-head, and cag-lover were all common.

Byron nodded. "We call that the Schism. For a time, a few North and South American territories stayed with the NWG. Quebec was one of the few territories that didn't secede. And what you probably don't know is that when the CAG invaded Quebec, it marked the beginning of the Silent War."

"The what?" Natalia asked. She wasn't the only one confused. Sammy had no idea what Byron was talking about.

"The Silent War," Byron repeated. "A war fought only by operatives—specially trained soldiers that are not part of an army. No war in the history of the world has been fought this way. During the twentieth century, the Cold War was a race to build up nuclear arms. Not a single bomb detonated nor one bullet fired between the United States of America and the Union of

Soviet Socialist Republic, but they did fight via smaller proxy nations. Since the Scourge, standing armies and weapons of mass destruction have been deeply unpopular in both governments. Human life is viewed as sacred. We are assured the CAG does not intend to build an army unless we build first. So when these rare exchanges take place, like in Quebec, we fight anomalies against other anomalies."

Sammy and the other recruits stirred uncomfortably in their seats and exchanged glances. Brickert paled and swallowed hard. Byron had not said that the Psions were in the middle of a war. Byron's repetition of the words "extreme danger" now took on greater meaning.

"How come I've never heard of the war?" Jeffie asked. Sammy liked watching her lips move as she spoke.

"There have been only five battles between NWG and CAG since the Schism. Four of those were in territories invaded by CAG. The last battle took place almost seven years ago in an Australian territory. NWG works hard to keep information away from the public and press."

"Why?" Jeffie asked. Her questions mirrored Sammy's own thoughts.

"To prevent people from losing faith. The concept of a worldwide government is fragile. We base most of our military strategies around intelligence gathering and surveillance, not invasion."

"And the CAG uses other Psions, like us?" asked Natalia.

"As far as we know, Psions do not work for the CAG. They use different anomalies. Before we even knew of an operation in Mid-Western America, the CAG had struck us the worst blow of the war in a former American state called Wyoming. It is a desert—a perfect place for an ultra-security holding facility for people discovered to be afflicted with Anomaly Thirteen—the anomaly discovered three years before mine.

"Have any of you ever heard of the Friday the Thirteenth Carpenter Killings? A teenage girl named Katie brutally murdered and then decapitated her family one morning. Then she went to school and stabbed twelve students, killing nine. Three were horribly mutilated. I have seen the pictures from the police reports. They are very disturbing. A battery of studies showed she had an anomaly affecting her brain in such a way that she possessed no sense of barriers to restrain her actions. People with this anomaly have no fear of consequences or authority. They are all but mad with their own desires. Even small whims can become obsessions. Anomaly Thirteens have been known to kill brutally, inflict prolonged torture, and rape without the least remorse. I have even heard reports of cannibalism."

Sammy looked at Brickert, whose faced mirrored the look of disgust on his own. *This is who we fight? A bunch of animals? No wonder Byron didn't mention this.*

"Why would anyone want to have those kinds of people on their side?" Natalia asked. "That's horrible!"

Sammy fully agreed with her, and Kawai silently nodded.

"Like I said, the loss of the Wyoming prison hurt us. The CAG was desperate for its own operative force and wanted to force the remaining American territories to secede. When CAG troops invaded Mid-West, they broke into the prison and bargained the Thirteens' freedom in exchange for their service. The Thirteens paid a minimal price of being tagged, and became free if they work for the CAG. They weed out CAG citizens who are still loyal to NWG. Watch this example of their brutality."

The screen changed from a world map half red and half blue to amateur film footage of a man and woman—presumably a couple—ragged and thin, taken into a bunker wearing thick magnet cuffs. The camera

- 58 -

followed them down a dilapidated gray-yellow hallway and into a room where two men sat in chairs laughing as if one of them had just told the funniest joke in the world. One man was skinny in a wiry way with thick black hair on his head and the rest of his body covered in tattoos. The other man was burly and had a bald head covered in dark scabs. Sammy wondered if someone (maybe the Thirteen himself) had ripped out all the hair from his scalp. Both men wore matching uniforms: blood red tunics that melted into black pants. Above the left breast was a jagged black thirteen emblazoned onto the tunic.

The mirth ended when the couple was forced into the room. When Sammy glimpsed the men's eyes, he saw more red. They had dyed their sclera to the color of blood. The soulless red eyes combined with the multiple scars on their faces and arms made them a terrifying sight. They stood and smiled at the couple. The smiles had no warmth. A tangible jolt of fear went from Sammy's head to the small of his back. He did not know these men. He could not comprehend them. Men without feeling or remorse. The couple must have sensed something similar because when the woman saw their smiles she screamed and fell helplessly to her knees. The man sat on the floor silent and defiant. The Thirteens laughed again; their laughter made Sammy sick.

The bald, scabby Thirteen made a small jerk with his head, almost as if he had a spasm. The tattooed Thirteen saw this, walked out of sight of the camera, and came back with a weapon that Sammy recognized from the old movie *Moby Dick*. A rusted harpoon gun. The woman saw it and shrieked louder, begging for mercy. She groveled on her hands and tried to tug on the tattooed man's pants when he kicked her with the steel toe of his boot in the face. She fell back and recoiled to the wall like a wounded dog, hands covering her face. The screaming stopped, and she simply collapsed into the corner bawling hysterically. Blood oozed out between her fingers.

The tattooed Thirteen aimed the harpoon gun at the man's leg and shot the harpoon clean through it. Sammy closed his eyes as the man's screams filled the air. He did not want to see this. He already understood what these people were capable of. More shots were fired and more screams of pain, but he did not look at the screen.

The sounds ended, and the screen on the wall disappeared. Natalia had tears in her eyes. Jeffie's face was flushed. Brickert's and Kawai's eyes were still closed. Sammy's thought a large rock had been dropped in his stomach, and his mouth had gone dry.

"This is what we face," Byron said. "I will not water it down or make our work sound glamorous because it is not. They are deadly. Even our trained Alphas never survive when alone with more than three of them. No one in the history of our training simulators has beaten four of them. They epitomize the words ferocious and merciless. Thirteens have never taken a Psion prisoner. They are always heavily armed. Unlike normal people who have visceral centers in the brain to tell them when they are fatigued or pushing their muscles past capacity, Thirteens have none, allowing them to fight longer, harder, and faster than normal people."

"How many Psions have died, Commander?" Brickert asked in a hoarse whisper.

"Fifteen." Sammy noticed the commander clench his hands hard while answering. "We have lost fifteen of our soldiers to these people. That may not seem like many, but there have only been eighty-nine Psions, including each of you. There are forty-eight Psions in the Alpha group, five more in Alpha Command, twenty in the Beta group including all of you, and myself.

The majority of those deaths were in the early days of the war, before we started the simulations and the Game."

Sammy's mind buzzed. Byron had said a Psion's life would be dangerous, but this was too much. Everyone else in the room seemed to be thinking the same thing. Brickert had his head down. Kawai stared at her hands. Natalia looked on the verge of tears again. Jeffie was less affected. She gazed hard at the commander, ready to hear more.

Byron seemed to read their thoughts. "I told you all this was a deluge of information, but I have learned the best way to introduce this is at the start. It is why you are here and why you must give your very best every day. You are each here for a purpose. Your training will be hard, it will stretch you to your very limits, but I promise you that if you give everything you have, you will leave here prepared to face whatever comes."

He paused, as he had already done so many times, to look each of them in the eyes and show them his sincerity.

"Do any of you have questions or comments before we go on to an equally serious matter?"

Sammy shook his head, as did Brickert. None of the girls responded.

"Do any of you now object to taking upon yourselves an oath of service to the New World Government as Psions?" he asked.

Again no one objected.

"Please stand, raise your right hand, and repeat after me."

They followed his instructions. Byron began the oath and paused after each line so they could repeat it. Pride swelled in Sammy's chest as he repeated the words. He thought of everything that had happened to him in the last year and hoped by making this oath, he could atone for the mistakes he had made. He thought less about his friends and more about his parents for the first time in a while.

"I am a servant of the people. On my own accord I declare my life is not my own. I will give my mind, my strength, and my heart to the service of the government so long as the government serves the interest of the people. With justice as my strength, I will protect the freedoms and liberties to which my people have a right. My life is not my own. I am a servant of the people."

"All right," Byron said, his eyes now a tinge redder. "I am so proud of each of you. Let me give you a tour of this fine building."

5 | Racing

THE RECRUITS FOLLOWED the commander around headquarters for the better part of an hour. Psion Beta headquarters had six floors and was shaped like a giant cube. According to Commander Byron, the perimeter of the building was almost two kilometers. Betas had access to the first five floors.

Combat simulations took up all the space on the fifth level. Byron briefly demonstrated how to operate the control panels in each room. All rooms employed state-of-the-art interactive holograms. The fourth level held a library and several classrooms each with a strange looking machine Byron called a Teacher. On the third floor they saw the exercise facility, a huge recreation hall, and, what impressed Sammy the most, a cafeteria.

The cafeteria boasted a fully-automated RoboChef. Sammy had heard of these amazing machines in his dad's tech magazines. All he had to do was enter in a recipe, and the RoboChef could prepare almost any dish. Even Jeffie seemed impressed. As they moved on, Sammy looked back forlornly and his stomach grumbled.

The next level down was the girls' dormitory, while the first floor belonged to the boys. Although a stairwell connected the two dorms, only an eye-scan allowed access inside them. When he showed them the eye-scans for each dorm, Byron looked at them all gravely. "You are not allowed in the dormitory of the opposite sex. Do not try me on this. Most of you have already agreed, but I will repeat it anyway: sexual contact of any kind is not allowed. My job is enough work without dealing with your relationships. While you are here, practice strict abstinence. I will say no more about it."

Jeffie, Natalia, and Kawai grinned at each other when Byron turned his attention to Brickert and Sammy.

"The boxes you carry contain your communicators. Or coms, as you probably call them. You can use those for texting or to speak to me and anyone else in the building. It will not make outside calls, but it will hold your daily schedule. Follow it as best as you can. The different simulators and classrooms are scheduled in rotation to allow everyone equal use during the day. If you have an emergency—medical or otherwise—just say your name and 'emergency.' It will activate the program. The personal statistics menu will show your rank based on your simulation performance in comparison to others. I feel competition and feedback tends to increase individual performance. If you do not wish to know your rank, that is fine, too. Any questions?"

Among all the little curiosities bouncing in his brain, one stuck out to Sammy. "Why are there no rooms on the inner walls?"

"Of course—thank you—I almost forgot. The whole inner part of the building is the Arena. You will learn more about that soon. Any others?" he asked, looking around. "No? Then, I will take my leave, and you can get yourselves settled in your rooms. They will be marked for you."

With one last glance at the girls, Sammy went down the stairwell to the first floor with Brickert behind him, banging his suitcase on each step. Sammy eye-scanned himself and Brickert into the dormitory floor. Like everywhere else, the layout was a perfect square, and each hallway had several doors on the outer wall.

"What's in the bag?" Sammy asked Brickert. Unlike the others, he had no luggage and was curious to see what Brickert had brought.

"Clothes. Pictures. Some other personal stuff. Where's yours?"

"I didn't need to bring stuff from home," Sammy lied to avoid awkward questions.

Brickert muttered something under his breath that Sammy couldn't quite hear. They walked the hall in silence looking for their rooms. After a moment, Sammy realized he had not been listening properly when Brickert had introduced himself. His mind had been on other things.

"Where are you from again?"

"I'm from the Irish Territory," Brickert answered, and for the first time Sammy noticed a slight accent in Brickert's voice. "Near Killarney." His words came tumbling out, giving Sammy the impression Brickert had been eagerly waiting for a chance to talk about home. "My parents were shocked when they found out about all this. My dad had more than half a mind to not let me come here, I'll tell you, but my mom insisted that one of her children amount to something more than a factory worker."

"How many children are in your family?" Sammy asked.

"I'm the ninth of ten children," Brickert replied.

Sammy swore loudly. "Ten kids?"

Brickert made it sound like everyone had ten kids. Sammy's parents had tried to have more children after him, but he had never met anyone from such a large family.

"Yeah, it's kind of a lot, huh?" Brickert admitted with an embarrassed look.

Sammy stopped walking when he realized he had made Brickert uncomfortable. "I mean . . ." he hurried to say, " . . . there's nothing wrong with that. I was an only child, so . . . you know, anything more than one seems big to me."

"Really? No brothers or sisters?" Sammy heard more than a hint of jealousy in Brickert's voice. "That must be really nice."

"Actually I always wanted a little brother," Sammy told him. "You know, to play sports with or chess or something. I had friends, but sometimes I only had my parents for that stuff."

"You can have one of mine . . ."

They continued walking again. Many of the rooms in the dormitory were vacant. The halls were all white, just like everywhere else, except near one room where a large chunk of wall sported a mural of two boys wearing VR helmets faced off in some sort of fight. The door in the middle of the mural said Reynolds/Reynolds. The one after it read Hayman/Petrov, and finally Berhane/Plack.

"Cool! That's you, right?" Brickert asked pointing at the names, and smiling for the first time since they had met. "We're going to be roommates."

Sammy saw the relief in Brickert's face. *The poor kid's probably been terrified he'd get a roommate that would eat him.* Rooming with Brickert was fine by him; at least he would not be stuck with some anal-retentive wacko. *Unless*

Brickert turns out to be some anal-retentive wacko. But from the little time they had already spent together, Brickert seemed okay.

"I don't think that I can reach that eye-scan," Brickert mumbled at the door, and he was right. He had to jump just a little to get his eye over the scanner.

"You're the youngest person here," Sammy pointed out quickly, "it's no biggie. It's not your fault someone didn't plan better." He put his eye over the hole and heard a click.

They went inside their new bedroom. It was much larger than Sammy had expected. A bunk bed stood against the left wall. He guessed he'd probably be sleeping on the top given Brickert's size. Two large desks stood at the back wall with a chair apiece, and spacious closets with mirrors were on the opposite side of the room from the beds. The furniture all seemed high quality and looked recently cleaned and polished.

"Wow!" Brickert said. "I can't believe I'm going to be living somewhere so—so posh!"

Posh was not the word Sammy chose to describe it, but he was still impressed. "Yeah . . . it's pretty nice."

"Let's see if they've brought us those suits Byron mentioned we're supposed to wear during the day."

In the closets, they found their personalized flight suits. All of Sammy's suits were white and light blue, but to add a little flavor, each had different colored embellishments on the sleeves and legs. He grabbed the one with gold trimmings, and pressed the collar tabs. When he stepped inside and pressed the tabs again, the front sealed seamlessly. He looked over and saw that Brickert's jumpsuit color was white and a soft green; Brickert had chosen one with white trimmings.

"Amazing, huh?" Brickert said, gesturing to the clothes. "I've never worn anything like this before, I'll tell you."

Sammy had worn seamless clothes before, mostly when his parents took him to fancy parties and important ceremonies, but he thought it best not to mention it as Brickert probably came from a poorer family and was embarrassed easily.

"Where are you from again, Samuel?" Brickert asked, trying to sound casual.

Sammy choked back a laugh. "Call me Sammy. No one calls me Samuel, not even my parents, except, well, unless I made them really mad."

"Sorry."

"Don't worry. I'm from Johannesburg."

"You're—you're the first black person I've ever met," Brickert said. Red spots grew on his cheeks just as they had during the orientation.

This time Sammy's laugh came out. "You kidding?"

"I'm—well—from a very small town."

"I'm actually only half-black. My mom—my mom's about as light-skinned as you," Sammy said. "How did you find out you were a . . . you belonged here?"

"I was fixing up our shed with my father and accidentally hit my finger with the hammer. I got so mad I blew a hole clear through both sides! It was a cheapo shed but my father saw the whole thing. Made me get checked in at the hospital. He was freaking out. I was there about three hours with all these confused doctors before Byron came in dressed as a doctor, too."

"Byron came?" Sammy asked.

"Yeah. I think he recruits everyone. He told me and my folks about this place, and then let us talk it over for a while. When we agreed, he said I'd have to wait a few months for the next recruiting period to end before I could come."

"So you've known for a long time now?"

"Yeah. He said I shouldn't try to experiment around or tell anyone. We had to sign stuff saying we'd keep it a secret. My family tells everyone I've gone to a boarding school in Melbourne, Australia, for the next several years on scholarship." Brickert chuckled. "Me? On scholarship!"

"Do you have any idea how to—how to do—whatever it is?" Sammy struggled to find the words to describe something he knew nothing about.

"No," Brickert said, shrugging.

"When do you see your family again?"

Brickert looked at him incredulously. "Don't you know? Sorry. I assumed they told everyone. We won't get to see our parents until we graduate. Didn't they tell your family that?"

"Of course," Sammy covered quickly. "I— I just wondered since maybe you are closer to home . . . you know, maybe they'd come visit or something."

"Nope. It was really hard leaving them, too. Tonight will be the first night I've ever spent away from home." Then Brickert suddenly became suspicious. "You're not going to tell anyone that, are you?"

"No. Course not," Sammy said. "You can trust me."

And he meant it. Brickert seemed loyal, much like Sammy's friends in the grocery store. Brickert's youthful innocence brought out a tamer side in him that he hadn't felt in a while. Sammy lost himself in his memories, missing Feet and Gunner and others. Brickert had to clear his throat to get Sammy's attention back.

"Sorry," Sammy mumbled, "just thinking."

"You didn't tell me how you found out about being a Psion," Brickert said. They were both sitting on their chairs wearing the new uniforms. Sammy had his feet propped up and Brickert was settling in as though he was about to hear a good story. But Sammy had a chance now to make a clean start with a new crowd; he wanted to make the most of it. Someone knocked at their door at that moment, saving him the task of thinking up a lie to tell Brickert.

Sammy got up a little too fast and crossed the room. The door opened to reveal a tall skinny boy with light-brown hair and blue eyes wearing a gold and white jumpsuit. He was definitely older than both Sammy and Brickert. He wore a monstrous grin on his face.

"Hey!" he exclaimed. "Can I come in?"

"Sure," Sammy responded, moving out of the way to allow him room.

"Albert Hayman," he said, shaking their hands heartily. "Everyone calls me Al. The commander asked me to keep an eye on you guys. Make sure you find everything okay."

"Thanks!" Brickert answered as if he had just won the lottery.

"What're your names?" he asked.

"Brickert."

"Sammy."

"Are you two the only nukes?" Al asked.

"What does that mean?" Brickert asked.

"Nukes . . . New recruits. Newcomers. Don't either of you game?"

Both Sammy and Brickert shook their heads.

Al rubbed his forehead. "Well, that's going to have to change if you want to fit in. Who else came today?"

"Three girls with us," Sammy answered.

"Really? Five? Wow. Biggest group I've ever heard of."

"How long have you been here?" Brickert asked.

"Me? I've been here forever. Over five years. Almost six now that I think of it. Second longest of anyone here right now, and I finish in about nine months."

"How many Betas are there?" Brickert asked, definitely eager to get his important questions answered. Sammy didn't bother reminding him Byron had already told them the answer.

"With five new recruits that brings it up to . . . twenty Betas."

"Does everyone get along?"

"For the most part. If you can tolerate being called a 'nuke' or worse for a few weeks. Are you guys hungry?"

"I'm starving," answered Sammy. In fact, he could not remember eating since the pizzas on the night the Shocks had come. Thinking about the Shocks reminded him of something else. "Al, what day is it?" he asked.

"It's the eighteenth."

"No, what day of the week is it?"

"Er . . . Sunday," Al replied slowly.

Sammy had been chased from the grocery store on Thursday night. *Two days completely gone, and I have no memory of what happened.*

"Come on," Al said, interrupting Sammy's thought. "I'll help you get food."

"Where's everyone else?" Brickert asked Al as the three of them walked upstairs to the cafeteria.

"Well, we spend so much time inside that on Sundays everyone just wants to get out. Plus, the commander doesn't want anyone inside during tours. Says it distracts the recruits."

Once in the cafeteria, Al gave them a more detailed explanation on how to work the RoboChef. Sammy ordered his favorite, a creamy chicken cordon bleu. The RoboChef made it perfectly. Brickert asked for a hamburger. Al ordered something Sammy had never heard of before. Fifteen minutes later, they were all eating.

"The RoboChef isn't going to break, Sammy," Al said, watching him with disgust and awe. "You can slow down."

Sammy almost choked through his laughter. "Sorry, I just—it's really good and I'm hungry." His diet while living in the grocery store had consisted of anything he and his friends could nick without being caught. And the cordon bleu tasted like a home-cooked meal.

"Mom isn't much of a cook, eh?" Al asked, now smiling again.

"Something like that," Sammy replied.

Brickert glanced at Sammy, but continued eating his burger. While they ate, Al kept up a steady stream of information about other Betas.

"Kobe and Ludwig are habitual practical jokers—watch out for them."

"Are there brothers here?" Sammy asked. "We saw a door that had identical last names above it."

"That's Kobe and Kaden. The Reynolds twins."

"Twins?" Brickert repeated. "Cool."

"Kind of a funny story how the commander found them, actually," Al continued. "They were playing one of those VR fighting games. You know the ones you can control with your mind? Street Fighter, I think. Anyway, Kobe, he's the one I just mentioned, he got really mad and blasted Kaden across the room. Kaden did it right back. By the time the commander got there, they'd caused a ton of damage and the cops were dragging them to jail."

Sammy and Brickert both laughed with Al.

"Can you show us what it is we . . . can do?" Sammy asked Al.

"Sure. What do you want to see?"

"Anything," Brickert said.

"Okay," Al answered, and then, after looking around, pointed to Brickert's half-empty glass of water. "Watch that glass."

Sammy and Brickert stared at the glass, and Al held his hand about ten centimeters away.

"Watching?" Al asked.

They both nodded anxiously.

The glass moved away from Al's hand all on its own at a steady speed toward the end of the table. It stopped only centimeters away from the edge.

"WOW!" Brickert exclaimed with unabashed applause.

Sammy swore softly. He had to admit it . . . it was cool.

"Thanks," Al said. "We used to have contests to see who could get the glass closest to the edge without falling, but the commander made us quit. We broke too many."

Just then Al's com came alive and a holographic screen dropped down over his eye.

"Hey," Al said. "Yeah, we're in the cafeteria, bring the girls up and have Kaden bring the guys. Okay. Bye." When his screen went away he informed them, "That was Marie. She's the oldest girl. Looks like we're going to have a little get-together in the rec hall. So everyone can get to know you."

The rec hall was empty when they got there, so Al took time to show Sammy and Brickert more than what they had glimpsed on the tour. Sammy couldn't help but be impressed, and everything astounded Brickert. The rec hall took up almost half of the floor. It had a miniature VR gaming area similar to what Sammy had seen in the best malls in Johannesburg, a small movie theatre, and lots of other games like pool and foosball. Plus, there were two racquetball courts, a basketball court, and an indoor turf field—all of it pristine.

"Dang, this place is nutty," Sammy commented to himself when Al finished showing them around.

They waited in a sitting area next to the VR center where Al had arranged almost two dozen gel chairs into a circle. Sammy and Brickert took adjacent empty chairs as other Betas trickled in. Marie came in with Natalia, Kawai, and Jeffie. She was a pretty girl with dark hair in a ponytail. She sat next to Al, and they began chatting at once. Sammy tried to catch Jeffie's eye so she would take the other chair next to him, but she didn't notice and sat with the other girls across the room.

"Where's the pukes?" a loud voice called from just outside the door. It belonged to a tall, athletic kid with spiked, bleach-blond hair ending in darkened tips and a cocky smile that filled the lower half of his face. "Where are they?" he said again, doing a mock duck hunt. "I just got back from the store with some fresh diapers. Commander Byron said they haven't been potty trained yet." Several other boys about his age followed him in, laughing at his joke. After glancing around the room, the blond boy sat down next to Jeffie and held out his hand. "Hi."

Jeffie smiled and shook his hand. "Hi."

"I'm Kobe," the blond kid said, his voice rich with charm. "Nice to meet you. Do you need your diaper changed?"

"Jeffie," she replied with an even bigger smirk. "And no, thank you."

Sammy's ears got warm as he watched Kobe expertly work his magic on Jeffie. Then Kobe introduced himself to Kawai and Natalia with the same fanfare.

"So Al," Kobe said, "Are we going to sit in a circle and sing Cowabunga?"

"Something like that," Al chuckled.

"Maybe we should just skip the talk and get straight to the nitty-gritty," Kobe said. "Who's good at gaming?"

Several people laughed.

"Told you," Al said to Brickert and Sammy with a wink. When all twenty Betas had arrived, the group got quiet and all eyes were on Al. "What?" he asked sheepishly.

"You're the one who called us here," Marie said.

"Fine. Let's just go around and introduce ourselves to the new guys."

"And girls," Jeffie added.

"Right," Al said, "and girls."

From the names and accents he heard, Sammy guessed they had a small sampling of almost every ethnicity on the planet in headquarters. Fortunately, English was NWG standard language, and everyone spoke it fluently. The names also told Sammy that seven of the twenty Psions were siblings from three different families.

No one paid much attention to Sammy when he gave his very brief introduction, and he didn't mind. This crowd was so different than his friends. He hadn't heard anyone swear, and a few of them talked in very proper English. Gunner and Honk sometimes liked to see how many times they could curse in one sentence. *Don't these people know how to relax?* But then he remembered how he had once been a lot like them.

When Brickert's turn came, Al pointed out that he was the youngest Psion ever. Kobe snorted and muttered under his breath, "That runty puke definitely needs his diaper changed," to the kid sitting next to him, who nodded and snickered. Brickert, who hated the extra attention, overheard Kobe's comment and his cheeks turned bright red. When Jeffie introduced herself, she received several open-mouthed stares from most of the other male Psions. On the other hand, several of the girls glanced back more than once at Kawai's strange bracelets and feathers, but she seemed unabashed as ever about her unusual style.

As soon as Li Cheng Zheng finished his introduction, Kobe jumped up and announced, "Let's break in the pukes with Star Racers."

Several Betas voiced their agreement.

"Do you guys want to play?" Al asked Sammy and Brickert.

"Sure," they both said. Sammy had very little experience gaming, but had always enjoyed watching the other kids play when he and his mom walked by the gaming stations in the shops.

"Don't embarrass yourself, Kobe," Kaden said.

Kobe made a rude noise. "Right. Like any of them have played it."

"I have played it, actually," said Jeffie.

"Oh, you have, have you?" Kobe asked, now even more interested in her. "Well, it just so happens that I'm the best here. King of the hill if you will."

Groans of dissent came from all corners of the room. Ludwig threw his gel chair at Kobe's head.

"Well, I am," Kobe told them as he ducked it.

"Talk is cheap," Kobe's brother, Kaden, said. "Let's play."

"Pukes—I mean, nukes—first," Al announced. "Brillianté, Levu, and Martin can play with them."

"Why us?" Brillianté asked?

"Because you're not very good," Kobe responded with a smirk. Brillianté shot a blast at Kobe which left his hair messed up.

Al, Marie, Kobe, Kaden, and Li Cheng Zheng took the five nukes into the VR stations. Each of the eight stations were built like small cubicles with the same brilliant white walls Sammy saw everywhere else. A pilot's chair and flight controls furnished the interior. A small projector hung overhead. Kaden, who looked very little like his brother and acted even less like him, explained the rules to Sammy and demonstrated how to work the controls to move, accelerate, shoot, and shield.

"Just like this?" Sammy repeated what he had seen Kaden do.

"Exactly." Kaden's smile was friendly. "You're a natural."

Sammy took his seat, and the playing area darkened while the projector turned on. The cubicle gave the perfect illusion that he sat in the cockpit of a fighter docked inside a gigantic star cruiser. He fingered the controls to practice, remembering everything Kaden had said. To his left and right, he saw identical racing fighters, only with different occupants. The projected image of Brickert looked back at him and grinned giddily.

Cool, Sammy thought. *Very cool.*

Numbers appeared counting down to the start of the race. When it reached zero, Sammy fired his reverse thrusters and shot backwards into the dock, banging his ship on the back wall.

Oops! Wrong way.

Fortunately, three of the others had similar problems accelerating as well. Only Jeffie shot clean out of the launching space. Sammy fumbled with the controls until he was able to gently ease the fighter out of the dock, then he took off into space with the others accelerating beside or in front of him. He sped past Brickert's ship, which seemed unable to fly in a straight course, and followed flashing green arrows that guided the racers. It surprised Sammy how quickly he acclimated to the controls. After only a minute of flying, the ship was merely an extension of his body.

A red light appeared on his control panel. This, Kaden had said, meant one of the racers was targeting him. He punched the shield button and directed the shields to the rear to absorb any hits he could not shake off. This meant he would lose some of his speed, but it was better than being blown up. After experimenting with a few other maneuvers, he shook the ship targeting him.

Out his left window, he saw Jeffie trying to accelerate past him. He moved left to cut her off. She went up and over him to prevent this, so he held back and fired on her engines. She easily shielded them, but he accelerated nose down and came up under her, firing on her belly. According to Kaden, this was the only part of the ship that could not be shielded. After a brilliant, but momentarily blinding explosion, Sammy went full speed ahead to reach the carrier first without any more difficulty.

The projector turned off, and Kaden came in congratulating him. "Pretty good flying."

"Thanks," Sammy responded. "How'd you see it?"

"The screens out there show the whole race like a movie so we can watch everyone."

Sammy got up to leave, but Kaden stopped him. "Hold fast. Let everyone else switch seats for the next race. You and Brillianté both stay since you were first and second."

"Gotcha."

"I'll see you in there this time," Kaden called out as he headed for his cubicle. "Good luck."

As Sammy waited, a huge grin formed on his face. *No wonder they're hooked on the game. It's a rush!* The race was intense, and with the holographic projection perfectly synchronized with his controls, the illusion of space was almost too real.

Six new players took their seats while Sammy waited impatiently. The projector came to life once more, and he saw new faces in the fighters next to him. Kaden and Al were on opposite sides, and Marie sat on Al's other side giving him a thumbs down.

The countdown began. At zero, Sammy shot out of the carrier with the others. The outside racers jockeyed for a better inside position. He fired his reverse thrusters just enough to get behind the small crowd of ships. Three ships moved in to occupy his space. Sammy fired on Kaden and Al. The ships on the outside pulled ahead of the middle ships and cut in toward the middle. When Sammy took out Kaden's ship and drew even with Al, Al gestured for a temporary truce.

Together they targeted the enemy fighters in sequence, destroying them all until only they remained. They both sped toward the landing ship trying to get into the best position, circling around each other's ships. As the intensity picked up, an odd sensation settled over Sammy.

He saw.

Just like the chess game.

He went into a nose dive exactly as he'd done against Jeffie, but this time he counted on Al recognizing what he was doing. Instead of actually diving, Sammy did a shallow dip and sped forward while Al went nose up to protect his belly. Sammy threw open his thrusters and raced forward. His target warning went off and he shielded Al's fire. Although it cost him in speed, he had gained enough distance to beat Al into the cruiser and win again.

From the cubicle next to him, Al cried, "You punk! You've never played this before, huh?"

"Never," Sammy said with a confident grin.

"Sweet flying! Let's see who wins the next one. Watch out for Kobe—he's not all talk."

"That's right, puke," Kobe gloated as he walked by. "Don't get a big head. Only I've earned it."

Al was right. Kobe played very well. He started on the outside, and quickly eliminated two ships on his side, drifting inward and targeting Sammy. Rather than shielding, Sammy sped in front of Al. Al's ship took the force of Kobe's fire and detonated. Knowing from experience that Kobe would be blinded from Al's explosion, Sammy quickly reversed his thrust and fell close behind Kobe, hoping Kobe would think he had picked off both ships.

Kobe set his sights on the remaining two racers. When they were both gone, a whoop came from a nearby cubicle.

He thinks he's won.

Sammy dived down, just as he had with Jeffie, and came up targeting Kobe's unprotected underside.

KABOOM!

Poor puke never saw it coming, Sammy thought with glee.

With no ships left in the game, Sammy sped off to the cruiser and gracefully landed—three games, three victories.

"No way!" Kobe's voice boomed as he came down the hall toward Sammy. "I blew you sky high. How did you get behind me?"

Just as Kobe appeared at Sammy's cubicle, Al put his hand on Kobe's shoulder, laughing hard. "No, no, no," Al jeered. "Don't be mad just because you got beat. Sammy—just—absolutely brilliant!"

Al and Sammy exchanged fives. Kobe just stood there, demanding to know how Sammy had won. Sammy shrugged ominously and walked out past him. He almost gave Kobe the bird, but better wisdom prevailed. Al was laughing too hard to explain anything, and this made Kobe hopping mad. Sammy didn't like Kobe, and he wasn't going to stand around and talk strategy with a guy who got in his face.

"Puke luck," he heard Kobe's voice grumble in the cubicle.

The comment angered Sammy, but he realized Kobe had a point. *How did I pick up on the game so fast? I was pretty good at the games back in the grocery store. Maybe I'm just good at games.* He exited the VR cubicles and saw Brickert beaming at him and Jeffie scowling.

Determined to make a good impression on her, Sammy approached her with an outstretched hand and a smile. "Good game?"

Jeffie rolled her eyes and walked past him into the cubicles. Everyone else congratulated him or remarked on how impressed they were with his playing. But none of it meant anything after seeing Jeffie upset. Suddenly she seemed a lot less attractive. *Stupid girls.* He turned to Brickert. "Tired?"

"Not really," Brickert responded. "Are you?"

"Yeah, kinda. I think I'm going to bed."

On his way down, Sammy got the urge to stop at the cafeteria. The idea of having so much food available on a whim excited him. He helped himself to a large bowl of coconut ice cream, his favorite. His mom and dad used to make it for him on his birthday.

He thought of everything he had been through over the last several days, even months—everything was so jumbled. *Maybe I'll just wake up tomorrow on a stack of cardboard boxes in the store . . . or in a white room for loonies.* Within the year, he'd gone from a home, to the Grinder, to being a runaway, and now here as a Psion Beta with some weird powers (if he even had them). Everything in his life now was based on Byron's promise that he had an anomaly.

A simple bowl of ice cream became too emotional for Sammy. Without really knowing why, he was blinking tears from his eyes. He was scared and missed his mom and dad more than he had in quite some time. He wished they'd been there when he'd taken the oath to protect people. His father, especially, would have been proud of that.

Someone came into the room, and he turned to see Al.

"Hey, I was wondering where you'd—" he stopped as he saw Sammy's face.

Sammy tried to turn back before Al noticed, but was not quick enough.

"Are you all right?" Al asked, moving over to sit next to him.

"Yeah," Sammy quickly answered, "I'm fine."

"You need to talk?"

"No! I mean—no, it's nothing, I was just thinking about . . . stuff," Sammy reassured him. Talking about feelings reminded him too much of the one-on-one and group sessions in the Grinder.

"What kind of stuff?"

"Just stuff," Sammy replied in his most casual voice. "What did your parents think about you coming here?"

Al seemed caught off guard by the question, and he took a moment to think. "It was really hard for me and my dad both when I came here," Al said. "My dad was worried."

"And your mom?" Sammy asked, thinking back to what Brickert had said about his family. "What did she think?"

Even more time passed before Al answered this question. "She was really . . . proud of me. Really proud." Sammy heard a finality in Al's as he said this. "You sure you're all right?"

"Yeah," Sammy answered, "seriously, I'm cool."

Al gave Sammy a friendly pat on the back and left. Sammy sat in silence for a moment, thinking about the conversation.

Feeling more tired than ever and embarrassed about being caught crying, he dumped the rest of his ice cream and went to his room. Without much thought, he undressed, put his com on the charger, and turned out the lights. *A bed*, he thought when he hit his soft pillow. *If Feet and the others could see me now. Sleeping in my own bed. Posh.* Then he fell asleep. He only woke up once during the night to the sound of muffled sobbing; he was not used to sleeping above a very homesick roommate.

6 | Headquarters

"GOOD MORNING, PSIONS. Good morning, Psions. Good morning, Psions," a calm and soothing female voice repeated over and over again, stirring Sammy from his sleep.

His eyelids cracked open, and he saw his body covered in sheets. The familiar scent of moldy cardboard was strangely missing.

Who's snoring below me?

"Good morning, Psions," he heard again, and then he remembered: he was a Psion. He reached for his com. Putting it on made everything real again. He couldn't help but be excited, especially when he thought about his training. If everything went well, he would find out if he had these abilities everyone talked about. Just as he thought to wake up Brickert, a loud thud shook the bed.

"OW!" Brickert cried in pain below.

Sammy laughed in pity as he hung his head over the side to look in the bottom bunk. Brickert clutched his forehead, hiding the purple lump forming there. He looked paler than usual and his eyes were a little red from being rubbed too much. Sammy guessed his roommate had not slept much last night.

"You okay?" Sammy asked over the female voice.

"My first night on a bunk bed," Brickert whimpered. "Don't worry, though. I'll get used to it."

As soon as Sammy turned the light on, the woman's voice stopped. He reached over his ear, activated his com, and saw the holo-screen. With one command, he called up his schedule:

```
0600-0700  Rise/Exercise
0700-0800  Breakfast/Shower
0800-1200  Instruction
1200-1300  Lunch
1300-1700  Simulations
1700-2200  Dinner/Recreation/Retire
```

"I'm surprised they don't tell us when to take a dump, too," he said to himself.

His life had suddenly changed from anarchy to rigid structure. He wondered what his friends were doing at that moment. He had half a mind to just stay in bed, but rather than make trouble for Byron, he let out a long sigh and grabbed his exercise clothes from his closet. He noticed that the jeans and hoodie he'd worn when Byron had picked him up had been laundered and hung up. He took his hoodie off its hanger and threw it on over his shirt.

As they talked on the way up to the fitness room, Sammy and Brickert realized their schedules were identical. Sammy hoped his schedule mirrored Jeffie's, too. He paused at the entrance. He hadn't expected to see the room so busy, but it looked like all the Betas had morning exercise. Al and Marie sprinted on the same treadmill, Al taunting her to keep up. Rosa, Marie's younger sister, ran alongside them. She looked like a miniature version of her sister, just with lighter hair. Kaden was surrounded by a bunch of guys his own age. *But where is*—And then Sammy saw her working out with Kobe, Natalia, and Kawai. A surge of jealousy pulsed through him. In the pit of his stomach, he knew Kobe had his eye on Jeffie . . . but did Jeffie already have her eye on Kobe, too?

The computer gave Sammy and Brickert their workouts. Sammy picked out two empty treadmills far away from Kobe, and said, "Let's go over there." Perhaps sensing Sammy's sudden mood change, Brickert tried to strike up a conversation about how the rest of their day would go. But as the treadmill picked up speed, he stopped talking to focus on breathing.

Sammy fueled his dislike for Kobe into the treadmill. The more he heard Jeffie and Kobe laughing, the harder he ran. He didn't care if he would feel the burn later or if he had to suck down air to avoid passing out; he welcomed it. *What does Jeffie see in Kobe? He's a douche.* As his mind raced, his feet flew gracefully on the exercise machine. Another thought struck him. Maybe Jeffie was more like Kobe than Sammy cared to admit. The idea occurred to him that maybe he wasn't jealous of Jeffie talking to Kobe, but that she wasn't talking to him.

As the workout wore on, he got tired of thinking about Jeffie. He wondered about the simulations in the afternoon. *What if I can't do it? Even if I actually am a Psion or whatever but I just sit in the simulation room for hours without accomplishing a thing?* A monumentally horrifying idea struck him: *Would they send me back to the Grinder? No*, he assured himself. *I'll be gone before they realize it.* But the possibility worried him.

Exercising in the morning was both invigorating and exhausting. When he stepped off the treadmill and threw on his red hoodie, his legs wobbled like jelly. He was looking forward to a hot shower. It had been almost a year since his last one. The Grinder only had cool water, and at the grocery store, when they started to stink, they borrowed someone's garden hose or washed in the restroom at the nearby Burger Palace.

Brickert and Sammy picked out their jumpsuits and took them to the common bathroom. He undressed and laid his clothes over the door of his shower, then stepped onto the cool tile inside. He felt giddy. He had no desire to hurry. As he soaked in the warm water, his palms turned to raisins. After three washes, his hair started to feel normal again. How had he lived without simple things like shampoo or a change of clothes?

He turned off the water and started the dryer until he felt windblown but clean. After putting on a deodorizing powder, he reached over the stall door for his new jumpsuit, but couldn't find it. His hoodie was gone, too.

Someone had taken them. Someone had taken his hoodie—a terribly foolish person.

He threw open the shower stall and scanned the ground. No clothes. Stark naked, he left the bathroom and marched down the hall to his bedroom. As he passed Kobe's room, he heard laughter inside. *Of course.* He pounded on the door, cursing and yelling, "Give me my hoodie back!"

The door opened and Kobe, Ludwig, and Miguel stood inside laughing hysterically. Sammy knew they had no idea what the hoodie meant to him, and he didn't care. He grabbed Kobe by the collar and yelled in his face, "Give me my hoodie back, dickhead!"

Ludwig and Miguel stopped laughing at once. Sammy was taller and built stronger than both of them. Kobe, however, did not seem to get the point.

"What's your deal?" Kobe shouted back, wrenching his jump suit from Sammy. "It's just a puke prank. Learn how to take a joke."

"Kobe," Miguel said, "maybe you'd better—"

"You really are a puke!" Kobe spat. "Here," he shoved the clothes back at Sammy, "take your piece of trash hoodie."

"Don't ever touch my stuff!" Sammy roared, even more infuriated by Kobe's response. "I don't like you, and if you take my things again, I'm throwing it down. Get it?"

Miguel and Ludwig both muttered apologies to Sammy as he passed them. Kobe, on the other hand, did not. Rather, he added for good measure, "Well, don't come into my room uninvited!"

Sammy didn't need an invitation to leave. He crossed the hall, still naked, and entered his own room. Brickert had finished dressing, but noticed the hurricane that accompanied Sammy inside.

"What happened, Samuel—Sammy?"

Brickert's question didn't register with Sammy. He was so inflamed from the encounter that his arms and hands shook. He clutched the hoodie to his chest, replaying the encounter over again in his mind, only each time he imagined himself saying something much worse and then punching Kobe in the face and stomach.

It took several minutes before the anger collapsed on itself, and he came to his senses. He paced around the room to calm himself, afraid that he might do something really stupid. Byron had warned him about his behavior. It was hard, especially remembering the fights he had gotten into at the Grinder over lesser things.

"Sammy, are you okay?" Brickert finally asked again. He sounded so young.

"Fine," he told himself more than Brickert. "They stole my clothes so I'd have to walk back here naked. I—I—argh!" The anger threatened to surge back again and he slammed his closet shut. For a moment, he thought he had broken the door. He blew out a long slow breath. "You wouldn't get it, Brickert. Sorry."

His mind went back to the day he got the sweater. *No*—Sammy corrected himself. *The day I won it.*

Sammy's father had many hobbies but few passions. Chess was one of his passions. "Territorial tournament champion two years in a row," he often told people, especially his son. He made it a point never to let Sammy win a game. "You've got to earn the win," he always said. "You'll appreciate it more."

One night after dinner, Sammy tried talking his dad into playing without a queen, and if not the queen, at least a rook.

"You know I won't go easy on you," his father reminded him, "because then—"

"—I'll always remember the first time I beat you," Sammy finished from memory.

"Go get the board, smarty pants."

I'm going to beat him, Sammy told himself, just as he always did before they played. He brought the board to the kitchen table, and they set up the pieces. Sammy was white, his father was black. Just as it always was. His father made a joke out of it because Sammy's skin was much lighter than his father's.

Though they occasionally played with a chess timer, tonight there was no rush. They sat opposite each other, Sammy Sr. still in his work suit, Sammy Jr. wearing jeans and a Drive Shaft T-shirt with a couple of designer holes. As was typical, his dad began with a strong Sicilian defense. Both took their time planning their moves. Sammy's mother moved in and out of the background clearing the table around them.

It was almost like magic when it happened.

Suddenly Sammy *saw* the square board differently. He saw not only pieces and movements, but he also repercussion, potential, and his father's flaws. Then he made his move.

His father stared at the board for almost a minute, then muttered, "Good move."

Sammy took similar amounts of time to think after his father's next few turns. He saw more flaws.

Absentmindedly, his dad loosened his tie and opened the top button on his shirt. "You're playing . . . well."

Samuel Sr. moved again.

There's the position I need.

Three more turns passed.

"CHECKMATE!" Sammy yelled, jumping up and down, screaming at the top of his lungs.

His father stared at the chessboard, mouth open. "Are you sure?" he muttered to himself.

His mother, Sarah, came back into the room to see what all the commotion was about.

"I beat him, Mom! I beat Dad!"

"Is that true, Sam?" she asked.

Sammy's father could only nod his head to acknowledge his wife.

"Wow, that deserves a celebration, don't you think?" she said, smiling down at Sammy. "Want to go to the mall and pick out something?"

"Right now?" Sammy asked. "I'm spending the night at Denton's house tonight."

"Well, how about I drop you off there on the way back from the mall?"

"Can I get a new pair of jeans and that red hoodie?" he asked.

"Anything you want," she answered. "You coming, Sam?"

Sammy's father didn't hear her. He was still staring at the chess board in shock.

No, Brickert, Sammy thought to himself. *You wouldn't understand at all. Not with your nine sisters and mom and dad, who may be poor, but still—*

He hung his hoodie back in his closet with care, and quickly dressed into a blue jumpsuit with black stripes. He left the room, ignoring the perplexed stare on Brickert's face. By the time he reached the third floor, he'd decided to skip breakfast. He was in no mood to eat, and didn't want to see anyone, particularly Kobe. Part of him felt embarrassed for getting so upset; he was already making waves, and had only been there one day.

But why did he have to pull a prank on ME?

It was time for instruction. The part of his schedule he looked forward to the least.

He found his name above a door and eye-scanned himself into the room. Instruction, Byron had told them, would not be held in a classroom setting. Rather, to facilitate maximum learning, each person could choose what he or she wanted to study for the block of four hours each day at a comfortable pace. To facilitate this theory, every room had a machine called the Teacher. It was a large armchair set on a large black platform that extended vertically, supporting a screen that faced the occupant of the seat. To Sammy it looked like a giant arcade game built for brainwashing people.

He sat down, and the screen automatically powered up to reveal Commander Byron's face looking back at him.

"Good morning, Psion. Today you begin your personal instruction. The education you will receive is based around a core of information you need to become an effective member of a Psion Alpha team. You are expected to learn and understand all of the material presented. Part of the Psion Panel, which you must pass to graduate from Beta, is scoring high enough on the exams you take after completing each subject unit.

"See the subject units in which your aptitude will be tested." An interface titled `Main Menu` replaced Byron's image.

"Basic mechanics," his voice continued, "weaponry, theory of combat, mission planning and execution, critical thinking, physics, history and political science, and geography. Parts of combat, mission functionality, and weaponry will be covered in your simulations and in the Arena; however, you must also learn the principles behind these subjects for the Panel. I encourage you to take advantage of the flexibility of your education. There is no homework, just exams. If you wish, both the Teacher's menus and the library are available for you to explore sections more in depth."

Commander Byron's face faded, and a tutorial appeared on the screen to teach Sammy more about the Teacher. It took him about five minutes to complete. Then the main menu appeared again. When Sammy touched a subject, it broke down into several units. All of these units had dozens of subunits from which to choose. He was staggered by the amount of information, and guessed it would take years to get through the material.

He chose history and started with the first subunit. The screen displayed information in the form of text, movie clips, news footage, and pictures relating to political history.

The format of the material made the presentation quite fascinating, but Sammy still found himself losing interest in the female voice that guided him through the information. The only reason he could think of was that she spoke too slow. He stopped the lecture to find the menu allowing him to adjust the speed.

After another hour, boredom set in again. He turned the speed up a little more. Then a little more. By the time his first session finished, the lady's voice sounded like she'd inhaled too much helium. On the other hand, Sammy got through over half of one subunit. He was pleased with himself as met up with Brickert. In the cafeteria, he ordered a sub sandwich; Brickert got a hamburger again.

"Geography was pretty cool," Brickert said with a mouth full of lunch. "It was mostly stuff about territories, major cities—you know, like that, but some of the other subunits that come later on look really cool. I think I'm saying cool too much. Anyway, a bunch of them deal with important geographical CAG sites. I can't wait to learn all that!"

"Didn't you think the lessons were too slow?" Sammy asked.

Brickert shook his head. "It seemed fine to me. Maybe it was just your lesson. I mean, it's totally different than school. You get to pick what you want to learn about. No busy work. I tell you, I wish my old school had been like this."

Sammy agreed with him. This new way was definitely better. If he didn't understand something all he needed to do was touch the subtitle, and the program would offer supplemental information to help him. Best of all, he had no distractions. What if he had to sit through a class with Kobe? Or worse . . . Jeffie? He'd spend the whole class sneaking peeks at her instead of listening.

"Hey guys," a voice behind him said. "Mind if we sit by you?"

Sammy turned to see Kawai carrying her food, her hair still done up in ribbons and feathers, only different colors today to match her outfit. Behind her came Natalia and Jeffie with their own trays. He stopped chewing his food and found that his voice was gone.

"Um—" Brickert hesitated, looking to Sammy.

"Sure," Sammy coughed out, shrugging casually back at Brickert.

Natalia sat down by Brickert, and Kawai next to Sammy. To Sammy's disappointment, Jeffie sat on the other side of Kawai.

"So how was instruction?" Natalia asked. Then she added with a smirk, "Wasn't it just so much fun?"

"Not bad," both boys said.

"What'd you guys study?" Kawai asked.

Brickert and Sammy told her what they'd studied.

"Jeffie and I did history, too."

"I started with physics," Natalia answered. "Well, I thought it said psychics—like talking about our powers. But I got so lost, I stopped it and went to geography."

"You thought we're called psychics?" Jeffie asked.

Natalia just shrugged, circled her finger around her ear, and made a silly face.

"Did you think the history lesson was slow?" Brickert asked the girls.

Kawai shook her head, "No, I liked it. Way better than my old school. Our tribal elders teach school. No kidding, this one guy used to fall asleep mid-sentence at least twice a day."

"I liked instruction, too," Jeffie said to Brickert. "Didn't you?"

"Yeah, I did," Brickert said just as he noticed his fingers were dripping burger grease. Kawai handed over a napkin so he could wipe his hands. "Sammy thought it was really slow."

"No—that's not—I just thought—"

"Yeah, we can't all be as good as Super Sammy," Jeffie said with a scowl just like the one she'd worn last night after Sammy beat her.

"That's not what I meant," he shot back. "I don't think I'm better than anyone."

He saw Kawai and Natalia exchange a wary glance. Brickert's cheeks turned red.

"Then why'd you lie about never playing Star Racers before yesterday?" Jeffie asked, looking past Kawai.

"I didn't lie," Sammy answered. *Why is she being so dumb?*

"Whatever . . ." she responded. "I played Star Racers a lot before I came here. I can tell when someone's played before."

Sammy didn't know what to say in return. Jeffie had never talked to him before, had no idea who he was.

"I—uh—I don't think he meant that . . . about the lesson, Jeffie," Brickert tried to say.

Sammy shook his head at his roommate. He appreciated that Brickert wanted to erase the damage, but the opportunity was gone. Kawai kept eating her food as if she couldn't hear Sammy and Jeffie, but Natalia's eyes grew to about twice their normal size and she just stared at them.

"Sorry," Brickert muttered so only Sammy could hear.

"It's not your fault," Sammy answered with closed eyes. "Some people are just so small they can't handle losing."

Jeffie started to fire off her next retort, but Sammy got up and disposed of his lunch before he had to hear it. *Maybe I should start eating in my bedroom,* he thought as he stormed out of the cafeteria. To kill time before simulations, he stalked the halls of the fifth floor to calm himself.

I can't believe she thinks I lied about the stupid game.

When it was time to start simulations, he went to the room assigned to him and tried to open it, but it was locked. He muttered a curse and slumped to the floor. He'd never had to put up with any of this crap before, even at the Grinder. If someone had pissed him off, Sammy punched him until the guards broke them up.

The stairwell door shut behind him, and Sammy looked to see who was coming. It was Jeffie. She saw him and looked away as she walked past him. Her room opened right when she eye-scanned the door. Just before going in, she turned and glanced at Sammy, her face expressionless.

Just go away, Jeffie.

Finally his sim room opened. A sweaty and tired Kaden stepped out. "Hey! You waiting for me to finish?"

"I guess so."

"Pretty excited for your first time?"

"Yeah," was all Sammy answered. He'd been thinking more about Jeffie than simulations.

"Don't worry if you don't catch on right away," Kaden told him. "It took me the better part of—shoot—an hour or two before I figured out how to do a blast properly. I think everyone's that way."

"Oh, really? That's good."

Kaden held the door open for Sammy with one hand and brushed his overgrown, dirty blond hair out of his eyes with the other. "I—uh—heard Kobe hazed you a bit this morning."

"Yeah," Sammy answered. "He's a real hilarious guy."

"He is what he is. He's my bro. I love him, but he hates losing, in case you couldn't tell."

"No, I had no clue." He tried to manage a grin for Kaden's sake, but he wasn't sure he pulled it off. "How come you and Kobe are so different?"

Kaden brushed his hair out of his eyes again. He wore his hair much shaggier than Kobe. "Fraternal twins, obviously. But we're alike."

"People play pranks on the nukes all the time here. Just something to get used to. I couldn't find my underwear for almost a week after I got here. Turned out Kobe did that, too, so maybe it doesn't count."

"I didn't mean to blow up at him. He caught me off guard. I'm trying to play it cool."

"Oh well, no biggie," Kaden called out as he left. "Good luck in there."

Sammy stepped into the room. It was much, much bigger than the instruction room. The walls were the same brilliant white that Sammy had come to expect everywhere, but the ceiling was dramatically different. Not only was the ceiling much higher here (he estimated it reached fifteen meters), but it was laced with micro-projectors. Micro-projectors had only one purpose: fully interactive hologram display. The floor was unique, too.

It was slightly more flexible and gave off tiny swirls of gray and white wherever he stepped.

The controls for the room were on a small touch screen near the door. As he read the display, all thoughts of Jeffie vanished.

UNIT ONE: Primary Skills:

Introduction	Advanced Jump Blasting
Precision Blasting	Hovering
Jump Blasting	Landing
Blast Variation	Aerial and Ground Agility

The only subunit that would open to his touch was the first. Apparently, the subunits had to be completed sequentially. Holding his breath, he pressed the icon for the first unit: Introduction.

"Welcome to Psion Beta Simulations," a voice said.

7 | Rankings

SAMMY SPUN AROUND, startled at the sudden noise. Then he laughed. Byron stood in the middle of the room. Sammy reached out and touched Byron's arm. "That's cool." The arm felt like real flesh, except it wasn't. It was a hologram.

"In the introduction unit you will learn how to execute a basic energy burst, or *blast* as we call it. In order to move onto the next section, you must repeatedly perform blasts from the palms of your hands. We have found it helpful to explain the mechanics of a blast to help you accomplish it for the first time."

The skin and bone around the hologram's head disappeared, allowing Sammy to see highlighted parts of his brain.

"Blasts are voluntary actions controlled in the motor region of the cerebral cortex. A signal is sent from the cerebrum, down the spinal cord, to the hands or feet or both. This triggers the specialized energy conductors in the skin to release the energy into the environment. In time, you will learn to control more aspects of the blast. In this unit, we are only teaching you to voluntarily release the energy. Say 'yes' if you are ready to continue."

Sammy said "yes" at once.

"Extend your arms, palms facing out like this." The hologram of Byron demonstrated the instructions. "Now imagine that you are releasing a blast out of your palm. Focus on the target."

A target materialized. Sammy stared at the rings of red circles and tried to imagine a blast of energy going from his hand to the bulls-eye. Nothing happened. He held his breath and tensed up as if he could push it out of his hands. His face turned red, but that was it. His arms shook from holding them up for so long, but still nothing out of the ordinary. When on the brink of passing out, he gasped for more air and tried again.

After five minutes or so, Byron appeared. "Do not be alarmed if nothing happens. This is common on first attempts. Often a motion or command can be used to trigger the brain. Say the word 'blast' out loud, and thrust your hands forward, palms facing the target. Continue this until you feel the blast."

Talking out loud to no one was awkward.

But if it works, it works, right?

"Blast!" he said, thrusting his arms out and palms forward as he was told. Absolutely nothing. His armpits and neck grew hot.

"Blast!" he said again, this time with more force.

Again nothing happened. He repeated it a dozen times until yelling 'blast!' seemed like the dumbest idea he'd ever heard. He sat down against the wall. After having such an easy time with the instructions that morning, why was this so hard?

Mind over matter. I can do it. I'm going to shoot a blast of energy from my hands to the target. When I thrust my arms, the blast is going to come out.

He climbed back to his feet and stared down the target. "BLAST!" he yelled with a tremendous thrust of his arms. Sweat fell down his brow as he dropped his arms to the side. All the doubts and fears he'd worried over since Commander Byron had told him about his abilities hit him again. *I'm no use to them if I can't do this. They'll send me back to the Grinder. I'm never going—*

"BLAST!" he screamed.

Warm energy left his hands. The target splintered and disappeared in dramatic fashion.

"I DID IT!" he said, throwing his arms up.

"Very good," Byron said. "Now try to do it again."

The target reappeared. Sammy stopped celebrating and focused himself.

"Blast!"

Nothing.

"BLAST!"

The warm feeling returned, rushing out of his palms and fingertips.

"Yes!" he yelled, jumping this time.

Byron's hologram requested that he repeat the task a third time. Sammy did it on his first try.

"Very good. Here are two targets; aim one hand at each and blast them simultaneously."

The two targets almost immediately disappeared. Sammy was almost beside himself with giddiness.

"It seems you now have control over both hands. A series of targets will appear randomly. If they appear on the left side of your body, blast them with the left hand. If on the right side, use the right hand."

For sixty seconds the targets appeared, and Sammy blasted them into oblivion. The computer put him through several other exercises designed to teach him to aim the blasts with increasing accuracy. An hour later, he'd finished them.

"Excellent work. You were nearly perfect. Now it is time to learn to use the soles of your feet. This is called a blast-jump. Remember your feet will give off real, physical energy. When you jump, you exert a force on the ground through your shoes, and are able to leave the ground because the ground exerts a force back on you, lifting you off the ground until the force of gravity pulls you back to earth. When your energy blast hits the ground, the returning force will follow the same principles, and push you off the ground. Sometimes beginners try to physically jump when performing a blast-jump, but this is unnecessary and, at the beginning of your training, counter-productive. The combined force of a jump and jump-blast takes practice and can throw you off balance. For now, try to blast through your feet without jumping. Above you is a high bar, see if you can blast yourself high enough to grab it."

A bar appeared five meters above the floor, suspended on nothing but air. Sammy bent his knees as if he were about to jump, but then remembered Byron's instructions. Against what came naturally, he stood with his legs fairly straight, and prepared to blast through his feet. The nervousness that had disappeared during the hand-blasting exercises returned.

"Blast!" he shouted, focusing on the energy leaving through his feet. Nothing. Thinking of the steps of the blast again, he prepared himself for a second try.

"BLAST!"

He shot from the ground four, five, six meters high. Not expecting to jump so high, he panicked and flailed his arms as he tried to balance. He grabbed at the bar, but missed and plummeted back down to the ground.

He cried out as he fell. His muscles tensed, and he braced for the inevitable impact. But the ground he hit was very soft, almost like a sponge. After the impact, the floor hardened again. He got up panting and laughing at himself.

"A good attempt," Byron commented. "The sensation takes some getting used to. Try again to blast through your feet, this time grabbing hold of the bar."

Wiping his sweaty hands on his jumpsuit, Sammy focused on the next blast-jump. Without vocalizing, he blasted up into the air, this time maintaining enough composure to grab the bar and cling to it.

"Very good. Release your hold on the bar, and the electro-gel floor will cushion your fall."

"Now you tell me," Sammy muttered as he released his grip and landed softly on his feet. He repeated the test three more times, and each time the bar was raised slightly higher. Then Byron congratulated him on successfully completing the third subunit and invited him to move to the next.

When Byron's hologram disappeared, Sammy shouted at the top of his lungs. "It's real. It's all real. I can do it!" He sent off another blast from his hands.

He went back to the computer panel and saw he had used up only ninety minutes of his simulation time. He eagerly began the next unit.

Byron appeared in the middle of the room again and explained how to control the amount of energy sent out in a blast. Then he put Sammy back to work. Almost three hours and two subunits later, drained and covered with sweat, Sammy left the simulators at the same time as the other new recruits.

"Sammy," Brickert exclaimed, "Did you—?"

"Yeah!" Sammy said, on the verge of freaking out again. "I did!"

"Me too!"

"It was so cool!" Natalia added.

"Did you do it, Jeffie?" Kawai asked.

Jeffie grinned. "Yeah . . . it was so awesome."

"How far did you get, Sammy?" Brickert asked.

"I got through—" He broke off as he saw Jeffie waiting to hear his response. "I just started the blast jumps."

"What was that like?" Brickert asked. "I only just finished doing hand blasts."

"It's unbelievable," Jeffie said as Sammy started to answer. "There's this trapeze you have to grab in the air." She glanced at Sammy with a smug look on her face, but he avoided her eyes by turning his attention elsewhere. His excitement vanished like a popped balloon.

On their way downstairs, he listened to the others discuss the sims in greater detail. No one had gotten as far as him, but their excitement was the same. They all sat at a table together during dinner. Every so often, a Beta passed by to ask how their first day had gone, but from what Sammy could see, everyone stayed in their own groups. Al stayed and chatted with them the longest.

When Brickert and Sammy got back to their room that night, they set up stuff all over the room for target practice: shoes, water bottles, just about anything not nailed down. For three hours, they shot blasts at them, laughing hysterically whenever one of them hit a bottle so hard it sprayed water onto the carpet. They talked about being Psions, the girls, and other hobbies. When Brickert asked about Sammy's home and family, Sammy steered the conversation away, always carefully guarding his secrets.

The next few days went much like Monday. Exercise, instruction, sims, and hanging out with the other "nukes" during mealtime. Sammy found the busier he kept himself, the less he missed his old friends. Still, he often lost himself in his thoughts wondering where they were, what they were doing, if they were okay. Almost every night, several Betas played Star Racers, and each time they did, Sammy had to turn down about a dozen invitations to join them. Everyone wanted another shot at beating him—Kobe in particular. Sammy was content playing pool, shooting baskets, or challenging whoever would play him to a chess match. The few games he played, he won easily. Soon, no one wanted to play him. And by the end of his first week, Sammy thought life was going to be fairly routine.

Then he had Friday sims.

Monday through Thursday, he had moved rapidly through the Introduction subunits. He had easily mastered high and low energy projections enabling him to hover and create a strong projectile shield. Blast acrobatics proved to be a bit tougher, but once he got the hang of bouncing off the walls and floor in a rapid succession using his hands and feet, it wasn't too bad.

He had just completed another section of the blast acrobatic unit when, as usual, Byron appeared, congratulating him on finishing the section. The green-colored Introduction subunits on the panel were gone. Instead was a new, longer list of units in blue.

The first one read: Elementary Combat. Sammy grinned and tossed his bottle aside. Combat sounded like something he'd like. With renewed enthusiasm, he touched the icon to start the new unit. Byron's hologram appeared:

"Welcome to the secondary units. Now that you have mastered the elementary skill of your psionic powers, you will learn to use them against simulated enemies. As you will see, these units gradually become more advanced, and will test your stamina and creativity. In most scenarios, there are many possible tactics or solutions for success. Some will be more effective than others; review the recordings of your performances to learn from your mistakes. If you need help with a particular unit, consult with other Betas or myself.

"In many situations, competition can improve performance. From this point on, you will be compared on a standard with the other Betas who have also reached this level and beyond in their training. If you wish, you may see how you rank in the personal statistics menu in your com. The areas of comparison are timeliness, accuracy, efficiency, and overall performance. The latter is an average of the first three areas weighted to their importance. You will only know your own rank out of the total number of participants."

Sammy activated his com and called up the stats option. In each of the four categories it listed him as the sixteenth of sixteen. He smiled to himself. *We'll see how long that lasts.*

The commander introduced the new unit. Sammy had to dodge enemy attacks without making any physical contact or using attacking blasts. When Byron finished speaking, a man in black t-shirt and torn pants appeared. The image reminded Sammy of Gunner, who only ever wore black. Then the man ran at Sammy. Caught off guard at the sudden reality of his situation, Sammy panicked and stumbled backwards. The man was quickly upon him and viciously kicked Sammy in the head. It was a strange sensation. Sammy felt the kick, but judging by how hard the man had struck at him, it should have broken his nose and caused a lot of pain. Instead it merely registered as a touch. The man disappeared, and Byron reappeared to demonstrate a few techniques used to evade attacks.

This time Sammy felt more ready. When the man came at him, Sammy blast-jumped and landed safely meters away. The man turned to attack him again, aiming punches at Sammy's head and chest. Sammy ducked and dodged them, finishing with another blast-jump away from danger.

He was surprised at the rush he got from the fight. The enemy was fake, but his brain reacted otherwise, flooding his body with adrenaline. The holograms became faster and more aggressive. Sammy made plenty of mistakes, but most often he successfully completed each trial the first time. After completing all of the evasive trials, Byron instructed Sammy how to use his appendages and blasts to block the blows of his enemy.

As his combat training continued, Sammy grew aware of certain patterns of combat. The enemies usually tried to force him into a corner because Sammy had the advantage in open space. They often aimed for the most vital parts of the body: the face, groin, and stomach. Friday's simulations worked him harder than any other so far. He left exhausted and eager for dinner. As usual, he joined the other four in the cafeteria.

"You're out of your mind," Jeffie said to Sammy while twirling spaghetti noodles on her fork. "Holo-films are way better than screenies."

"She's right," Kawai told him. "Everyone in my village goes to holo-films."

Sammy could barely suppress a smirk when Kawai spoke. Brickert grinned, too. They had noticed whenever Kawai talked about something really important her head had a funny way of wagging, making the feathers in her hair stick up taller. It reminded Sammy of the peacocks in the zoo.

"But of course you're not biased," he remarked to Jeffie, "because your mom is the only Norwegian holo-film director. Holo-films are too limited with what they can do. Screen films are way better and make more money."

"My mom says holo-films cater to a more elite audience," Jeffie responded. "You know, people who understand the intricacies of art. I guess you're just too shallow—"

Kawai cleared her throat loudly, and Jeffie stopped her sentence. Sammy noticed this was happening more and more frequently. Either Kawai had a cold or she'd decided to help Jeffie censor herself. "Never mind," Jeffie finished, glaring at Kawai.

Jeffie came from a very wealthy Norwegian family. Her father had been a professional athlete in multiple winter sports, and her mother was heavily involved in the entertainment industry. She had five siblings (all brothers) and from the sound of it, her life before coming to headquarters had been one great adventure. Her parents often took the kids on expensive excursions to tour the sets of big-budget movies and to watch high-profile sporting events all around the eastern world. In fact, at the NWG World Cup in 2084, Jeffie had her first taste of her psionic abilities.

As she told it, Norway trailed Portugal 3-4 with only a few minutes remaining when a vendor trying to sell drinks blocked Jeffie's view. Furious, Jeffie accidentally blasted the vendor into a crowd of people. After taking care of the damage, Byron visited the Tvedts and told them their daughter's "telepathic experience" was really an anomaly that could be exercised and controlled in the proper setting. They were thrilled at the prospects of their daughter's next big enterprise, and Jeffie was still mad that Norway lost.

"So what did you think of hovering?" Kawai asked, obviously steering the discussion away from something Jeffie wasn't so defensive about.

"Still working on it," Brickert mentioned half-heartedly.

"Don't worry," Natalia said as she examined her new purple hairstyle in the reflection of her spoon. "I heard it took Gregor a month to finish the Introduction units."

"Who'd you hear that from?" Sammy asked. Natalia had a way of knowing how long it took everyone to do everything.

"Asaki," she answered.

Sammy nodded. Asaki was Natalia's roommate and seemed a perfect fit for her. Two gossip queens who could sit up all night and share hard-earned information with each other.

"Natalia, stop staring at yourself," Kawai said, snatching the spoon from her. Natalia tried to grab it back, but Kawai tossed it to Brickert. Brickert looked at Sammy for a moment, trying to decide what to do, then gave it back.

"I'm not sure I like it," Natalia said, holding a few strands out. "Maybe I should have done blue—like the light blue on Sammy's clothes."

Jeffie smirked at Sammy and then made a face.

"So . . . back to the sims," Sammy said.

"I thought hovering was pretty easy—" Jeffie started to say, but under Kawai's look she added, "—harder than blast variation, though."

Sammy suppressed an urge to roll his eyes. Jeffie seized every opportunity to brag about how far along she was.

"How far are you again, Sammy?" Jeffie asked.

Sammy picked at the ravioli on his plate and toyed with the idea of telling Jeffie that he had already finished the introduction units. However, he did not want to risk getting on her bad side again, and even more, he did not want Brickert to feel inferior. So he made the choice to maintain his carefully crafted lie of how he was always just behind Jeffie.

"I'm just about to start the subunit you're on," he told her.

Jeffie gave him a polite nod. "We should play some Star Racers tonight. You up for it?"

Sammy was about to tell her that he would have to take a rain check when a small group of Betas, led by Al, approached their table.

"Which of you is it?" Al asked, his voice intentionally mysterious.

The five each looked at each other to see who knew what Al was talking about. Apparently nobody did.

"Is what?" Kawai asked Al.

"Which of you started secondary units today?" Kobe answered for Al.

Sammy tried to put on a face to match his friends. He had forgotten the older Betas would see a new competitor on their rankings.

"Oh, come on," Kobe said. "One of you cracked through the secondaries already. We all know it."

"How would you know?" Jeffie asked him.

"Because," answered Al, "our per-stats show sixteen people in the competition, not fifteen like the last couple months."

"And the only way that can happen," Kobe added, looking at each of them with mock suspicion, "is if a puke already finished the introductions."

Sammy tried to act as surprised as he could. He didn't want to think about what Jeffie or anyone else would say if they found out he had just lied to them.

"Come on, out with it. Which of you was it?" Kobe questioned. "I can guess it probably wasn't you, Bricky boy. Being the youngest and smallest doesn't carry any advantages around here."

A couple of people laughed, but bright red spots appeared on Brickert's cheeks.

"Shut up, Kobe!" Sammy snapped. "For all you know it was him, being young doesn't mean jack—"

"Dude, chill out." Kobe said, waving Sammy off. "I know it wasn't you, either."

"Are any of you going to confess to it?" Al asked. "Because whoever it was, one week through the introduction is the fastest I've ever heard of, and I've been here five years."

Natalia's eyes got really big at this piece of news. Kawai and Jeffie still shrugged. When they saw no one was going to confess, the older kids dropped it and left.

"So which of you was it?" Natalia whispered as soon as they were alone again. "Was it you, Jeffie?"

"No, but I'm really close," she answered. "Maybe they're already counting me in. Was it you, Kawai?"

"Nope," she said. "Sammy?"

"I already told you where I am," was all he could think to say. He said it with the most honest expression he could muster. They all seemed to believe him, but Brickert's eyes lingered on Sammy a little longer.

Jeffie wondered aloud, "So weird. If it wasn't one of us, how could that happen?"

"Maybe there was some kind of an error in the system," Kawai offered.

"Or maybe one of us just doesn't realize we've finished the introduction," Brickert said. "You know, like maybe you finished the last part of it as you left, Jeffie."

"Yeah, that could be," Sammy quickly agreed.

After exhausting that topic, the five friends launched into a discussion on plans for the weekend. They were so involved with food and conversation that no one noticed when Commander Byron entered the cafeteria. Everyone else stopped talking and looked up.

"No need to stop anything on my account," Byron said.

It surprised Sammy that he had not seen the commander since Sunday, and yet Byron's absence already seemed normal. Byron did not otherwise interact with the Betas on a daily basis, but when he came into a room, everyone gave him full attention.

"I need to see the five new recruits, please," he said.

"Oh. They have to learn about the Game," Rosa said to Marie and Miguel.

Sammy had completely forgotten about the Game. He knew from snips of conversations that it was played every Saturday, and Natalia, of course, had tried to press people for more information, but almost everyone she talked to had insisted the information only came from Byron.

Natalia, Brickert, Kawai, Jeffie, and Sammy followed Byron to the exercise room where he waited for them to get comfortable.

"How was the first week?" he asked.

Everyone nodded or mumbled something positive, except Brickert who said "awesome" too enthusiastically.

"What made it so awesome?"

"I don't know," Brickert hesitated to answer. "It's fun here."

"I hope all of you are having an 'awesome' time," the commander said. "I want a few minutes to tell you about tomorrow's Game. First of all, it is a training tool, a place for you to put aside your egos, your prejudices, and learn cooperation and execution. Every Saturday, at a random point in the day, you will be alerted when it is time to play. When that happens, go to your room, change into your special jumpsuit, get your helmet, and go to the cafeteria for your assignment.

"Each week I assign different honchos to lead the teams. Eventually you will have turns, but not until you reach a certain point in your sims. You may think the Game is about winning; it is not. It is about learning to execute an assignment, or, when you are honcho, learning to be a leader. This is the best training you will have to fight Thirteens when you become Alphas. Inside the Arena, you will be challenged to develop adaptability, technique, and above all—" he momentarily glanced at Sammy, "—trust. Have fun tomorrow, but remember what this is all about.

"Second, some basic things you need to know. We usually play a set of Games. The computer will inform you how many wins are in a set. Your suits are made of noblack and are specially designed to absorb enormous amounts of shock, but you can still get hurt if you fall a long distance. So be careful—the floor inside is not electro-gel like in the sim rooms. Your helmets will be your enemies' targets. If you ever get hit in the head, your helmet will blind you, and your suit will become immobilized. Protect your head. Listen to your honcho. Work hard. Anything else you need to know, you can pick up inside the Arena as you play. You are all dismissed."

They walked back to the cafeteria talking about the Game. Natalia was the most excited, as she had pried some information out of her roommate. Jeffie, Kawai, and Brickert hung onto her every word.

"Each Game has a different scenario. Sometimes they're really long and we only play one, and sometimes they're all really short and we play best of seven. Asaki even said that one time—"

"Are you guys going to play Star Racers?" Li interrupted.

"Of course," Jeffie said.

The other three also voiced their willingness, then they turned on Sammy. Despite his protests, they forced Sammy to join them. Even his best excuses would not work. Al kept reminding him that it was a Friday and he had nothing better to do. Since Sammy knew they all wanted another chance at beating him, he agreed.

He ended up playing several games. Just like before, he saw what he needed to do to win, and never lost a game. What made the night even better was Kobe refusing to give up his seat, even when he finished third or worse. He kept insisting that he would win the next game. Sammy made it a point to take Kobe out first whenever he could. They never spoke about it—their private vendetta was beyond words.

Jeffie, on the other hand, had no problem venting her frustrations. To her credit, she never lost her temper, but Sammy could see that losing chafed her badly. He wanted to apologize after the gaming finished, but she shot him a look; it was civil, but warning. Unlike last time, Brickert left for bed with Sammy. Kobe stayed behind. Sammy chuckled at the thought of Kobe trying to prove he was still second best.

Brickert was quiet as they walked downstairs with Kawai and Jeffie's roommate, Brillianté. They came to the girls' floor, and Brickert, blushing, barely managed a simple "goodnight" to Brillianté. Sammy did not even try to figure out why his roommate was so tongue-tied. The silence continued as they descended one more level. No sooner had the door to their bedroom closed then Brickert turned to Sammy and blurted, "It was you!"

"What was me?" Sammy froze in the middle of taking off his jumpsuit and looked at his roommate.

"You passed the introduction units. I know it was you."

With all the talk of the Arena and his intense pleasure in blowing up Kobe in Star Racers, their earlier conversation had slipped from Sammy's head, but Brickert must have been waiting to say something all night.

"Why do you think it was me?"

"Sammy, you're the best at everything, I'll tell you. I'm your best friend; I can tell when you're lying."

"Oh," Sammy laughed. "You can read me like a book, huh?"

"Pretty much," Brickert said, smiling back. "I'm right, aren't I?"

Sammy let out a long breath. "Fine, yeah, it was me. But please don't tell anyone else. I don't want more attention or jealousy from Jeffie. You know how she gets, even over that—that stupid game."

"Do you like her?" Brickert asked suddenly, not even bothering to hide the grin breaking out on his face.

Sammy nodded, and they both burst out laughing. "I can't even figure out why," he explained. "She's so annoying and . . . impossible to get along with."

"Yeah," Brickert acknowledged. "Well, she's hot."

"What about you? You like her, too?"

Brickert's cheeks immediately grew red. "Brillianté."

"That girl we just—? Jeffie's roommate?" Sammy asked with a gaping mouth. "She's—dude, how old is she?"

"Sixteen," Brickert finished, the spots on his cheeks now blended in with the rest of his face. "I know—Natalia told me."

Sammy snorted loudly.

"I won't tell anyone you lied, Sammy. I promise. I still feel bad for telling them that stuff about your instruction speed."

"Thanks."

He and Brickert undressed and readied for bed in silence. As Sammy took off his com and placed it in the charger, Brickert spoke up again, "Tell me one more thing?"

"Sure, what?"

"Your rank." Brickert had a crazy look in his eye now.

"Oh, sure." He hadn't even thought to check what his rank might be. Putting his com back on, he called up the per-stats from his menu. What he saw stunned him.

"That can't be right."

"What? What is it?"

"You're not going to believe me if I tell you."

"Try me."

"Look for yourself," Sammy said, and tossed his com to Brickert, who caught it.

"Oh my—!" Brickert cried out. He dropped the com as if it was hot. The screen lay open for both of them to read:

```
Accuracy: 8/16
Timeliness: 5/16
Efficiency: 4/16
Overall: 5/16
```

8 | Game

SAMMY'S FIRST SATURDAY began early. "Good morning, Psions," the familiar voice repeated.

"No . . ." Sammy moaned. "But it's Saturday."

"Get up, it's game time!" Brickert told him, already putting on his noblack suit.

"It's waking us up for the Game?"

"Yes. So hurry."

"What time is it?" Sammy asked as he crawled out of bed.

"It's probably better you don't know," Brickert answered, now grabbing his helmet. "Do you want me to wait for you?"

"Sure, I'll just be a minute."

"Well, at least brush your teeth." Brickert took a step back from Sammy. "Jeffie won't want to talk to you if you reek of mouth fungus."

"Geez, thanks so much."

He snatched his toothbrush off his desk, threw on his suit, grabbed his com, and left with Brickert. They arrived in the cafeteria to find most everyone already there, many staring wearily into their breakfast plates. Sammy spotted Jeffie sitting between Kobe and Brillianté, eating a bowl of fruit. With a scowl, he ordered his cereal and sat down with Al, Marie, and Marie's younger sister, Rosa. His view was such that, from across the room, he could spy Kobe flirting unabashedly with Jeffie. He ground his spoon into his cereal bowl as he looked on.

"Did you see today's orders?" Al asked them, pointing to a brightly glowing panel on the wall that until today had been blank and dark.

"No, not yet," Brickert responded.

"Go check it out," Al told them.

A handful of people stood around the panel, but Sammy and Brickert worked their way through and saw this:

Team 1: 3rd Floor	Team 2: 5th Floor
Covas, Marie (*)	Berhane, Samuel
Covas, Miguel	Alanazi, Cala
Covas, Rosa	Morel, Brillianté
Enova, Levu	Hayman, Albert
Ivanovich, Natalia	Plack, Brickert
Nujola, Kawai	von Pratt, Gregor (*)
Petrov, Ludwig	Reynolds, Kaden
von Pratt, Parley	Reynolds, Kobe
Trector, Martin	Yoshiharu, Asaki
Tvedt, Gefjon	Zheng, Li Cheng

Victory: 3 Games of 5
Maximum Game Length: 1 hour
Start Time: 04:40

"We're on the same team!" Brickert said, high-fiving Sammy as they walked back to their seats.

"Teams look pretty even, don't you think?" Al asked Marie.

"Seems okay," Marie said, "but no one knows who's good among the new batch and who . . . needs work." She grinned sheepishly at Sammy and Brickert to show she meant no offense.

"Do the stars show who the honchos are?" Sammy asked through a yawn. He couldn't fathom how Marie could be so bright-eyed this early in the morning.

"Yep." She smirked at Al who seemed too tired to open his eyes until Martin brought over a mug of hot chocolate.

"Mmm, thanks," Al said.

"Is this your first time as a honcho?" Brickert asked.

"No. I've done it plenty of times. Haven't I, Al?" She poked Al several times in the ribs while saying his name.

"She's pretty good," he said, "for a girl." Marie poked him even harder until he conceded. "Okay! She's really good. But, you know, I'm surprised Byron didn't decide to have four teams with so many new recruits."

Marie just shrugged. "Either way you're going to lose again."

Martin laughed into his own mug, and Sammy wondered if Al and Marie kept a tally of wins like he and Feet used to do.

"I don't think so, lady," Al said.

"Definitely not, Hay-man," Kobe said, sitting down next to Al.

Sammy rolled his eyes at Brickert, who returned a smug grin.

"Not if we have anything to say about it," Kaden added.

"Where's G, our fearless leader?" Kobe asked.

"Over there," Al said, nodding across the room.

Sammy followed Al's gaze to Gregor, who sat by himself looking pale and glum. Sammy did not know much about Gregor except that he was much older, and looked it. He was of average height and skinny, and his brown hair had started to recede back prematurely, exposing his pale white forehead. Natalia had told Sammy once that Gregor was a year older than everyone, including Al.

"How's he holding up?" Kaden asked Al.

"So-so," Marie answered. "This is his first time as honcho since he failed the Panel."

"He failed the Psion Panel?" Brickert repeated.

"Sh!" Al hissed. "Don't go yelling that stuff around. He's just got a thing with nerves, is all. He's scheduled to take it again a couple months after me. No one's ever failed it twice."

Brickert's cheeks went as red as apples as he stammered to apologize.

"Yeah, but no one did as abysmally as I've heard he did," Kobe snorted.

"Don't," Kaden said. "Who needs to know that?"

"So you pukes must be pretty nervous for your first time in the Game," Kobe said. Looking at Brickert he added, "I've got a spare diaper in my room if you need it."

Brickert's spots threatened to cover his whole face.

"Why do you have diapers in your room, Kobe?" Sammy asked. "You have a problem with wetting the bed?"

Milk spurted out of Kaden's nose, and Kobe got up to sit with Jeffie again.

It was getting close to start time. Brickert and Sammy got up to take care of their dishes.

"Good luck, Marie," Sammy said as he left.

"Thanks, but Al will need it more."

Al shot her a covert wink, and Marie turned away to blush. Sammy caught all this as he followed Brickert upstairs.

Gregor's team chatted excitedly except Al and Gregor, who joined them in the last few minutes. Sammy heard Al muttering a constant stream of encouragement to Gregor, who looked even more nervous now.

When they got close, Gregor whispered to Al, "Don't worry. I'll be fine once we get in there."

Al gave him a pat on the back and sat down next to Sammy and Brickert.

"Ready?"

"Yeah," they both answered.

"Piece of cake, and don't worry about him. He's a good leader—just psyches himself out, you know?"

The lights in the hallway dimmed, and the calm female voice said, "Game one, begin."

"Alright ... let's go," Gregor said. The lack of enthusiasm in his voice scared Sammy.

"Go where?" Brickert asked.

In answer to his question, the inside wall opened and widened like an enormous pale mouth. Behind it was another solid black wall. Then Sammy realized that he was staring at the opening to the Arena.

"Clip your com inside your helmet," Al told them, showing them how to secure the com. "Touch here on your helmet when you want to talk to your honcho."

The noblack material was hard to see in the darkness of the Arena, even with Brickert walking a meter ahead of him. As they descended a very long staircase, Sammy's eyes adjusted.

The Arena housed enough space to fit at least two football fields side by side, five stories high. Everything inside, from the floors to the walls, had a dull metallic glaze. It amazed Sammy the entire room actually fit inside headquarters. It gave him new perspective into just how big the building was. Giant cubes, ranging from three to four meters high and spaced about two meters apart, covered the entire floor.

Gregor's voice came over the com, "Two-fold attack. I want half of us on the floor, and half on the cubes."

He divided them up, putting his five best players on the floor, and the weaker or newer ones on the cubes.

Despite the obvious flaws in Gregor's plan, Sammy didn't say anything. They spread out in the darkness, coordinated by the honcho's voice, and hunted for opponents. It didn't take long to realize that during the Game only the honcho's voice was broadcast over the coms. In turn, Sammy's com only linked to Gregor's.

Trouble found Sammy quickly. When two of Marie's people ganged up on Brickert, he hurried over to help. As soon as he got there, more of Marie's troops converged on them. The seasoned Betas knew what they were doing, and Sammy could not fight in six directions at once. He called out to Gregor, but a blast hit his helmet just before he could tell his honcho that Marie had deployed all of her troops on the cubes. As Sammy lay on a cube, awaiting the end of the Game, the thought struck him that he hadn't managed to hit one player with a blast.

The second Game did not go well for Gregor's side, either, although this time the match did stay close. After regrouping in the hallway for a few minutes and listening to Gregor's pep talk, they returned to the Arena to find the cubes gone. In their place was a dazzling network of thick vertical bars jutting out of the ground and rising up at least thirty meters. Gregor's instructions were to go with one of two groups of three people around the perimeter, trying to force Marie's team inside, where his four solid fighters would be spread out to do the most damage.

Gregor's plan was moderately successful at best. Sammy began to see that Marie was simply a better strategist than her counterpart. From what he gathered, Marie sent in two scouts to see what Gregor had decided to do, and after getting a general idea, counteracted his moves. Almost mocking Gregor's last Game plan, she divided up her forces into two bodies, took out the perimeter forces, and converged in the middle to sweep up the final four. The bars made it too difficult for Sammy to send a blast farther than two or three meters, and once he was surrounded, his helmet shut off. And he still hadn't deactivated a single person.

Annoyed with being the first to black out in both Games, he stomped up the stairs, dreading another motivational speech. Gregor, however, did not say a word. He slumped down in a heap in the hallway and closed his eyes. Sammy's frustrations melted into pity.

Gregor is doing his best. That should be enough for me.

"Hey guys, let's do this!" Al said with more enthusiasm than he probably felt. "We still have one more chance to win. Those first two Games—just bad luck is all."

Al talked on until everyone's spirits had improved. Gregor pulled out of his stupor and discussed how they could improve their situation. Al pointed out some advantages he noticed they had over Marie's team. Gregor made adjustments to capitalize on Al's suggestions.

"Game three, begin."

With a renewed desire to win, and hope mixed with a touch of cockiness, they headed back inside much more ready for the next Game. The entire Arena was flat except for a giant fifteen-meter-high wall in the middle of the floor separating the two teams. Whoever got on top of the wall first would win.

Obviously Gregor realized this because he talked fast: "We need a human ladder at the bottom of the wall." He named off Sammy, himself, and two others. Then he organized two attacking teams. "Those teams climb as soon as we're in position."

The ladder was composed of four boys standing on each other's shoulders with their backs against the wall. Only by blasting off the top of the ladder could the climber grab onto the ledge of the wall. Fortunately, the suits absorbed most of the weight of the boys above and, for Gregor on top, the force of the blast off his shoulders.

Brickert was an attacker, and being the smallest, he climbed the ladder first. Each person's hands helped him step up higher and higher until he blasted up and grabbed onto the ledge of the summit. Hugging the wall, he hoisted himself up top, and signaled to his team how wide the wall was: nearly one and a half meters. Kobe and Brillianté followed Brickert, forming the first attacking team. Then Sammy helped heave up Al, Asaki, and Li.

Gregor's team seized the wall so speedily that Marie did not have a chance to retaliate. Those on her team attempting to climb the wall were quickly dispatched first, their helmets easy targets from above. The remaining players huddled at the back in a defensive stance. Gregor ordered a two-prong attack: Al's team from above, Brickert's team on the ground. Al's hovering team was especially lethal.

Gregor's attack was so perfectly executed, not a single player was deactivated. This time it was their turn to celebrate as Marie's team marched away dejected and beaten. Everyone congratulated each other in the hallway; even Gregor seemed elated.

The fourth Game, though closer, also went to Gregor's team. They fought in a small room that sealed itself off as soon as both teams entered. The darkness was almost pitch black. On Gregor's orders, Asaki, Brickert, and Sammy sacrificed themselves to get Al and Kobe behind the other team. Though they'd been quickly taken out, their efforts were the turning point of the Game.

With two wins apiece, the score was even, but Gregor had momentum on his side going into the deciding fifth Game. Still, Sammy was angry he hadn't been in a real battle. Every order he had received was a sacrifice for someone else. He needed to show Gregor that he could contribute.

Before the last game began, the panel gave them each a different entrance to use on the floor. Li and Sammy's was a small hole above their heads. They used hover blasts to make it easier to hoist themselves into the cramped space.

After a short, uncomfortable crawl, Sammy dropped head first into the Arena, rolled on a hover blast, and stood up. Li dropped right behind him. They stood in a tightly enclosed space with a narrow stairway leading upwards. Sammy started up the stairs, but Li pulled him back.

"Wait for orders," he warned. "It's more important now than ever."

Seconds later Gregor's voice came over the com. "Is everyone in?"

Li and Sammy both confirmed.

"Here's the plan: Al, Kobe, Kaden—meet up as attackers. Target Levu, Martin, and Marie."

"Marie's best players," Li told Sammy.

"Brickert and Brillianté scout together—"

"Brickert won't complain about that," Sammy chuckled to himself.

"—and Sammy and Li scout together. Everyone else stay on defense, but keep moving. Find a position out of sight and sneak up on whoever comes around you. Everyone should always have someone watching their back. Clear?"

Sammy sighed. Scouting. In other words—no fighting. Li explained the basics of scouting to Sammy as they climbed the stairs. He tried to make it sound interesting, but Sammy thought his job was a crock. All they had to do was find the position of the enemy and report it back to Gregor.

"Why does scouting even matter if the labyrinth changes every five minutes?" Sammy asked Li.

In answer to his rebellious thought, the words of Commander Byron rang in his ears: *a place for you to put aside your egos, your prejudices, and learn cooperation and execution.*

They reached the top of the stairs, coming to a large corridor with several doorways on each side. Sammy made to go in, but Li stopped him, shaking his head.

"Going in the open means death. Just wait a little longer."

They stood there, silent, watching the empty corridor for a full minute until Sammy's feet started to rise in the air.

"Wha—!" he started to say, but Li shushed him.

He turned to Li and saw him rising, too. The whole floor was elevating.

He caught one last glimpse of the corridor they had been watching. Many of its doorways were closing off and a large wall rose up, dissecting the corridor in half.

Then the floor stopped moving. They were no longer on top of a flight of stairs, or even in a doorway, rather, they stood in the middle of a long half-pipe.

The walls were too steep and slick to climb, so they jump-blasted out onto the edge and sprinted along, looking for cover. The ever-changing lighting in the Arena grew dim, making it difficult for them to find a hiding place. For one frantic minute, they raced back and forth looking for anything to help them get out of the open. Then, in the dark, Li smacked head first into a pole and fell onto his back, shaking. Sammy thought Li was having a seizure. Then he heard Li laughing.

"It's a ladder," he whispered to Sammy. "I found a ladder."

"What?"

"Look."

Sure enough, the pole was the side of a ladder going up at least one level.

They ascended cautiously. Li even climbed facing outward to keep an eye out for anyone wanting to catch them off guard. Sammy reached the top first and peered over the ledge. He could see into a small room with stairs leading out of the back. Judging by how high they had already climbed, he suspected those stairs would take them to the highest level of the labyrinth. Once Sammy was sure the room was empty, they crawled over the ledge and ran up the stairs.

Halfway up, the stairs came to a plateau, splitting into three different directions. Li led them down the path headed right. "Always go right," he said. All that waited for them ahead was more blackness, but Sammy also heard very soft sounds like people whispering. He grabbed Li's suit and put his finger to his ear. Li nodded. *He hears it, too.* They retraced their path a few steps and told Gregor their position and what they heard.

"It's not someone on our team," Gregor answered. "Follow them, but don't engage," he ordered. "I'm sending Al and the twins your way."

They went back into the blackness, hanging just around a dark corner where they could watch and wait virtually unseen. As they waited, the Arena grew lighter again. Sammy took a gamble and glanced around the corner. Facing the other direction, watching through another doorway, were two boys and a girl. He was almost positive the girl was Jeffie, judging by the blonde hair peeking out of her helmet—blonde hair he had studied rather meticulously over the last week. One of the boys turned in Sammy's direction, but Sammy withdrew back into hiding.

"They're still there," he hissed into his com.

"Al says he's almost found you," Gregor responded. "Just hang tight for another moment."

Within a minute, silent as spring breezes, three black shadows rushed past the spot where the two scouts were hidden.

"They're here!" Sammy heard Martin Trector shout.

Spying around the corner again, Sammy saw Kobe, Kaden, and Al fanned out, blasting shots at Parley von Pratt, Martin Trector, and Jeffie. Parley and Martin held their own fairly well, but Jeffie, in her inexperience, struggled to stand her ground. Sammy squelched an urge to rush in and help her. Al dove under a blast sent by Martin, aimed low at Jeffie, and knocked her off her feet. It gave Sammy the impression that she was struck down by an invisible force. The whole situation was comical: a battle where no one threw punches, only thrust their palms out at each other. After knocking her to the ground, Al terminated Jeffie, and the battle turned that much worse for Martin and Parley.

Before Kobe or Kaden could cut off their retreat, Martin led Parley out of the room and into more darkness. Al and the twins gave chase. No sooner had they left the room, than three more shadows flew past Sammy and Li, following Al's group.

"That bunch didn't look friendly," Sammy whispered to Li.

"No, they didn't." Li informed Gregor of what just happened.

"Follow them," Gregor said.

Li and Sammy sprinted past Jeffie, through a doorway, and into another larger room beyond. From inside they could see Al and the Reynolds twins surrounded by Marie's team on another staircase.

The labyrinth began to shift. The staircase was disappearing, a wall cutting them off from their teammates. They ran as fast as they could, but could not make it in time. Sammy yelled and banged his fist on the wall.

"We got cut off," Sammy reported.

Gregor swore. "Just a second."

While they waited for orders, Sammy and Li searched for an escape route from the room. The lighting in the Arena grew brighter again, helping them.

Gregor's voice came back. "They're all right so far. They took out Parley before they were ambushed."

"What do we do now?" Li asked.

"Keep scouting."

Great, Sammy thought darkly. *Not much good that has done.*

After extensive searching, Li found a small hole in the corner of the floor just big enough for a body to pass through. With the increasing light, Sammy and Li saw the ground below about two stories down.

"Can you do drop blasts?" Li asked.

"Yeah," Sammy responded. "I think so."

"Can you or can't you?"

"Uh . . . I can."

Li gave Sammy one last skeptical look and said, "Follow me." Then he jumped through the hole onto nothing but air.

Taking a deep breath, Sammy imitated him. The exhilaration of the drop almost made him forget the steps to a good landing. *Fire strong blasts followed by weaker ones to cushion the landing.* He slowed his descent and landed neatly next to Li, just like in training.

"Very nice." Li actually seemed impressed.

As they scouted again, they found some success. Judging by the updates they received from Gregor over the next thirty minutes, they had lost half their team, including the Reynolds brothers. That left only Al, Cala, Gregor, Li, and Sammy. Cala and Al had already managed to find each other, and, thanks to Sammy and Li, were hot on the trail of Marie's team. Gregor estimated she had between four and six players remaining.

None of this made Sammy feel any better. *How am I supposed to learn if I never get a chance to battle until I'm surrounded by Marie's best fighters?* He silently complained. *All I've done in this labyrinth is find people for Al to fight.* Even Brickert had gone down fighting Ludwig, a much older boy.

But who found Ludwig? Li and I tracked him down twenty minutes ago. Maybe Li didn't mind scouting, but Sammy needed a fair chance to show Gregor and the others that he could fight. He wanted to prove himself. Otherwise, he'd be stuck pulling the same boring assignments every Saturday.

Li led Sammy through a maze of rooms, halls, and stairs. Eventually, they came to a large corridor that looked exactly like the one they'd scouted at the beginning of the match. *No, it is the same corridor. It's repeating the cycle.* An idea clicked inside his mind. A risky idea.

The time was getting close for the next change in cycle. He made up his mind. It was worth the risk. While Li was checking behind them for enemies, Sammy took off at a sprint for the middle of the corridor. He heard Li calling for him, but didn't stop.

"I see someone!" he yelled over his shoulder.

The wall—the same wall he had seen before—rose up in the middle of the corridor, and he blast jumped over it, not giving Li enough time to follow.

He safely landed and turned to see nothing but solid metal.

"Sammy, what are you doing?" Gregor demanded. "Why did you leave Li?"

"I—I thought I saw someone on the other side of the corridor," he lied.

"You're supposed to stay together. You need to hook back up with him immediately. Got it?"

"Yeah. Got it." But Sammy had no intention of following orders.

You'll understand that I did the right thing, Gregor, after we win.

He climbed some stairs and entered a room at a jog. His stomach gave a lurch as his feet went out from under him. He landed hard on his chest and slid down a long slope into a very large bowl.

"Sammy, what are you waiting for?" Gregor asked.

"I'm kinda stuck."

On reaching the bottom, he scrambled to his feet and tried to climb back out of the bowl. But, like the half-pipe, he found it too slick, and had to blast out. It took him some time because the bowl was so wide, but he finally managed his way out.

After almost fifteen minutes of good light, the Arena grew dark. As it became more and more difficult to make his way through the passages, he wished he had Li to keep an eye out behind for attacks.

"They got Li," Gregor announced. "There's a group of three out to track us all down. Get to Al. He's near a half-pipe near the dead center of the Arena. If you can make it there, he'll find you."

"Okay," Sammy said, cursing under his breath.

My fault. I stranded Li. If I'd stayed with him, I could have helped. And I'd have had a chance to get some people.

He hoped his selfishness hadn't ruined his team's chances. He pointed himself in the right direction of the half-pipe, and ran toward it. Just as the half-pipe came into view, he heard Gregor calling out over his com, "Help! I'm surrounded!"

"Where are you?" Sammy shouted back in panic.

No answer.

"Sammy? Where are you?" Al, the de facto honcho, asked through the com.

"I'm right next to the half-pipe. Gregor said you were there."

"I'm here with Cala, but there's too much of a risk that you'll be ambushed if you run out in the open. We think Marie's been tracking us, so she may spot you. The Arena is about to change again, just sit tight and wait for it."

"Okay." He ducked down to the floor and counted. When he reached forty, everything changed. Four walls went up around Sammy.

"Cala and I just found cover in a small room off a big corridor. The room's partially bisected by a wall, so you'll have to climb over it to even see us." Then Al gave him a good description of what the corridor looked like. "Can you find us here?"

"I'll find you."

Fresh guilt surged through him. He pushed it aside. He did not want to—could not think he had caused his team to lose the fifth match. He ran in and out of rooms, trying to find his team so he could fix his mistake.

It was almost pitch black again. He came to an area matching Al's description. Investigating inside one of the rooms he saw a wall that rose about a meter off the ground, easily enough space for Al and Cala to be hiding behind.

"Al?" he whispered. "Are you in here?"

"Sammy, I don't think you're in the right room," Al said over his com.

Sammy figured if the rooms were that identical, he must be close. He made to leave the room when he heard something outside. He jumped over the wall and hid.

"Al, I think they're near me," he breathed into his com.

"You're sure he went in here?" Sammy heard Marie whisper.

"Yeah," Miguel answered.

"They're definitely here," Sammy hissed.

There were at least two enemies in the room. Sammy knew he could eliminate one of them with the right element of surprise. Laying on his stomach, he flattened his hands against the floor, flipped his legs into the air, and while standing on his hands, blasted blindly with his feet.

Someone hit the ground. *Were they ducking or falling?* Using one arm, he hovered just high enough to see over the wall, and held the other arm out in front of his head using a blast shield.

Two more people had entered the room. Sammy recognized all of them: Marie, Levu, Ludwig, and Miguel. Two boys and two girls, all at least two years older than Sammy. All ready to jump the wall and surround him. He blast-jumped into the air trying to rain down blasts with his palms on the two closest enemies, Marie and Ludwig, but missed. He launched himself again.

After a series of jumps and attacks, he had still managed to hold off Ludwig and Marie, but was unable to get a head shot. Miguel and Levu stood guard in the doorway of the room, blocking off his escape.

"Where are you, Al?" he cried.

"I don't think we're as close as we thought," Al said. "Just hold on!"

In a move of desperation, Sammy curled up his body, resting knees and hands on the floor, feet against the back wall. He shot his body upward with hand blasts, and extended his legs, pushing off the wall. Then he shot a blast off the wall with his feet for maximum velocity. He shot toward the exit like a bullet, firing blasts at Miguel with one arm, protecting his head with the other. Miguel went down, and Sammy fired both palms at Ludwig and Marie.

"Woohoo!" Sammy yelled in uncontainable excitement.

Ludwig went down next, but Marie seized a chance to take careful aim at his poorly protected head.

Direct hit.

The fibers in Sammy's jumpsuit stiffened, forbidding any more movement. His com turned off, his helmet expanded over his eyes, and everything went black.

9 | Dantès

THE MISERY SAMMY ENDURED at the loss of his first Game was compounded by Gregor's sullen mood for the next several days. With Gregor's low confidence, Sammy should have been determined to carry out his honcho's orders implicitly. He wanted to confess his fault for abandoning Li, but he was too embarrassed. And since Gregor showed no hints of anger, Sammy said nothing. The only person suspecting anything was Al.

Sammy didn't know how Al knew, but he knew. He never mentioned it, but his attitude toward Sammy was noticeably icy for the next few days. Sammy wondered why no one got in his face and yelled at him. That's how he'd done things with his old friends, and it worked fine. His respect for Al made him resolve never to be the cause of his honcho losing again.

Jeffie, on the other hand, was thrilled Sammy had lost. She told Natalia and Kawai she thought it was good for him—something about building character, as Sammy heard it from Natalia. Jeffie never said anything directly to Sammy, but hinted around it regularly. For the next three weeks, she took advantage of every opportunity to remind Sammy her team had beaten his in their first Game. Brickert and Sammy got very good at rolling their eyes and holding their tongues. By the Sunday of his fourth week at headquarters, Sammy was pretty much over his crush on Jeffie.

Because it was still too cold on Capitol Island in March to do much outside ("except make spit icicles on your tongue," Brickert liked to say), most Sundays they spent inside relaxing. The Betas rarely did anything as a large group except gaming, but Al and Kobe decided to organize a slam dunk contest ("now that all the pukes aren't so pukey anymore," as Kobe put it). Sammy pointed out that if they weren't pukes, then he should drop the title, but Kobe pretended not to hear.

Al and Kobe made everyone play whether they liked basketball or not. Kaden arranged the competition into a tournament of sorts. Each round half of the Betas were knocked out of the competition by receiving the lowest votes from their peers. Sammy wasn't much of basketball player, his experience was limited to a recreation team in grade five. It was part of his parents' theory that he should try every sport at least once. American football was his favorite.

Sammy made it past the first round using a big blast to give himself plenty of time to do a 360° turn before dunking the ball, but his ball handling skills weren't good enough for him to stay in the mix for any longer.

"What a waste of size," Jeffie teased as she gave him his lowest score: 5 of 10.

Sammy went out in the second round, but he was content to watch the others. The five Betas who stood out the most were Kobe, Levu, Kaden, Li, and Jeffie.

The competition heated up as these five took the court. Of course, Sammy knew Jeffie had played basketball at the Junior Olympic level, but he had no idea she was *that* good, after all, she was still a girl. Everyone used blasts to get high enough to dunk, but she controlled the ball as well as anyone Sammy had seen. She had a graceful poise that even Kobe lacked with all his finesse. So it wasn't a surprise when the championship round was between Jeffie and Kobe.

Kobe went first, dribbling the ball from the half court line to the tip of the three-point arc, then launching himself into the air with a blast. His movement was fluid, his body frozen in an angular pose. At the peak of his jump, he performed an aerial somersault, pulled the ball high over his head, and jammed the ball home.

Despite being genuinely impressed, Sammy barely clapped.

Jeffie had that gleam in her eye that Sammy had seen before. She needed to win. Dribbling a few times, she sprinted down court up to the free-throw line and blasted hard—much stronger than Kobe—until even her feet rose above the rim. *Oh wow, she's going through the hoop.* It was the perfect choice because her frame was just slender enough to fit through. Kobe, with his more athletic build, could never hope to duplicate it.

Her legs went through cleanly, but she had too much forward momentum for the rest of her body to get through so easily. She must have realized this because she tried to grab the rim to stop herself.

Use your landing blasts! Sammy shouted at her mentally.

The panicked expression on Jeffie's face told him enough. He threw down his score sheet and tried to cover the distance from the sideline to the hoop before she hit the ground. Jeffie's sweaty hand missed the rim and threw off her balance even more. Several people gasped as she toppled onto the floor with a gut-twisting *CRACK!*

Sammy just missed her by a second.

Jeffie moaned in pain, squirming on the floor, trying to grab her ankle. The blood in her face was draining fast.

"Are you okay?" Sammy asked as several other Betas ran to help her. Kobe was among the first.

"I'm fine," she groaned, "just give me a second to get up."

"No," Sammy insisted, "Let me help you. You don't look so good."

"I'm fine!" she repeated louder, but as soon as she was upright, hobbling on one foot, her face went glue-white, and she fell again. This time Sammy caught her.

He picked her off the ground in his arms, and turned to Brickert. "Can you call Byron? I'm taking her to the cafeteria."

"You got her okay?" Kobe asked with genuine concern.

Sammy hoisted her up to improve his grip and pushed through the crowd until they parted for him. "Yeah, thanks."

Inside the cafeteria, Sammy lay Jeffie down on a table and made sure she was still breathing. After a few seconds, she recovered from her faint but was still quite pale. Just before she vomited, Sammy grabbed a garbage bucket and held it for her while she emptied her stomach.

"Feel better?" he asked when she finished.

"No," she mumbled. Sammy could see in her face that she was determined not to cry in front of him. "Dang it. I hope it's just broken."

Sammy put the bucket of barf down and wiped his nose to try to change the smell in his nostrils. "Why would you hope it's broken?"

"Breaks can be fixed in a week; sprains take like a month."

"I heard a crack, so that's a good sign, right?"

Jeffie nodded and wretched again. Sammy only just got the bucket in time. A little splashed on his hand, and he thought he might retch, too. Her face regained a bit of its color. "I looked so stupid out there."

"No, you looked great. You're better than I'll ever be."

She lay back down and closed her eyes.

"Byron should be on his way. Brickert called him as soon—"

"Had you ever played it before?" she blurted out. Her eyes were still closed and her hand was on her forehead, concealing her eyes, but Sammy wondered if she was peeking at him.

He had to think about her question. Finally he asked: "You mean Star Racers?"

Jeffie nodded. He wished she would open her eyes so he could see them now.

"No. I haven't—I mean I have, but not before here."

She frowned weakly, her face still pale, but attractive nonetheless. "I'm such a freaking idiot."

Sammy dug his finger in his ear. "I think I broke my hearing. Can you say that again?"

"You heard me," she told him with a fragile laugh which quickly turned into a grimace. "Don't make me laugh, it hurts."

Sammy nodded complacently. Despite the smell of barf on her breath, he wanted to kiss her. He wanted to kiss her very badly. But all he said was, "Yeah, I'll work on that."

"Thanks for trying to catch me, though."

Her hand twitched like she made to catch something, and then the cafeteria door opened. Commander Byron entered pushing a wheelchair and behind him came a man with very brown skin wearing a doctor's coat. Several curious Betas looked in over his shoulder.

"How are you, girl?" Brillianté called out from behind.

The doctor's attention went from the trash can where Jeffie had vomited, to Jeffie, and finally to Sammy. He looked at Sammy for a long moment. His strange smile made Sammy feel weird. He shined a light in her eyes and briefly examined her ankle. "Let's get you out of here," he told Jeffie in a voice Sammy was sure he'd heard before. "I'll have you fixed up in no time." He picked her up tenderly and put her into the wheelchair.

Just like that, she was gone. As she left, he wondered to himself, *What would she have done if I'd caught her?*

⑤ ⑤ ⑤

The days at headquarters came and went a little quicker as the routine settled deeper. Every few days or maybe once a week, Sammy thought about his friends, especially Feet, and missed running the streets with them. The strict life of a Psion at those times seemed too tedious, but between the Game and sims, enough adventure was still packed within the four white walls of headquarters to keep him interested.

As Jeffie predicted, she was out of her cast in a little over a week. She claimed to use the time in her sims to become the most precise hand blaster ever. Sammy wanted to write her off as an arrogant snob, but he'd come to accept that Jeffie had claimed for herself a little piece of his heart that he couldn't quite take back. No matter how much she grinded his nerves, he couldn't shake her. And he hated it when she spent time around Kobe.

Kobe and Jeffie aside, Sammy's biggest problem was the growing disparity between himself and the other nukes in instruction and sims. The burden of constantly crafting his lie and the paranoia of being caught made him feel like he was in a pressure cooker. What had started as a little lie to protect himself from Jeffie's jealousy had snowballed into a mammoth whopper, and only Brickert knew that Sammy was actually kilometers ahead of the others.

But even Brickert didn't know that Sammy sat back in instructions while the Teacher raced through film clips and pictures in rapid succession while his brain soaked everything in like a dry sponge. Sammy didn't understand what it meant, and he didn't care. He just didn't want his friends to think he was a freak. He feared someone, Jeffie especially, might walk in and see him zipping through a subunit, listening to a chipmunk on amphetamines.

What he did care about, and quite passionately, was his steady ascent in the ranks on his per-stats. He was at least fourth now in every category. At the conclusion of each training session, he checked his stats, priding himself when he climbed another spot. He hadn't forgotten his goal to become number one in everything.

Saturdays and Sundays were his favorite. He loved the Game. In the Arena, it was almost like being back in the grocery store. The competition swallowed him up, and he forgot all his troubles. He'd kept his promise to follow his honcho's orders whether he agreed or not. On Sundays, with the warmer weather, the Psions almost always left headquarters. Sammy enjoyed exploring the nearby areas on Capitol Island while Natalia told him and his friends all the latest gossip.

Brickert and Sammy were like brothers. They created new blast games to play in their room and looked for ways to sneak into the girls' dormitory. Natalia said she'd heard that two Betas tried this and once were caught by Commander Byron. Brickert, besides having grown enough to barely reach the eye-scan on the door, eventually got over his crush on Brillianté. It wasn't hard since he'd never had a real conversation with her. Days later, he confided in Sammy that he liked Rosa Covas. As close as he and Brickert were, Sammy could not understand why his roommate fell for the older girls.

Life at headquarters took a turn for the worse after a grueling simulation focused on weapon disarming. As usual, Sammy checked his per-stats and saw that he'd earned the number two ranking in timeliness and jumped to number one in efficiency. In celebration, he ordered his favorite meal, chicken cordon bleu. When he sat down to eat, he noticed someone missing.

"Where's Jeffie?"

Kawai tried to hide a smile with her milk glass. "She said she's staying behind to finish up her sim unit."

"Combat sucks," Natalia said, throwing down her french fry and splashing her ketchup onto Sammy's arm. Her hair was now a dull gray, a side-effect from too many dyes. "How the heck am I supposed to beat up people twice as big as me? They don't even flinch when I punch them."

"So blast them in the face," Sammy answered as if it was a no-brainer, only to get a kick under the table from Brickert.

This launched the four of them into a discussion on some of the finer points of combat. Kawai and Natalia were arguing over targeting the groin or the face when Kobe came bursting into the room. Jeffie came in only a few seconds later.

"You!" Kobe said, pointing dramatically at Sammy.

Everyone in the room stopped talking and eating to watch.

"Yeah?" Sammy asked.

"What's your rank in timeliness?" Kobe demanded.

Brickert pushed past Kobe with his second tray of food and asked, "What do you care?"

"Shut up, uber-noob. This is my business."

Brickert's cheeks went bright red, and he sat back down next to Sammy. Noob was a rude name to call someone, but *uber-noob* was downright offensive.

"It's not your business, Kobe," Sammy said without giving Kobe the courtesy of even a look, "so leave me alone."

"I've heard stuff," Kobe continued. "Li told me about the moves you could do in your very first Game. Like a perfect landing blast. You were the first one in your group to pass the primary units. You lied to me . . . and everyone else." His eyes flickered to Jeffie.

Now Sammy's face turned red.

"But I also know that someone has been rising quickly through the ranks since then. So I'll ask you again, what's your rank?"

The cafeteria became deathly quiet as everyone waited for Sammy to answer. Furious and embarrassed at being put in the spotlight, he was tempted to show Kobe two of his fingers (the middle and the thumb), but instead answered, "Twenty," and returned to his meal.

Brickert burst out in laughter, then stopped at a look from Kobe. It was Brickert, not Sammy, who held the number twenty ranking, but Sammy knew Brickert didn't mind.

"Liar," Kobe spat, reaching over the table at Sammy, trying to grab Sammy's com. Sammy jumped up from his seat and leaned away from Kobe's reach. "What have you got to hide?"

"Get away from me!" Sammy got up and shoved Kobe backwards.

"Keep your dirty hands off me!" Kobe shouted back, now in Sammy's face.

Everyone now was either yelling or rushing toward them to stop a fight. Brickert got in the middle first simply by standing up—unfortunately it was just as Kobe aimed a blow at Sammy—and got punched right in the eye. When Brickert fell backwards holding his face, Sammy tried to knock Kobe down with a quick sweep, but Kobe jumped over it and aimed another punch at Sammy, connecting with the side of his head.

Suddenly, Sammy wasn't at headquarters anymore, he was back at the Grinder where fights started every day if a bigger kid wanted someone else's dinner roll. He blasted Kobe in the chest, propelling Kobe toward the wall. Kobe neatly stopped himself using a backward blast off the wall, then blast-jumped over Sammy, grabbed the com off Sammy's head, and landed on the other side of the room. Sammy would have gone after him, but Martin Trector and Li Cheng Zheng tried to stop the fight by grabbing Sammy.

Before Sammy could get free, Kobe manually accessed his per-stats. With a grim face, he threw the com back at Sammy. "I knew it."

"Kobe, you are way out of line!" Kaden stood in the doorway of the room with Al, both breathing like they'd heard the news and come running.

"I'm out of line?" Kobe asked. "Why is he lying to everyone? I bust my butt in that room everyday so I can be the best, and he just sits back and wins everything! How is that fair? He's top in almost everything. It's a bunch of bullsh—"

"Shut your mouth!" Kaden interrupted. "It's not your business. Al just told me he's dropped a ranking, too, but he's not mad about it. You don't know how hard he works. You don't know anything."

"That's crap—"

"All you care about is winning. You've never taken time to get to know Sammy. Just get out."

Kobe opened his mouth to argue.

"I said GET OUT!"

If anyone else had said that, Kobe would have either laughed or gotten angrier. Kaden, however, possessed a certain influence over his brother. When Kaden spoke, people listened—even his twin. Kobe gestured rudely to Sammy and stomped out of the room.

Kaden awkwardly muttered something that Sammy didn't hear, then followed his brother. Sammy appreciated Kaden's interjection, but he was concerned now with the looks everyone else was giving him. Some stared at him curiously, others jealously, and Brickert with a swollen eye full of pity. It was Jeffie's hard glare that made his heart sink. She had the distinct look of someone who felt betrayed, and—as he began to notice— so did Kawai. Natalia just seemed fascinated by the whole event.

"Jeffie—Kawai—I—" he started to say, wanting to explain why he had kept up the act for so long, but not able to grab the words.

With one last look of disgust, Jeffie shook her head and walked out with Kawai in step. Sammy stared stupidly at the door.

"It's so stupid!" he vented to Brickert as they hurried down the stairs. "Man, I hate Kobe. I freaking hate him. Why can't he just grow up?"

"I'm sorry, Sammy," Brickert said, struggling not to say anything more. Sammy noticed his hesitation and turned on him.

"What? What are you thinking?"

"Let's get in the room first."

When the door had closed behind them, Sammy asked again. "All right, what?"

"Listen, everyone knows there's something different about you. You never lose in—in Star Racers. And everyone is beginning to see how good you are when we play the Game. If you don't believe me, ask Natalia. She knows everyone's opinion about everything, I'll tell you."

Sammy didn't want to admit it, but Brickert's words rang true. Ever since Marie told everyone about the impressive moves he performed and how he single-handedly held off four opponents in that room, he was much more involved in the Game. And for the last few weeks, the honcho whose team he played on consistently earned the victory.

"But so what? Why do people even care?"

"So what?" Brickert cried, throwing his head down into his hands. "No one understands you. You're so . . . frustratingly secretive about everything. Everything, I tell you! It's like you don't trust anyone."

"I do—"

"Including me. Don't you realize you've never told me anything about your life before you came here? You know me like—like—I don't know . . . but you know me really well."

Sammy forced a laugh. "That's because you talk so much."

Brickert laughed, too. "When I'm around you, I do. But for all I know you could've been raised by Martians—plus, you've got to understand the way everyone else feels. You're better than all of us in almost everything, or you will be soon. Why?"

"I don't know," Sammy answered. Then, seeing the look of skepticism on Brickert's face, he added, "I'm being serious! It comes easily to me. Things have for a while now. Ever since . . ."

His voice trailed off as embarrassment overcame him.

"See what I mean?" Brickert told him. "You're doing it again."

"I'm sorry, but there are things in my past, things I've done, that I don't want people to know. Everyone loves to tell the story of how they found out they were Psions. Not me. Mine wasn't good."

"Like I said, you don't trust anyone."

"I trust you. You're my best friend. I just don't want . . . people to know about the things I've done."

"Why?"

Sammy blasted a piece of paper hanging from the ceiling by a paper clip and made it twirl. The spinning cleared his thoughts. "Because they won't like me. They'll think I'm a freak. Or they'll pity me."

Brickert blasted the piece from his side and made the spinning stop. "Right. Trust issues. You don't trust us to accept you or your past."

Sammy was about to disagree, but didn't. Brickert was right, even if Sammy wouldn't admit it. He took off his clothes, hung up his com, and went to bed. He lay silent for a long while thinking about everything that had just happened. When he heard Brickert starting to snore, he said, "Hey, Brick, you'd better put ice on your eye."

🌀 🌀 🌀

Saturday's Game went well. Gregor was honcho again, but Kobe was also on the team, and only referred to Sammy as "hot shot." After winning, Sammy repaid his debt to Gregor, who led the team to victory in four Games of five over Ludwig. He'd hoped that by following Gregor's orders exactly he would be relieved of his guilt.

He wasn't.

Jeffie was assigned to Ludwig's team. After the Game, she congratulated Kobe with an unnecessarily long hug, then walked past Sammy with her hand outstretched to compliment Gregor. Natalia and Kawai spoke to him, but he could tell they still held a grudge. At lunch, the three girls sat at a separate table with their roommates. It made Sammy feel weird.

"How long do they stay mad?" he asked.

"It's only been a day," Brickert explained. "Girls need more time than guys."

"Well, then they're stupid," Sammy commented while trying to stab a tomato with his fork. "Salads are stupid, too. Why did I even order this?"

"One time I mixed peroxide into my sisters' shampoo—you know, as an April Fool's prank. Only two of them used it before they realized what I did. I'll tell you, I honestly thought they were going to kill me—all because of a stupid joke. I mean, it's not like it's so hard to just dye it back to the way it was. No sense of humor at all—worse than the time I hid their make-up. . . ."

Sammy was flabbergasted by Jeffie's behavior. He assumed things would go like the last time she'd been mad at him: if he just stayed calm, remained friendly, and waited for her to come to her senses, things would turn out fine. However, rather than shooting him scathing looks like before, her behavior was dramatically different.

She had always been good friends with Kobe, especially since Kobe was considered one of the "older Betas." And it wasn't uncommon for them to flirt as they sparred in a game of Star Racers. But that Saturday she spent the whole day attached to Kobe's side, laughing at everything he did and said. She giggled especially hard when Kobe used the term "hot shot" with his friends. Kobe clearly did not mind the extra attention.

This new behavior went on into Sunday. With the weather unseasonably warm, many of the Betas headed to a park for a game of Frisbee. In no mood for socializing, Sammy went to the library and chose a book. Very few books in the library were fiction, but he found a dusty old copy of *The Count of Monte Cristo* and decided to try it. While the others divided into teams, he parked himself under a nice big tree and started reading. Brickert and Kaden tried to get him to join, but they saw he had no interest. Brickert, of course, was chosen last. From where Sammy sat, Brickert didn't mind. Sammy envied the way his friend didn't let things bother him.

He left this train of thought as the tale of Edmond Dantès unfolded. A sailor with a promising future who falls in with a band of smugglers, an incredible transformation into a fabulously wealthy and mysterious count—Sammy saw parallels of his own life as he lost himself in the book.

The game lasted over two hours. During one of their breaks, Kaden jogged over to where Sammy sat in the shade.

"Hey, you all right?" he puffed.

"Yeah, fine," Sammy said in an absent-minded, leave-me-alone tone. "I'd just rather read than play."

"When did you start that?" he asked.

"Huh?" Sammy snapped out of his trance. "Oh, uh, just today. Why? Have you read it?"

"Yeah. It's awesome. Are you really already that far into it?"

Sammy looked at the book. He hadn't realized it, but he had finished well over half the book. And the book was fourteen hundred pages.

"No! Uh—no . . . I know it drives people crazy, but I just like to skip around."

Why am I still lying?

"Are you cool about yesterday?" Kaden asked him.

"Don't you think it's funny how when Kobe does something stupid, you're the one who apologizes?"

Kaden grinned and chuckled, but Sammy thought it sounded hollow. "Well, I'm not apologizing for him, but I do want to uphold the family honor. Look, dude, I don't care if you're number one or number ten in the rankings. We just do our best. I hope you don't think everyone cares about all that stuff."

You didn't see the way everyone looked at me on Friday night, he thought, but only said, "I don't think that."

"Good—well, you know what they say, 'never get between a man and a good book.'" With that, Kaden joined a group of Betas heading back to headquarters for lunch.

"I thought it was 'never get between a hungry man and a meal,'" Sammy called after him.

Kaden just grinned again and shrugged as he walked off.

Sammy went back to his book, but was immediately interrupted by a loud clearing of the throat. Brickert wanted his attention. When Sammy looked up, Brickert pointed to something in the distance. He tried to see what it was, but only saw a bunch of Betas. Brickert pointed again with a jerk.

Sammy finally saw it.

It was Jeffie. She was holding Kobe's hand as they walked back into headquarters.

Brickert gave Sammy a helpless look and mouthed, "Sorry."

Sammy wanted to act like it didn't bother him, but he couldn't. Something deep inside him smoldered powerfully and for a brief moment a feeling of terrible strength swept over him. *How can she be so stupid? Hasn't she seen the way Kobe treats me . . . or Brickert? The way he takes everything way too seriously? Why—how could she like him?*

Worst of all, Sammy hated that he still cared for her. He still wanted Jeffie. Why couldn't the poisonous thoughts erase that? Despite everything negative and horrible he thought about her for taking the slightest interest in Kobe, he still liked the way her blonde hair bounced when she walked, the way the corners of her nose stretched when she smiled, and her fiercely competitive nature about everything from Star Racers to spinning her plate on her finger.

The poisonous inventions of his mind battled with the ache in his heart and made his stomach ill. He wanted to scream and storm and rage, but for what good? Like a fire with no fuel to burn, the storm wore itself out and he was left with a deep sense of emptiness. He sat wondering what to do, how to react. Was he ridiculous for even taking an interest in her, for getting so hung up on her after only a couple of months? He closed his book and made to go find Brickert when he realized what he truly wanted. He reopened the book and flattened the pages so he could read more. The story would inspire him.

After all, *Monte Cristo* was a story of revenge.

The next two weeks went by slower than normal as Sammy watched and waited for his chance to strike back at Kobe. Even after one day, the new thing to talk about was Kobe and Jeffie. Natalia's efforts alone made sure of that. She would go on and on at mealtimes about how cool it was that a sixteen-year-old and a mature fourteen-year-old could forge a relationship. Her goal now was to hook up Kawai, almost sixteen herself, with some of the seventeen- or eighteen-year-olds.

Of course, to be a couple in headquarters did not carry much weight, especially with the strict rules of conduct between the opposite sexes (for which Sammy felt extraordinary gratitude). While all Jeffie's attention went to Kobe, she didn't spare Sammy a word—not even a glance. He hated seeing them talking, laughing, and especially touching. A viper slept inside him, and whenever he saw them together, it bared its fangs and coiled to strike. Eventually Sammy couldn't even take eating with Kawai and Natalia, so he and Brickert sat alone.

"Kawai doesn't even think Jeffie likes Kobe," he told Sammy over a lunch of Philly steak and cheese sandwiches. "She says Jeffie just likes being liked."

"What does that even mean?" His conversations with Brickert about girls often left him even more confused.

Brickert just shrugged.

Sammy put his hot dog down and leaned to Brickert so they could speak privately. "The girls don't know I like Jeffie, do they?"

"I didn't talk, but I think they suspect something."

"How could they suspect something if you didn't say anything?"

"Girls have a sixth sense about that stuff," Brickert answered. "Like my older sister—the one right above me."

When did he suddenly become the expert on girls? Sammy asked himself as he watched Brickert take an inhuman bite out of his sub. *He doesn't even talk to the girls he likes. He just has eight sisters.*

"It's really weird," Brickert continued as he swallowed, "my sister could always tell when guys liked her friends. Always. But then, a guy liked my sister, she could never tell. I don't get that."

"Yeah, that is weird." Then he asked in a whisper, "Do you think they would tell Jeffie if they do suspect?"

"I don't know. Would you tell me if you knew that a girl liked me?"

Sammy had to think about that. He had never been in that situation. "Probably—I guess so."

"Then they probably wouldn't."

Sammy was about to ask more, but the calm female voice sounded over the room. "Prepare for the Game, Psions."

"Oh man!" Brickert exclaimed. "I'll tell you, I hate playing on a full stomach."

They ran over to the flashing panel.

Team 1:
Alanazi, Cala
Covas, Marie
Covas, Rosa (*)
Enova, Levu
Morel, Brillianté

Team 2:
Hayman, Albert
Plack, Brickert
Petrov, Ludwig
Reynolds, Kaden (*)
Tvedt, Gefjon

Team 3:
Berhane, Samuel
Ivanovich, Natalia
von Pratt, Parley
Reynolds, Kobe (*)
Zheng, Li Cheng

Team 4:
Covas, Miguel
Nujola, Kawai
von Pratt, Gregor
Trector, Martin (*)
Yoshiharu, Asaki

Victory: 3 Games
Maximum Game Length: 40 min.
Arena Rotation: None
Start Time: 13:10

"Suck a duck!" Brickert moaned. "You're on Dopey's team. Sorry, man. Could be worse. Could be on Rosa's all-girl team."

"You've got Al on your team," Sammy pointed out.

- 154 -

"Lucky me. We'd better go change."

As they ran downstairs and into their dorm to dress into their black suits, Brickert spoke up, "This is Rosa's first time as a honcho, isn't it?"

"I think so," Sammy answered.

"She got a pretty good team. All the older Beta girls."

"Even still, I doubt she wins."

"I don't think Dopey could handle Rosa winning on her first time," Brickert said. "The only people he can tolerate losing anything to are Al and Marie.

"Isn't Kaden the other honcho?"

"Uh-huh."

"Interesting," A thought formed in his head. A truly wicked idea.

Brickert stopped dressing with one leg in his noblack jumpsuit, the other frozen in mid-air. "No, Sammy," he said. "Don't even think it."

"What?"

"I know what you're thinking. It's—it's nutty. If anyone finds out, you're in deep doo doo."

Sammy burst out laughing. "Brickert, you're on Kaden's team. You shouldn't mind. Dopey has this coming. It's perfect! The only person he hates losing to more than me is his twin."

"That doesn't matter. It's not about personal vendettas; it is about cooperation and teamwork. What you're thinking goes against all of that. Remember what you did to Gregor?"

Sammy winced. He shouldn't have told Brickert about that. *Still, Gregor is Gregor, and he deserved to win. Kobe doesn't.*

"I'm not ruining Dopey's life." He stared at Brickert. "Are you going to tell anyone?"

Brickert opened his mouth, then closed it quickly. His cheeks turned a bright red and he looked down at the floor. "No."

"Thanks, Brickert."

"Please don't do it," Brickert pleaded one last time. "If Dopey—Kobe—finds out . . . I mean, what's the point?"

"The point?" Sammy repeated with a grin. "To understand that you'd need to ask Edmond Dantès."

10 | Revenge

"DIPLOMACY," KOBE SAID right before the Game began, "is the key to winning these Games. If we sit back and let the other teams fight, we win the first, and maybe even the second Game easy. Then they'll start coming after us. Li, Natalia, Parley, and I will play attackers when most of the other teams' players have been taken out. Hot-shot, you play defense."

It was a slap in the face and everyone knew it. Sammy knew they knew it by the way they watched him for a reaction, only he did not give one. He wanted to give Kobe no reason to suspect him.

As if Providence truly wanted Sammy to carry out his plan, visibility in the Arena was very poor for the first Game. Each team entered from a different side of the third floor. However, once they got inside, it appeared as though all the honchos shared Kobe's strategy. Judging by the permeating silence in the Arena, no one dared to be the first to enter the bizarre grid of randomly placed walls and platforms that formed this Game's setup. Kobe adapted his plan with a flexibility that surprised even Sammy.

"We travel as a team. Stay as elevated as possible, but keep your body low and undercover. Never be more than five meters away from a teammate. Move."

For the time being, Sammy followed his honcho's orders perfectly. High in the air they moved, creeping behind walls whenever possible, and swiftly along platforms when unprotected out in the open.

They met Rosa's team first, and just as Sammy predicted, she was unable to coordinate an effective defense from her lower position. One of her players escaped Kobe's onslaught, but Sammy wasn't sure whom.

"Let someone else pick off the last bone," Kobe said with an unmistakable brag as they watched the sole member of Rosa's team retreat.

Despite his orders to play defense, Sammy had taken advantage of opportunities to take out two of Rosa's four players. He knew Kobe wouldn't make special mention of him, but he wanted it to look like he did his part to help the team.

They continued the hunt through the large, angular jungle of metal. Sammy stayed right in the middle of the group, careful not to let himself be separated too far from his target. Not much time passed before Martin's group surprised them with a three pronged attack: two on each side, and Martin himself from above.

The attack would have been deadly if Kobe hadn't been so quick to fall back. Finding safer ground, they mounted a strong counter-attack, forcing a standoff. Kobe lost Natalia and Parley, but Martin lost Miguel and Asaki, his left flankers. Both honchos knew that if Kaden's team went untouched, they would lose. Martin slunk back into the darkness with his remaining two; Kobe went back to the high ground to try and surprise Kaden with an all-out aerial attack.

Martin's team found Kaden first. Eight Betas were locked in another battle when Li spotted them. It was the ideal time for Kobe to employ his plan of diplomacy, but the honcho caught Sammy off guard when he ordered them to launch into battle.

When Li questioned him, Kobe explained he didn't want Kaden and Martin teaming up on them, but Sammy knew the truth. Kobe did not want Martin to have the pleasure of eliminating Kaden before he had a chance.

They went as high as they could climb before dropping down, using hover blasts to stay just above the heads of their enemies. Just as Sammy thought, Kobe persisted on trying to take out Kaden single-handedly. Both Kaden and Martin's teams stopped blasting at each other and directed their attention to the three fliers: Li, Sammy, and Kobe. Sammy blocked their assaults using feet blasts and landed a few meters away from the battle. While Kobe was engaged in a free-for-all battle with the other honchos, Sammy aimed a blast at his helmet from behind.

As always, Kobe had no clue what hit him.

Sammy's heart triumphed, glorying in his lack of honor. Seconds later, Li was deactivated by Martin. This left Sammy alone to join the fight against Martin's team, helping Kaden cruise to an easy victory. Kobe's brother only lost one player: Brickert. Sammy didn't even mind when Kaden's team ganged up on him. He went out with a smile.

The layout for the second Game was a completely level playing field with nothing else in the Arena. It quickly turned into a melee. Kobe's attack was more cautious, keeping his team near the outside, but Sammy still found his chance to eliminate him. It came when they were finally pulled into the middle of a huge brawl between all four teams. His opportunity came even quicker than the first Game because they were all surrounded by opposing players, trying to watch their back and front sides at once. As it just so happened, Kaden also won the second Game.

Martin's team handily won the third Game, but Sammy played smart. He intentionally let himself get blacked out early.

Before the last Game started, Sammy almost felt sorry for his honcho. An edge of desperation laced Kobe's voice as he spoke to the team while they entered the Arena. The layout was a large network of connecting pipes. The teams had no choice but to enter the network, as the portals fed directly into them. Kobe came up with a great strategy. They searched until they found two pipes that formed a T. Then he ordered them to lay in wait at either end of the top of the T for a team to come up through the base. Easy ambush. However, if either or both ends were attacked, they could retreat into the base of the T, regroup, and hold that tunnel in defense.

The Game was tedious, taking almost the entire forty-five minutes allotted. Several small battles broke out between Kobe and Martin and Rosa in which no player from any team was deactivated. Finally Kobe made a bold move to rush Martin's team lying in wait a few pipe junctions away. The attack was successful, decimating the enemy team in a moment of confusion, but it placed Kobe's team at a positional disadvantage between what was left of Rosa and Kaden's teams, who had just finished their own battle.

Sammy could only assume that Rosa did not realize the advantageous situation that had been handed to her, but Kaden did. Leading his team forward at Kobe's, Kaden yelled out to Rosa's team, "Ambush! Ambush!" It only took moments for her to catch on. Kobe's team made some small headway against Kaden and his three, but was trapped when Rosa came with her two from behind. Sammy, Li, and Natalia were faced against Kaden's front attack, while Kobe and Parley guarded the rear.

Sammy fought hard alongside his teammates, waiting for the right moment to finish his vendetta. However, Brickert and Jeffie made a terrible error, which Li exploited, driving Jeffie back and Brickert to the floor, deactivated. Kobe's team stood on the verge of winning. If he was to change the tide of the Game, Sammy had to act fast.

Behind him, Parley cursed when a blast hit his helmet. Seizing the moment, Sammy raised his arm over his head, palm facing away, and blasted two random blasts behind. Kobe went down. Natalia looked at Sammy with surprise. Sammy's heart thundered in his chest. *Does she know what I did?* He turned around and feigned shock when he saw Kobe fall stiffly to the ground.

"Was that me? I was only trying to help!" he cried.

Natalia hesitated a moment too long, and a blast from Kaden hit her helmet. Sammy pretended to get confused from all the commotion around him. By now, it was only a matter of time. He and Li were toast. But had Natalia had actually believed his farce?

"Come on, Li!" he roared like a general making his last stand. "Fight to the—"

Kobe wasn't angry that Kaden had won three out of four Games. He was outright livid. As they left the Arena, he wasted no time pointing out that even the "hot-shot" had been unable to pull out a win under such conditions. All guilt Sammy might have felt vanished, and even Brickert managed a smug wink as they grabbed a snack. Revenge tasted pretty darn sweet . . . on Saturday.

Then came Sunday.

And on Sunday, Battle of Ages arrived at headquarters. Battle of Ages was the latest VR game boasting complete mental immersion. Everyone wanted to try it out—everyone except Kobe. Gone was the outspoken sarcasm and loudmouthed ranting from the day before. Instead, he kept to himself and watched movies on the big screen while everyone else took their turn in the game. Twice, Sammy caught Kobe watching him with an unreadable look in his eye. It gave Sammy the chills. Even when Sammy won several games in a row, Kobe made no comment.

This new attitude unsettled Sammy and stayed on his mind all evening. He waited until he and Brickert were back in their bedroom to discuss it.

"Are you absolutely sure he doesn't know?" Brickert asked.

"No, not absolutely," Sammy replied after thinking it over for the hundredth time, "but I'm pretty sure. The only way he could know is if Natalia guessed what happened and told him."

"What if Natalia said something to Jeffie— "

"Natalia? Spread gossip? No way, José."

Sammy chuckled. "—and then Jeffie repeated it to Kobe."

"Maybe Kobe doesn't know. Maybe he just suspects."

"Yeah, maybe." Sammy pulled off his jumpsuit and climbed onto his bunk. "I guess I just can't give him any reason to suspect anything."

"Maybe I can say something—casually—to throw off any suspicions about your intentions."

"That would be a bad idea."

"You think so?"

"Yes, I do." Sammy remembered the times Brickert mentioning something casually had caused trouble. "But thanks, though."

For the next few days, they kept an eye on Kobe and listened out for any rumors, but they heard nothing. Sammy was glad to put the matter behind him. He had something more important to worry about: his history exam. Though he knew Natalia would tell him he set some kind of record by how fast he finished the history unit, he worried if he could remember the vast amount of information taught him in two months' time. On Friday, rather than following his usual morning schedule, he skipped exercise and breakfast for extra study time.

After a thorough review, he sat in his Teacher and took the five hundred question exam. Two and a half hours later, he left with a big smile. He had correctly answered four hundred ninety-eight. And he was pretty sure he knew the two he had missed.

He went downstairs for a quick brunch. Some of the older Betas were already there.

"What are you doing here, Sammy?" Al asked.

Sammy took a seat by him. "I sat my first exam today. The instructions said I could leave when I "

"You finished your first unit already?" Gregor asked. Al and Marie had similar looks of disbelief on their faces.

Sammy caught himself before saying anything else. "Er—well . . ." *Think up a way to get yourself out of this one.* "I was home schooled for—uh—some of my education. My parents didn't like the curriculum that the school board set for its students. So for history they—my mother—she taught me quite a bit before I got here. I just barely finished up the rest of the work." He took a large gulp of water from his glass and spilled several drops on his clothes. "I mean—wow—the test was really, really hard. I'm—I didn't do very well. But I think I passed."

Gregor and Marie seemed to believe his story. But Al didn't seem convinced. Still—perhaps in respect to Sammy—he said nothing else. Instead he asked, "How do you think the exam went?"

"You need an eighty percent to pass," Gregor told him. Sammy hadn't spoken to Gregor much outside of the Games. It surprised him how much older Gregor looked than the others. Natalia said he was almost twenty. "Did you get at least that?"

"Uh . . ." Sammy responded, acting as if he was calculating his score in his head. "Yeah—just barely."

"Great."

"Good job."

"Oh, yeah. Thanks."

He searched for a topic to change the conversation, finally resting on the Psion Panels the three Betas had coming soon. Al's was first, coming up in only three months, then Gregor would retake his two months later, and Marie was only a month or so after that. Apparently the Panels lasted several weeks, so some of their testing would overlap.

"After you pass the Panel, what happens?"

"We have a little ceremony here," Al answered. "I'll be grafted into an Alpha Squadron, and go to Alpha headquarters."

Marie stared at her plate as Al explained about going into Psion Alpha. At that moment it dawned on Sammy that the two were dating.

"Do your parents come for that?" he asked.

Marie shot Al a nervous glance.

"Actually, yeah, parents are allowed to attend the ceremony. The government even flies them here in a private atmo-cruiser. It's a pretty big deal."

"Cool! Are they coming?"

"Um . . ." Al hesitated, ". . . my dad will definitely be there."

Sammy didn't catch the subtlety in Al's voice until the words left his mouth: "What about your mother? Isn't she coming, too?"

Everyone at the table stirred uncomfortably. Sammy noticed it and wanted to take the words back.

"My mom passed away when I was really young. But she'll be there in a way."

"Oh." Sammy wanted to choke himself on his sandwich. "I—I really had no idea." The words stumbled out of his mouth. Each word was like a glass ball rolling another step down the stairs until the inevitable crash. "You talked about her before—and I just thought—I'm sorry . . ." Before he could stop himself, he asked: "How did she die?"

Marie and Gregor looked on as if they were watching a car wreck happen right in front of them. And Sammy felt like the victim.

"She was killed in an accident."

"Oh."

"But I'm sure she's proud of me."

Al managed a smile the whole time. It made Sammy feel like maybe he hadn't made such a big fool of himself. Another question popped into his mind, and he let it fly. "How can you think that if she's dead?"

"Because I believe our dead family members watch over us. You know, like life after death. What do you believe?"

"I don't know," Sammy answered. "Sounds nice, though." His mind went somewhere else, thinking about his own mother:

"Don't you think it's just a bit silly?" Mrs. Berhane said. Her laugh never had a trace of malice. Sammy's dad called it a gentle laugh.

"You said I could get any outfit I wanted," Sammy reminded her. "My treat for beating dad at chess."

They stood next to a clothes rack inside the Snow Gears department store at the Johannesburg mall. Being in the middle of summer, the store was nearly dead, but a group of five kids with long hair were checking out helmets. Sammy guessed they were hardcore boarders or skiers who knew the summer was the best time to get new gear for cheap.

"I'm just surprised you want winter clothes in the middle of summer," she answered. "What if you outgrow them before it gets cold?"

"We can buy them extra big, plus I'll wear the hoodie around the house, it gets so cold sometimes."

Her smile flickered for a second. Sammy noticed it, but said nothing. He had not meant to say that. He knew why the house was kept so cold, but he'd been sworn to secrecy.

"Well, I like the red one the best," she said, pulling it off the clothes rack and holding it up to him.

"But Mom," Sammy whispered, his eyes wide with fear, "red is the bad color."

His mom pursed her lips to keep from laughing again. Sammy Sr.'s favorite rugby team, the Springboks, wore green and gold, their rivals, red.

"You look so good in red. You need more in your wardrobe."

Sammy rolled his eyes so his mother could see. "Fine." He knew better than to argue with his mom about wardrobes. He was just glad she wasn't dwelling on his comment about the house being cold.

The rest of Sammy's lunch passed in relative silence. His thoughts lingered on what Al had mentioned about death.

"Well," Al said as he got up from the table, "if you're going to be threatening my other spots at number one, I've got to put in a little extra time in the sims."

"I didn't know you had—"

Al snickered at Sammy's embarrassment. "Kidding. It's cool you've got a special talent for this stuff." Then Al was more serious than Sammy had ever seen him. "The real enemies are the Thirteens, not other betas. Remember that if someone comes along and dethrones you."

As Sammy nodded, Al patted him on the back and walked out. Sammy wolfed down his sandwich, then decided to skip exercises to take a shower. He went downstairs and got clean clothes. Resting his com on top of the stack, he climbed into the wash unit and turned on the water.

"GAH—!" he cried out, jumping out of the streams of water coming from all directions. The water was set to 1°C. People (particularly Kobe) thought it was funny to change the settings. His body shivered as goose bumps formed up his legs and arms. It brought back fresh memories of what he'd been thinking about during his conversation with Al. He turned the water up as high as he could tolerate, sat down in the stall, and cried until he felt normal again. *Mom never knew that Dad once told me why it was always so cold in the house.*

As he dressed for simulations, his com light blinked. Brickert often texted him funny thoughts or a question about simulations while they were in separate rooms. He rarely received messages from anyone else. He hurried to finish, then picked up his com and fitted it around his ear. The message was indeed from Brickert:

How did it go?

The test. He spoke into his com with a grin. The computer converted his speech into text:

`Nearly aced it.`

He didn't have to wait long for Brickert's reply:

`Knew you would!`

Laughing at this, Sammy ran upstairs and entered the sim room, just ahead of schedule.

A couple weeks earlier, Sammy had finished the combat unit and started weapons training. The weapons unit started with simple things like hand guns. Sammy struggled to develop good accuracy. When he mastered the basics, Byron moved him to automatics, then assault rifles. Sammy liked these weapons more. After rifles, nastier things came along. Things like shrapnel spreaders, flesh jiggers, and explosives like the syshée he was using now. It was by far the most difficult unit he had done—even more than the tricky disarming units in combat.

The large black syshée was so real and warm in his hands. It never ceased to amaze Sammy what technology could do with holograms. The large human-shaped target loomed ten meters ahead of him. His finger rested gently on the trigger. He remembered the techniques the program gave him for aiming a weapon: *Relax the fingers, comfortably support the weapon, visualize the most precise target possible, take a full breath and exhale, momentarily hold the breath while firing.*

Holding as still as possible, he pulled the trigger.

The syshée made a hissing noise that sounded like someone in the room wanted to get Sammy's attention: *Psst!*

A black projectile no larger than the marbles he had used in the grocery store flew from the business end of his syshée and struck the target right in the heart. A small flash and bang erupted from the impact with just enough force to burst through the rib cage and inject the enemy's heart with microscopic, lethal barbs. If hit square over the left breast, the barbs would embed themselves in the coronary arteries and veins, maybe even in the aortic crest; the enemy would bleed to death in seconds.

Not bad aim. I'm definitely getting better.

When Sammy first began the weapons and demolitions unit, he was anxious to blow through it so he could move on to bigger and more important things like Advanced Enemy Training. But overlooking the importance of doing well in weapons hurt him in the stats, causing him to fall a few ranks. He sobered up after falling as low as fifth in accuracy and fourth in timeliness. As his attitude and performance improved, he bounced from fifth to second in the accuracy rating, and fourth to first in timeliness.

Though the weapons sims were not as aerobically demanding as earlier units, his skin glistened with a sheen of sweat from the intensity he exerted in order to excel. He prepared to fire the syshéc again. Two consecutive shots this time . . .

Psst! Psst!

Two perfect hits.

The rest of Friday's simulation went well. Between almost acing his exam and having the weekend in front of him, Sammy's spirits soared. He drank deeply from his water bottle and dried his face and hands on a hand towel. When the screen on his com flipped out, it almost startled him. He had another message, this time not from Brickert.

From Jeffie!

Sammy, I want to talk to you in private when you finish your sims. Meet me in sim room 3.

His heart leapt to his throat and he tripped as he hurried to the door. *She wants to say she's sorry.* he thought as he ran down the hallway and turned the corner. He was so excited to mend the tear in their friendship, he overlooked that Jeffie's message should have appeared as "From Gefjon," just as the messages he sent to Brickert always appeared as "From Samuel."

He eye-scanned the door and went inside. The room was empty and a little cold. Jeffie probably hadn't finished her own sim yet. He looked for something to distract him from the mounting anxiety and began absentmindedly toying with his sock, pulling on the threads and releasing them so the elastic would snap back against his ankle. His heart thumped harder inside his chest.

Any minute now.

A thread came loose in his sock, and his hands began to work it around his index finger. He wondered why she wanted to meet in a sim room of all places. Perhaps she didn't want Kobe to know they were meeting.

The string seemed to have no end and was soon wrapped around his first two fingers.

He thought about the last time she'd apologized to him. They'd been alone in the cafeteria and he had wanted to kiss her.

Maybe she decided she likes me and wants to ditch Kobe.

Three—six—ten minutes passed with Sammy impatiently waiting for her. The top of his sock was a frayed bundle of loose threads, but he didn't notice. Auditioning in his head were the different things he could say after she confessed her sorrow for the way she'd treated him.

I shouldn't play too hard to get, she might get mad again. But if I appear too willing to forgive maybe she'll think I'm a push over.

As the strings wrapped around a third finger, he played several different daydreams in his mind, each one ending in a waterfall of tears from Jeffie. Just as his imaginary scenarios reached the pinnacle of emotion and passion, they were abruptly cut off with a flicker of light in the room.

Appearing from thin air, Kobe and Jeffie were suddenly sitting in the middle of the sim room, on a park bench surrounded by green shrubbery, bound in a very romantic kiss. Sammy swallowed hard.

Someone must have fabricated it. Kobe must have . . .

But a second voice spoke reason to him: *A fake holo-recording? Kobe doesn't have access to that kind of equipment.*

It felt like a boulder had been dropped into his stomach, but despite his disgust he couldn't tear his eyes away from the scene. *She wouldn't kiss him.*

She IS kissing him!

Why would she show this to me? What kind of a sick person does that?

In the background of the recording, he heard Ludwig's voice. "Why does he even want us to record this anyway?"

"I don't know. He wouldn't tell me." The second voice was Miguel's. "Just hold the camera steady."

"Kobe is one weird dude. Does she know we're recording this?"

"You don't honestly think she'd let him, do you?"

"Does it record sound?"

"Yeah, but it's on mute . . . oh, crap. It's not."

The large stone in Sammy's stomach burned white hot and then spread into fire throughout his whole body. He shot a blast through the hologram. It blew through Kobe's head like air through a window screen.

Kaden was down the fifth floor hall with his head in another sim room. When Sammy's door shut, Kaden pulled out and ran toward him. He looked frantic.

"There you are."

Sammy didn't stop. He didn't even acknowledge Kaden's presence.

"Sammy, wait!"

"Don't," he snarled at Kaden with a wild gleam in his eyes.

He leapt down the stairs using small blasts to cushion the landings and blew like a tornado into the cafeteria. Kobe sat on the far side of the room eating a large bowl of ice cream with Jeffie, Ludwig, and Kawai.

Sammy barely noticed the look of terror on Brickert's face when he came into the room. Bristling with raw energy ready to be used, he aimed for his target. Kobe only just had time to look up before the first blast hit him. The ice cream flew off the table and splattered his target with a confection of colors. Impotent background voices, however urgent, did not have time to register in his mind, it focused on only one thing:

Destruction.

Kobe was merely a target, startled—perhaps even stunned—at the sudden shower of ice cream, watching stupidly as Sammy blasted away chairs and tables between them. It gave Sammy sadistic pleasure to see the shock on Kobe's face. Jeffie, eyes wide in fear, screamed for Sammy to stop, but he hardly heard her. Ludwig pulled Kawai and Jeffie out of the way just before Sammy reached their table. Some of the Betas yelled for Sammy to stop, others shouted or ran for help, but they all seemed so far away.

Kobe aimed two quick blasts at Sammy's chest, but he dodged the first one and parried the second, advancing closer. Kobe sent one more worthless blast and then blast-jumped over the table in a vain attempt to escape. Sammy met him in the air and knocked him into the ceiling with his own jump. Kobe grunted in pain. They fell down together in a twisting ball of fists emitting howls of rage at each other. Sammy used every punch from physical combat he knew as Kobe tried to block his attacks.

Strong hands grabbed Sammy around his chest and head, pulling him off of Kobe. He squirmed and writhed to fight free, but Byron's voice shouted in his ear: "Enough."

11 | Friends

SAMMY STOPPED STRUGGLING. Commander Byron's voice boomed out again, "Kobe, get off that table and follow me."

Byron set Sammy down on the floor and ushered him out of the room by his collar. Sammy had to assume Kobe was following because he did not dare look behind. The commander marched them down the hall, then abruptly stopped and said, "Open one and two."

Two doors opened in the hall to reveal identical, brilliant white rooms. The doors blended in so perfectly with the wall that Sammy had not even known they were there. He recognized the room on the left as the one he'd woken up in on his first day at headquarters.

"Solitary—both of you," Byron said, pointing each of them into different rooms. "Kobe in there. Samuel in there."

The door closed, leaving Sammy to sit and shake from the rage that still pounded in his veins. He wanted out of the room. He wanted out now so he could pound Kobe's face some more.

The best thing he could say about solitary was that at least he was not restrained like the first time. A few minutes after Byron left him, one of the walls turned into a screen and a movie began playing. Sammy cringed when he saw the title: Psion Training Protocol Session 4: Conflict Management. After watching the film twice, Sammy's rage had run its course. Then Byron's more effective punishment took effect: leaving Sammy alone to suffer through the guilt and embarrassment of what he had done.

What would Dad say? he asked himself over and over again. *All those talks about stepping up and being a man were wasted on me.*

It was tradition in the Berhane household that once every three months, father and son went on an overnight fishing trip. His dad had four great loves in his life: Sarah, Sammy, chess, and fishing. While Sammy never loved fishing as much as his dad did, he enjoyed their trips. It gave them time to talk, and talking with Sammy Sr. was fun. When Sammy was still twelve, his father proposed a trip only a month after their most recent outing, but Sammy assumed his dad just had the urge to fish again.

Once they got in the car to drive to the lake, Sammy sensed something different. His dad's usual excited chatter was forced. His smile looked wrong. He didn't sing the "Wishin' You Were Fishin'" song. But Sammy knew his dad would talk eventually. Sammy simply had to wait until that time. When they rented the boat, he helped row a half kilometer onto the lake, never going too long without sneaking a glance at his dad. It was about an hour after they set up their rods when his dad finally spoke.

His father stared out over the water and the low sun reflected pricks of light off his pupils. He stirred for a bit, then spoke. "Sammy, Mom's going to be gone for a while."

"Why?" Sammy asked, straightening up on his little fishing chair. "Is it because she's sick? She seems sick lately."

"Yes. In a way." His voice dropped off, and he mumbled something to himself. Sammy wanted desperately to know what he'd said. "Can you keep a secret from your mom if it's really important?" He turned and looked directly at Sammy.

From the countless times he'd watched his dad take calls from clients, Sammy learned the way to determine the seriousness of a conversation: counting the wrinkles on his dad's forehead. The more wrinkles, the more critical it was. Right now, Sammy Sr. had too many wrinkles to count.

"I'll keep a secret," Sammy Jr. answered.

"You remember when she lost the baby last time?"

Sammy nodded.

"It was harder for her than you realize, buddy. She tries to be very happy for you and me, but she really hurts inside."

Sammy nodded again, but he didn't fully understand what his dad meant. It was a while before either spoke. A large fish broke the water several meters off, breaking their silence.

"Remember when we had that long talk about drugs and how sometimes people will try to trick you into taking them? Do you remember that, Sammy?"

"Yes," he said, but didn't understand what that had to do with Mom.

"There's a reason. Your mom was given some pills from a—from someone she thought was a friend. Those pills, son, weren't what she thought they were. They were pills—stimulants— no, well, they were drugs, Sammy. And your mom . . . has been unable to stop herself from taking these for almost a year. Her friend has been using her to make money off us."

The weight of his father's words and the undertone of anger in his voice sunk deep into Sammy. Now he got it. *My mom's addicted to drugs.* He felt guilty for not noticing. Sammy's mother, Sarah, was a more than just a homemaker. She was his best friend. She was his confidante. Sarah Berhane always waited for him outside when he came home from school so they could talk. Before his dad came home, they ate a snack she'd baked or played sports at the park. The idea of all that being gone was like a punch to the gut.

"How long will Mom be gone?" He blinked quickly to stop tears from forming.

"Probably three months. She doesn't want you to know, buddy, because she thinks you'll look down on her. You won't, will you?" Sammy heard a pleading tone in his father's words. "Can you step up and be a man now?"

Sammy shook his head, tears now freely flowing down his cheeks. "No, Dad, I won't think bad of her, and I won't tell her anything."

Samuel Sr. reached over and hugged his son so they could cry together.

Exhaustion set in as Sammy lay on the bed in solitary, but he woke early and couldn't fall back asleep. It was Saturday. The Betas might be in the Arena right now. Strangely, it didn't bother him that the Game would go on without him; he didn't care if he ever played a Game again.

By noon the boredom had really set in and the idea of never playing the Game seemed like unending torture. He would have even welcomed another showing of the cheesy Psion Training movies. "Why not show me a movie about how to get a girl to like me?" he yelled at the wall. It was as if a vortex had formed around the room itself, and the day had become a revolving eternity.

Sammy had finally gotten used to the pervasive silence, and it was just lulling him back to sleep when the door opened. It startled him so badly that he jumped off the bed. As he composed himself, Commander Byron entered carrying a covered plate of food.

"Come with me, please." That was all he said, then he walked back out.

Too scared to ask questions, Sammy followed him out of the room. He wondered if Byron planned to lock him and Kobe in the same room to make them talk it out, but Byron headed for the stairs. They climbed up to the fifth floor and stopped at the top of the stairs. Only Commander Byron had access to go any higher. The commander scanned his eye and led Sammy up one more flight. He stopped at a landing with two doors. One said: Roof, the other: Commander Byron. Sammy went through the latter door.

They entered a beautiful sitting room with plush rugs hiding almost every centimeter of the floor. Several pieces of exotic Mediterranean furniture upholstered in bright, vivid colors waited for use. Dozens of holo-pics decorated the walls. It was a nice home, but even Sammy could see it needed a woman's touch.

This must be where Byron lives.

Byron gestured for Sammy to sit down at the dining table, then set the plate in front of him.

"Here, eat," he said pushing the plate toward Sammy, who reached to uncover it.

Chicken cordon bleu. His favorite. How did Byron know? Sammy looked at it, shaking his head. All the shame of what he had done came rushing back, replacing his hearty appetite with hot, sick guilt.

"Do not tell me you are not hungry."

"I don't deserve that," Sammy said weakly.

"I know you feel that way, but you have not done anything so unforgivable that it merits starving yourself. Hunger will not help you deal with your problems—only add to them. I thought you had learned that in the old grocery store you snuck into."

Byron smiled.

"Why aren't you angry?" Sammy asked. "I thought you'd kick me out."

"Because I understand things better than you," Commander Byron answered. "You are not the first Beta to brawl like an uncivilized baboon."

Sammy smiled and took up his utensils. Food rarely tasted so good.

Commander Byron said, "I will talk to you while you eat. If I say something surprising, you have my permission to spit anything out so you do not choke."

Sammy laughed.

"Do you remember our first conversation a few months ago? When I recruited you as a Psion?"

Sammy nodded and chewed.

"On that day I said you had anomalies? Do you remember? Well, you never asked me what that meant. I still find that interesting. Why have you never asked me what that means?"

"I don't know," Sammy said through a bit of food. After swallowing, he finished his thought. "It didn't mean anything to me. I didn't even believe that I belonged in this place."

"So it meant nothing to you because you were not even sure you had the abilities I talked about?"

"Yeah, I guess so." Even now, Sammy couldn't grasp what the big deal was.

Byron nodded thoughtfully. "I have monitored your progress closely, Samuel. Perhaps closer than I have with most who have passed through this facility—and not because of favoritism in your behalf or a prejudice against you."

He paused, but Sammy showed no reaction. *Why would Byron care more about me than the others?*

"Have you learned about Anomaly Eleven since you began your instructions?"

"No."

"But you do remember that I told you that you had this anomaly also?"

"Vaguely." He stopped chewing again because his stomach was starting to hurt from eating too fast. "Most of that conversation is a blur."

"The reason, Samuel, that I have observed you so closely is because you are the first and only Anomaly Fourteen with—" He paused again. Sammy couldn't read the commander's face, but his expression scared Sammy a little.

"—multiple anomalies. Anomaly Eleven, like Fourteen is categorized with five stars. NWG puts a high priority on employing those with it, as you can imagine. In fact the first five-star anomaly to be discovered was an Eleven—a young boy named Ivan from Ukraine. Nice man, I hope you get a chance to meet him someday. Loves math, though. Math makes my head spin."

The commander gave Sammy a little wink.

"People with Eleven use a higher percentage of brain neurons—they have a higher mental capacity. Sharper memory, extended planning ability, faster capacity to absorb information. Truth is, Eleven is still a mystery. You, for example, grasp concepts very easily in your instructions. You play your instructions at the highest possible speed because your brain works faster than most people's, allowing you to break down the information easier. It's also helped you identify combat patterns easier in the sims. Your brain has learned to focus a gun faster than most people do."

Byron caught the look of surprise on Sammy's face when he heard this. "Oh yes, I know all about your instruction habits. I said I was watching you closely. Now while there are many others with Anomaly Eleven, some of which have a much higher capacity than you, I think you can understand what an extraordinary contribution you can make to our war efforts."

Sammy's brain buzzed and he could only nod. It explained so much: the chess game, instructions, Star Racers. He couldn't wait to tell Brickert. But would the others understand? Would Jeffie or Kobe stop feeling the need to compete with him, or would it make him even more of a freak? Either way, he liked having answers.

"Can you see why I watch you so meticulously? I want you to succeed. And you have! Today you received a perfect score on your history exam. Most students struggle to get the required eighty percent."

"But—No—I . . ." Commander Byron simply raised his hand and Sammy fell silent.

"You were going to say you did not achieve a perfect score. I know. I intentionally put two questions in your exam that were more subjective than the rest of the test. Of the five answers you were given to choose from, one of them was the correct answer that any textbook would have you pick. Another one of these answers was a morally correct answer. You missed both of those questions because you picked the correct choices in my answer key, not the computer's. So in reality, you scored perfect marks on the test."

"Why did you do that?"

"I have my reasons," Byron answered mysteriously, but waving it off with his hand. "More important is how you performed overall."

"But sir," Sammy said, "why are you telling me this now? Just because I got in a fight with Kobe?"

"You have great potential, Samuel. You may possibly contribute more to bringing our world to peace than anyone else. I have great expectations for you."

He drove home these last words, looking directly into Sammy's eyes. Sammy was grateful for the information, but nothing Byron said changed how he felt about Kobe.

"Let me show you something," the commander said, getting up from the table. He was only gone from Sammy's view for a few seconds, and came back holding a holo-pic. He showed it to Sammy. The picture was framed in gold adorned with silver flowers and birds.

"It's beautiful," Sammy whispered. He wanted nothing more in the whole world than to hold a picture of his mom and dad, but he had none.

Byron handed the picture carefully to Sammy. It was much heavier than it looked. The gold and silver in the frame gleamed brightly, boasting of the care the commander must frequently give it. He looked into the picture and saw a younger commander posing with a stunning brown-haired woman. Both of their gazes were fixed below the frame at something Sammy couldn't see. The joy in their faces reminded him of his own parents.

"She was more beautiful than any picture could capture, Samuel."

"I'm sure."

Byron's expression was wistful and far away, lost in his own thoughts. Sammy sat silently, occasionally glancing at the picture, but letting the commander have his moment.

"She was one of the first I trained, you know."

"She was a Psion, sir?"

"Yes. And very talented—very enthusiastic about life. We fell in love and were married in secret about twenty-five years ago. It was wonderful—just wonderful. After we told our superiors we had wed, she lived here and we trained the Betas together.

"Not long after our second honeymoon, the first battle of the war happened. We were part of several missions to rescue refugees, including Kobe and Kaden's parents. Many people wanted to come to the NWG, but were stranded, cut off, and hiding in the sewers. All of the missions we did were dangerous. The CAG caught onto us and sent the Thirteens to trap us. They overwhelmed us and the battle turned . . . deadly.

"Emily, my wife, fought like a warrior. Like a warrior-princess," he added with a half smile, but his hands trembled badly. "I always called her my princess. So many of them. A handful of us. We got through the worst of it, but she caught two braxels in the back."

Sammy almost lost his lunch. He knew from weapons training what a braxel could do. Braxels were small, blunted projectiles carved into drills and fired from a flesh jigger. They were specifically designed to continue burrowing after impacting into the target's body. He had seen some of the worst things they could do to the human body, and it made him sick to think the commander's wife had suffered such a painful death.

"She was still alive when we got into our atmo-cruisers, but they had already dug so deep, one into her heart, we could not stop all the internal bleeding."

Sammy understood the emptiness the commander felt from such a loss. "I'm very sorry, sir."

"Thank you, Samuel," Byron responded, and his face became more firm again. "I know what happened to you in Johannesburg—why you lived in that grocery store. Can you see now how petty and insignificant your argument with Kobe is in perspective to what people have lost because of this war?"

Sammy nodded soberly.

"I watch the Games, too, Samuel. I know you targeted Kobe—made him lose on purpose. I also know why. I heard what Kobe did to you in the simulators. I understand why two ordinary boys would lose their tempers in such a situation. But think about this, Samuel: you and Kobe are not ordinary boys. You do not have the luxury to fall prey to your petty rivalry. You took an oath. You took upon yourselves the responsibility of fighting in a war. A war that killed my wife, and may someday claim the life of someone else you care about. Maybe Brickert or Gefjon. The harder you train, the more successful you will be in protecting the ones you love. Okay?"

"Yes sir." He knew Byron was right. He did not have to like Kobe, but he should not let his personal feelings overshadow the more important issue. The greater good.

"Work hard. Be a great person, a great friend, and let Gefjon sort out her own feelings. Take that as the only love advice you will ever receive from me," he said, smiling again. "Can I have my picture back now, please?"

Sammy adjusted the frame in his hand and gripped the handle over a dove carved into the silver. It depressed slightly under his hand. He must have activated a switch or something because the picture leapt out of the frame into a hologram hovering in the air. There stood the commander and his wife, Emily, as they looked down on a tiny infant they held together in their arms. Byron took the frame from Sammy, and the hologram disappeared almost as soon as it appeared.

"I—" Sammy swallowed hard and watched Byron's face for signs of anger. "I'm sorry, it just—it was an accident."

"No need to apologize," Byron said, giving Sammy a reassuring look. "But please keep the information that I have with you shared about myself, and my family, very private. Just between the two of us."

"Yes sir, absolutely."

"Thank you," the commander said, standing up. "You will become a capable Psion, I have no doubt."

"Thank you, sir," Sammy said sincerely, standing up as well.

He shook the commander's hand, and turned to leave, assuming he was excused. He reached the door, and was about to open it, when Byron called to him.

"Yes sir?" he asked.

"Two more hours of solitary," Byron said, smiling.

When Sammy returned to solitary, the door opened by itself. Everything was exactly the same as before except for a small person with unruly black hair facing away from Sammy on the restraining table. This boy wore a bright yellow prison uniform and battered shoes that dangled carelessly in the air.

"*Feet?*"

The shaggy head turned around to reveal the small face of Sammy's long lost friend. Grinning from dimple to dimple, Feet laughed when he saw Sammy. They ran to embrace as old friends who thought they'd never see each other again.

"Brains!" Feet cried. Sammy hadn't heard his old nickname in months. "You're really alive. What happened to you? Are you okay? Who are these nutty people?"

"I live here," Sammy still couldn't stop smiling. "How'd you get here?"

"Bunch of stiffs in suits found me in the Grinder," Feet explained when he calmed down. "They pulled me into the office up front and got in my face. 'Do you know Samuel Harris Berhane, Jr.?' they asked." Feet quoted them in his best deep-man voice. "Totally nutty dudes, Brains—I even forgot that Sammy was your real name. They told me if I came with them to talk to some commander, I'd get six months knocked off my time."

Sammy barked a laugh.

"I'd have come whether they knocked off time or not, though."

They lounged around on the floor, talking about everything. Sammy had so many questions about his friends, and Feet answered them all. They had new plans for breaking out of the Grinder. Since Sammy had orchestrated their last attempt, he offered his advice. At one point, Feet dropped his voice and asked, "Are you here because of what you did in the alleyway? You know, your teleka—your powers?"

Sammy smirked. "I told you I don't have any powers."

He said what he could about life at headquarters, but he knew better than to say much. From the way he described things, he was in a government program for youth. He told Feet about how he lied to his friends, how he beat everyone at VR games, his rivalry with Kobe, and his crush on Jeffie. Feet listened and laughed.

"You should hear yourself. You're a total cake-eater again."

Sammy could not help chuckling, too. Being with Feet was like peering into a looking glass, but seeing exactly how much his life had changed. The jarring pieces of his life now fit together into a sharp timeline starting with his comfortable life at home to his time at the Grinder and ending here.

Suddenly Feet became serious. "Brains—listen—the reason they brought me here is because I gotta talk sense into you. Remember the games we played in the old Save-o-Mart or whatever it was?"

"Yeah, I wouldn't forget, Feet."

"You know why you lost all the games toward the end there—just before we got caught?"

"Yeah," Sammy answered. "I do. I always knew."

"Good. Because I figured it out, too. Took me a while, but then I sorta used it against you. It was almost like you wanted to lose."

"I never wanted to lose. And you didn't beat me every time."

"Almost. Toward the end, almost every time. You counted on yourself to do everything. Chuckles and Honk hated being on your team."

"That wasn't what I meant by it. I just—"

"You didn't think they could do everything perfect. Chuckles used to get so pissed at you. He told me you always chewed him out whenever he messed up."

"I do trust—" he started to protest, but Feet cut him off.

"No, you don't. Your commandoid guy—" His voice dropped to a hush, and Feet glanced around the room looking for spy cameras. In the Grinder, if they were speaking about an adult, they had to be cautious. "—that white-haired dude told me about how you don't trust anyone here, either. How you won't talk about your past like it's some kind of mark on you. We had to survive. All of us came from bad places. You, too—especially you! You don't have to be ashamed of that."

"It's not the shame that stops me from talking to them."

"Then what is it?"

"I don't know," he answered in an empty voice.

"Yeah, you do. Tell me."

Sammy's face grew hot. He did not want all this emotion to happen, but he did not think he could stop it. With everything he had experienced over the last forty-eight hours: the fight, the hours of solitary, the overwhelming information given to him by Byron, and now the ecstasy of seeing his best friend from long ago, it was all he could do not to cry. In a torrent of emotion and words, he poured out his feelings. He spoke of his paralyzing fears of what his friends might think, his mixture of pride and terror at being the best at everything, and the new burden of responsibility Commander Byron had placed on him.

"Why don't you tell this stuff to . . . what's his name? Big Bird?" Feet asked.

Sammy chuckled, though his voice was still thick from his outburst. "You mean, Brickert. I don't know—I should, shouldn't I?"

"Yeah, you should. But not all at once or he'll explode."

Sammy laughed even harder. Commander Byron was even smarter than he'd suspected. *He brought the one person I could talk to.* "Do you want to grab some food downstairs?" he asked Feet. "I'll introduce you to some people."

"I can't, Brains. I was blindfolded when they brought me into the room. The commandoid said I can't leave without him. Made me promise." Then in a fake whisper he added, "I don't think they want me to see too much around here—like anyone's face."

The door opened. Commander Byron appeared in the frame. Sammy understood it was time to bid farewell. It was harder than he thought, and he almost wished for a parting like they'd already had where no goodbyes were uttered. But he was grateful for the chance to see Feet once more before they traveled too far down their respective paths. As Feet turned to walk out the open door, he called out, "Hey Brains! If anyone can save the world, it's you."

Sammy nodded. "Thanks." Byron led Feet out of the room. Sammy watched them go, then went downstairs to his own room. It was late into the night by then, and Brickert was already asleep.

12 | Girls

THE SENSATION SURROUNDING the fight in the cafeteria died down faster than Sammy expected. He and Kobe avoided each other now and Jeffie still didn't talk to Sammy, so things were pretty much back to how they'd been before the fight. At headquarters, routine was like a tiger trap: so easy to fall into. Before he realized it, weeks had gone by, and he hadn't kept his promise to Feet. It wasn't that he forgot, he just had a lot on his mind.

The summer threatened to end unseasonably early, and Brickert wanted to visit the NWG Museum of History before the weather turned sour. Sammy agreed to go on a Sunday afternoon, thinking it might be his opportunity to open up to Brickert about his past. However, Capitol Island was known for its fickle weather, and a severe rainstorm forced them to postpone. This didn't bother Brickert. He was dying to play the new game at headquarters: Star Racers *Turbo*.

Sammy wasn't so eager. Most of his problems stemmed from consistently beating people at games. And since Star Racers Turbo was not that much different than Star Racers, he flatly refused each time someone invited him to play. He didn't mind spending the day in the rec hall playing pool and catching glances of the Turbo matches on the screen, but he frequently caught himself silently critiquing the playing styles of his friends. After watching a handful of matches, he figured out exactly how he could win every game using the new weapons and features.

That night, as he stared at the stark whiteness of the ceiling from his top bunk, Sammy thought about Jeffie. She'd dumped Kobe the moment Byron let him out of solitary. Brickert had told Sammy all about it while Natalia filled in the juicy details. And though Kobe never showed signs of being upset, Jeffie just wasn't the same.

Does she miss Kobe? The thought made him queasy.

But what irked him the most was that even though the crimes he and Kobe had committed were enormously different, she punished them the same. All Sammy had done was lie to her so she wouldn't be jealous. Kobe had filmed them making out and used the tape for revenge. How could she think those two transgressions deserved equal punishment?

What has she got against me? The question bit at him like the fleas he'd gotten once from sleeping in an old junkyard while on the run. He needed more information. And the only person he could turn to was Natalia. He approached her at breakfast the next day.

"You should have seen her when she found out what Kobe did, Sammy," Natalia said, not even touching her bowl of cereal. "And with her own camera."

They were huddled in a corner of the cafeteria with Brickert, who was keeping a watch out.

"Me and Kawai had to physically stop her from going to solitary and finishing what you started. I mean—wow—you know? She was so scary, it was like—"

Brickert interrupted Natalia's description with a stream of nonsense words as Jeffie walked by looking distinctly uninterested in what anyone around Sammy could be doing. They all pretended to be doing something other than talking. Brickert tied his shoe slowly so he could see where Jeffie was going. Sammy took a few bites of oatmeal and Natalia stared with wide eyes just like any other time she got excited.

"Hi, Jeffie!" Natalia announced in a voice so perfectly happy, no one would have guessed she'd just been gossiping about her friend.

"Hey, Natalia." Jeffie's voice was glum and flat, and she moved on to sit with Brillianté across the room.

Sammy did not bother greeting Jeffie. She hadn't talked to him in almost two months, and seemed to think of him as a non-entity. "So what am I supposed to do to make her happy?" he pleaded. "I just want to be her friend again."

Natalia looked at him like a doctor about to tell a patient terrible news. "She only wants one thing: to emasculate you just before pushing you off a building with your wrists locked in magna-cuffs so you can't blast to save yourself."

"Wow . . . it ought to be easy then, right?" Brickert asked smugly.

Natalia left, and Brickert tossed several more ideas at Sammy, but each one seemed more and more like what Jeffie wanted to do to him already. He and Brickert discussed it again that night, lying in their bunks long past bedtime until Brickert exclaimed in frustration, "I'll tell you, I'm as clueless about girls as you are about losing!"

Life continued like this, and Sammy spent a good deal of his free time desperately searching for the key that would unlock the secrets of the female psyche. He found it in the most unusual of places on a Friday night.

After another successful week in the sims, moving up in the rankings and advancing through weapons, Brickert caught Sammy in such a good mood that Sammy finally accepted a challenge to play Star Racers Turbo. His one condition was he would only play in the new team mode. No one seemed to mind, the mere fact that Sammy had agreed drew every Beta to the rec room like flies to rotting meat. They all wanted a chance to beat him. Just like the very first time Sammy played, Kaden explained how to use the new features. Sammy didn't bother confessing he'd been watching closely enough to already be an expert.

His team handily won each game, even if he was the only player left. Many of the new dynamics in the game made it even easier. Like a gaming addict, Sammy's anticipation peaked before each new race. His impatience for the next one to start made him antsy. Then, around the fifth or sixth match, team mode ended and a free-for-all game started. Feeling a little peeved that no one informed him, he almost quit. But he wanted to win again. Winning was fun. Winning made life good. He went into automatic mode, no longer thinking about the controls, only acting and reacting. He won the race with ridiculous ease, and was in such a fine mood, it seemed harmless to play another.

The projector in his cubicle came back on for the next game and showed the other seven ships docked in the star cruiser. Sammy saw a familiar blonde head sit down in the ship next to him and take the controls. He stared as she maneuvered herself into position and prepared for the countdown, flicking strands of hair out of her face. The need to win left him, replaced with an even greater desire. *Come on, Jeffie. Just look at me. I'm right here. Just look over here.*

But he knew Jeffie wouldn't look at him. She would continue to pretend he wasn't there. If he beat her, she'd get up and be pissed, though never showing it.

He knew what to do. He saw the solution. It wasn't *seeing* like when he won so many games. It was different, but he knew he was right. His gut told him so. The countdown began. *It has to work. It has to.* Three seconds now before blast off. The countdown reached zero.

He launched into space and targeted the fighters on the side farthest from Jeffie. He knew her style. She would avoid a fight with him as long as she could. After clearing out all three ships on his side, he came for Jeffie and the other two fighters remaining. The two ships teamed up against Jeffie and Sammy, until one turned on the other and dispatched it. Jeffie got the next kill shot, leaving her and him alone. As if thinking the same thing, both ships turned and raced toward the star cruiser that marked the finish, taking only an occasional pot shot at the other ship.

Make it look real, he reminded himself. *It has to look real.*

From Jeffie's cubicle, he heard her voice muttering, "Come on. You can do it. Come on."

Only a quarter of the race remained. Sammy knew he had the better angle, which gave him a greater chance of winning, but he and Jeffie were nose to nose, and the ships bumped and pushed for position. If he were to surrender his slight advantage and end up losing, it might look suspect. Fortunately, Samuel Harris Berhane, Jr. had never been known for letting races play out. No one survived if he could help it.

He pulled away from Jeffie, giving up his small advantage. He called up his weapon selections. Jeffie shielded her flank and pushed on, playing it very safe. Sammy shot a space mine just ahead of her ship. It was too close for her to safely blow it up with her lasers. She easily dodged it, but it cost her the better position he had just given up, forcing her to fight dirty with him . . . which was exactly what he wanted.

For the rest of the race, they engaged in a fierce battle with Sammy owning the upper hand. In a desperate move, Jeffie made a sharp turn, sharper than would have been possible in the older version. Her nose aimed straight for his ship. He seized the chance to roll his ship over, allowing his turret to have a better shot at her underside. This counter-move exposed his own turret, which was more costly to shield. Setting the stage for his ruse, he dropped his shields, rerouted power to the weapons, and focused all his fire power on Jeffie. Predictably, she put a mine of her own in front of Sammy, one he could have easily avoided, but instead ran fully into it with the front of his ship unprotected.

BOOM!

An explosion ripped through the cubicle; fire on every side consumed all the oxygen in the ship. Yet the noise of the explosion was nothing compared to the screaming coming from the cubicle next to him.

"*I WON!*" she shrieked as she ran down to the main rec hall. The sound of every Beta clapping and cheering her name met her. Kawai and Natalia tried to raise her up on their shoulders, but collapsed in a heap. Sammy stayed in the cubicle wondering if he should appear happy or miserable or angry over his first loss. He chose happy. It seemed the best way to go. So with a big grin, he joined Jeffie in the tumultuous common area.

"Tough loss, Sammy!" Kaden shouted to him over the roar.

"I knew it had to happen someday." He shrugged it off as the next hand grabbed his shoulder.

"Never thought I'd see you lose," Al told him. "Way to take it like a man."

Perhaps it was her elation, but in the midst of Jeffie's excitement, she forgot to mention anything—not even to gloat—to Sammy. In fact, she made no effort or gesture to him at all. Before Sammy had any chance to try to break the ice, a band of girls surrounded Jeffie, all chattering or shrieking energetically, and carried her off like a flock of seagulls. As Sammy watched her leave, more comments came his way. It seemed no one realized the truth.

And for now, that was enough to make him smile.

He stayed a little longer to watch Brickert's last games. After those ended, they left the rec hall for the dormitory. Standing in the hall, Jeffie's voice carried from the cafeteria. He peeked inside and saw the girls gorging themselves on pizza and ice cream.

Brickert went in and offered his congratulations, but Sammy didn't dare. What if he gave something away? The decision was difficult. He wanted very badly to talk to Jeffie, but knew it wasn't time. Brickert brought back some pizza to share. They sat in their dormitory and ate in silence until Brickert suddenly started laughing.

"What?"

"Nothing," Brickert said apologetically, then filled his mouth with more food. About ten seconds passed, and he let out another loud giggle.

"*What?*"

Brickert had to cover his mouth as he laughed again. After swallowing he said, "She doesn't have a clue. Are you ever going to tell her?"

Sammy knew what Brickert meant. And he knew by now better than to play stupid with his best friend. "How did you know?"

"Please!" Brickert snorted and choked on his next bite. "No one's studied your moves more than me. I would never believe you lost that game from someone outplaying you. Not in a million years, I'll tell you. You're too good."

"I may tell her . . . someday. When she doesn't get so worked up about that kind of stuff."

Brickert offered Sammy another slice, but Sammy declined, rubbed his stomach, and lay on the floor. "How long do you think that will take?" Bricker asked.

"Mm. Don't know. Ten—maybe twelve years."

They shared a laughed.

"And until then?" Brickert asked. "I mean, she didn't even talk to you after the game."

"Keep giving her the only wins over me—" he said. The plan was all thought out. He would be cautious and calculating, never giving himself away. "—every now and then, of course."

"Oh, yeah . . . of course," Brickert said with a sly grin. He seemed to be catching on to Sammy's game. "And you're sure it'll work in the end?"

"The way I see it, every time I lose that game, *I win*," Sammy said. He snatched up the slice and took a big bite. "S'dangoodeetzza," he said with his mouth full.

"Yeah, but win what?"

"Her heart."

"Ladies and gentleman!" Brickert announced, laughing and gesturing dramatically to Sammy. "Casanova!"

The next day was Saturday. Sammy sent a text to Natalia and Kawai, asking them to meet him and Brickert in the cafeteria. Only Kawai came.

When she arrived, she had one of those mysteriously knowing smiles she sometimes wore. "Let me guess, you're wondering what Jeffie said about you last night."

"How did you know?" Sammy asked. "And where's Natalia?"

Kawai grabbed Brickert's plate of food and slid it in front of her. Like always, she pulled her bracelets up her arms so they didn't get in her food. "Natalia doesn't feel like she should talk to you right now. She stayed at the party longer, and Jeffie told her a bunch of stuff. But don't worry, Natalia told me everything Jeffie said."

"And you're just going to tell me?"

Kawai was still grinning when she said, "Why not? This business between you two needs to end."

"So is Jeffie cool now that she beat me?"

Kawai covered her mouth with a napkin as she swallowed her food. Her manners were always impeccable. "Er—well—actually—I think it made Jeffie really happy to beat you. I wouldn't say she likes you any better or worse."

"See? That's why girls are insane!" Sammy exclaimed. "Why didn't Natalia just come tell me this herself? She was there."

Kawai picked at the rest of Brickert's food. Her tone sounded as if the answer should've been obvious. "It's a betrayal for her to tell you directly what Jeffie says about you."

"But it's okay for Natalia to tell you, even if she knows you'll repeat it all to me?"

Brickert snorted his agreement.

"Duh, Sammy," Kawai said. Again, this was supposed to be obvious to him. "And by the way, you'd better be willing to play more games now. Everyone wants to beat you."

Kawai wasn't kidding. Interest in Star Racers Turbo exploded now that he'd lost. Betas played almost every night after dinner, and those who didn't play, watched. And Sammy did not disappoint the waiting audience. Over the next few weeks, he lost convincingly to Jeffie three more times, never letting anyone else claim the honor of defeating him.

Sammy searched for a sign that things between him and Jeffie were improving. Two weeks after her first win, she glanced at him without a scowl or frown. He considered it a step in the right direction. Days later, at lunch, she muttered, "Pass the salt."

Sammy dismissed this until he saw the salt right in front of him. But before he could react, she quickly added, "—Brickert." But still . . . it was something.

And only two days ago, during dinner, her foot accidentally kicked his. She pretended not to notice, but Sammy wondered if she had meant to do it. When he mentioned it to Brickert, his friend gave him a strange look.

With such thin strands of hope to cling to, Sammy was grateful for anything to boost his spirits. Free time on Sundays, passing his Geography exam, and time in the Arena all helped, but nothing compared to the day he finished his sims session and saw this:

```
Accuracy: 1/20
Timeliness: 1/20
Efficiency: 1/20
Overall: 1/20
```

This pleasant surprise was followed by another, less-welcome one the next day. Sammy stumbled into the cafeteria early Saturday morning. It was

0210, and his eyes barely focused on anything. He had gone to bed just over two hours earlier. Only a few other Betas were there before him. He looked into the flashing panel for the Game instructions and waited for the blurriness to leave his eyes.

Team 1:	Team 2:	Team 3:
Covas, Miguel	Alanazi, Cala	Berhane, Samuel(*)
Covas, Rosa	Covas, Marie(*)	Hayman, Albert
Nujola, Kawai	Enova, Levu	Ivanovich, Natalia
Plack, Brickert	Morel, Brillianté	von Pratt, Parley
Reynolds, Kaden	Petrov, Ludwig	Trector, Martin
Reynolds, Kobe(*)	von Pratt, Gregor	Tvedt, Gefjon
Zheng, Li Cheng	Yoshiharu, Asaki	

Victory: 3 Wins
Maximum Game Length: 75 minutes
Start Time: 0245

"I'm honcho?" he muttered to himself. "I'm honcho and he gave me the smallest team?"

His oatmeal tasted bland and landed hard in his knotted stomach. *What's Byron playing at? I can't win in these conditions.* Al soon came in with Marie, and before sitting down to eat, offered Sammy a few reassuring words and a hearty pat on the back. When Brickert saw the panel, he laughed so hard he couldn't breathe.

"Figures it'd be Kobe the first time you play honcho. And you only have six guys!" Brickert's grin stretched ear to ear. "With Li and Kaden on our team—we're gonna waste you."

Sammy flipped his oatmeal at him, but Brickert shielded it away.

"Should I hope you do well or hope you lose?" he asked Sammy. "I mean, it won't give me any pleasure to see Kobe beat you, but he is my honcho."

"Just play your best game, and I'll play mine," Sammy grumbled as he noticed the look of displeasure on Jeffie's face as she read the panel. Across the cafeteria, some of the older Betas on Kobe and Marie's teams were huddled together, talking quietly. Sammy wondered if they expected to be beaten in the Game just like in Star Racers.

"You'll do great," Brickert continued. "You got Al and Martin, plus Parley and Natalia won't give you any grief. "

Sammy lowered his voice. "Do you think Jeffie will try to sabotage me?"

"Not everyone thinks like you," Brickert said, giving Sammy a playful shove. "Besides, hurting you means helping Kobe—you think she wants that? If she has any ill feelings toward you, it's a hundred times worse toward Kobe, I'll tell you."

At 0235, twenty tired Psions plodded to their starting places. Sammy saw how groggily everyone moved and decided to lead his team in some warm-ups. Afterwards, he felt much more awake and noticed his team did, too. The lights dimmed, and he ordered his team into the dark Arena.

Marie won the first Game, and then the second. Kobe won third Game, and then the fourth. But these were more than failures; Sammy's team was routed every game. He couldn't explain it: he knew exactly what he needed to do to win, but he couldn't go through with giving the orders. What if his team didn't agree? What if they decided to do something different? He had no way of knowing if they'd follow him. And why should they? He had disobeyed orders from Gregor. And Kobe. They had no loyalty to Sammy. He was younger than almost all of them. How did he know they wouldn't abandon him?

It was just like when he played games with his friends in the old grocery store . . . he ignored his gut instinct. Only now he knew his "gut" was really his anomaly. His stupid anomaly that gave him the upper hand in almost everything. Instead of using a winning strategy, he placed upon himself the majority of the responsibility and gave his team simple jobs and basic directions. If his orders were followed, great. If not, no big loss. It was only good fortune that Kobe and Marie had drawn in the first four matches. One more win by either honcho, and Sammy could go back to sleep and feel miserable the rest of the day.

His team waited in the hall laying or sitting on the floor. Everyone was exhausted, ready to be done with the Game. Sammy sat alone with his eyes closed, hating himself for being who he was, but unable to change anything. Someone sat down next to him. Sammy peeked through his hands.

It was Al.

"Can I talk to you please?"

Sammy thought Al sounded rather stern. Rather than answer, he sighed and dropped his hands so Al could see his face.

Al tugged on Sammy's sleeve. "Alone."

Reluctantly, Sammy got up and followed Al around the corner. Al stopped and surveyed him angrily. "Marie is never going to feel about you the way she feels about me. You're way too young for her."

Sammy gawked stupidly. At first he thought he'd misheard Al, but he'd understood Al perfectly. *There's no way I'm having this conversation—especially right now.*

Al continued, poking a finger into Sammy's chest. "You're losing on purpose because you think you can win Marie over, the way you lose to Jeffie in Star Racers so she'll like you, right?"

"I—I—huh?"

Al broke into a huge smile. "Just kidding. Why are we losing, Sammy?"

"I don't know. Things just aren't going right."

"I wasn't born yesterday. Why are we losing?"

Sammy frowned and looked away. It was amazing how Al could talk to him in almost the same way that Byron did when giving correction or advice.

"Al, I just can't do it," he said helplessly. "I know how to win, but I'm—I'm scared of everyone messing up."

"Why?"

"I don't know. What if Parley or Natalia screws up? Or if Jeffie loses on purpose—"

"Like you did with Kobe?"

Sammy's face felt hot but his answer was defiant. "Sort of, yeah."

"Where has it gotten you so far?" Al waited for Sammy to answer, but Sammy knew he didn't need to. "Maybe you should change tactics."

"But what if—" Sammy started to say.

"Save butts for the chairs. You can trust me, Sammy. I'll do whatever you tell me to do, because I trust you. Start there."

He gave Sammy that familiar pat on the back and walked away.

Sammy blew out a long slow breath. *Okay—okay—I can do this. I can do this.* He walked around the corner. Most of his team stared at him. He gave them a weak smile, but he felt really awkward trying to give a pep talk to a bunch of older Betas.

"Okay. Um—we have three Games to win," he told them. The more he spoke the firmer the conviction grew in his voice until he almost felt like a real honcho. "The other Games don't matter. We can still win. We will win! Does anyone doubt that?"

"Not me," Al said. He had a stupid, cheesy grin on his face, but Sammy was still grateful for his vote of confidence.

"Because if you do, go back to bed now."

"Martin, Parley, Natalia . . . Jeffie?"

"If I'm going to be up this early, I'd better win," Martin shouted. Then he let out a war cry, and smacked the others' helmets to fire them up.

Everyone laughed.

"We don't have to beat them, they have to beat us," Sammy said as the lights began to dim again. "Here's our plan …."

Sammy's ideas worked, and two Games later his team was one win away from victory. The matches had been rough; there were some close calls, but Sammy managed to stay active through both Games. The depressed feeling in the hallway had transformed into jubilance. Tired, but elated. Everyone, including Jeffie, tasted the victory. He discussed some things that went wrong and made suggestions for improvement. He liked that they all listened to him.

The Arena setup was unusual. Rather than a different layout for each new match, the Arena format stayed exactly the same. This made each match last longer than the one before, and meant strategies constantly had to be altered during and between games.

Byron had designed a dark and complex labyrinth of tall thin halls, but the halls didn't shift or move as previous ones had. As the three teams came to know the labyrinth better through consecutive Games, specific spots were fought over to gain better position; sometimes a honcho's approach became more cautious, while others evolved more aggressive tactics.

Sammy led his team to their dumping room. He called it this because their entrance grew more and more narrow until they dropped five meters into a single room with only one exit. He ordered his team to keep close together, assigning three people as short range lookouts.

The labyrinth had two levels. All teams entered on the bottom deck. The upper deck was too high to reach by blast jumping, even off the walls. One wall in the dead center of the Arena had a ladder climbing it, and as far as Sammy knew, that was the only way up. Kobe's team had won the first Game because they'd been the first to find it. Brickert had guarded the access point while the rest had rained down blasts on their opponents from the upper platforms. In each of the six Games, almost all the battles had centered around the ladder. Sammy expected the final Game to be no different.

He hurried his team toward the center, a circular intersection where seven narrow hallways met. Along the way, he ordered Al, Jeffie, and Parley to take an alternate route. They ran through a zigzagging maze of narrow halls, and stopped at the intersection.

"Al, where are you guys?" Sammy asked.

"We're hidden behind the corner, but we can see the ladder right now. Just waiting on your orders. "

"You see anything?"

"Nope."

Staring into the intersection reminded Sammy of an old game show he used to watch. "*Samuel Berhane, what's behind door number four?*" He couldn't see Al, Jeffie, or Parley, but knew where they were. The question remained: where had Kobe and Marie chosen to take cover? If Kobe and Marie's teams weren't already lurking around one of the other corners, they would be very soon.

An idea struck him. He didn't pause to wonder if it would work. It felt right.

He spoke quickly and quietly on his com: "Everyone but Jeffie will wall-blast to the top of the halls. The five of us who are up top will fire concentrated blasts into all the other passages until we flush the other teams out. As soon as you see movement, stop firing.

"Jeffie, I need you to be a diversion. You need to stay down and fire blasts at them from ground level. Draw enough of them underneath Al and Parley so they can do some real damage. If you make it far enough away, double back on a different path and try and get behind some of them. Everyone clear?"

Everyone was clear.

"Let's do it."

Wall-blasting was a hard technique to master. It required blasting off opposite walls in a continuous upward direction without turning around in midair. The backward blasts in particular took hours of practice to perfect; the timing and ankle work had to be right on target. It had been one of the hardest elementary techniques for Sammy to master before moving on in the sims.

In near perfect formation he, Natalia, and Martin blasted up the walls. They caught themselves near the ceiling, suspended only by the friction of their feet against the walls, using their arms for occasional support or balance. They staggered themselves vertically, positioning their bodies so each had maximum targeting range.

"Is everyone in position?" Sammy asked.

All replies were affirmative.

He paused to revel in the moment and then said, "Fire at will."

Together with Martin and Natalia, Sammy blasted into the three other passages he could see from his angle. He heard cries of surprise in two of the halls and relayed the information to Jeffie. Moments later, someone from either Marie or Kobe's team sprinted into the intersection to scout out Sammy's position. Whoever it was, he or she moved too quickly to be taken down and darted safely into another passage. Sammy ordered everyone to keep up the barrage of blasts into the neighboring passages. Eventually one team had enough and seven players rushed into the intersection firing blindly in all directions, but mainly up at the second floor platform. Sammy recognized Kobe and Brickert in the group.

They think we're already up on the second level. He smiled wryly, waiting for them to spot Jeffie and run after her. "Take them out."

Sammy's team finished off three of the seven invaders before Jeffie was spotted. The remaining four chased her down the hall into Sammy's trap. Al reported that two of those four lay motionless beneath him and Parley, and Jeffie had gotten away safely.

One team down. Sorry, Kobe, but not really.

Sammy ordered renewed blasts into the other five passages, concentrating on the ones the scout had left and entered minutes ago. He figured as long as they guarded the second level entrance, they held the advantage. This went on for a couple of minutes when Natalia screamed.

Sammy looked back in time to see her falling about twelve meters to the floor, landing hard on her stomach, helmet closing down on her. Sammy swore under his breath, not because of Natalia's fall—her suit would absorb most of the impact—but because he'd been caught off guard by the two stragglers from Kobe's team firing up at him and Martin. Martin turned with Sammy to finish them off when Al yelled, "Buckle up. Here we go!"

Marie's team of seven poured into the intersection, focusing their fire into Sammy's hallway. Martin's position was more suited to defend against Marie's attack, so Sammy ordered him to defend against them while he took care of the two from Kobe's team.

"Jeffie, we need you back here now!" he shouted.

"I'm coming!" she answered.

Between the seven in the intersection, who fought with more coordination than Kobe's team had, and the two from Kobe's team in the rear, Sammy's perched players were caught in a very tight place. He had just managed to take out one of Kobe's two when Martin fell from his spot and crashed to the floor deactivated. Al reported that he and Parley were just barely holding on as four of Marie's surrounded them below.

Great. That leaves four to me.

A well-aimed shot knocked his leg loose from the wall, and he was forced to launch himself from his perch. He tried to deactivate the remaining member of Kobe's team while still in the air, but couldn't, and so he landed behind him.

Parley's voice came over the com: "We took out one of Marie's— aurgh!"

"What happened?" Sammy screamed, louder than he meant, still aiming a blast at the head of the person he just realized was Brickert.

"We just lost Parley," Al answered.

"Jeffie, we need you now," Sammy cried.

"I'm trying to find you guys, but I'm a little turned around!" she shrieked. Her voice was shrill and desperate, more so than he could ever remember hearing it.

"Please hurry," Sammy answered.

He and Brickert were locked in a battle that needed to end quickly. All of Marie's team had left to gang up on Al.

"I need help here real bad, Sammy," Al said. "There are five of them on me!"

"I'll be right there," Sammy said in a cool voice, then to Brickert he added, "Sorry, buddy." He performed a dazzling array of acrobatic blasts and jumps, leaving Brickert completely turned around.

"That's not right!" his roommate cried out in frustration.

In a neat flip off the right wall, Sammy gracefully soared over Brickert's head and laid a hand on his roommate's helmet. A gentle blast deactivated Brickert. Then Sammy landed in the intersection.

He looked up to see Al moving in a flurry of defensive blasts and foot attacks, letting go of his hold on the wall just long enough to blast and regain his footing. As bizarre as Al's movements were, Sammy was impressed he'd had managed to stay up so long. Two of Al's enemies turned on Sammy as soon as he appeared in the intersection. Sammy parried and evaded their blasts, sending out his own from the ground and from the air in mid-jump.

Two more of Marie's stopped attacking Al to help take out Sammy. Desperately, Sammy launched into an all-out barrage of attacks, figuring his defensive maneuvers were now worthless against four. Just as Al picked off the one who had stayed to attack him, Sammy hit Marie in the helmet, but the cost was a shot to his own helmet from Cala. As Sammy arched backward from the blast, slowly falling through the air, his eyes caught hold of something just as the helmet covered his face.

Help had arrived for Al, and she was beautiful.

For about five or ten minutes, Sammy could not tell for sure, he lay in darkness hoping that his team had managed to pull out the win. He found out the answer as soon as his helmet lifted. Al pulled Sammy up to his feet, smiling broadly. Natalia ran up and hugged him, screaming, "You did it! On your first try! We won! We won!"

"Yes!" Sammy shouted, pumping his fist into the air. "I knew we could do it."

The turning point of the Game was Jeffie; she had wall-blasted unseen, high above the competition, just as the others had done. Between her sharp-shooting skills and Al's near invincibility, they deactivated the last three on Marie's team. A come-from-behind victory winning three straight games. Sammy thanked the members of his team for their outstanding performances. Jeffie merely blushed and stared at the floor when he complimented her shooting ability.

"I'm serious," he told her. "Without you, we never would have won. Al can only handle about two by himself."

"Pardon me?" Al interrupted with a grin. "I can handle at least three." He patted Sammy hard on the back. "You were real good, Jeffie. And you, Sammy."

"See?" Sammy pointed to Al to emphasize his point.

"Thanks," was all Jeffie said, still looking at anything but him.

Just then Marie tapped him on the back, and he turned to face her. "You little punk," she teased. "Good work. Don't give Albert all the credit. You had a great plan—it worked really well."

"I'll remember that," Sammy answered. "Good game."

He turned again to face Jeffie, but she had already left with Al, and instead he saw Kobe walking swiftly past him. When their eyes met, Kobe grunted something that sounded like "Gh—game," without breaking stride.

The seven Games had lasted over five hours.

"Can you believe it's not even eight the morning?" Brickert griped on their way downstairs to change. It was obvious he was still a little sore about losing to the team that was on the brink of a shutout.

"Sorry about taking you out like that in the last Game, Brick."

Brickert waved it off. "It was too impressive to make me mad. I think I stopped blasting just so I could watch you. I've never seen Al move the way you did."

"Whatever," Sammy retorted, but his face turned hot in embarrassment. For him, Al would always be the standard to look to. The rankings didn't mean a thing. Al was simply the best.

Sammy just wanted to sleep. The high of winning had worn off and a deep feeling of fatigue settled in. But Brickert refused to let him lie down, claiming Sammy might throw off his sleep cycle.

"Then what am I supposed to do? Pass out standing around? Everyone else is going to bed."

"Let's celebrate. Ice cream for breakfast." Brickert had a maniacal look in his eye, but a bowl of ice cream sounded better than an argument about circadian rhythms. The cafeteria was almost empty. Jeffie sat by herself in one of the corners stirring something in front of her. She didn't look up when they came in, and Sammy wondered if she was even awake.

"You didn't even win," he reminded Brickert when they got to the Robochef, "how can you have ice cream?"

"Well, let's see. Your first victory as honcho . . . you're my roommate . . . and do I really need an excuse to eat ice cream?"

They sat down at a table nearby, watching to see if Jeffie would notice them. Brickert leaned over to Sammy and hissed in his ear. "Has she talked to you at all, since—whenever?"

"A little during the Games ... when she had to."

"Not after?"

"Not really, she just said 'thanks.'"

"Girls are so . . . nutty."

"I know." Sammy smiled at Brickert's use of the word he'd taught him.

It was a lazy Saturday, and Sammy struggled all day to stay awake. The few Betas who didn't sleep sat around the rec room—some studying, some playing games. After the nerve-crunching intensity of the Arena, no one was up for VR gaming. In the late afternoon, Sammy and Brickert played doubles in pool with Kawai and Natalia. Sammy sometimes pretended not to see the exact geometry of the game so he and Natalia could lose a few times. Brickert inconspicuously rolled his eyes, but kept silent.

A rare event occurred that night: all of the Betas got together to watch movies. Cala and Asaki wanted to watch an *X-Men* film, but got vetoed.

"Pick something realistic," Kaden argued.

Martin and Li chose a boxing film, *Rocky IV*, about a fight between a Russian and an American boxer. Everyone booed when the American won. They followed it with a romantic film for the girls.

Near the beginning of the second film, Sammy got cold and ran downstairs to grab his red hoodie from his room. When he passed the girls' dormitory, the door opened. He almost flattened whoever was coming out.

"Watch out!" he cried in surprise, stopping just in front of Jeffie.

"Sorry!" she said, blushing as badly as he had ever seen.

Neither of them moved. Sammy couldn't go down the stairs until she closed the door, and she made no sign that she intended to. This went on for several uncomfortable seconds. Sammy stared at her, wondering what to say.

"I was just—"

"I didn't mean to—" they said at the same time.

The second silence was worse. Sammy might have laughed had he not felt like the world's biggest idiot. In a movie like the one playing upstairs, he could just say the perfect line and she'd fall into his arms for a passionate kiss. Or he could stand there, say nothing, and look like the dumb friend who always loses the girl.

Say something, he urged himself.

"Well," he finally said, "sorry." He nudged the door aside and went down the stairs. His ears and neck tingled with a white-hot heat and a bead of sweat ran down his left armpit. *Great job, moron. Looks like you get to be the stupid sidekick.*

He had just eye-scanned the door to the boys' dormitory when he heard, "Sammy, wait!" Jeffie came running down the stairs and stopped a meter away from him. Her face was definitely setting a record for redness.

"Sammy, I'm sorry. I know—" She took a deep breath. "I know we've been through all this before, and I overreacted when I got mad at you for lying—but I didn't realize you did it because you didn't want us to feel stupid for being so far behind you in everything. And now I completely get why you did it. I know I should have said it earlier and not ignored you for so long, but I just didn't know how to say anything after being so rude to you again—and it meant so much to me that you stood up for me after what that jerk-off Kobe did. And I felt even worse after all of that—and it was even harder to talk to you, but I've really wanted to all along."

She paused to breathe again. "Does that make sense?"

Sammy tried to tread water, but Jeffie had flooded him in a deluge of words. For all of his brain capacity and listening to instructions at incredible speeds, nothing she said had registered in his mind . . . but she looked really beautiful. And in the end, all that mattered to him was that she had chased him down the stairs and apologized. She had done that for him. His feet were glued to the floor, his mind oblivious to her question.

The thought occurred to him that he should also apologize.

"I—I shouldn't have lied to you," he said. "I don't have an excuse for it. I'm really, really sorry. I hate it when you're mad at me. Do you forgive me?"

Jeffie laughed and covered her mouth to stop herself. "Do you forgive me?" she asked, her eyes never breaking from his.

Sammy couldn't pull his gaze away from her eyes. Everything negative he had thought or felt about her melted. *Please stop looking at me like that!* he wanted to scream. He wanted to kiss her. He wanted the nothing in the world but her closer to him.

Closer. Closer. Melting closer. Her breath filled the air around him. It was mint. Beyond that he smelled roses. She smelled like roses. He noticed a small freckle she had on her left cheek. He liked that, too. Then she made a tiny noise, clearing her throat. She looked at him expectantly.

He cleared his throat, too, and said, "Yeah, of course I forgive you. But do you think that, maybe, you could please just . . . talk to me next time you feel hurt by something I do?" Even as he said the words, they reminded him of something his father would tell him after Sammy had acted inappropriately.

Jeffie laughed again. The sound of it made Sammy feel stupid and wonderful and unsure. "Definitely," she answered. "I can do that." Her white teeth gleamed in her smile.

"Thanks."

"Um—so what's going on upstairs?" she asked. "And why did you come down here?"

"We're just watching some movies. I came down to get my hoodie."

"The red one? You always wear that one."

"Yeah. It's my favorite. Be right back."

"Okay, I'll wait," she called after him as he disappeared through the door.

Sammy grabbed the hoodie from his closet and looked at himself in the mirror. His hair sucked but it could have been worse. He tried to remove the huge grin on his face before he re-emerged from the dormitory. When he returned to the rec hall with Jeffie behind him and sat down beside her on the floor, he had to suppress another laugh. Out of the corner of his eye Brickert was shaking his head, obviously very perplexed.

14 | Paradigms

SAMMY HAD HEARD about the phenomenon where best friends become worst enemies, and worst enemies turn into best friends, he had just never experienced it. Over the summer months, after he and Jeffie reconciled their differences for the second time, their friendship became forged with something different than anything he'd experienced with anyone else—even Brickert. It was palpable but still intangible.

Before the big fight, he and Jeffie had eaten together because they were scheduled to eat at the same time; they talked about the same Beta stuff because they had been recruited at the same time; they acted friendly more by association (and often because Kawai made them). Now he could see this friendship metamorphosing into something better—much better. As this transformation continued, his feelings for her blossomed.

He never dared to show how he felt. He had no experience whatsoever with girls or dating. Other than Brickert, he had no one to talk to about these new sensations. And Brickert only knew stuff from overhearing his sisters. Sammy worried that everything he felt was just in his head. What if Jeffie just wanted to be friends? The possibility of putting himself out there, telling her his feelings, and then being rejected mortified him. So he chose the safer path of doing everything he could—short of spending less time with her—to hide his true feelings.

In some ways, he suspected Jeffie must already know his heart. She knew what Kobe had recorded and shown in the sim room to piss Sammy off. She knew the way Sammy had reacted to it. But if she had any clue about his true feelings, she gave no sign. And that was fine by him.

Sammy was careful not to ignore Brickert. No one had been so true a friend to him through thick and thin. If anything, his newfound friendship with Jeffie brought the five friends closer as a group. They were almost always together in their spare time playing games in the rec hall or planning things for the weekends. But it was after everyone else had left for bed, long into the Friday or Saturday nights, when Jeffie and Sammy stayed up alone to chat, eating ice cream until they laughed uncontrollably from sugar rushes. And soon, even these things became part of Sammy's routine.

ⓢ ⓢ ⓢ

"Sammy, wake up," Brickert said, shaking him urgently.

"Uh-uh. Sunday," Sammy murmured into his pillow. "Leff me 'lone."

"You have to get up!" Brickert said more earnestly.

"I'll tell you about my night with Jeffie later. Need sleep now."

"Har har," Brickert laughed sarcastically. Then he dropped the bomb: "Alphas are here."

"WHAT?!" Sammy said, jumping up. "Alphas?"

"Yes. Alphas. Here."

Sammy sat up straight so he could stretch his arms out without bumping the wall behind him. The stretch felt good. Even though he was still a little tired, he loved that sense of cheating time by staying up late and getting up a little too early the next morning. "Why are they here?"

"Because Al's Panel starts today."

Sammy smacked his forehead. "Crappy crap. I forgot all about that. Did you actually see them—the Alphas?"

"No, Commander Byron came into the cafeteria and called for Al." Brickert snickered and kicked the bed. "I'll tell you, I don't know who looked more nervous."

"What do you mean?"

"The commander or Al. They both looked really nervous."

"Yeah. I'll bet Byron gets like that every time a Beta goes through the Panel."

"Who cares? Let's go already." Brickert smacked him with his own pillow and threw back the sheets on Sammy's bed. "He's been gone for four hours. Should be finishing up soon."

"I swear," Sammy groaned, climbing down from the top bunk, "sometimes I think you're my mother."

After speeding through a shower and throwing on the first jumpsuit he saw, Sammy headed upstairs with Brickert. Everyone had turned up in the cafeteria. Sammy grabbed food while Brickert sat down with the three girls. The low roar of conversations filled his ears while he waited in line at the Robochef. The same topic was being covered in the separate circles: Al's Panel. Sammy got his bowl of steaming oatmeal and caught Jeffie's eye on the way back to his seat. She smiled warmly at him. It made him giddy.

"Hiya," she said brightly as he took the seat next to her.

"Hiya back," he grumbled.

"Sleep well?" she asked, grinning around the spoon handle protruding from her lips.

"I got to bed kind of late, actually," he informed her, though she already knew he'd been up until almost three. He had been with her. "Brickert wouldn't let me sleep in."

"That's because I made him go get your lazy butt up," she said. "I knew you wouldn't want to miss this."

"Did any of you see the Alphas this morning?" he asked the other girls.

"Kawai did," Natalia said.

"Kind of," Kawai corrected. "I caught a glimpse of someone in the hallway, the Alpha doctor, I think."

"The who?" Sammy asked, at the same time, blowing on his bite of oatmeal to cool it down. That was one thing about the Robochef, cooked food always came out piping hot.

"The Alpha doctor," Kawai repeated. "He gave us all health examinations us when we were recruited. Remember?"

Truthfully, Sammy did not remember ever being examined by a doctor. Either he had been unconscious for it, or they had just not done one on him.

"You remember him, Sammy," Jeffie said with a meaningful look. "He's got a heavy Indian accent and came here when I got hurt. My leg . . ."

"Oh, yeah. Him."

"How many Alphas are on the Panel?" Kawai asked.

"Five," Natalia answered. Sammy knew she'd pestered Al and Marie all about the Panel over the last few days so she could know more about it than the rest of them. "One Alpha for each of the five sections: combat, mental aptitude, leadership, psychological fitness, and mission functionality." She listed them off like a roll call.

"How do you know all this stuff?" Brickert asked.

"I ask," Natalia told him at once.

"He's doing the psycho fitness test today." Jeffie smiled at Natalia as she said this because Natalia hated having her thunder stolen from her.

"Yeah, but from what Al said, it's cake," Natalia said, refusing to be outdone. "The one he's really worried about is the last. Leadership."

"Why?" Kawai asked

"Because leadership is the main focus of the Panel, and it's the last section," Brickert told him. He shot Natalia a roguish wink when she scowled at him. Jeffie snickered into her glass of orange juice. Natalia was probably the only person Brickert had the nerve to stand up to.

"Al and I talked about that one a couple days ago," Brickert continued. "But it was really late, and I was tired. I think he said it means that Al has to go on a mission, right?"

"Yes and no," Natalia jumped in. Sammy grinned to suppress a laugh at her need to divulge information. "The leadership test measures how well Al can direct a mission. After he passes his first four sections of the Panel, an Alpha Commander will tell him what his mission will be. Then he chooses the other Betas who will go with him."

"You mean some of us are going to get to go on a real mission?" Kawai asked in utter disbelief. "Uh . . . isn't that dangerous?"

"Al's mission won't be dangerous," Natalia answered, "and none of us will go. Al will only choose the older Betas. And the missions are always simple, non-confrontational stuff. They're just to test Al on how well he can operate under real conditions in command of other Psions."

"But it's still scary," Kawai said. "Do you think Al's nervous?"

"No, he's been on other missions before. So has Marie and a few others," Brickert answered. "He still has a while to prepare for it, though. His mission isn't for like three months."

"What happens if something goes wrong?" Her question was almost a demand. Sammy understood her fear, though. The missions didn't sound all that safe to him, either. "Why doesn't Byron go with them, just in case?"

"Well," Brickert began, "there's a team of Alphas standing by for mission recovery if something happens."

"No wonder why Byron's so nervous," Kawai said. "I'd be worried too if my students were on their first mission."

Just then, Al came into the cafeteria followed by a woman who Sammy thought looked to be in her late thirties. She was not very tall and her short hair style fit her well. She smiled knowingly as the conversations died down upon their entrance. When Commander Byron appeared in the doorway (not looking worried at all, Sammy noted), the woman turned and greeted him. She shook Al's hand with a genial smile and left with the commander in deep conversation. Al watched them go, then faced his fellow Betas.

"How'd it go?" asked Marie, sitting closest to him.

"Great," Al said, but his big grin had already answered the question.

Marie shrieked and jumped into his arms. Sammy joined the rest of the Betas who preferred to just clap or cheer. He personally congratulated Al later.

The rest of the weekend flew by. Monday morning, Sammy suffered through an awful instruction lesson on engine mechanics. After bolting down a quick lunch, he literally ran upstairs for sims. He was grateful to see that Kaden had already left the room. Without letting another moment pass, he started up the sim.

Today, after several long weeks of weapons units, Sammy would start the unit he had been waiting so long for: Advanced Enemy Combat. He eagerly pressed the panel screen, and the familiar voice of Byron sounded behind him.

"Congratulations on your completion of the Weaponry and Demolitions Training Unit. Thus far nearly all of the units you have completed have been standardized, requiring you to complete a specific task in order to advance to the next level of your training. You will no longer be following this format. All the necessary tools have been given to you to think for yourself and decide how to defeat enemies in combat. This will help you know how to accomplish assignments in a mission.

"Today you will begin learning to fight the real enemies: Aegis and Thirteens. It is essential for you to understand the abilities of the enemy before you can continue into mission functionality. Thirteens rarely attack Psions one-on-one. They know they will lose. Therefore if you see one, you can reasonably deduce there are more nearby. NWG reports tell us that in the beginning of the Silent War there were two hundred thirty-seven Thirteens in maximum security. We have confirmed the deaths of forty-nine since then. Still, they outnumber us almost four to one. Just as Psions often work alongside the Elite in our missions, Thirteens train operatives they call the Aegis, who are almost as deadly and cruel as Thirteens themselves.

"You will start by learning to fight the Aegis, then Thirteens. The further you progress through these sims, the harder your training will become until our data reports that you have reached your maximum potential, your plateau. This information is important. It will tell you when you must fight, and when you must withdraw to save your life in real battle. Good luck."

From countless previous experiences in combat training Sammy knew that as soon as Byron disappeared from view, the task at hand would appear, in this case: his enemy. He particularly remembered the disturbing session when his holographic enemy had appeared behind him and shot him with a splinter gun. He felt the splinters prick his skin, scaring him half to death; there was no pain, but still a shocking lesson that enemies can attack from any direction, at any time. Ever since then, without fail, he waited against a wall for Byron to disappear, watching the corners.

The lights dimmed slightly. A single Aegis materialized in a corner of the sim room. Sammy relished the feeling of adrenaline flooding his system—his breathing quickened, his reflexes sharpened, and his heart drummed a rock song in his chest. Still shrouded in darkness, the figure fired his weapon at Sammy. Sammy recognized the noise and identified the weapon immediately. Using a blast shield, he easily deflected the bullets. He continued to use the shield until he drew close enough to see the figure better. It was a man with strawberry blond hair and a heavily pitted face. His uniform was different than Sammy had seen Thirteens wear in the videos. Rather than the red and black of Thirteens, the Aegis wore a uniform of murky brown and green blotched together in such a way that it played tricks on Sammy's eyes, making it difficult to focus on any one place.

Drawing upon skills already mastered in personal combat, Sammy continued warding off bullets, moving in closer to disarm his enemy with a blast. The Aegis was harder than any single enemy Sammy had fought so far, and there was one close call where a bullet passed close by his ear. But without any real difficulty, he disarmed the man. The Aegis' weapon had a fingerprint scanner on the grip, making it useless to Sammy.

It took little effort to get himself into position to disable the Aegis. Using a jump-blast, he brought his foot down hard on the exposed neck. The crunch of the Aegis' bone made his stomach lurch. As his enemy's eyes closed and his body crumpled lifelessly to the ground, Sammy could only watch, knowing that he had just killed a person . . . and yet he had not killed anyone.

It wasn't the first time he'd killed an enemy in the sims. Often, a voice in his mind, the one always urging him to do anything he could to win Star Racers, told him this was only a game and the Aegis wasn't real, but Sammy felt differently. Of course, he realized as a Psion he would have to take human lives, but he didn't look forward to it. He didn't look forward to being a killer.

Maybe that's what part of the oath was all about, he decided, *a promise to be responsible.* But at the same time he couldn't answer another nagging question: *who am I to be given the power to kill?*

The thought scared him.

The next trial introduced a smarter, tougher Aegis, carrying a better weapon. Disarming him wasn't too difficult, but subduing him proved to be a more arduous task. The third Aegis—armed to the teeth—almost proved too much for him. Intelligent, quick, and strong, she kept him at bay with a hand cannon capable of shelling out a large spread of shrapnel. When fatigue forced Sammy to ease his attacks, the brutish, ugly woman launched her own deadly offensives, trying to force him into a corner. Fortunately, Sammy had been in predicaments like this before in the Arena. He dove off the wall into the woman, bowled her over, and landed a bone-crushing elbow on her head.

Then the simulator threw two Aegis at him. In the first combination, they hindered more than helped each other. Sammy handily won. But the next pairs were always smarter and tougher, appearing on his sides, working together to flank him. It took four tries before he defeated the hardest combination of two Aegis. Then three appeared. By the end of his first day in Advanced Enemy Combat, he'd beaten three Aegis at once on the second-easiest setting without taking a vital hit.

He noticed that the more he fought, the less the deaths of his enemies affected him, though not all simulations had to end in death. His attention was not on the bloodshed but on mastering his technique and increasing his killing efficiency. The holographic blood did not seem as real. Their wounds had no true tangibility. Perhaps he was not really killing after all.

As the days passed, Sammy became absorbed in the simulations. He rushed upstairs each day, shortening his lunch more and more, eager to continue the new training. It was better than anything he'd done before—more exciting than any game he'd played. Here his actions meant something. Things mattered. Winning translated to staying alive. He saw more difficult combinations of three or four Aegis take form, and he threw himself against them. He discovered a certain kind of freedom in the violence, a wild beast inside him that could be unleashed for a short while.

After his losses, he reviewed recordings from different angles to find his flaws and determine where he could improve. He often grew frustrated when he lost twice in a row, but used his anger to focus himself back into the simulation, remembering what Byron had said about his great expectations. At the times when he felt he hadn't quite given it his all, he stayed late into the evening working on particularly difficult trials. With every new attempt he got better, until finally he defeated a very difficult combination of four Aegis.

"Congratulations," the hologram said. "You have progressed far enough to start combating Thirteens. As I have informed you, Thirteens are responsible for the training of Aegis. Thirteens, however, are different in important ways. They have little to no conscious visceral sensory perception. In other words, they will only be able to feel the most extreme forms of pain, and their brains do not process the body's natural warnings from the muscles and tendons when they approach their limit of natural function. This allows them to exert their bodies in fascinating, but dangerous ways. They are swifter, stronger, and more lethal than a normal man or woman.

"Also unlike Aegis, they often wear blast suits. These suits copy the science of metallic atom interaction. As electrons spread over a large surface, they are capable of absorbing more energy. Applied to blast suits, the energy of our blasts can be safely absorbed without affecting its wearer, similar to the noblack suits we wear in the Arena. However, if you damage these suits, the metallic-like flow of electrons is hampered, and the suit can no longer absorb your blasts. Therefore a top priority should be to damage a Thirteen's blast suit, or aim for the face, which the blast suit does not cover."

As Byron continued speaking, Sammy's skin grew warm. Hot blood flushed his face and his palms were sweaty but cold. He hoped Byron's instructions would go on forever. The simulations used images of captured enemies or known targets scanned into the NWG data banks. Real people. Sammy didn't want to look into their cold red eyes. Lifeless, but not dead.

He had thought he would be excited to fight them, but he was not. He was terrified. He was more scared of the Thirteens than he had been of the Elite several months ago.

Unsympathetic of Sammy's feelings, the simulation computer obeyed its programming and called up the first Thirteen. It was a woman. She had long dark hair, olive skin, and large brown eyes. Perhaps before her transformation into a sociopathic killer, she had been attractive. Sammy would never know. Her hair was matted and filthy, her skin sallow and crusted, her face reminded him of a rotten potato. Her eyes fixed on Sammy, and he froze. Her face contorted into a sickly grin at his inaction.

The computer programmed all of this, even her reactions. It's not real.

He told himself this over and over again, trembling from head to toe, and still unable to move. He didn't know terror could be so real. She advanced on him, her expression now a dull scowl. Fighting to regain control, he watched her raise her arm, point a deadly weapon to his head, and squeeze the trigger. Just in time, he jerked himself out of his reverie of panic and leapt sideways.

BLAM! BLAM!

Projectiles sailed centimeters away from his face.

The battle commenced, rampaging across the whole sim room. Sammy attacked her with blast after blast, but she either dodged them or skillfully used them to give her distance from him. Despite the woman's deadly precision with her weapon, her true lethality was in her ability to move. The way she could jump, twist, and attack so acrobatically caught Sammy off guard. She was lithe and agile like a ballerina from hell, her body a force to be respected even unarmed. As he worked her into a corner, easily fending off her volleys, she leapt animal-like off the wall, springing at him. He went into the air with a blast from his feet, but she flipped her body over, and her feet came crashing down around his head, legs gripping his neck and twisting. He would have felt it, but the safety mechanisms of the simulation obeyed the programming, saving his life.

"No!" he shouted angrily into the air, "No! I wouldn't have been hurt." But his words fell on deaf ears.

He picked himself up and marched over to the panel. With a touch of two buttons he called up the three-dimensional replay of the scenario and watched echoes of himself and the devil-woman grapple in silence. Sure enough, the Thirteen had his head in a fatal grip.

I should be dead, he thought, not for the first time. He marveled at her ability to move in such unimaginable ways. Byron had understated how much more capable the Thirteens were than Aegis.

How can someone move so fast with such prolonged intensity? he wondered as he replayed the video a second time. He made a mental note to completely overhaul his exercises in the morning to focus on speed. Prolonged speed. If he couldn't move like the Thirteens, he'd never beat them.

He restarted the trial with only a shadow of the trepidation he'd experienced previously. On his second attempt, he focused on exploiting the Thirteen's weaknesses he'd seen in the replays. The trial lasted longer, but she still killed him. On the third go, however, Sammy caught her off guard with two strong blasts to the legs. When the fight finished, Sammy's sim time had ended. He was down-to-the-bone exhausted.

One after the other, Sammy battled Thirteens for the next several days. It took time to see improvement. His body wasn't conditioned for the level of intensity the battles required. Each morning he worked to increase his speed and agility, pushing his body harder and longer than ever before.

After the first week, he noticed only small changes for the better. After a month, he was handling two Thirteens at a time.

The constant interaction with Thirteens was not without some side effects. Sammy began having nightmares. Often in the middle of the night, he lapsed into the same dream:

As an Alpha on assignment, he runs through the streets of Johannesburg, stalked by faceless bodies in Thirteen's uniforms carrying shockers. They call his name over and over and over and over like it's the chant to some perverse ritual of death. Their gravelly voices grow deeper until they sound as if they rose through blood-choked throats to reach him.

Every time, he ends up in the same dead end where he and Feet met the Shocks. Sammy picks up the broken pipe on the ground and holds it as if only this weapon stands between him and fate. He turns to see an army of Thirteens circling him, laughing inhumanly. The shockers they'd been carrying are gone. Instead they have cannons, mini-guns, jiggers, and syshées. Finally, right before they fire their storm of weapons for the kill, the middle of the crowd parts to reveal two bloody, murdered corpses.

They always ended the same. Just before Sammy could shout the names of his parents, he awoke, shaking and sweating almost every time. The topic of these dreams came up during one of Sammy's late night conversations with Jeffie. He described them to her in so much detail that she had to set aside her bowl of ice cream.

"That's horrible! I'd want them to stop, too. When did they start?"

"Right about when I started fighting them."

Jeffie rolled her eyes and smiled. "I still can't believe you're already fighting them. You're like . . . light-years ahead of me, Brainiac!"

Sammy shrugged as though he were helpless to do anything about it.

"You're lucky I'm not the jealous type," she said.

Ice cream came out of Sammy's nose. "Jealous?" he repeated with fake astonishment. "Have you ever been jealous of me?"

"I don't know. Maybe once," she answered with a coy smile.

"A week," Sammy added.

"I just love being second best at everything. Even Star Racers!" Then she rolled her eyes at herself. "With five older brothers, I can't help it."

"Do you get the competitive edge from your mom or dad?"

"My dad for sure. He almost competed in the NWG Olympics twice. One time he missed out because of an ankle injury in the qualifiers. He always says, 'You got to do whatever it takes to win.' He even showed me little ways to cheat in basketball when the refs weren't looking. Step on players toes when you're jumping, pull on their jerseys for a rebound. Stuff like that."

"That explains a lot," Sammy said.

Jeffie returned him a mocking glare. "So whose faces do you see in the crowd?" she asked. "You know, the dead ones at the end."

Sammy just shrugged. "So your mom's not very competitive?"

"Not like my dad or brothers. And nice job changing the subject. You're a pro."

"Thanks." He grinned even though he was peeved she had caught him at it.

"But really, Sammy, what about you? You've hardly told me anything about your parents." She swiped her spoon at him playfully, trying to get ice cream on his cheek. "What are they like?"

Sammy's first reaction was to make a joke out of Jeffie's question. Then he remembered his conversation with Feet in solitary. He'd promised Feet to be more open with his friends and he still hadn't done it. *Maybe this is the right time. Maybe I'm supposed to tell Jeffie.* He tried to think of the words to say how he felt.

"I, uh—I guess it's not a very fun subject."

"Sammy, I've been wondering about this for a while. I've even asked Brickert about it. Just once. I was really surprised that he was clueless about your family. So if you don't want to talk about it, you don't have to tell me anything." She stared at him hard, but in a way that communicated to him how much she cared. "Was there something wrong with your parents? I mean, did they hurt you? Because you've got this side to you that's—I don't know. Dangerous, I guess."

"No, nothing like that," he replied. He wanted to laugh, but could not because of what he planned to say. "I don't talk about them because the year before I came here was extremely . . ." He looked around the empty cafeteria searching for the right word.

"Difficult?" she asked, smiling now, like she thought this was a game. "Were you a rebel child?"

"No."

"Extremely long?" she guessed. "Maybe you were a very boring child."

"No," he said again, getting very uncomfortable now.

But Jeffie didn't seem to notice. She raised an eyebrow and whispered, "Extremely paranormal? Your parents are vampires or werewolves?"

Sammy shook his head, afraid to say anything.

"Give me a hint, then," she said looking at him.

He tried to say something, but he didn't have the words.

Jeffie's countenance fell when she saw his face. "Oh Sammy, I'm sorry! I shouldn't have treated it so lightly."

"No, no—it's okay. Do you really want to know about my family?"

Jeffie looked him in the eyes and nodded.

"I don't want you to think differently about me," he added.

"Trust me." She had a funny look in her eyes, that Sammy liked, though he wasn't sure why. "Trust me, Sammy. I won't—I can't think differently about you."

Sammy paused for a moment, deciding where to begin. *The chess game.*

The words came slowly at first as he described to Jeffie how his mom had become addicted to drugs trying to deal with several miscarriages. How his dad had told him all this in a canoe in the middle of a lake in South Africa.

"My mom didn't stay in rehab for the whole time," Sammy said, thinking back to the day his mother came home, how he and his dad had thrown her a small welcome home party with almost burned cake and a way-too-big banner hanging in the dining room above the table. "She did really well while she was there, plus she hated it—being away from her family—well, us."

Jeffie nodded in an understanding way.

"But she was still—you know—detoxing. Yeah. She'd wake up in the middle of the night in hot sweats, so we kept the house pretty cold at night. So I got the hoodie to wear at night. But my mom—she also got claustrophobic, panicky, so she started taking walks late at night. Dad said the doctors told him those urges would eventually wear off."

Sammy swallowed hard and shook his head. His tongue stuck to the roof of his mouth, it was so dry. He tried to wet his lips, but it didn't work. He got up and poured himself a drink of water. From her reflection off the metal of the dispenser, Sammy saw Jeffie watching him carefully.

"My mom took a walk the night she bought me the red hoodie. I watched her sometimes from my window even though she thought I was sleeping. She always walked the same route. But I didn't watch her that night. She dropped me off at a friend's house to sleep over. From what they said—"

"From what who said?" Jeffie asked, but Sammy could tell she already knew from the way her face had gone white. Her eyes were wide in shock.

"Shocks—police. Someone must have recognized her—maybe they had seen her walking late at night before—because that person followed her home. I'm sure my mom had no idea. She got to the front door, scanned it open, and whoever was following her attacked her as soon as the door opened. . . ." Sammy's voice failed and for a second he was not sure if he could continue.

The images were fresh in his mind as if it had all happened moments ago. The countless times he had woken in the middle of the night, sweating, seeing it all over again—they made certain the images stayed fresh. His eyes stared blankly into space and his voice dropped to a rough whisper.

"He—maybe she, I don't know—slit my mom's throat and then stabbed my mom over and over again. He found my parents' bedroom and did the same thing to my dad while he slept. Nothing was stolen. No rape. He just left the house. It was a Saturday. I'd slept over at a friend's house that night—but I should have been there. I was supposed to be back early to help with chores, you know, around the house. So when they dropped me off and the front door was already open, I didn't know anything was wrong. The house was so quiet. I called out for my parents, you know, to see where they were. No one answered. And—and—and the first thing I saw was blood. Lots and lots of blood." He had to really try to keep it together. He could smell the house now: the carpet, the potpourri his mom hung, the river of blood staining the floor. He could smell and see everything perfectly. "I just—I followed it, knowing, until I found my mom. When I saw her, I ran up to their bedroom to get my dad. And—and I lost it. I completely lost it. I just screamed and screamed and screamed. The front door was open still—the neighbors heard me. After that—I don't know—everything else is a blank until the investigators were talking to me. No one ever got caught. They think that it was someone who my dad had prosecuted a long time ago. They had a few suspects, but some of them they couldn't find, others had alibis. No one ever got caught, but I get to see my mom and dad's faces when I dream."

"Sammy, I'm sorry," Jeffie said. He could tell she didn't know what to say. Tears glistened on the lids of her eyes and a stream flowed on each cheek. For a moment, Sammy watched as more drops fell from her chin onto her clothes. "I'm sorry—I understand why you didn't want to tell me or—or anyone else about this."

Sammy nodded. He was still in the reverie of horror that fell over him whenever he relived that day: the sights, the sound of his own voice screaming forever in sheer terror, and the smell of all the blood.

"The thing that never makes sense is when I ask myself why?" Saying these things made him feel like his insides were all exposed to Jeffie, and he wondered what she was thinking while he spoke. "Yeah, my mom was beautiful. Yeah, we were rich, but none of that seems to have mattered. In the end it was nothing more than two random . . . murders. It's sick."

"Was it," Jeffie dropped her voice even lower to the point that Sammy almost couldn't hear her, "one of *them?*"

"I don't think so," he said. "Sometimes I pretend it was. It helps me fight better."

"What happened after that?" Jeffie asked.

"I spent a couple of weeks at a center for trauma victims. That sucked. Just a bunch of people trying to get me talk about how I felt. Then Family Services put me in a surrogate home. They were nice, it was just—I don't know—too soon. The dad, his name was Calven, he was a cool guy. The mom was okay, too, but it was Calven who really tried to get me to like him. After a month, right when I'd started to get to know him, you know, and we'd warmed up to each other, he had a massive stroke and died."

Jeffie gasped and covered her mouth. "Oh no, Sammy, that's—I mean—"

Sammy let out an angry snort. "Bad luck."

"Yeah."

"I didn't want to wait around for Family Services to find me a new home. So I ran off. That's when I started stealing."

He told Jeffie about his life as a runaway: how he was caught and sentenced, how he escaped from the Grinder. Then he talked of his life in the grocery store, and how he first used his psionic abilities.

Jeffie looked amazed. "So this is what you've been trying to hide?"

Sammy just nodded.

"You're ashamed that you were a fugitive?"

Again he nodded.

"Sammy, don't you realize if you told everyone about how you became a Psion they'd think you were the coolest person ever?" Jeffie said. Her smile turned into a look of shock. "Not about your parents, I mean. But that you were a fugitive or whatever you want to call it. That's kinda cool.

In fact, it's really cool. It's something none of us know anything about. Even Kobe would be impressed."

Sammy chuckled a bit.

"But I understand why you don't want to tell people. It brings up too many questions. But you don't need to be ashamed of what happened to you. You could have turned into—no offense—a quack after seeing all that. But you're not, you're normal—well, as normal as you can be," she added with a wink. "Do you understand what I'm trying to say, though?"

"Yeah." He didn't want to look at her. He hated the sympathy she was trying to give him. He didn't want it. He'd rather bury all of his past in a deep hole and forget about it.

"I can't believe—!" she started to say, but could not finish for laughing too hard.

"What?" he asked. But then, without even knowing why, he began to chuckle, too. Soon Jeffie was snorting through her snickering, which made Sammy chuckle harder. For almost five minutes, they did nothing but laugh at each other.

When the amusement finally died down, and Sammy could wipe the tears of laughter away, he asked: "What did I say that was so funny?"

"I can't believe you attacked the police!" she cried out, almost falling out of her chair. "I can't imagine you doing something that crazy."

"I was desperate." He threw his arms out as if he were helpless, but he had a grin the size of a half moon on his face. Laughing and smiling felt incredible after airing out all his baggage for Jeffie to see.

"I'm sure you were." Her smile rivaled his, but it dazzled him.

They looked at each other until Sammy's mind became fuzzy. He again had that need to say something clever or charming, *But what do I say?* Jeffie broke eye contact, roses growing on her cheeks, and said, "Actually, I can see you doing something that crazy now that I think about it. You've already done some pretty wild things since you've been here."

"I guess so," he chuckled. "It's funny what people do when—" he stopped himself short, mortified he had even gone so far.

"When what?" A light appeared in Jeffie's eyes and a smirk on her lips like she'd caught him right where she wanted him.

"You know, when we're really . . . really . . . angry," Sammy finished. The conversation needed to end before it took a nasty turn into super-uncomfortable land.

But Jeffie just sat on her gel chair looking at him in her funny way. The scent of roses was there, as it always was when she was close.

He faked a yawn until it turned into a real one. "Well, I'm getting pretty tired. I think I should go to bed. You?" He got to his feet and offered his hand to help her up.

"Oh, okay," she said with an undertone of something like disappointment.

She accepted his hand, and he let go as soon as she reached her feet. They walked down the stairs together in silence. Stopping in front of the girls' dormitory, Jeffie opened the door and leaned against it, looking at Sammy with the same funny look. *What is she trying to do? Read my mind?*

"Well . . . good night," he said lamely, wondering what he else was supposed to say.

Jeffie smiled mysteriously, "Good night, Sammy."

He was puzzled. The "good night" part of their late night talks had never been this awkward. Was it because he had told her so much about himself, and now she thought he was weird or had too much baggage? He shifted his weight uncomfortably, thinking he should leave now.

"Okay, well . . ." he said, trying to make his exit. *Is she trying to make this harder for me?*

"And thanks."

"For what?"

"I don't know. Everything," she said, then ducked behind the door, disappearing from his sight.

He stood alone on the landing of the second floor watching the door close. When it finally did, he thought, *I will never understand girls.*

ⓢ ⓢ ⓢ

As the weeks of summer dwindled, Sammy found himself pulled in several directions: Jeffie seemed to want more and more attention from him, Brickert asked Sammy multiple times for help in some of the combat trials in the sims, Betas tried every night to get him to game with them—but the strongest pull of all was the Thirteens.

The extra effort in his morning exercises had started paying off, and he propelled through the two- and three-Thirteen sim units. As the difficulty increased, so did his interest. Even Saturday's weekly Games seemed insignificant compared to the challenges he found in the four walls of his sim room. So what if he didn't hang out with Jeffie every single Friday or Saturday night? So what if Brickert had to figure some things out on his own?

Then Sammy hit the wall that every Beta before him had met: the insurmountable four-Thirteen sim trial. This wasn't like the earlier units when the Aegis tripped over each other. Even on the first trial, the Thirteens worked too well together. If Sammy gave too much attention to any one Thirteen, the other three's combined efforts quickly forced the sim trial to shutdown to protect Sammy.

The first time he had fought three Thirteens, the Byron hologram introduced the skip option. In effort to prevent Betas from becoming too frustrated with one trial, it became possible to pass on a subunit after twenty failed attempts. Sammy's skip option for four Thirteens had long been available, but he'd set his mind to beat the unit. He wanted to do something no one had ever done before.

Day after day he fought, planned, observed, and fought again, but he didn't seem to be getting any closer to victory. He mentioned to Brickert and Jeffie his struggles, but what did they know? They weren't there yet and wouldn't be for months or, perhaps, years. He needed to talk to an older Beta—someone who could relate. Knowing his mechanics examination was coming up soon, he waited until the day of the test when he could have lunch with the older Betas. Li Cheng Zheng was the only Beta eating when Sammy finished the exam.

"Hey, Li," Sammy said, carrying his plate of food. "Mind if I sit with you?"

"Sure." Li pointed to the chair on his left.

Sammy took the seat and ate several bites before starting the conversation he meant to have. "Hey, I have a question that's been bugging me."

"Shoot."

"What's your opinion on the four-Thirteen sim?" Sammy tried to sound as casual as possible.

Li's eyes narrowed whenever he became serious, which was more often than not. He'd grown up in a very traditionalist Chinese home and wasn't exactly known for having a strong sense of humor like Kobe or Miguel. "It depends who you ask. Some of the older Betas think it's intentionally setup to be impossible to teach us how to know when to retreat. But others—Al, Marie, a couple more—they think it's beatable."

"And you?"

"I don't know. It was a nightmare when I was in it," Li said. "I must have attempted it about fifty, sixty times."

"Wow. Did you ever get close to beating it?"

"No. I don't know anyone who's even killed two of the four. Al's probably closest. I think it took him about five hundred tries to finally give up. No exaggerating. And I think he still gives it a go about once a week."

"That doesn't surprise me," Sammy said grinning. "Can anyone do it? Byron? Other members of Command?"

"No one's ever beaten a four-Thirteen sim, Sammy," Li told him, shaking his head. "It's just not possible."

"Nothing is impossible," Sammy replied, masking his frustration. "Nothing."

Now Li's eyes were like slits. Sammy could tell the subject bugged Li. Failing at the four-Thirteen sim still bugged many of the older Betas. "Yeah, well, tell that to the dozens of Betas who've passed through here, faced the same sims we have, and all failed."

"Just cuz no one's beaten it doesn't mean it can't be done," Sammy mumbled.

"Ask anyone," Li insisted. "That's why they put in the quit option. Some Betas got more obsessed than Al did. Not many, mind you, but a few. I think at some point everyone thinks they can do it. I remember the first time I killed three of them. I thought I could take on a whole army. Then I faced four and got the beat down of my life. Over and over and over again." Li looked Sammy dead in the eyes. Sammy saw the same look of grim acceptance he'd seen in every other Beta he had mentioned the four-Thirteen sim to. "It's just not possible."

Sammy nodded his head. He remembered the feeling Li was describing. Beating three was an amazing experience.

"I'd love to stay and debate some more," Li said, getting up, "but I've got to go. I'm late for my instructions."

Sammy watched Li leave the cafeteria. *That wasn't much help* . . . Then Jeffie slid in Li's chair and bumped his arm

"Hiya," she said, flashing her beautiful smile at him.

He almost jumped. "Hiya back."

"You have a look. What's on your mind?" Jeffie was wearing Sammy's favorite uniform, the white and pink with blue stripes that matched the blue on his uniform. He liked to believe that she wore this one more often for him.

"Nothing . . . the same stuff."

"Same old stuff."

He nodded glumly and offered her his food. His appetite was gone.

"Feeling down on yourself?"

"No . . . I don't know. I just—"

"You have to do this," she finished for him.

Sammy nodded again. He'd said those exact words to her two dozen times in two dozen different conversations. That she understood the way he felt meant a great deal to him.

"I know you think that. But at the same time, you've done so much so soon. Don't feel bad if you get stuck, just remember how much you've accomplished. And . . ." Her hair fell over her half her face, concealing a toothy grin. ". . . remember all the time you could be spending with me and the others if you weren't so fanatical about it."

"What's the point in just getting the same things done but in a faster time? No one thinks this can be done, Jeffie. Doesn't that bother you? I don't want to believe that."

"That's good. You're doing the right thing by not giving up easily. But don't think of yourself as a failure if you—"

"Fail?"

"No. If you don't succeed."

"Sounds the same to me."

"Someone who doesn't succeed isn't a failure. He's just . . . someone who gives all he has without the results he expected."

Her efforts to cheer him were generous, but he couldn't explain the need to beat the sim. She wasn't there yet and she didn't understand. It wasn't her fault. *Maybe I am obsessed.* "I don't know. Maybe I'll give it until the end of the month." As soon as he said this, he knew it wasn't true.

"Sounds good," she said, giving a playful wink. "If anyone can do it, though, it's you."

Their conversation turned to other things as they were joined by Brickert and the others, but Sammy's thoughts kept turning to the faceless Thirteens that stalked him in his nightmares. He tightly clenched his fork in his hand and ground it into his leg until the pain jerked him out of his reverie. The fork had poked through the cloth and left four deep bruises on his leg.

I will kill all of them.

As soon as lunch was over, he headed upstairs to the sims with the other four recruits, determined not to leave until he succeeded. It was late in the night when Sammy no longer had the energy to fight, and had to call it quits.

Instructions became increasingly difficult over the following days. Thoughts about the four Thirteen trial consumed him. He often stayed in the sim room until 2100 or later, sometimes with only enough energy to stumble to bed. That weekend, when he wasn't in the Arena, he spent more time in the sims, avoiding Brickert and Jeffie intentionally so he wouldn't feel guilty about ignoring them.

As the next week wore on, signs of deep fatigue became more evident, even to Sammy. He hardly ate, his appetite had all but disappeared. At mealtime, his friends tried to voice their concern, but he assured them he was fine. The dream came back every night now, and a few times his screaming or crying was loud enough to wake Brickert. On Wednesday during breakfast, he caught Brickert and Jeffie discussing whether or not they should go to Byron with their worries, and chewed them out until Jeffie was nearly in tears.

"I'm fine!" he told them in a voice so loud that half the cafeteria stopped to listen.

The incident only made him bury himself deeper into his work. At 2200 that Thursday, Sammy was still in the sim room. He had battled the same four Thirteens for hours. Fighting, then watching the recording. Then fighting again. Then watching again. No success. He'd stopped caring about how many attempts he had made on the trial. It didn't matter.

"This is not impossible. It can't be!" he screamed at the top of his lungs after another failed effort. "Why am I beating myself up like this?"

He sat on the floor, his back against the wall, breathing hard. His energy was sapped, but he wasn't ready to call quits yet. "This has to be worth it. This has to mean something!"

He shoved himself off the ground, determined to give it one more go before going down for dinner. Without bothering to review the fight, he restarted the trial and the same four persons appeared. No sooner had the sim begun than he vividly remembered a conversation with his father from several years ago.

"You're locked inside a paradigm," his dad had told him. It was a bright and sunny afternoon and they sat outside on the back porch at a picnic table. His mom lay on a hammock, reading a novel and keeping an eye on them. Sammy rested his chin in his hands as he glumly surveyed the chess board after another annihilation from his dad. "You have to let go of it."

"What do you mean a paradigm?" ten-year-old Sammy asked.

"Sometimes we get locked into a box of thinking a certain—"

"What box?"

"A box in our minds that surrounds us—blinds us from seeing the truth because we believe so strongly in the wrong thing. And when everyone is thinking only one way, no one can change things for the better. Look at examples from history: people used to believe the earth was flat, they believed in spontaneous generation—you know, that maggots were born from meat—the four minute mile. Things like that."

"The four minute mile?" Sammy repeated.

"Yeah, didn't you know? People used to think it was impossible to run a mile in under four minutes—that the human body was not capable of such a feat. Then Roger Bannister set out to break the mark. And he did it way back in 1954. Once he did it, people started beating his time of three minutes and fifty-nine seconds. You know why?"

"Why?" Sammy begged to know.

"Because Bannister destroyed the paradigm. Before him, no one believed it was possible, but as soon as they saw it was, it broke down the barriers in their minds. They knew it could be done, so they did it. It's the same in chess. Playing piece for piece is the weakest way of thinking. You have to break through the paradigms your teachers taught you. They don't know how to think in chess. You need to play your defense like a Sicilian, or attack like the Grand Master Kasparov in your offense. Position, options, strategy: these are more important than exchanging a piece for a piece. Stop believing you can never beat me, and start learning how you can. Paradigms, Sammy. Paradigms rule the world until someone brave enough challenges them."

"Oh." That was all little Sammy could say in response, but his dad's words made him think.

Sammy held his ground against the four Thirteens, trying to calm his mind despite the insanity and turbulence raging in the room as holographic shrapnel bombarded everywhere around him. *Let go of the paradigms. Let go of it all.* Pushing out a long slow breath, his brain steadily became clearer just as it had so many times before, and he *saw*.

"I can do this," he muttered through gritted teeth. And he knew he could. Maybe it wasn't fair that he had Anomaly Eleven, and no other Beta did, but Sammy knew he'd been dealt a good deck of cards, and neither heaven, hell, nor four Thirteens would stop him from using them.

The very room he was standing in changed. It was no longer a rectangular box. It was a giant chessboard. *I am a rook. They are pawns.* He saw new ways to exploit his enemies. Running into a wall with two Thirteens following him, he blasted himself into the air, and shielded himself from behind. As he reached the peak of that blast, he planted his feet firmly onto the wall and blast-jumped again, aiming for the wall sharing the corner. He barely caught the third jump blast and used it to reach the upper rigging of the room that held all the projectors. Hidden in the darkness above, he looked down on the four Thirteens trying to spot him and picked out the one with the best weapon. He wondered if he were to launch himself downward, would the computer shut down the simulation to protect him?

Only one way to find out, he thought and let go of the rigging.

To achieve maximum velocity, he used his hands to blast off the ceiling, then used a second blast from his feet off the rigging. He shot down like a bullet, feet-first, projecting a broad blast shield with his soles to protect himself from the hail of shrapnel being blown at him. All the while, his mind was cold and clear, calculating the exact moment he needed to act.

Dropping from the sky, he moved too fast for the Thirteens to react properly, and snapped the neck of one particularly ugly Thirteen just before throwing out his hands for a strong hover blast to cushion the rest of his fall. When he stopped his fall, he rolled into a defensive crouch behind the dead Thirteen, keeping the others at bay with blast shields. Deftly propping up the dead body in front of him as cover, he reached around to the front and used his knife to sever the middle finger of the dead Thirteen. When the blade hit the Thirteen's finger bone, Sammy thought he was going to barf. Fortunately, he hadn't eaten since breakfast. Only his concentration through the intensity of the moment got him through it.

The Thirteens moved to encircle him, but he grabbed the dead Thirteen's hand cannon and held the dissected finger against the fingerprint identifier on the handle. *Now things are much more interesting* . . . Laying on his back, using his feet as shields, he took aim holding the gun between his knees. The Thirteens fell back immediately.

Even with their incredible ability to move, they could not avoid the large spread of shrapnel Sammy's hand cannon dished out. All of them took damage, but even with blood oozing from their gaping wounds, the Thirteens wouldn't give up. They relentlessly emptied their ammunition at Sammy, and spent every last ounce of energy they possessed struggling to kill him. Even nearing death, their bloodlust knew no bounds. Sammy had to carefully defend himself against two of them while he targeted the third with the hand cannon until he put enough holes in him that the man collapsed.

Taking down the third Thirteen was easier, but it cost Sammy the last of his ammo. With just one wounded enemy left, Sammy saw the checkmate. Her two automatics were useless against Sammy's shields, plus she had a limp from taking shrapnel to the knee and thigh. And when the inevitable moment of reloading came, she tried to dodge Sammy's attacks, but he used a strong jump blast to pummel into her, jam his elbow into her jaw, and crush her windpipe.

It was like another win among the countless he'd already had, but tears dripped down his nose as he knelt down on the floor, supporting his weight with his hands. He'd done what no one believed was possible. He was exhausted, but he was happy again. He was free.

I did it!

Over two months of hard and focused exercise and hundreds of hours spent in the room with Aegis and Thirteens—the training and fighting and reviewing footage—all for this moment.

I DID IT!

For several minutes, he knelt in silence. The emotional shock finally wore off and fatigue crept over him like a suffocating blanket. He stood on shaky legs, cleared his throat, and wiped his eyes. Cool air flooded him when he opened the door. Just before leaving, he turned back and saw the lone finger, the pools of blood, the bodies, and the bullets—all of it resembling a scene of horrific carnage—disappearing like magic from the walls, floor, and himself. The computer could not erase everything, however. It was real. Even if the finger had been just a hologram, Sammy had cut it off. He had shot them. They were dead and he'd done the killing.

I did it.

When he spoke it was reverently. "I did it for you, Mom and Dad. A new paradigm."

Craving sleep, he walked downstairs and climbed into bed. He wondered who he would tell about this and when. He promptly drifted off to sleep, not thinking at all about blood, corpses, or Thirteens.

The next day was Friday, and Sammy went to the sims again. Everything was different, most importantly, his outlook. The computer threw a five Thirteen sim trial at him, and Sammy beat it in ten tries. He spent the rest of the day feeling like someone had grabbed a big chunk of the sun and stuck it right in his chest. It felt good, and it stayed that way all day. After dinner, his body ached worse than anything he'd ever experienced, and he went to bed early before anyone could bug him.

15 | Stonehenge

THE NEXT MORNING, Sammy had an urgent desire to talk to Byron—or anyone else, for that matter. Other Betas needed to know it was possible to do what he'd done. But he didn't know how to bring it up without sounding like a show-off. Somewhere in the back of his mind, he knew Commander Byron was already aware of his accomplishment. Why couldn't the commander help him get the word out? Why had Byron said and done nothing?

When Sammy finally got out of bed, Brickert, only half-dressed, blocked the door.

"I'm not moving until you talk to me." His cheeks were bright red, his dark hair, which had only grown much longer over the last few months, fell over his eyes. He looked as nervous as the day he'd arrived at headquarters.

"Did Jeffie ask you to do this, Brick?"

"I'll tell you, you're hurting yourself with all this extra work. I'm—we're really worried about you. What's happened to you?"

Sammy chuckled. Brickert had made everything much easier, whether he'd meant to or not. "Well—something has happened, Brickert."

"Something happened? Wh—" Brickert saw Sammy laughing and threw his shirt at him. "Did you kiss Jeffie?"

Sammy caught the shirt without really thinking about it. "No, I didn't." As an afterthought, Sammy added, "I definitely wouldn't mind, though."

"So, what is it?"

"You're not going to believe me." Sammy threw the shirt back at Brickert, who tried to catch it, but missed. It hit him square in the face.

"We've been through all of this before. With you anything is possible."

Sammy got up and dressed without speaking. The irony of Brickert's statement was not lost on him, but the comment about kissing Jeffie had taken over his train of thought.

"Well, say something."

"Okay, sorry. You remember what I've been doing in the sims, right?"

"Yeah, getting your butt kicked around by Thirteens."

"Right. Well, the other day. I—uh—I passed the trial."

"The Thirteens? You killed four Thirteens at once?"

Sammy couldn't help a small grin. That little piece of sun buried inside him flared up again and the only outlet for it was through his smile. "Yeah, and then yesterday I beat five."

"Holy—!"

Brickert smacked the wall with a loud BANG! "OW!" He grabbed his hand and winced in pain. "Sammy, do you know what this means?"

"Yes, I know what it means."

"It means you're the greatest Beta ever! In the history of the world!"

"No." Sammy looked sharply at Brickert. "That's not what it means. See? We all have the potential to do the same thing. And everyone needs to know about it, I just don't want to be the one to tell them what I did."

"Why not?"

Sammy threw his hands up. How could Brickert not know the answer to that already? "Because I don't want the attention! I don't want people to talk about me."

"No one is going to think you're a freak, Sammy. I don't."

"They don't know me like you do. Some of them still aren't comfortable with my Anomaly Eleven. Without it, I couldn't do all this stuff. It's not me, it's the anomaly."

Brickert's cheesy smile told Sammy that he didn't seem to get the point. "It is you."

"I'd just be a crappy video game player and a so-so fighter without the anomaly."

"Please . . . they're going to think you're a god."

"No—no." The thought of any more jealousy repulsed him.

"Then what do you want?"

"Don't you think everyone should know how to do it?" Sammy asked back.

"I guess," Brickert said sarcastically. "I'll let you know when I've gotten that far in training."

"See? That's what I mean."

"I was joking!"

"Yeah, well, you're joking, but what is everyone else going to think? Sammy the brain! Sammy the hotshot! Sammy the anomaly!" He whipped his hoodie against his bed with every name. "Still fourteen years old and he's done something no one else can do—before some people two and three years older than him have even had a chance to try to do it."

"Why don't you talk to Commander Byron about it?" Brickert suggested patiently.

"I was waiting for him to say something to me."

"He's super busy," Brickert reminded. "Call him, send him a text."

"Yeah . . . yeah. That's a good idea." Sammy blasted lightly to get back on his own bed and stared at the ceiling. He felt a little better now.

Commander, you probably know I passed the four Thirteen unit in sims. I want to talk to you about it. Any chance we can meet? I'd really appreciate it. I think I have some ideas to help other people. Thanks, Sammy.

That was the body of the text that Sammy sent Byron. A few hours later, he got back this:

Samuel,
I am aware of your recent progress, as is Command. I think to say congratulations would be a gross understatement. Therefore, I will forebear until we are able to talk adequately. I apologize that I cannot meet. Unfortunately, we are not on the same continent, and I will be stopping at headquarters only briefly for Albert Hayman's Panel. Please forgive that I cannot say more. What you have done is extraordinary. Continue meeting your expectations.
CWB

The Betas played a short Game early in the evening and spent the rest of the day celebrating Al's final achievement: passing the last test of his Panel. All he had left now was the mission. Al tried to act modest about his prospects, but Sammy knew better. Al was thrilled and excited about becoming an Alpha. Festivities went late into the evening, but some people turned in earlier than expected. Sammy found out why the next morning.

When he turned up for Sunday brunch, the cafeteria was buzzing.

"Sammy!" Natalia cried as soon as she saw him. Her eyes were as big as Sammy had ever seen them. "Al's upstairs being briefed on his Beta mission at this very moment."

"Huh?" The cobwebs in his head filtered out every other word Natalia said. All that mattered was getting a glass of orange juice and a muffin.

"Serious. According to Marie, three Alphas came a couple of hours ago and called for him. And when he comes back he's going to have the names of the people who are going on the mission with him."

"Are you sure?" he asked.

"Of course. Everyone's been talking about it."

Sammy hurried and got his food. While he waited, Jeffie and Kawai came in and sat down. Natalia had already ordered food for the other girls. She wasted no time filling them in on everything.

"So who do you think it's going to be?" Jeffie asked the group.

Sammy shrugged. "Probably Martin, Gregor, Li . . . all the oldest Betas."

"Marie, too," Brickert added. "She's right up there with Al—"

"Obviously not Marie," Kawai interrupted.

"Why not?" Brickert asked her, blushing small spots on his cheeks.

Sammy glanced at Jeffie. He knew she would be trying to catch his eye, and he was right. She gave him a secret nod.

One night, less than a month ago, Jeffie had told him she was sure Brickert liked Kawai. Sammy, being the friend he was, vehemently denied it even though he knew it to be true. Brickert had bound him by honor to say nothing. Kawai was, after all, the oldest of the girls in their group of friends. It made sense Brickert would crush on her eventually. He said her exotic look was exciting and unique.

Sammy shook his head back at Jeffie. She responded with a raised eyebrow and a skeptical expression.

"Yes, why not Marie?" Natalia repeated.

"Because Al loves Marie," Kawai said as if it were the most obvious piece of information in the world, "and they want to get married after she passes her Panel. Why would Al do anything to risk the life of his girlfriend?"

"Because she's one of the most talented Betas at headquarters," Natalia responded for Brickert while he recovered his nerve to speak, "and he won't be risking her life. The missions aren't dangerous."

"Do you think she will be the only girl Al takes?" Jeffie asked Brickert.

"No, Levu and Cala are both likely to go," Natalia said.

"Three girls, I don't think so," Sammy said, teasing Jeffie while he said it.

"One girl soldier is worth twenty boy soldiers," she responded with the mocking face that always made him smile.

"Well, he's definitely going to take Kaden, Gregor, and Martin," Natalia said.

"Kaden's only sixteen," Kawai objected, as she was barely the same age.

"But he's one of the highest-ranked fighters here," Natalia answered back.

"I guess it depends whether he wants skill versus more experience," Jeffie commented. "I bet he'll probably take some of both."

"What about you, Sammy?" Brickert asked in a careful voice. "Why wouldn't he pick you, too?"

Everyone at the table looked at him as though they'd also thought this, but didn't want to be the first to voice it. Sammy had no reply. The idea had crossed his mind, too, but he'd quickly dismissed the notion because of his age and inexperience.

"I don't know," he finally answered. "Don't you think I'm too young?"

Brickert was about to add something when Commander Byron walked through the door, looking quite solemn. He was accompanied by a man Sammy had never seen, wearing the same flight suit as Byron: smoke gray with the Greek symbol of alpha emblazoned on the front over the left breast, and a gold star on each shoulder. The new man looked to be in his forties. He was tall and good-looking with brown hair beginning to show gray around the edges. His sharp eyes took in the whole room at once. From the way he and Byron were speaking to each other, Sammy guessed they were old friends, or at least knew each other very well.

The room fell silent at once, which Sammy thought was funny. The new man smiled, too, holding the silence with a dramatic pause. Finally he spoke: "Hello and good morning. Most of you know me, but for those who don't, my name is Commander Wrobel. You all know why I am here. Your friend Albert Hayman passed every part of his Psion Panel . . . except one." He paused again. Sammy could tell he was enjoying his effect on the crowd. "He's just spent the last few hours receiving information on his mission assignment and choosing eight other Betas to accompany him."

He stopped for a moment and his smile changed from friendly to parental. "Now I always like to say before I read the list that there should be no hard feelings about not being chosen. Al didn't pick people based on talent alone or by how much he likes you, but based on how he feels you will work with him and his unique qualities to accomplish the specific tasks he has. So please support him whether or not you'll accompany him on his assignment."

A few whispers of quick conversations broke out, but all fell silent when Wrobel cleared his throat and began reading from the com screen over his eye. "Here are the eight Betas Al has chosen . . ."

Sammy felt the tension in the room grow, especially among the oldest Betas.

"Marie Covas."

Brickert turned to their table and mouthed, "I told you!" Kawai rolled her eyes so well she reminded Sammy of Jeffie.

"Kaden Reynolds."

There was applause. Sammy saw Kobe clap his brother on the back, both brothers smiling.

"Kobe Reynolds."

More applause. Kobe looked smug and satisfied.

"Martin Trector."

That was an obvious choice as well. Al and Martin had always worked well together in the Arena.

"Gregor von Pratt. Cala Alanazi. Li Cheng Zheng."

Sammy nodded along with names. All were solid, older Betas with years of experience under their belts.

"Samuel Berhane, Jr."

Several people looked at each other when Sammy's name was called, but none of his friends seemed surprised. Marie grinned at Sammy from across the room, Kobe frowned and his nose wrinkled like he'd just smelled something terrible, and Brickert clapped Sammy on the back.

Why would he choose me? His jaw fell and he looked at Brickert "How did you guess?"

"Oh, don't act shocked, Mister Number One at everything," Jeffie said with a dangerous edge in her voice. Natalia and Kawai laughed.

"Everyone whose name I read, please come with me!" Wrobel shouted over the roar of voices.

He and Al were friends, sure, but Sammy was still the third youngest person at headquarters. Being good at games was one thing, but he wasn't ready for a mission. *Why would Al pick me?* He got up amidst smiles from his friends and walked out the door along with the other seven Betas. They followed Wrobel upstairs and into a sim room.

The room was furnished with comfortable seats, one of which was occupied by Al. He wore an expression of anxiety eerily similar to the one Sammy had seen on Byron's face not long ago. Al stood up when the commanders entered the room and tried to smile, but it came across as a nervous grin. His face was too tight and his grin too toothy. Marie took the seat closest to Al and slipped her hand in his for a brief moment, squeezing gently. Sammy sat between her and Kaden. Commanders Wrobel and Byron waited for everyone to settle.

"Congratulations for being selected to assist Al on his mission." His tone contradicted what he'd said earlier about it not mattering if they were picked. Sammy felt like Wrobel was welcoming them into an exclusive secret club. "For four of you, this is your first time participating in a Beta mission, so I will explain some of the basics. The missions we assign to Betas are elementary, non-confrontational, and very low-profile. Our primary interest is always your safety. You'll need to do some additional preparation for your assignments. Even with our desires for everything to go smoothly, you need to realize Al is your leader, and your responsibility is

- 257 -

to follow his orders to the letter. With that bit of advice, your commander and I will step out of the room and leave you to Al's care."

Al stood up and moved to the front. Commander Wrobel headed for the door and waited for Byron, who followed. Al watched them leave with an unreadable expression on his face. When the door closed, Al turned to his team. Now he looked confident. But this wasn't friend-Al. This was leader-Al. There would be no bantering like normal. Leader-Al would be all business.

Al used the panel on the wall for a moment, and a podium shimmered into view. Stepping behind it, he pressed a few buttons, and a large transparent building appeared in the air.

"This is an old factory in Rio de Janeiro. CAG-controlled territory. It was once owned by a large communications firm used to manufacture prototype nanotech electronics. CAG troops shut it down by force when they discovered it was also a secret operating facility for NWG resistance fighters. Our intelligence reports have confirmed plans by the CAG to convert the factory into a major producer of short-range thermal armaments. They predict this to be the next step in Silent War weaponry. We have surveillance of CAG operatives being trained with prototype thermal weapons: liquid nitrogen cannons, napalm grenades, and blitzers. When—"

"Sorry, Al," Sammy interrupted with a half-raise of his hand. "What's a blitzer?"

"A blitzer is a large weapon that discharges superheated discs hot enough to cut through a blast-shield. Only very concentrated blasts can deflect them."

"Oh . . . thanks."

"So when the prototypes test successfully, the factory is scheduled to undergo moderate remodeling. Full-scale production should begin in about thirteen or fourteen months. That's why we've been given this assignment. The building will be desolate for another three to four months. Our job is to go there four weeks from tomorrow and plant hidden surveillance equipment armed with Class B detonation devices. The tricky part is we have to do it without being seen—without making the CAG aware of our presence. Totally covert."

The miniature holographic factory spun slowly in the air on two axes. It was huge. Al punched some buttons on his podium, and the factory stopped pivoting.

"We'll arrive by air in the early morning via stealth atmo-cruiser, low enough to allow us a safe drop using landing blasts. We'll set up base in the shipping yard." He highlighted a large open space with only a few large storage crates dotting the landscape. "Two of you will enter here, two here, and the other four here." Three doors were highlighted. "I'll stay in a mobile hut in the yard and command the operation from here. Any questions so far?"

No one said anything, but Sammy already felt tense about the mission. He glanced at the Reynolds twins and saw that at least two other people in the room felt the same way. After living safely in headquarters for several months, who wouldn't be nervous about flying straight into enemy territory?

"Even though the building is empty, there are security devices throughout. Luckily, only a couple areas concern us. They've got smart cameras, motion detectors, and hot fields. Some serious stuff, but nothing we can't handle."

Sammy did not know what a hot field was, but it sounded more than serious.

"I've chosen each of you for your strengths in handling certain aspects of the mission. Gregor and Li will be our cloakers. They'll go in first and hack into security, load up pre-recorded footage for the cameras, and turn off selected motion detectors. That should enable us to get in and out without making our presence known, and it allows Martin and Cala unrestricted access to the control room, where they can create localized power outages to shut off the hot fields and some other cams. The building is definitely old enough that this won't look suspicious. Once those are out of the picture, Kaden and Marie can plant three bomb-cams each on the lower levels, Kobe and Sammy will place four each on the upper level."

"Whew!" Kobe exclaimed. "For a second there, I thought it was going to be complex, but now I'm very reassured."

Everyone except Sammy laughed. Even leader-Al allowed himself a chuckle. Sammy was too busy thinking about being teamed up with Kobe for this assignment. They hadn't spoken so much as a word to each other since the incident—as Jeffie liked referring to it—and Sammy had hoped to keep it that way. Now he'd be working with Kobe intimately, trusting his life to him. Sammy didn't think he was ready for that.

Maybe I can back out of this . . . tell Al I'm not ready for a mission.

Al spoke again, interrupting Sammy's thoughts: "Here's how the training will break up over the next four weeks: Starting tomorrow, Monday, everyone will be either learning or refreshing their skills on covert operations in sims. That will be the first two weeks. The second two weeks of your sims will cover mission functionality. Some of you will have part of your sims cut off early those last two weeks so we can train as a team and run scenarios. Until then, just work hard on the tactics that are thrown at you. Any questions?"

No one said anything. If they were anything like Sammy, they had too many questions floating around to know what to ask. He envied those who had already gone on Beta missions. Certainly they were less nervous than he was right now.

"Okay. You're all dismissed—except for Sammy." He turned his gaze to Sammy. "If you've got a second, I'd like to speak to you alone."

"Sure."

Kaden and Kobe cast curious glances over their shoulders to see what was going on, but Al just waited patiently for them to exit.

"Surprised?" Friend-Al was back with a big grin on his face.

"Yeah—completely. Brickert said he kinda suspected it, but I thought I was—"

"Too young? Yeah, that's what I thought, too. I was planning on bringing Levu. She's good. But I went through a much more detailed briefing this morning and Command gave me a list of everyone's state. The list changed my mind. It's actually kind of fun to see what everyone is doing—where they're at in instructions and sims. I already knew you're ranked number one in everything, Sammy, but something else I saw blew me away."

He did not need to guess what Al referred to, but stayed quiet all the same. Al sat down, staring at Sammy like he'd never seen him before. The look was almost reverent, and made Sammy squirm. *They'll think you're a god!* Brickert's words echoed loudly in Sammy's skull.

"You really passed the four-Thirteen sim?" Al asked.

"I did. It happened just a couple days ago."

"Sammy—wow, dang—that's incredible! You realize what this means? What that says about you?" Al's reaction was remarkably similar to Brickert's.

"I don't think it says anything about me, Al. It says something about all of us. What our potential is—or could be."

"Exactly. That's why I wanted to talk to you. I'd like to ask a huge favor."

"What?"

Al's face was lit up like a spotlight, and in his eyes Sammy saw some of the same fervor he'd seen in his own. That need to win burned strong in Al. "Will you teach me how you did it?"

"You think I can teach you?" Sammy asked. He'd never taught anyone anything before.

Al nodded, his expression was feral.

"Are you sure it's okay? I mean—uh—when would we be able to do it?"

"I've already spoken to the commander. Your instruction time is while I'm in the sims, and he said you are far enough ahead that you could take— you know—a sabbatical for a while if you want to. Besides, your sims for the next while won't be so demanding, you'll be learning covert ops and mission training."

"Then I guess I can do it. I should warn you, though, I might be really terrible at it."

"No worries," Al said, giving him a pat on the back, "I really appreciate this. I do."

"Sure, no problem."

"If it does work—who knows—I could teach your technique to the Alphas when I graduate. One other thing," Al added just as Sammy thought the conversation had ended.

"What?"

"I need you to put aside your crap with Kobe and work with him. This may sound crazy, but I have a good feeling you two could be very successful together."

Sammy snorted but quickly turned it into a cough.

Al was not fooled. "I'm serious. You're the most capable Psion here, possibly ever. That's why I picked you."

Nice flattery.

"I'm not flattering you, either," Al said as he read Sammy's face. "You're crippling yourself to carry this grudge. And you'll be crippling my team. Can you put aside your feelings and cooperate?"

Sammy honestly didn't know. He tried to imagine himself laughing and joking with Kobe like they were friends, but he couldn't see it. But if thought of himself working with Kobe in a dangerous situation, he decided they might be able to maintain a civil relationship.

"Ok, Al, I'll do that."

"Great. I'll see you tomorrow morning in sim room five."

He watched Al leave and wondered what he'd just gotten himself into. *Teaching? Me?*

ʕ ʕ ʕ

"I still can't believe it!" Brickert exclaimed as he tried to push more cheesecake into Sammy's hands. Brickert always looked for reasons to solemnize an occasion with extra desserts. "I mean, I believe it. I kind of expected it. But still . . . it hasn't really clicked."

"It is pretty cool, Sammy," Natalia agreed with an admiring smile. "I've asked around. You're the youngest person to go on a Panel mission that anyone's heard of."

"Great . . ." Sammy glanced at Jeffie, still trying to interpret her reaction.

He'd filled them in on the briefing, trying to give them all the details that he could remember. Jeffie tried to be excited along with the rest, but Sammy saw through her attempts. She was too quiet. Something was wrong. As a result, he omitted the part about Al asking him for private tutoring sessions during his instructions.

"Anyone up for some gaming?" Kawai suggested.

"Actually, I am." Sammy found himself quite keen to escape for a while. "Jeffie, are you coming?"

"Um, yeah, I'll play for a bit," she answered, forcing a smile. "Can I pick the game, though?"

No one objected to her request. They went to the rec hall as a group. Sammy slowed his pace to match Jeffie's so they could walk side by side. He hoped she'd take the opportunity to talk to him about what was bothering her, but she said nothing, and he knew better than to push the subject.

Brickert, Kawai, and Natalia wanted to play Crazy Mazes, one of the newest games, but Jeffie chose Battle of Ages. They hadn't played it for several weeks. Sammy thought it was too gory, and since he got enough blood and guts in the sims, he'd never been a fan of the game. But he had told Jeffie she could pick, so he felt obliged to agree.

Both games were hands-free, meaning the players only needed helmets to play. Sammy chose his cubicle and got his helmet from a small cubby built into the floor. The helmet was all white, but scuffed from months of use. It had a long metal visor that blocked out all light once it was worn. Reaching up blindly, he found the twelve screws on the helmet and tightened them until he could feel a dozen metal pads touching his scalp.

When he turned the helmet on, he could see again. This time, however, it was not with his eyes, but rather through the electrical impulses being transmitted into his brain via the metal pads. Although he had a general understanding of the technology of brain wave manipulation, "seeing" through blinded eyes took some getting used to. The game booted up and linked the five players together.

"CHOOSE YOUR CHARACTER!" the game said.

Mentally, he selected his character. After waiting for the others to choose, the game opened onto a random setting: Stonehenge.

Sammy's character was a tall, powerfully-built Mongolian man with long flowing black hair and a matching beard: Genghis Khan. He wielded a long wooden staff with deadly metal spikes embedded at each end. Across the rock formation, standing under a rectangular arch of stone, he saw William Wallace—Brickert, no doubt—toting two large swords. Kawai appeared as Hannibal of Carthage, and Natalia was a small but agile ninja in traditional black garments. She carried with her a dazzling assortment of daggers and stars. Jeffie arrived as a beautiful Amazon warrior clad rather scantily in an ugly, B-movie leather bikini, expertly holding two wickedly curved scimitars. A blinding bolt of lightning violently struck the ground in the middle of the sacred site, signifying the start of the blood bath.

Now able to mentally give his virtual body commands, Sammy rushed straight for the ninja amid the smoky remains of Salisbury Plain. The scent of burning grass and dewy moss filled his nostrils. The ninja threw a deadly star at him, mid-stride. He was just able to dodge it by sliding on the grass underneath. In his peripheral vision, he saw William Wallace and Hannibal locked in their own raging battle. Reaching behind her lean black-clad body, the ninja pulled out two more stars and flung them at Sammy. One of them he was able to evade, but the other had a truer course. Using his fat wooden staff, he blocked the disc just before it hit his face.

The wood vibrated in his hands, and he almost lost his grip. With one of his giant hands, he jerked the star out of the wood and whipped it back toward the ninja. A spry leap was all she needed to sidestep the danger. The ninja advanced menacingly on Sammy, armed now with two crooked daggers. Before Sammy could even engage the ninja, the busty Amazon woman sprinted silently from on top of the rocks. With a soaring leap, the Amazonian flew into the air and ran the ninja through with one of her wicked scimitars. Even more impressively, she used the momentum of the falling ninja to cartwheel neatly onto the ground only a few meters away from Sammy, still clutching both weapons, one gleaming silver, the other now dripping with crimson red.

Sammy let his barbaric cry echo across the plain, and raised his staff in challenge to the ravishing gladiator. Her lovely face etched in fury, she dashed toward him, scimitars ready. Genghis Khan met her with a ferocious swipe of his staff, blade aiming at her chest. She parried his blow with surprising strength and struck with her free blade at his neck. In one continuous movement, Sammy used the top of his staff to knock away death. As the battle intensified he became oblivious to everyone else at Stonehenge, focusing solely on Jeffie's Amazonian avatar.

Their furious battle raged over and under slabs of rock. Sammy had never seen Jeffie play with such passion. He could scarcely find chances to go on the offensive despite his greater size. Each time he used his brute strength to beat her back, she redoubled her efforts, returning stronger— deadlier. Steel clashed against wood over and over again until her blade sliced his staff into two. One half of his staff hit the ground, and Sammy was forced to give up turf as she pressed her attack.

Jeffie, what has come over you?

But her wrath continued and he had hardly any room to maneuver. A glint in the grass called his attention. He risked a glance to see one of Natalia's stars lying nearby. Desperately, he kicked up an anthill into Jeffie's face. She raised one arm to block the dirt and ants from her eyes, then swiped the air in front of her. He had little time to act before she regained her composure.

He seized the star and raised his staff just in time to ward off her next blow. Just as she attacked, he hurled the star at her. It struck her in the sternum. Horrified at what he'd done, he watched as she gazed down at the small star protruding from her chest.

Jeffie threw herself upon him with such ferocious blows that he was forced back once again until his back hit solid rock. Jeffie raised her left scimitar and struck the remains of the staff out of Sammy's hands. She put the other to his throat. Helpless to do anything, he watched her pull the star out of her chest; blood pouring freely from the wound. Her face twisted as she jabbed the star into his chest, forcing it between his ribs. Her expression morphed into one of pure triumph. Sammy was amazed at the depths of anger Jeffie displayed. She stepped back on her left leg and kicked the star deep into him with her right.

The game ended, the screen went black. Sammy took off his helmet, extremely disturbed at what had just happened. Half expecting to feel the star in his ribs, he looked down and ran his hands over the area just to make sure he was okay. *Still alive!* he reassured himself. But what had made Jeffie act so primal? He left the cubicle and went into the common area to watch the rest of the match. Natalia was already there amusing herself with ping-pong, so Sammy sat down in a gel chair in front of the screen.

Wallace had just laid waste to Hannibal (who lay dead, impaled on his own triton), and was locked in combat with a very bloody Amazon-Jeffie. Her movements were slower now, the avatar unable to respond to her mental commands. Her virtual body was dying. This put her at a huge disadvantage to Wallace, who was nearly unscathed.

In a beautiful dance with two weapons apiece, they battled across the terrain for nearly five minutes. Jeffie, paling visibly, nearly stumbled to the ground, but quickly caught herself, parrying a blow to her head. As Wallace pressed down harder on her, she fell to the ground, twisting her body around as she did. In one gruesome, but fluid motion, she sliced off Wallace's lower leg. He, too, fell to the ground, but not before sticking his sword through Jeffie on his way, impaling her to the grassy floor. Jeffie's look of fatal surprise stayed on her face until the game ended, Brickert the victor.

Brickert whooped loudly from his cubicle and jogged out to take a bow. Jeffie gave him a playful push. She didn't seem at all angry. Instead, she had that glow about her—the one Sammy recognized every time she won. Yet something deep inside told him that all was not well with her.

"Well, tomorrow's Monday, and I need sleep," Kawai said.

Others agreed. Sammy still wanted to talk to Jeffie, so he stayed to straighten out the gel chairs and tidy up. "Hey, Jeffie!" he called out, just as she was leaving with Brickert and the girls.

She turned.

"Can you give me a hand with these?" he asked, pointing to the chairs. He tried to appear as if his request was innocent, but doubted Jeffie would buy it.

She said goodnight to the girls. When Jeffie had turned her back, Natalia rolled her eyes at Kawai, who answered her with an exasperated smirk. Sammy wished he knew why girls had to do that. Once they were out of earshot, he asked Jeffie: "Are you okay?"

"Of course I am." She straightened up the gel chairs without looking at him.

"That was an intense game, don't you think?"

"Wasn't it fun?" When she glanced at him, her face was in that tight smile again, the one she'd worn while everyone had been congratulating Sammy for getting picked for Al's mission.

"I—no, not for me," he said as he surveyed the room for anything else to do. It looked pristine.

She stood with her arms folded, tapping her left foot against her right, and stared at him. "Mad because you lost to me?"

"No, of course—" He wasn't going to play her game. "—you know me better than that."

Now she seemed torn between dropping her façade and putting up an even stronger front. *Competitive to the end, aren't you, Jeffie?* He met her stare and waited. The depths of her eyes went on forever. In them he saw her powerful will and an indomitable spirit. A great part of her was wild and exciting and beautiful. Finally, her face relaxed some. He'd won the battle.

"Sorry, Sammy. I was just taking out some frustrations on you, that's all. I'm not angry."

He believed her. Over the last few months, their friendship had taught him many things, some of them more valuable than others. One of the most priceless pieces of information he'd learned was that when her eyes shifted back and forth between his, she was lying. And she did it every time. He guarded this little tidbit from everyone, even Brickert.

"Do you need to talk?" He felt stupid as he asked it, but nothing else came to mind. "About whatever is bothering you?"

"No. Not right now," she said with a sigh. "Thanks, though."

Sammy was tired, but not ready to sleep. They walked downstairs together and said quiet farewells. In his room, Brickert was just getting into bed. Sammy was glad his friend was still awake. He needed a guy to talk to. For a while, they lay on their bunks and mulled things over out loud. Sammy lamented about the strange behavior of the female sex while Brickert complained about how none of the girls he liked ever reciprocated the feeling.

"You're the youngest guy here and you like older girls, what do you expect?"

"I don't know," Brickert answered. His speech was slurred and heavy. "Girls are so . . ."

Sammy waited for Brickert to finish his sentence. When Brickert didn't, Sammy leaned over the edge of the bed. Brickert was sound asleep.

"Stupid," Sammy finished. It was Brickert's favorite phrase. "Girls are so stupid."

16 | Walls

"GOOD MORNING, PSIONS. Good morning, Psions. Good morning, Psions."

"I hate you, woman!" Sammy yelled huskily while Brickert laughed at him from below. "Gotta start getting more sleep."

He forced himself out of bed and barely made it through morning exercises. In the cafeteria, Brickert pushed something in front of him, and Sammy ate it. He had a vague feeling he was forgetting something as he sat down in the Teacher, but pushed the thought away. Just as he selected a subunit, his com screen flashed out in front of him displaying a message from Albert:

Sammy, are you coming? I'm in sim room five.

Sammy let out a colorful string of curses and dashed out the room, still swearing at himself all the way up the stairs. When he knocked on the door of the sim room, Al ordered it to open.

"That was fast," Al commented with a friendly smile. "Forget?"

"Yeah, sorry."

"No big deal. Let's get started."

"Sure . . . right. Do you want me to just show you what I do?" Sammy asked.

"No. That won't work. The sim room is configured only to me, the Thirteens won't respond to you being here."

"Oh, right. Duh. Go ahead and start it up, I'll just stand in the corner and give you some suggestions."

"Make sure you put on a zero suit," Al said, pointing to a closet door in the corner.

Sammy opened the door and saw a light blue suit hanging amongst other equipment. "What's that?"

Al grinned broadly. "You've never worked with Commander Byron, have you?"

Sammy shook his head as he pulled the suit on, complete with a thin metallic mesh that zipped around his face.

"If you don't wear a zero suit when you're in someone else's sim, you could get killed by a stray bullet or something. Zero suit makes you immune to holograms."

Al started up the sim Sammy had faced countless times. Even now it amazed him how fluidly the Thirteens moved. He tried to shout instructions as Al battled the four Thirteens, but everything was moving too fast for Al to react properly to everything going on. If Sammy had not already known Al was a great fighter, his first impression would have been dismal at best. The Thirteens killed him in under two minutes.

"I'm sorry, Al, I—I really don't know how to teach. I've never done anything like this before."

Al waved him off. "Don't worry. I didn't think about how difficult it would be for you to coach in the middle of a trial. I don't think it will work that way."

"Well, let's watch the replay and talk through it. Is that okay?"

They reviewed Al's recording together. Sammy saw several things Al could do better. "You can't let them get around you like that, you give them too much target," he said as they watched his fatal mistake of allowing the Thirteens to surround him. "You either need to back up or go high."

"But they're so fast, how do you prevent it?"

"You've got to be faster." Sammy explained the rigorous exercise routines he forced upon himself to quicken his movements.

"This is going to be harder than I realized."

"Ready to try again?"

"Yep."

Sammy spent the next few hours watching over two dozen fights, then discussing each replay. Sometimes he was afraid of being too blunt, but Al encouraged even brutal honesty. It took time for Sammy to accept that Al sincerely wanted help, but once he did, he molded into the role of instructor smoothly, answering questions, demonstrating techniques, and offering criticisms. Al learned quickly and showed mastery over most of what he was taught after two or three trials.

Of course, it helped that Al had more skill than any other Beta. He was fast, smart, adaptable and, like Sammy, he threw himself—mind and body—into the fray. The reckless abandon with which Al fought struck a familiar chord in Sammy. Something deeper pushed Al to perfect his technique. He already possessed the ability to defeat four of them, he only lacked refinement and raw speed.

His progress was tremendous. He worked tirelessly. After a few weeks of intense training, Sammy witnessed what he had told Brickert would happen: someone else defeated the four-Thirteen sim.

"You did it!" Sammy shouted. Al was bent over, hands on his knees in the middle of the room, catching his breath. His clothes were stained with sweat and blood and pieces of Thirteen. He stared down at the four bodies that would quickly disintegrate into nothingness.

"Yes!" he growled in a primal voice, and pounded on the floor. Then he straightened up and clasped hands with Sammy. "I spent months on this unit, maybe almost half a year. Marie finally convinced me to move on, reminding me that there was more to being a Psion than just fighting Thirteens. But the day I stopped I felt like I'd done something wrong. So every so often, maybe twice a month, I gave it another go. That feeling is finally gone."

"I knew it," Sammy exclaimed, his face glowing. "I knew other people could do it."

"Can you give me more time?" Al asked. "A few more days?"

"Do you think you need it?"

"Well, I've only done it once. I want to be able to beat them consistently. You said you beat five, right?"

Sammy nodded with only a touch of the old embarrassment he used to feel.

"I don't think I can do five." Al massaged his ribs as he said this.

Sammy knew well the ache and exhaustion that came from hours spent on the trial. He also knew that Al was right. He might be able to beat four Thirteens, but not five. "Okay. First, let's talk about what you did right."

Al threw his head back and let out a tired laugh. "That's a very tactful way of putting it."

⑤ ⑤ ⑤

To prepare for the upcoming mission, Sammy began covert operations in his own sim time. It was unlike anything he had experienced before.

It was fun.

Gone were the room's bright white walls, the appearing and disappearing enemies. Rather, with each different trial, the room transformed into a new setting. Byron gave him one or more assignments to complete within an allotted time. In his first trial, the sim placed him in an old building with no cameras or motion detectors.

"Your objective is to enter the guarded room without your face being seen," Byron informed him.

The floors were littered with moldy paper and broken tiles and the wallpaper peeled back in several places. A flickering light bulb hung over Sammy's head, swinging in its socket each time a puff of warm air ejected from an air vent on the ceiling. Sammy smiled at the dramatic effect. He crept down the hall keeping close to the wall. Around a corner, he spied a guard standing in front of a doorway marked "Restricted Access." Sammy doubled back to the light and smashed it with a simple blast.

The guard cursed and called in the damage while turning on his flashlight. Sammy stole farther back down the corridor until he came to a fire extinguisher hanging from the wall. Quietly, he detached it and gave a test spray. A white fog burst out of the nozzle, filling the hall with a heavy chill. Sammy sprayed the fire extinguisher ahead of him as he walked the rest of the distance.

- 275 -

"What's going on? Someone there?" the frightened voice called. The flashlight's beam lit the fog up like lightning in a heavy storm.

Sammy heard the guard's footsteps running toward him and dropped onto his belly. The moment he saw the man's feet, he blasted them. The guard hit the ground with a dull, "Ooof." Sammy grabbed the man's head and forced it into the dirty broken tile, ignoring the muffled, panicked cries. With his other hand, he yanked the keycard off the guard. No sooner had he crossed the threshold of the restricted room, then the entire hologram disappeared.

He progressed through dozens more of these trials quite rapidly. They grew more challenging as past units had. Sometimes the missions focused completely on stealth; occasionally a Thirteen or Aegis would surprise him; and other times Byron asked Sammy to pull off several objectives with nearly perfect timing. Sammy enjoyed them all. They were a nice break from the constant violence-demanding combat units. He was careful to learn the principles involved, knowing they would be needed not only for his own Panel, but during Al's mission to Rio.

Between the covert sims and training Al, the weeks flew by. Sammy's feeling about the mission was like a pendulum swinging between apprehension and excitement, changing hour by hour depending on who was speaking to him.

And if the looming mission and all its pressures weren't enough, Sammy also worried about Jeffie's increasing distance from him. Since their disturbing duel and the cryptic conversation that followed, she'd noticeably withdrawn from their group of friends. She spent more time with her roommate, Brillianté, went to bed early on the weekends, and though she was just as friendly, Sammy felt that spark they had between them had been lost.

Sammy could not, as Brickert suggested, pass this off as a bizarre side effect of Jeffie's menstrual cycle. He looked for moments during the week to get her one-on-one so they could talk, but they never seemed to be alone at the same time. When the weekend came, he hoped to find an opportunity during their ample down time, but Saturday's Game was long and grueling. And on Sunday, Jeffie fell ill and didn't come out of her room.

"How do you know she's sick?" Sammy asked Brilliante when she gave him the news. "You're not a doctor."

Brilliante gave Sammy a sour look. "Duh, Sammy, she's been in the bathroom all day."

"Doing what? Throwing up?"

Her expression turned impatient as she turned to leave. "As if it's your business."

He kicked the wall, sending a dagger of pain up his leg, and wrote it off as a bad day.

Monday morning, Sammy's com informed him of a change in his schedule. He would be let out early from simulations, have a half-hour for dinner, and then meet the mission team in sim room ten for special training. He knew he should've been excited about the mission training sessions, but all he saw was less time to spend around Jeffie. And so, later that day, after wolfing down a lonely dinner, he ran up to the sim room to find everyone already there and waiting for him.

The sim room was much larger than Sammy's normal training space. He wondered if it was designated specifically for this type of use. Everyone became quiet as Al spoke.

"We have two solid weeks to run through the most accurate simulations Command can give us before we go to Rio. We'll be branching out to different sim rooms to work out the finer points of your individual assignments. But today we're going to spend the majority of our time working together in this main room.

"We need to learn how to react to different scenarios as a team and in our smaller groups. We'll start by learning every step of the mission together, so everyone knows exactly what everyone else is doing. Let's plan on spending at least three hours here each night."

They spent the first training session walking through each step of the mission as the sim room replicated different parts of the building using the reconnaissance of NWG satellites and intelligence photographs. Al led them up to the security room to show Gregor and Li exactly where their work would be taking place. He took them to the control room where Martin and Cala needed to be to turn off localized power systems so the other four could do their work, and he made sure Sammy, Kaden, Kobe, and Marie knew where each bomb-camera would be placed.

The factory had three floors. Sammy and Kobe had to plant four bomb-cams on the top level. Sammy was in charge of the left side, Kobe the right. The entire floor was a large, open manufacturing center with an enclosed inner room in the middle. Both the outer floor and the inner room were designed for mass-production: a vaulted ceiling with large skylights, dozens of automated robotic arms, conveyor belts, and other modernized factory equipment were all there. Sammy and Kobe had to ascend the walls and place the bomb-cams where the wall met the ceiling. The demolition of the building required the bombs to be set exactly right.

The climb reached about seventeen meters. The only tools they had were their blasts and a pair of slivers. Their slivers were razor sharp and fortified with tungsten carbide, shaped into long, thin daggers with thick handles. The super-hard blades easily plunged into reinforced brick or anything softer. Al also gave them special shoes with two-centimeter-long spikes built into the toes. Between blasting, the slivers, and the climbing shoes, they wouldn't have any problem scaling the wall. The trick was learning to stay balanced on the wall while mounting the explosives in the dark corners.

It was impossible for the room to simulate the height of the factory walls, so Sammy and the others couldn't practice the climbing. Instead, they focused on mounting the cams while using their slivers a few meters off the ground.

Staying up was tricky. If Sammy leaned back much at all, his center of balance tipped, and recovering it was almost impossible. His movement had to be slow and deliberate. The four of them spent several hours practicing and laughing at each other when they fell. Once, Sammy even saw Kobe chuckling with him. But for the most part, the two partners spoke as briefly as possible, and only when needed.

When the four climbers weren't rehearsing the mounting process, they watched the other team members do their work. Al wanted everyone knowing exactly what the others were doing at any time during the mission. They worked and worked at it for a week until Sammy believed he could mount each cam blindfolded and drugged. When he told this to Al, the response was, "Good, that's exactly what I want."

Al's team was excused from the Game on Saturday so they could begin running mission scenarios. Sammy felt no sense of loss; by the time Al called it quits, he had an ache in every "climbing muscle" in his body. On the way to his room, he saw his friends in the rec room, but didn't stop to hang out. His eyes almost needed props to stay open, and he'd have time to do all that tomorrow. After days of consuming work, and with an even more stressful week ahead, Sunday promised to be a nice break.

Nine months ago you were nothing more than a juvenile anarchist, Sammy told himself as he stared at his reflection in the bathroom mirror. *Now look at you. Don't even have time to hang out with your friends.* The thought almost made him laugh, but he realized it wasn't very funny. In fact, it wasn't really funny at all. *Who have I become? I'm nothing like the person I was a year ago.* The questions danced in his mind late into the night.

He awoke late the next morning with a headache and a sore body complaining that it hadn't finished sleeping. After showering, he headed to the cafeteria. A few Betas were hanging around, but none of his friends. He sent a text to Brickert asking where he was, and ate breakfast while waiting for a response. When nothing came, he sent a second text.

Still nothing.

He had a nasty feeling that he'd been left out, and he tried to shake it by searching headquarters for his friends. He asked around, but no one had seen them. Frustrated, lonely, and hurt, he went back to his room, picked up a book he'd grabbed from the library, and flopped onto his bed. He hadn't been reading for more than ten minutes when Brickert poked his head in the door.

"Hey, Sammy. Come on, let's go."

Sammy sat up in bed. "Where have you been? Why didn't you answer my texts?"

"We're out on the grounds goofing off."

Sammy saw the pink spots on Brickert's nose and cheeks, the watery eyes stung by cold. "Are you crazy? It's November."

Brickert just shrugged it off. "It's not bad out today." Sammy started to argue, but Brickert cut him off. "Are you coming out or staying in, Mr. Bookworm?"

He gave Brickert a petulant stare. "I'll come outside, but I'm taking my book . . . just in case."

"Just in case what?"

"In case you-know-who isn't in a good mood and ignores me all day."

"She's not evil, I'll tell you. And she's been talking about you all week—saying nice things, too."

"Why didn't you tell me?"

"Probably because I've hardly seen you since Sunday, and whenever I do see you, you're just running off somewhere else."

"Come on, not my fault. I hardly get time to eat."

"Relax," Brickert laughed as he pushed Sammy out the door. "I'm not saying it is your fault."

"So . . ." Sammy dropped his voice so no one might overhear. "What's she been saying?"

"Oh, you know, she wants to marry you—have your kids—that stuff."

"Har. Har." Sammy pushed Brickert in the back and messed up his hair as they walked onto the grounds.

Brickert had been right. It was an unusually sunny day for early November, but the wind had teeth. Not that it mattered. All Sammy thought about was how Jeffie had been "talking highly" of him.

They found the girls lounging on a sunny spot of grass with Asaki and Brillianté. Sammy could hear them talking in the distance, laughing at something. They sounded almost . . . mischievous.

The laughter ended the moment Sammy arrived. Something was fishy, and when he looked at Brickert, he could tell his friend knew something about it. Then, almost imperceptibly, Jeffie scooted over from Brillianté so he had room to sit by her. How could she go from evading him the past two weeks to wanting him next to her? The answer didn't really matter. He was happy with what he got.

"Hiya, buddy," she said with a goofy smile.

"Hiya back," he answered. "What have you guys been doing all day?"

No one seemed to want to answer until Kawai finally spoke up. "Nothing much. Just hanging out."

"Uh, huh." He didn't believe a word of it. "What's the plan for the rest of the day?"

"We were thinking of checking out the water works they just put in over by Hilltop," Jeffie answered. "Want to get wet?"

"Serious? I'm already cold just sitting here. If you're really going, I'll just watch."

"Sure you will," Jeffie said, smiling wickedly.

The afternoon spent at the water works with his friends was the only real bright spot in Sammy's week. Monday sent him back to the grind, with extra hours after sims to prepare for the mission. The days slipped away quickly, and before he knew it, it was Saturday, and they were conducting their last rehearsal before show time.

"NO!" Al shouted to Kaden during one of the run-throughs. "In an emergency, use the nearest exit. For you, that's the one in the back of the factory."

It was Saturday afternoon, two days before the mission, and tensions were peaking. They'd been working scenario after scenario the last five evenings, and Al had thrown the latest and toughest at them: a detonating bomb-cam. They had practiced it several times, but still struggled to meet Al's expectations. His frustrations mirrored the rest of the team's.

"Sorry, Al," Kaden responded as he wiped the sheen of sweat from his forehead, "it's just that all of the other exits are on the other side of the factory. I keep forgetting about the one in the basement."

"I didn't mean to lose my cool. My bad." Al looked even sorrier than Kaden. He checked his watch and made a grimace. "Let's take a fifteen-minute break. Sammy, can you stay behind for a bit?"

"Yeah," Sammy answered, not at all surprised by Al's request.

Jealously, he watched everyone else file off to the cafeteria and went to Al who was staring at his hand-held panel, digesting the information it contained.

"I don't know, Sammy," he said, shaking his head as he read more data. "Do you think we're going to be ready by Monday morning?"

Sammy did not bother to hide his dumbfounded expression. "Are you joking me?" he asked Al.

Al did not answer him.

"Al, this team is very ready to go."

"But you just saw that we still can't—"

"Get out in the minimum amount of time. In the worst possible scenario. One which we have almost zero chance of facing. I understand, Al. You're worried. You're supposed to be. But we've all made it out way under the maximum amount of safe time on several runs. Be optimistic. Everything's going to be fine. I'm not lying. This team is very ready."

Al's serious expression gave way to a reluctant smile. "You're right. Thanks. I get it from my dad. I always get really worked up about the unknown, you know?"

"It's cool."

"How do you feel about the hot fields? Better?"

Sammy shook his head grimly. He hated the hot fields. "Truthfully, not much better. Why not send one of us into the inner room? It'd be so much—"

"Mission rules. You have to be within viewing distance of another Beta at all times."

Sammy kicked the floor lightly with his shoe. Stupid rules. "I'd like to have a few runs through it again . . . just in case."

"Okay. Then let's do it again."

One of the scenarios Al threw at them was based around a temporary return in power from a secondary source. This caused the hot fields on the top floor to come back to life, and cut off access to all escape routes for Kobe and Sammy.

The inner room on the top floor had no windows or doors. The only way in or out was via one of two long, low hallways about six or seven meters in length. Within these hot fields were a dozen revolving heat beams threatening anyone who dared to attempt unauthorized entry. The beams were hot enough to burn clean through human flesh and bone, leaving a surprised intruder with a finely cauterized stump.

Normally power in the halls turned off when Martin and Cala flipped the breakers, but if a backup system kicked in while Kobe and Sammy were in the inner room, they'd be stuck. The only way to turn a hot field off was manually deactivating it at both ends of the hall. And that meant someone had to go through first. Al had appointed that task to Sammy. In his first few attempts getting through, he'd "lost" three legs, four arms, an ear, and half of his head.

The hot fields were nasty enough with the lack of maneuverability and extreme danger, but the heat rays were also completely invisible. Learning through trial and error, he'd figured out where the beams were by watching which direction the beam emitters faced. After several attempts, he'd made it through without touching a beam, but his success rate was still only about sixty percent.

After the break ended, Al asked each partnership to go and work on their toughest assignments. Sammy went to a sim room with Kobe and loaded up the hot field scenario. His partner leaned lazily against the wall, observing. His first attempt ended badly, caught in the back by a beam. He didn't even realize he'd messed up until the hologram shut off. He suppressed a long string of swear words and went back to the panel. On the other side of the room, Kobe let out a long audible sigh. Sammy was about to say something rude, but held his tongue.

He was more wary during attempt number two. Moving into the field, he gingerly sidestepped the first beam, keeping an eye on both the next one and the one behind him. *Here it comes . . . Here it comes . . .*

"Watch your heel, it's about to sweep back your way."

Kobe's voice surprised Sammy. He'd never offered his help before. But without thinking, Sammy pulled his foot to a safer spot, then swiftly slipped under the next beam.

"You have just a few seconds now before it doubles back and takes your head clean off."

Again following Kobe's advice, Sammy hovered in a squat to allow one beam to go over him while the other passed harmlessly under him. Kobe kept up a constant stream of direction, and Sammy managed to get through the hot field in record time. He loaded it again. This time he relied more on Kobe to watch his back.

Just after his sixth attempt without a mistake, Al summoned everyone back to the Arena for one last run through. It went very well, despite a kink thrown in as a surprise. In fact, Al could not think of a single point of improvement. "Great work, guys. I don't think anything will happen on Monday that we can't handle. Tomorrow is off. Monday morning we leave for Rio."

There were no cheers as the team broke up to gather their things, no high fives, just an anxious silence. Al approached Sammy as everyone else was leaving.

"How did the hot fields go?"

"Real well. I think Kobe and I can guarantee you that if we need to make it through, we can do it."

"I'm sure you won't, but I'm happy." Al gave Sammy a pat and left the room.

With a slight frown, Sammy watched Kobe put on his regular shoes. He did not know what to think about him now. Kobe had given him so much trouble. But all of a sudden, he didn't seem like such a terrible guy. In fact, Sammy felt a certain kinship knowing that if nothing else, he could trust Kobe with his life.

"Hey, Kobe—thanks."

"No sweat." Kobe shrugged his shoulders so casually that it looked anything but casual. "But this doesn't mean we're friends."

"Believe me, I know."

Kobe let out a bark of a laugh. "And I'm still gonna call you hot shot."

"I wouldn't have it any other way."

⑨ ⑨ ⑨

Sunday morning was long. Trying to avoid thinking about the mission only made Sammy think more about the mission. The gnaw of fear, the wrenching in his stomach, the sweaty palms were all constant reminders of what waited for him tomorrow. To make things worse, he had the oddest sense when he woke that he was forgetting something. He checked his com calendar, but nothing appeared on his schedule.

To help keep his mind off the mission, Brickert and Jeffie forced him outside even though the temperature had dropped dramatically in the last week.

They played blast ball, a game Al said had been invented long before his time at headquarters. Jeffie was probably the best at it because of her accuracy with blasting. She particularly enjoyed knocking Sammy's ball off course. Thanks to her, he came in last every game. When they'd finished, he again had that same sense of forgetting something.

"What's that look for?" Jeffie called over to him, reading his face as only she could. Brickert tossed a ball to Sammy, who blasted it midair and caught it.

"Nothing," he said, then he threw the ball at her.

She redirected the ball via blast back to Brickert. "C'mon . . . tell me."

"It's just one of those things, you know, when you feel like you're forgetting something."

"I know what it is," she teased.

Sammy feinted a low throw and Jeffie bit. Before she had time to react, he changed to a high throw and it sailed past her. "You can't possibly know what I don't know."

"Oh, but I do." She wasn't lying. And he could tell she wasn't going to tell him, either. "You hungry?" she asked Sammy, but she also glanced back at Brickert who was jogging toward them now.

"I don't know. Are you?"

Jeffie rolled her eyes and snagged the ball from Brickert so she could bump Sammy's head with it. "How can you not know if you're hungry? Let's go."

He was glad to get out of the cold. It took him a while to warm up once they were inside. He missed South Africa's warm Novembers. *November* . . . A light went on in his head. He stopped at the doorway of the cafeteria and said, "I remember! It's my—"

"HAPPY BIRTHDAY!" a tremendous roar shouted from inside.

"—birthday," he finished slowly, in awe of what he saw.

The cafeteria light flickered on, revealing seventeen Betas wearing pointed hats and smiles. Festive decorations had been splashed from ceiling to floor. Streamers, banners, and more than anything else, large number 1s hung on the walls. Sammy just stared, too stunned to react. Several hands reached out and pulled him inside. One pair put a party hat on his head, another shoved presents at him.

All the preparation for Al's mission had driven his birthday from his mind. It did not help that he had not properly celebrated his birthday in two years.

"You sneaky devils!" he declared to Brickert and the three girls as they grinned happily, quite pleased with themselves for pulling everything off behind his back.

It was a great birthday party. Someone had made the Robochef work overtime. Everywhere he looked was more food: pizza, chicken, coconut ice cream, pies, a layered cake filled with cream and yogurt, and cheesecake just for Brickert. The food was delicious, the games were fun, and it seemed that everyone had bought Sammy a present. His favorite part of the evening, however, was when everyone sang "Happy Birthday" in a strange but beautiful mixture of languages and tunes.

After two years of receiving no presents, Sammy was overwhelmed with gratitude. Only two people had any clue what the gifts really meant to him. But instead of crying, he laughed himself silly when he opened the presents, revealing the contents of each one to be different articles of clothing. Apparently during his nine months at headquarters, someone had taken notice that he either wore jumpsuits or the same red hoodie and jeans that he'd worn on his very first day. All told, he received two new pairs of jeans, four new hoodies, some tee shirts, a few new pairs of shoes and socks, and lots of under-shorts. The only person he could not find a present from was Jeffie.

The festivities continued into the evening with dancing. But at 2000 Al asked everyone who would be leaving the next day to retire. The mood quickly became somber, and about half the Betas left. Sammy stayed a little longer to thank everyone a third time for his gifts. Brickert told him not to worry about cleaning up and gave him half a hug, wishing him the best of luck on tomorrow's mission. Sammy looked around for Jeffie, but she had disappeared.

He deliberately took his time walking downstairs in case he might catch her, but he never saw her before reaching his dorm. In a last attempt, he sent her a short text asking where she was. When he remembered that she had not been wearing her com at the party, he gave up. Betas typically did not wear coms on Sundays, especially if they were all together.

Reluctantly, he undressed and showered knowing he wouldn't want to when he woke up early the next morning. It was awkwardly quiet in the bathroom and passing other Betas in the halls. The usual bantering as they stood side by side at the sinks was starkly missing. After stalling as long as he could, Sammy went to bed. He didn't think he'd be able to sleep with all the jumbled and pent up emotions flooding him. He was wrong. All the work he'd done had a toll, and it was collected that night. He fell asleep almost immediately and had no dreams of Thirteens chasing him into bloody dead ends.

17 | Rio

AL SHOOK SAMMY awake.

"O-four hundred," his voice whispered. Sammy couldn't see Al's face and wondered if he was dreaming. When he smelled Al's morning breath, he knew the truth. "Come on, Sammy, time to get up."

No more words were needed. Sammy knew exactly what was going on and what he needed to do, a mark of how well Al had prepped his team for the mission. His mind was alert—very alert given the early hour. He drew in a sharp breath as the realization hit him like ice cold water: *We're really doing it. Right now.*

He jumped out of bed and dressed in the uniform issued to him especially for this mission. It clung to him differently than his normal jumpsuits, and he wasn't sure if he liked that. Smoky gray, just like the Alphas', but emblazoned with a Greek beta symbol instead of the usual alpha symbol. The beta symbol acted not only as a homing device so Al always knew his location, but it also monitored Sammy's heart rate and respiration.

He climbed the stairs alone and crossed the second floor landing where he had stood awkwardly fumbling out good nights to Jeffie so many times. Just as he was passing, the door opened quietly. Still wearing her night clothes, hair angelically tousled from sleep, Jeffie slid through the crack of the opening, smiling at Sammy. It was an incredible wonder to him how she could look so beautiful straight out of bed.

She smiled brightly at him. He wondered if the beta symbol was already registering his increasing heart rate. *Hopefully not.*

"Hiya," she said sleepily. Her voice sounded somewhat huskier because her nose was stuffed. Sammy thought it was really cute.

Jeffie, you are perfect. "Hiya, sleepy," he replied.

"Nervous?" she asked.

"No, not really."

"Liar." Her smile got bigger. "I wanted to see you before you left. Sorry I disappeared last night, but I got your text."

"Where did you go?"

"Dealing with stuff."

What could she possibly have to deal with on my birthday?

"Don't worry about it," she said when she saw his perplexed look. "I have to give you your birthday present."

"Oh. No, you don't have to—Don't worry about it. I can't even take it with me right now," he said.

"Shut up, Sammy," she said with a little push. "You can take it with you."

He opened his mouth to tell her that she was wrong, but Jeffie was moving closer to him. His brain buzzed softly, clouding out other thoughts, and whatever he had thought was important became utterly immaterial.

Wait, he wanted to scream out. *She's so close to me. What is she doing?*

He tensed up, his back stiffened into a board. Since his parents' deaths, touch had become a foreign language to him. But Jeffie seemed to ignore his hesitance, and softly slid her arms around him in a hug. The embrace was amazing. No one had touched him like this before. It was much more . . . romantic? *Is that what this is? Romantic?* Gradually, he relaxed and hugged her back, trying to mirror the intensity he felt from her.

What does this mean? Is she trying to tell me something?

But he knew she had never hugged him like this before. She was so close to him, filling his senses with only Jeffie. For several seconds, he stood apart from the world, holding Jeffie and savoring every smell, every texture, the sound of her breathing, the sight of her so close to him.

When she pulled away, a piece of him went with her, and he doubted he would ever get it back. It would always be hers. Her eyes were redder than he had noticed before, and he thought they might even have tears.

"Are you okay, Jeff?"

"I'm fine," she answered him with a fleeting smile and a downward glance.

He decided it was not the time to argue the point. "Okay."

"I'm only going to give you half of your birthday present now. The other half you get when you come back safe. Got it?" Her voice was huskier than ever.

"Yeah. I got it."

"Close your eyes and don't open them until I tell you."

Sammy did what he was told, thinking of how strange she was being. He felt Jeffie's lips press against his cheek. With eyes still closed, he jerked his head back slightly, then got control over himself. His head went light as blood rushed from his brain, which only buzzed more noisily. *This means she likes me, right? She actually likes me?!*

The place on his cheek where her lips had touched tingled. He reached up and lightly felt the spot. His nostrils filled with that rose scent he had come to associate with only her. Her warm breath tickled his ear, warning him again of the nearness of her presence. Then he heard the faintest of whispers: "I'll miss you, so you'd better come back to me . . . fast."

The door to the girls' dormitory emitted a soft snap, and Sammy realized he was alone again on the landing. He squinted through his eyes, just to check. She was gone. His face had gotten awfully warm and his fingertips tingled a little. His heart was doing jumping jacks up to his throat. And the mother of all smiles stretched from ear to ear.

I could die right now. Brickert's wrong. Girls aren't stupid. They're amazing.

She'd had such a powerful effect on him that he had briefly forgotten about the mission to Rio de Janeiro. He stood there for a moment longer with eyes glazed until it popped into his brain that he needed to be upstairs with the team. He hustled up the next flight of stairs and joined the team in the cafeteria. Inside, Al was making everyone but himself eat breakfast.

No one spoke much. Sammy was able to get down some oatmeal, but his stomach must have shrunk. He mentally ran through the mission to ensure himself he would not forget a single step. At 0440 Al stood up.

"Any last words before we go?" he asked.

No one said anything. Sammy grabbed his glass of water and started chugging it because his mouth had gone very dry.

"Let's move out."

Almost in unison, everyone put their coms on. Sammy swung his leg over his chair and followed Al to the roof. They took the special staircase past Commander Byron's suite and came to the roof door.

The sun hadn't risen and the sky was clear enough to see a few stars. Sammy was glad for some reason. He rarely got to see stars. The air was pleasantly nippy and smelled fresh. In the middle of the roof a small, elegant atmo-cruiser waited for them. The noblack exterior told Sammy this cruiser was built for stealth first, everything else second.

It was an average-sized cruiser, capable of carrying no more than a dozen or so. With the noblack coating, a group could get in and out of an area without triggering any form of scanning surveillance. The structure of the ship was made to absorb radio waves, conceal thermal and electronic detection, and, in dark enough surroundings, block reflection of most light off its surface.

A door in the cruiser's side opened. The rear of the ship contained a small cargo area, which besides containing the team's packs and Al's portable command station, also doubled as a small medical station with several emergency supplies, fire extinguishers, and food rations. The rest of the ship held seating for two pilots and ten passengers.

Sammy and the rest of the team went to the cargo space and grabbed their packs. The pilot was an Elite. Sammy heard the pilot's voice in the cockpit, hailing NWG Flight Command for departure clearance. The team moved to the passenger area. The climbers put on their climbing shoes and secured them. Sammy strapped himself into his seat as Al slipped into the co-pilot's chair. Then he and the pilot began methodically preparing the cruiser for take-off.

The engines hummed as the ship came to life. The pilots exchanged low murmurs of conversation going through the starting up cycle. Sammy glanced nervously at Marie. She smiled back at him as if to say, "Don't worry. He's a good pilot."

In a matter of minutes, the cruiser was cleared for take-off and began its rapid ascent from the ground. "Estimated time of travel: two hours and twenty-three minutes," Al announced.

Sammy gazed out the window as the cruiser headed west, picking up more and more speed. It was not long before the landmass of Capitol Island disappeared from view, replaced with the inky blackness of the Atlantic Ocean stretching out impossibly endless in every direction.

Far above the ocean, the cruiser passed through a storm that spattered bullets of rain on the small windows. Thoughts and memories chased themselves through Sammy's mind. He'd arrived at headquarters nine months ago, almost to the day. All of this because of his anomaly. Anomaly Fourteen. Had it not been for the abilities, he would be back in the Grinder right now, trying to figure out another way to escape. It seemed to him miraculous that such opportunities had come along in his life, changing him so drastically. Without them, he would never have met Brickert . . . Jeffie . . . . everyone . . . wouldn't even be on this cruiser right now. He took comfort in the idea that when it was his turn to lead a mission, his best friends would be coming along.

"We're now flying over CAG territory," Al announced. Everyone understood what that meant. The cruiser slowly dropped in altitude, and their speed noticeably decreased. It was only a few minutes later that land came into sight. The great city of Rio de Janeiro.

The city itself, divided into several zones, boasted world-famous beaches and historical sites. It was the industrial North Zone of the city that housed the factory they would be sabotaging.

High enough to discourage curiosity, and low enough to quickly dip down for a safe blast-landing, Al skillfully flew the cruiser over the beaches and into the heart of the industrial district of the city. Several enormous skyscrapers passed by on the south. Sammy saw a red button blinking on the cruiser's control panel. Al reached up and pushed the button. That was the team's cue to move to the cargo area.

"Your ship," Al told the Elite pilot. He unbuckled himself and joined the others in the cargo space. "About thirty seconds until we fly over our jump site. Everyone get ready."

The side door of the cruiser opened again, letting cool air swirl around the cabin. The air smelled different to Sammy, dirtier and heavier than the air around Capitol Island. The ship flew relatively slow approximately a hundred meters above the ground.

"Hold on to something," the pilot warned them. In one smooth movement, the cruiser turned and sharply dipped down. Sammy could not see the factory yet, but Al began counting down.

"Three."

Al stepped to up to the doorway. Sammy thought he could see the factory now.

"Two."

The factory landing space was coming up fast.

"One."

The cruiser leveled off a little over one hundred meters above ground, still too high for a Psion to safely land with blasts. Al jumped out the door, free falling in a spread eagle formation to slow himself as much as possible. Everyone quickly followed him out. Sammy was the last. He tried not to think too much before he leapt. Giddiness, terror, and perhaps some craziness were all bundled up inside him. All he could do was grin and throw himself out. The cold air nipped his ears and nose, and whipped his curly hair as he fell. Seeing the ground rush up closer and closer gave a high nothing else could match. Down below, Kobe and Kaden whooped and laughed. Sammy grabbed two small loops on the sides of his suit and pulled hard. Two large flaps of cloth like miniature wings billowed out, reducing his velocity by over a third. This made it possible for him to land-blast without dying.

He dropped his feet and blasted hard several times to kill his speed. His feet touched down on the dusty earth over fifty meters past where Al landed. After zipping off the flaps and stowing them into his pack, he craned his neck upward to see Al's portable command station gently floating down on its parachute. It landed only a few meters beyond.

The landing area was an unpaved square open at one end to an industrial back road that appeared fairly well-used. The rest of the square was enclosed by the factory's horseshoe-shape extensions on two sides and a long loading dock that faced the road. The dock had two large ramps and several heavy-duty rolling doors for deliveries. The team met up at the portable station and moved it into the shadow of one of the ramps.

It took less than ten minutes to nestle it into place. Al ran checks to make sure he could communicate with everyone over their coms. Then he gave Gregor and Li the go to enter the building.

The U-shaped factory was by no means picturesque, but Sammy thought it could have been much worse. At a glance, he could see that the center section of the building had been built first, the wings added on later by what must have been a penny-pinching owner because the original section looked in better condition than the additions. It was a windowless stucco building. Once a magnificent, gleaming-white facility built to impress the eyes, produce cutting-edge communication products, and prevent industrial espionage, now it looked dirty and forgotten. The paint was chipping badly and cracks in the stucco were racing several long vines up the walls.

Sammy, Kobe, Kaden, and Marie split from Cala and Martin. The four climbers jogged up one of the ramps onto the dock and crossed its length. A small metal door used for parcel deliveries had been built right next to an employee entrance on the far side of the dock. Fortunately, it was wide enough that if they took off their packs any skinny person could fit through it.

"We're in position," Marie reported to Al in her com.

"Great," Al answered. "Hold tight. The others are still working."

The four climbers already had a good idea of how long they had to wait. Routine practices had taken no more than ten minutes and no less than seven for Gregor and Li to handle the security. Then it took about fifteen minutes for Martin and Cala to reach the power station in the right wing basement and shut off the selected systems. A slight breeze blew across the square, carrying dust that stung Sammy's eyes if he looked into it. Marie's hair billowed in a mesmerizing sort of way, so he watched that instead. No one had any reason to speak, and the silence both comforted and scared Sammy. The quiet here seemed watchful, but he knew it was only his nerves. He checked the clock on his com every couple minutes. After waiting twenty-three minutes, Al spoke: "So far so good. The security system is hacked. Power's off. The cameras won't be seeing anything interesting. You're clear to enter."

Marie grabbed the handle of the mail slot and pulled, but the door didn't budge. She yanked harder, but it only creaked.

"Al, we're having trouble opening the mail portal."

"Hold on a sec." A brief silence followed. "They're sure they killed the power. You should be able to open it."

Sammy saw the rust collecting all around the exterior of the mail door and got an idea. "Let me try for a second, Marie."

Marie stepped aside. He spread his hands out and blasted as strong of a spread blast as he could. There was a dull crunch of metal on metal, and he pulled again on the slot handle. It opened right up.

"What was that?" Kaden asked.

"Rusted shut," Sammy said, pointing around at what he'd seen. "Just needed a little jarring."

"We're going in now," Marie reported.

"Hopefully, that was the worst of our problems," Kobe said.

"That wouldn't be bad at all," Kaden said. "In and out."

In and out, Sammy told himself. Jeffie had told him to come back fast. That sounded good to him.

One by one they removed their packs and crawled into the large square hole. Sammy entered last, giving Kobe a few moments to get through. He scrambled through two meters of claustrophobic tunnel and entered the factory.

The docking area of the factory reminded Sammy of his old grocery store. It was dirty and dark, with an out-of-order, industrial-sized elevator in one corner and stacks of broken pallets in another. The only sounds came from the tiny feet of mice scratching the floor. Sammy imagined that in a few months there would be a fleet of heavy-lifting equipment in this area. Surveillance would be needed to see who was dropping off raw materials for CAG production and in what quantities. Kaden and Marie would be planting the cams in this main room and in the basement.

Sammy and Kobe headed for the stairs.

The large double doors echoed loudly in the stairwell. The flight of stairs was a long climb surrounded by walls of dull gray cinderblock and abnormally tall steps painted black, chipping and crunching under their weight. Occasionally their climbing shoes made a sharp tink-tink when the spiked toe struck against a stair, creating an oddly wild reverberation around them. The sounds set Sammy on edge.

The production floor was darker than the ground level. A thick layer of soot covered the skylights and the only illumination came from a few emergency lights above the doors. Sammy's eyes needed a minute to adjust to the dimness, but as they did the landmarks he expected to find came into view.

The outer room was equipped for mass production of standardized communications equipment. The inner laboratory was where delicate precision robotics had been used to engineer cutting-edge nano-communication technology. Save for the hot fields on opposite sides, the inner lab was surrounded by a thick wall which completely enclosed the area like a small box inside a much larger box.

As the Betas crossed the room, Sammy noticed the clean floor. He'd expected to see an inch of dust across the floor, but there was none.

"We're at the top," Kobe reported to Al.

"Copy that," Al replied. "Keep me regularly updated on your progress with the mounts."

"Gotcha-gotcha."

They set down their packs and unloaded their equipment. Sammy took out both of his slivers and stuck them in the holders on his suit. Next, he removed a pack that could be secured around his waist and put the first cam in it. Last, he clipped a small light onto his com and attached a thin power cord to his com's own battery.

There was no need for words; they had practiced enough times that each knew the other's routine perfectly. Sammy went to his first corner in the outer area and gazed up at the wall. At seventeen meters, the cams would be well concealed. The lighting in the room, even at its brightest, did not adequately illuminate the ceiling corners.

If everything went perfectly, a single bomb-cam took a little more than forty-five minutes to mount, from scaling the wall to putting in the last mounting clip. Everything had to be done very slowly so his balance wasn't upset.

He climbed onto a machine that looked like a gigantic golf ball made of chrome. Crouching low, he sprung as hard as he could and launched himself high into the air toward the wall. Just before colliding, he pulled out his slivers and stabbed them into the white-painted concrete. The spikes in his shoes dug into the wall making tiny but sturdy catches. He ascended like a spider, taking his time, careful not to make a mistake. It took him ten minutes to reach the ceiling. At the top, he dug his feet into the wall and positioned the slivers so they could act as supports for his arms.

Balancing delicately on his feet, he extracted the mounting drill from the pack around his waist and drove four small holes into the wall. These held the mounting grips. Once the grips were in place, he assembled the mount itself. The mount was small, no larger than a business card on each side. Each of the three pieces had to be locked into place.

His hands were more slippery than during practice. As he finished assembling the mount, he took a moment to wipe them with an alcohol pad. Then came the tricky part. With almost a motherly tenderness, he retrieved the bomb-cam from his pack. Into the mounting it went. He steadied it with one hand and brought out the mounting clips with the other. The mounting clips locked the cam securely into the mount.

In several of the earliest simulations, Sammy or Kobe had accidentally dropped the cam from seventeen meters up. About one out of every six times the cam fell to the floor, it detonated the bomb, all depending on which part of the cam hit the ground first.

It is not good to drop the cam, Sammy had often joked to himself. Right now, it didn't seem funny at all. He held the cam tightly in place while securing it with the clips. More sweat formed between his fingers and the smooth metal of the cam. His fingers slipped right off the cam's surface, smacked hard against the wall, and the cam tumbled out of the mount.

Sammy gasped and fumbled around frantically to catch it, but could not get a good hold. As a last resort, he pulled his spike shoe out of the wall and turned his foot in. The cam bounced painfully off his ankle, giving him just enough time to make one last lunge . . .

Caught it!

Balancing precariously on one foot and clutching the bomb in the ends of his fingertips, he drew it back up. Holding onto the cam with one hand, and a sliver with the other, he put the cam back into the mount and awkwardly thumbed in the first clip with a sigh of relief; the rest of the clips went in much easier. After double-checking his work, he pulled out his slivers and tucked them safely into their holders. Then he pulled his feet out of the wall and dropped silently to the floor. He guessed that by now Kobe had already finished his first cam. Kobe seemed to manage all the clips and drills better. Sammy filled his waist pack with another cam and more mounting equipment.

The next two bomb-cams went in uneventfully. They reported to Al that they'd finished three of the four mounts, and he asked them to take a quick break, no longer than fifteen minutes, then finish the fourth cams. Kobe and Sammy sat together, quietly eating a light meal found in their packs.

Five minutes later, Al's voice came through. "Sammy and Kobe? Marie and Kaden have finished their three cams. They're coming out now. Have you started the fourth?"

"We're both still eating," Kobe answered. "We'll be done in under an hour."

"Okay. I'll set my watch."

The last two cams had to be installed in the inner lab. As Al had assured them, the hot fields were turned off. This did not stop either of them from walking very briskly through the tunnel just in case something unexpected happened.

The inner lab was even darker than the outer area. But this was expected. Having been in a simulation of the room dozens of times, Sammy made it across the lab to his corner without relying much on sight. Because of the delicate nature of the equipment in the inner lab, they had to scale the walls without blasting off any machinery. For the last time, Sammy filled his pack and blast-jumped into the air. Like a cat extending his claws into a predator, he dug into the wall and climbed.

The final install went smoothly. Sammy had just finished assembling the mount and was now ready to put the mounting clips in and secure the cam. About six hours had gone by since the team had taken off from Capitol Island. He felt quite ready to go home.

"Sammy? Kobe?" Al sounded a little tense this time.

"Yeah," Sammy responded.

"I'm having some trouble contacting Martin and Cala. Marie and Kaden are going in to check on them."

"What's the problem?" Sammy asked.

"Probably some interference from their location. How close are you to being done?"

"Fifteen minutes or less," Kobe answered. He was a little bit behind Sammy this time.

"Great. Tell me when you finish."

The two went back to work finishing the cams. Twelve minutes went by and Sammy had barely finished. Kobe was putting in his last clips.

"Guys, get out of the factory now!" Al screamed. It startled Sammy so badly, he almost fell.

"Why? What's up?" Kobe asked.

"Martin— Cala! They're— they've—Oh my—"

"What happened, Al?" Kobe shouted.

"Martin and Cala—" Al said, his voice beyond the edge of panic. "You've got to run. Marie and Kaden found them. They're all bloody. I think—I think they're dead. *GET OUT!*"

In less than a second, a thousand thoughts went through Sammy's reeling mind.

Dead? No. That can't be right.

People don't die on Beta missions.

We aren't really even in danger on these missions.

There must be a mistake. Maybe someone got hurt.

But something clicked in his mind. That voice wasn't Al. Not Leader-Al. Al wouldn't act like that unless something had gone terribly wrong.

Sammy did not want to ask it; he already knew the answer to the question, but he could not stop himself asking. "Who did this, Al?" he half-spoke and half-whispered into his com.

"Thirteens! I—I don't know how, but they're here! Please get out."

13 | Unlucky

FOR THREE SECONDS Sammy froze on the wall, paralyzed. His brain kicked into high gear, analyzing all possible outcomes of the situation. He looked over his shoulder across the room at Kobe, whose com light pointed back at him.

"What do we do?" Sammy flicked off his light, wondering if the Thirteens were somehow already here.

"I've hailed the cruiser to get us. It's coming right now. It will be here in—in under five minutes with its weapons ready in case— in case they come out into the loading area. Just—just make it out here."

"What about Martin and Cala?" The question came from Kobe as his light dimmed to off.

"Marie and Kaden got them. You guys just . . . stay alive."

Kobe and Sammy released their holds on the wall, holstering their slivers. They made their way through the maze of machines to the hot field tunnel. Kobe was closest and ran in the tunnel first, Sammy only steps behind. The lights in the tunnel burst on just before Sammy entered. The hot fields came to life. Kobe stopped in his tracks about halfway through.

"No!" Kobe turned around, then turned back again, uncertain of where to go. "Oh crap. CRAP!"

"Stay calm. You have a few seconds before they heat up. Stay calm! Just do exactly what I tell you. Keep your eyes ahead, and I'll be your eyes behind. Got it?"

Kobe looked ahead and behind, twitchy nervous glances. "I got it!"

Click. Kobe threw himself against the wall to avoid the first beam.

Sammy bent all of his attention on the beams, trying to watch three of them at a time. "Duck."

Kobe ducked as the beam behind him cut over his head. Immediately, he rolled over in a ball across the width of the hall to escape two beams closing in. Another beam moved toward him angled down at his legs.

"Jump!" Sammy ordered.

Kobe blast-jumped too high, crashed into the ceiling, and fell into a curled up slump on the floor.

"Get up, Kobe."

He didn't move.

"*GET UP NOW!*" Sammy screamed.

Struggling to his feet, Kobe obeyed. Where he'd just collapsed, two beams converged making a figure eight. A wisp of smoke trailed from the leg of Kobe's flight suit, and Sammy smelled the unmistakable stench of burned hair and skin.

"Okay, you're clear from behind for a whole rotation. Go as fast and as far as you can."

The collision with the ceiling had left Kobe dazed. He reacted much slower to Sammy's instructions, moved too cautiously. Three times he came close to being burned again. Nearing the end of the tunnel, Kobe paused. Sammy continued guiding him.

"The beam behind you is coming back. You've got to get above it, but still stay under the beam in front of you."

Sammy held his breath. This was tricky. Kobe jumped without a blast, jackknifed his body as the beams passed simultaneously above and below him, and rolled out of the field. Sammy muttered several colorful words in relief. His arms trembled badly and he had to rub them to make them stop. In unison, they flipped the manual releases and shut off the hot field.

"Thanks, man." Kobe took Sammy's hand. "I don't think they're here yet."

"Does that hurt?" Sammy asked, pointing at Kobe's leg.

Kobe shrugged it off. The dazed look in his eyes had disappeared. "I'll worry about it later."

Sammy's thoughts swirled like he'd stuck his brain in a blender. He tried to block everything out but one thought: *Get to the stairs.* Once out, they would either fight or make a clean getaway. *But first we have to make it to those stairs.* Kobe and Sammy sprinted through the outer room toward the stairs.

The doors flew open, slamming into the wall with a *crack.* Instinctively, both boys threw themselves behind the nearest machine. Even in the darkness, Sammy could see the shining blood red tunic that melted into black pants covering a tall lean masculine figure. Blond hair stuck out in tufts from the hood of his blast suit.

Sammy's heart pounded so hard he felt it in his throat. Kobe let out a low groan next to him. Another figure stepped in behind the man, this one more feminine, but with no hair, then a third person, and a fourth. Sammy heard a loud metallic sound coming from across the floor. *The other doors.*

More were coming. He reached down to his side and drew the slivers out. Every part of his body seemed to be aware of the moment. Every hair stood on end and he felt more alive—and more mortal—than he'd ever been.

In his lowest voice he said, "Al, we're trapped up on the top floor. At least five of them are here."

"The Aegis are blocking our entrance!" Al said. His breath made loud hissing sounds in Sammy's ear. "We'll be there as soon as we can!"

Even with all Sammy's training, even with the lifelike holograms, it had not adequately readied him for real battle. He felt a quaking fear growing in his chest. It expanded outward until his teeth rattled and his arms shook again. His eyes watered, and he wanted nothing more than to curl up in a ball and cry out for his parents. Slow, deep breaths helped a little.

If you want to make it out of here alive, control yourself!

The blond-haired Thirteen in front made a sharp gesture with his head. His sudden movement gave Sammy a better view of his face. It was so severely scarred it gave the impression of having been badly mauled by a wild animal. Still, this was nothing compared to the eyes. He had seen their blood-filled eyes in countless sims, but the real thing was much worse. In the darkness, the eyes were more visible than any other feature of his face. Instead of reflecting back the natural light, the dim light only enhanced the blood-colored sclera surrounding each light-less pupil. The effect was two ghostly dots of faded red.

In response to the man's head gesture, the bald female Thirteen ripped something from her belt, kicked open the door, and threw a small object into the stairwell.

BOOM!

A loud explosion sounded behind the steel doors. Small, chilling chuckles followed. The stairs were gone. The other set of doors opened.

BOOM!

Another ripping blast came from the far side of the room. Both stairs were gone. More mirthless chuckles erupted from the Thirteens.

Sammy and Kobe slunk back further into the shadows of the factory, hiding behind the bulky machinery. More odd gestures, like jerks of the head and muscle ticks of the shoulders, came from the lead Thirteen.

They're communicating, Sammy realized. *Why didn't the simulators show this?* The answer came quickly. *Because they can't translate it.*

"Let's split up," Kobe whispered to Sammy when they were behind a conveyor belt that stretched across a large portion of the back of the room. "Make it harder for them to find us."

"No," Sammy hissed. "If we stay together we have a better chance at surviving. Just don't let yourself get cut off from me. They'll be trying to separate us, make us weaker."

Kobe followed him behind the conveyor belt to the far back corner of the room opposite of the side they had seen the Thirteens come in. There they saw five more. At least one was an Aegis, maybe more. Nine enemies total. Who knew how many more were downstairs?

"Kill the Aegis first," Sammy said. "Grab any weapons you can use."

"They'll be useless!" Kobe said, breathing fast. "They'll have identifiers on them."

"Cut off their middle fingers, then you can use the weapon. You don't need ID for explosives, which apparently they have. And if you can't get the finger, break the weapon so they can't use it."

Kobe nodded but with a tinge of paleness in his face.

Sammy knew the Thirteens would try to surround them. He knew their tactics from the sims. *When outnumbered, the attack comes from as many sides as possible.* Only then, would the Thirteens move in.

He led Kobe around the room. *Keep the enemy in sight. Pick them off one by one.* In order to survive, they had to be the hunters. And Sammy was determined to get out alive. He had to live long enough to get back to Jeffie—to get that kiss.

"Sammy! Kobe! The doors to the stairs—" Al shouted. "We can't open them!"

"They've blown the stairs," Sammy's whispers were urgent, desperate. "Find us another way out of here."

"We're working on that right now."

Sammy slunk low behind the base of a gigantic plastic presser. He peeked around the corner and saw an Aegis moving toward them, carefully checking all the little nooks and crannies he passed. Sammy knew they could drop back and find more cover, but sooner or later, they would have to stand and fight. He motioned a quick plan to Kobe, who acknowledged his understanding.

Kobe stood tall, tensing his muscles for one swift movement. Lunging around the corner, he hurled his right sliver at the Aegis. The Aegis reacted quickly, crying out, but he was not quick enough. The sliver stuck him in the chest near the heart. Sammy snuck up behind and sank his own sliver into the Aegis' neck, stopping near the hilt. The cry transformed into a death-filled gurgling sound, still loud enough to attract others.

Footsteps came from three directions. Sammy knew he should run away—knew he had to—but couldn't. The sight of the Aegis dying mesmerized him. He had done this. He had killed someone. It took several seconds to realize he had his hand pressed tightly against his mouth to ensure he didn't vomit.

Every detail that the sims hadn't been able to duplicate etched in his nearly perfect memory: the smell of the blood and sweat, the sound of gurgling blood, the lights going out in a man's eyes. All the kills in the sims had not prepared him for what it would really be like to take a life. He would never forget it. The guilt and confusion would have to be dealt with later. Only survival mattered now. He sliced off the dead Aegis' middle finger and gave it and the gun to Kobe, who accepted them hesitantly.

"Use it sparingly," he told Kobe. After yanking the bloody slivers from the dead man's throat and chest, he and Kobe sprinted on.

A horrific animal-like shriek came out in bursts behind them. *Vocal communications. They don't want their enemies to understand them at all.*

Bullets tore into the machinery and floor sending a shower of metal and debris that landed around them like hail on a tin roof. Sammy held out one of his hands behind him as a blast shield, listening carefully to the gunfire to know what weapons they had. Having no way to escape, he went to the best location in the room to mount a defensive stand. It was a section away from most of the machines so the enemy couldn't shoot down on them.

He could see all of them now: six Thirteens, two more Aegis. Their movements confirmed his predictions. They'd spaced themselves out to try to encompass Sammy and Kobe. Once they were successful, they would tighten the noose.

The tall female Thirteen with no hair made a complicated gesture with her head and hand. It might have been comical in any other situation. Gunfire erupted from three sides. Sammy shielded defensively during the first round of volleys. Always, in his mind, he was counting shots. The sims had taught him it was a key to survival. Then, when two of them had to reload, Sammy wielded his slivers like daggers and ran furiously at the Thirteens who opened fire on him. Behind him, he heard Kobe screaming in anger as he rushed his own targets.

Again and again the Thirteens and Aegis communicated in their bizarre spasms, gestures, and garbled shrieks, coordinating their efforts to surround or separate Sammy and Kobe. But the two Betas were always one step ahead. Every time the Thirteens tried to move behind them, Sammy and Kobe responded by dropping back with shields. This tactic stretched out the Thirteens' offensive, allowing Sammy and Kobe to attack the nearest enemies.

One time the Thirteens nearly did cut them off, but Sammy shielded both himself and Kobe while Kobe used his gun to open up a new hole for them to move through. It was a game of chess being played in one of the deepest dungeons of hell, except that Sammy and Kobe were queen-less because, unlike the Thirteens, their ammo would run out much *much* sooner.

Sammy focused on trying to damage the Thirteens' blast suits. His slivers, though sharp and deadly, were too short to make good weapons unless he used them as throwing knives. But how was he supposed to get them back once he'd thrown them? He settled with slashing and stabbing at the Thirteens when he got close enough, but they were too fast and dodged his attacks.

The Thirteens, it seemed, had figured out that Kobe was the less skilled of the two Betas, and pressed harder on his side. Eventually, it became too difficult to shield himself and Kobe with the slivers in his hands, so Sammy put his weapons away. As he did this, he realized that his fear had all but vanished for now. His mind had reverted back to the cold, calculating methods he had so often practiced in his simulations. They were, in essence, his survival instincts. Kill or be killed. *Til death do us part.* He did not allow any doubt into his mind. Somehow he would survive this, and he preferred to have Kobe leave with him.

Kobe ripped shots at the Thirteens until he ran out of ammo. They moved so quickly, he hadn't been able to hit any of them. Seizing their advantage, the eight mounted a strong offensive, trying to form a tighter circle. Sammy cried out in frustration, blocking another round of fire from three Thirteens. He blast-flipped himself into the air, extending his foot out and connecting hard with the chin of one of the Thirteens. It was the lean man with blond hair. The Thirteen fell back with a dull thud. The toe-spike had split his skin like rare steak, exposing his white jawbone. Blood spilled onto his neck. The man grinned devilishly, wiped the blood off his chin, and licked it off of his hand.

Sammy grimaced as he fell back to help Kobe. Several shots came close to hitting them, but so far they were unscathed, and so were the eight trying to kill them. The noose began to tighten again, and this time it appeared the Thirteens might do it.

A chance appeared when three of them had to reload at once. Sammy's bullet counting had paid off. "Cover my back and follow me!" he told

Kobe. He charged at the Thirteens, Kobe shielding from behind, and ran to the back of the room. Nothing was working. They had nowhere to go. Sammy checked his com. That little battle had not even lasted ten minutes. *What's Al doing!?!?*

They hid once more among the machinery. The Thirteens gave wild chase, making awful high-pitched sounds but barely moving their mouths. Sammy desperately looked for anything he could use as a more effective weapon.

"Sammy! Kobe! You guys still alright?"

Kobe quietly informed Al of their situation.

"We've found an exit for you. The largest robotic arm has its own power feed that runs through a square column right beneath it. That column runs all the way up from the basement to the top floor. There should be small access panel near the floor. Climb down to the ground floor, and we can get you out of here. Do you know which robotic arm I'm talking about?"

"Yeah," they both said.

"Can you make it?"

"Do we have a choice?" Kobe whispered.

"Good luck," Al said. "We're doing all we can . . . and praying for you."

Al sounded like he might break down any moment. *Keep it together, Al. We need you.*

The robotic arm Al referred to was in the outer room near one of the hot fields. Sammy guessed they were about sixty meters away from it. Moving as fast as they dared, they darted in and out of cover, jogging over to the arm. The Thirteens had spread out to look for them, and their angry shrieks echoed from every direction. The robotic arm was close, a beacon of hope just meters away.

But when they rounded a corner, they saw a problem. A Thirteen and an Aegis stood between them and the arm. There was no other choice. The screams of some of the Thirteens behind them were getting louder. Sammy became aware of the warm air radiating from the hot field. It was surprisingly palpable, causing beads of sweat to race down his forehead onto his nose. He blew them off and signaled to Kobe what to do.

Shields ready, they rounded the corner. The two attackers immediately opened fire. Sammy held them at bay while Kobe forced opened the panel with a crushing blow from his spiked shoe. Dozens of wires cramped the working space inside the column, but left enough room for them to access the thin ladder. Kobe went in feet first and waited on the ladder. Sammy shielded until the Thirteen was forced to reload his jigger. The Aegis, out of bullets, dove forward to prevent Sammy from dropping his shield. Sammy blasted him back as he crawled into the space. The Aegis tried to grab Sammy's legs, but Sammy responded instinctively, blasting the Aegis in the chest with his feet. The Aegis flew backward and let out a high-pitched scream that gave Sammy goosebumps.

He could not help but look back as he climbed down the ladder. His eyes confirmed what he already expected to see. The Aegis had landed in the hot field, suffering the wrath of the flesh-searing beams. His body lay in pieces.

At least it was quick. I may not get that luxury.

He climbed even faster, Kobe urging him onward. From above, he heard the Thirteen shouting out to the others scattered about the floor. Kobe spoke to Al via the com, informing him of everything that had happened. When they reached the ground floor and found the exit to the column, it took a solid minute of pounding and kicking to pop open the door.

They were back in the receiving area. This raised Sammy's hopes marginally, but they still weren't outside yet. Somewhere along the line this factory had come to feel more like a giant prison cell. The area was brighter now than before, with thin shafts of light streaming inside around the rolling doors along the south wall. Sammy had expected to see Al and the others waiting for them, but they were nowhere to be found. Yells and shouts leaked from under the door of the nearest stairwell.

"Where are you!?" Kobe yelled into his com.

"On our way!" Al answered.

At that same moment, the stairwell door burst open, and two Thirteens charged out, their blast suits covered in dust and rubble from the fallen staircase. Sammy and Kobe shielded themselves, but the Thirteens ignored them and ran to the large delivery doors.

"What are they doing?" Kobe asked.

They watched the Thirteens stop every ten meters and then continue running. Sammy looked back and saw red lights blinking on each of the doors.

"Al, stay back from the dock!" he shouted. "They're putting proximity mines all along the south wall. You can't get near it without blowing yourself up! We'll use our blasts to set them off and come through the wreckage."

"If that doesn't work, your only other choice is to head for the exit in the basement," Al said. "Which one's easier?"

The infamous basement exit. The one Kaden always forgot about in their scenarios. "We'll try this first." They ran for the proximity mines as more Thirteens emerged from the bombed-out stairwells.

Like ants coming out of the woodwork, Thirteens and Aegis appeared from everywhere, cutting Sammy and Kobe off from the mines. They arranged their positions perfectly, keeping far enough away from the proximity mines not to trigger them, but close enough to prevent the Betas from using their blasts to set any off. Two more Thirteens blocked off any retreat to the basement.

Sammy counted them: eight— ten—*twelve.* They moved close to the tall column for better cover.

"What do you want from us?!" Kobe's face twisted in rage and spit flew from his mouth as he screamed. The panic in his eyes frightened Sammy. "How many of you do we have to kill before you leave us alone?"

The Thirteens didn't answer in words, but in a storm of bullets which Sammy and Kobe again shielded. At the first opportunity, Kobe went into the air and bounced off the tall column. The two Thirteens blocking their way raised their guns high, faces focused upward like hunters trying to take down a bird. They were getting too anxious, and Kobe had somehow noticed that. Or he was just being very stupid. Either way, one of the Thirteens paid dearly.

With their focus on Kobe, Sammy only needed one hand to shield. He gripped the hilt of his sliver and in one fluid movement sent it flying through the air into the stomach of the bald female. He'd aimed for her chest, but knife throwing wasn't something he'd ever gotten very good at in practice. The fatal intrusion of the sliver into the Thirteen's abdomen didn't even make her blink. Blood and other stuff poured from her wound, but she continued shooting with an intensity bordering on psychotic, perhaps pushed to a more frenzied state knowing her death was imminent. Kobe landed behind her and the other Thirteen blocking their path.

Sammy took advantage of the moment again. His second sliver went straight into the other Thirteen's back, piercing his heart. He fell immediately. Out of the corner of his eye, Sammy saw one of the Thirteens take aim at him with a hand cannon. Just as the trigger-finger pulled taut, he blast-jumped into the air, leaving the bleeding female Thirteen exposed. Her body was riddled with shrapnel.

The path to the basement was clear.

Kobe ran ahead, yelling into his com; Sammy raced to the steps in the back of the receiving area that led downstairs. Behind them, the Thirteen who'd shot the female, roared and screamed unintelligible things at the others.

Sammy slammed the steel door shut behind them, throwing down a locking bar securely across the doors. He felt no sense of relief when the lock clicked. They jumped down the stairs and blast-landed safely at the bottom. They entered an enormous stock room filled with row after row of towering empty shelves that formed a labyrinth of zig-zagging halls. The air smelled dirty and stale, but it was much cooler down here. A gritty dust covered the floor, and Sammy could see Kaden and Marie's footprints in the filth.

Pounding echoed in the distance. "The bar won't hold them for long," he called out to Kobe.

The two Betas leaped through the shelves rather than navigating around them. Cobwebs stuck to Sammy's face, but he moved on, faster and faster as though the devil rode his tail.

The stock room took up over half the basement. The other half was devoted to three hallways lined with administrative offices. The paint on the walls, probably once pristine and white, peeled yellow and brown like someone's business left in the toilet. The floor's threadbare green carpet looked like the surface of an algae-infested pond.

This is it, he thought in jubilation as he ran through the halls, *We've made it! We're going to live!* But as he got nearer to the exit he noticed something was wrong.

Something was very, *very* wrong.

The entire wall—the wall where the exit was supposed to be—was sealed off in fresh red brick.

"No!" Kobe yelled. "NO. NO. NO."

"This can't be right!" Sammy shouted both to Al and Kobe.

"What's the matter?" Al asked. "Are you at the exit yet?"

"It's bricked off!" Kobe screamed and pounded and blasted furiously at the bricks, but did no damage. "What are these bricks doing here, Al? You were supposed to have good intel."

"What are you talking about?" Al asked again.

"The exit is bricked off." Sammy shot off several blasts of his own at the wall, but it held strong. "There is no exit."

"How can that be?" Al asked.

"What do we do now?" Kobe asked.

"Stall them!" Al ordered. "Stall them until we get there. We're going to get in one way or another."

"And how do we do that?" Kobe yelled.

"I have an idea," Sammy said. "Follow me."

He led Kobe back through the halls to the stock room. As they ran, his mind turned wheels about the brick wall.

They knew we were coming. Somehow they knew. This whole mission's a trap. The brick wall must have been added after Command took surveillance of the factory. The Thirteens forced us this way knowing we were running into a dead end. Trapped. Just prey now.

The panic spread through him like a malignant disease, quick and lethal. *I have to slow them down,* he told himself. *Prolong the moment when they come to kill us.* It was with great caution that they opened the door to the stock room. Sammy heard sounds in the far distance. The Thirteens were in the stock room, but nowhere close by.

"We need to push over these shelves," he told Kobe.

Together they shoved and pushed against the closest giant shelf, but could not get enough leverage to topple it. The voices were getting closer, but still out of sight. After resting for a moment to regain their wind, they tried a new tactic. Climbing to the top, they put their backs against the wall and their feet on the edge of the metal and pushed as hard as they could.

"Use a blast," Kobe grunted through his teeth.

Sammy strained until he felt the shelf give.

The massive wood and metal shelf tipped over onto the next row, upsetting two more shelves. When the combined force and weight of three shelves fell over onto the third row, the effect began to spread like dominos. Shelves toppled everywhere. Thirteens shrieked warnings in the distance, and the two Betas ran back into the office hallway. The offices were locked. Rather than trying to force their way inside, Sammy and Kobe took refuge in a bathroom.

The bathroom reflected the same neglect as the rest of the basement. It reeked of human filth. One light above the sinks still worked, and when they flipped it on the squalor of the room came into view. The floors were filthy, the toilets full of mildew and excrement. A long mirror that graced the wall of sinks bore so much dust that it barely reflected anything. All of this felt fitting to Sammy. It resonated with the way he felt. No sooner had the door closed than the panic inside overtook him. He sank to the floor, covering his face with his hands.

The dam of emotion broke. The terror, the exhaustion, the killing, and the madness raging as a malevolent storm all erupted at once. The emotion flowed down his cheeks in hot tears, wetting his hands. He didn't know what to do, and he couldn't figure a way out of this. Especially not with so little time and so much at stake.

We're backed into a corner. We're the king in the corner surrounded by ten queens. "Checkmate," he whispered so Kobe could not hear him.

The Thirteens had ten, maybe more of them, in blast suits. He and Kobe had no space to fight. No weapons. No hope of winning. He was going to die in a stinking hellhole of a bathroom and be buried underneath the rubble of the walls and ceiling.

"What are you doing?" Kobe pulled at Sammy to get him to his feet. "Get off the floor and figure out a way to save us!"

"I can't, Kobe. I can't do it anymore." Sammy brushed Kobe's hands away. He knew he was on the verge of hysteria. It was like standing on the edge of a sheer cliff, toes hanging over the side, and a strong gust of wind blowing at his back.

"You have to!" Kobe grabbed Sammy's shoulders and got into his face. "You're the one with the brains! You're the one who is supposed to be able to do anything!"

"They're going to kill us in here. It's checkmate."

"Then we're both going to die!"

"I DON'T WANT TO DIE!" Sammy screamed back, leaning over the abyss of insanity now.

"*NEITHER DO I!*" Kobe answered him. Sammy hid his face back into his hands, but was instantly jerked again. Kobe had grabbed his collar and shook him hard. "So get it together so we can give it our best shot. That's all we have left."

The shaking calmed Sammy down. Kobe was right. There was still one last choice. The very last choice. Go down fighting, or go down without honor. Like a coward.

I'm not a coward. I am a servant of the people. My life is not my own.

It took him several deep breaths before he was ready to get off the floor. He wiped his eyes and looked at his partner. "If we do make it out of here alive, no one needs to know about that little bit of craziness, right?" he asked Kobe, almost smiling.

"Sure they do," Kobe said.

They shared the shortest of laughs. Two boys, now friends, waiting for an incoming tide of death to roll over them. Sammy thought about his parents, wondering what they might say to him in a situation like this. He had no idea, but he remembered how proud he'd been when he took Byron's oath his first day at headquarters. He remembered the day he'd beaten the four-Thirteen sim. Each of those days he'd felt pride, not coming from himself, but from the feeling that his parents somehow knew what he'd done and were pleased. His parents would want him to fight on. Fight forever. Fight to the death.

"Sammy?" Kobe asked, sounding very worried. "Sammy?"

Sammy broke out of his trance. "Huh? What?"

"What's going on? You all right?"

"Just—just reflecting."

"Well, enough reflection. What are we going to do?"

Kobe's words struck Sammy. New energy filled him. "That's it," he said. "I've got an idea."

"What?"

"We need to break into one of the offices and steal a desk," he said with a small grin. "I'll explain the rest in a second." They hurried to the nearest office. The door, like all the others, was locked. Sammy checked his sliver holders, and remembered his were both gone. "Give me your sliver."

Kobe handed one over.

Sammy jammed the blade into the lock. "I'm going to pick this lock."

"How?" Kobe asked.

Sammy held the sliver firmly in place with one hand, then kicked hard into the butt of the handle. The sliver split the door knob in two. "Like that." The door swung open from the force.

Inside, coated in a layer of dust, was a simple office desk. The legs wobbled and the wood felt like cheap plastic, but that was good since they had to carry it back to the bathroom. They stood it upright near the door, leaving just enough space for the door to open without interference. Then they took down the bathroom mirror. All in all, preparations took less than ten minutes.

It's not much, Sammy thought as he looked over their work, *but it'll have to do.*

They stood side by side like kids in a tiny sandcastle waiting for a huge tidal wave to wash over them.

"Seems silly now, doesn't it?" Kobe asked right before Sammy thought the silence might drive him crazy.

"What's that?"

"All that fighting we did . . . you know, back home."

"Oh, yeah. That. I guess so."

"I'm sorry, man," Kobe said. "For all of it."

Sammy heard something in Kobe's voice that he had never heard before: humility. It touched him deeply. "Me, too. I was just jealous of you and Jeffie."

"So was I. Of you."

For some reason, perhaps they needed a break from the hopeless despair they felt, chuckles came from both of them. Then it was quiet again.

Sammy wasn't sure, but he thought he heard voices in the distance. "Kobe, listen, if somehow you make it out of here and—" He found himself choking up at the thought of it. He swallowed hard and forced himself to continue, "and I don't—for whatever reason—could you tell Jeffie something for me?"

"Sure, anything," Kobe said. His voice was soft and didn't sound at all like a sixteen-year-old's should.

Sammy heard the sound again. It was definitely a voice. People were coming. He was sure Kobe had heard it too. He smiled to himself wistfully, and touched his cheek, imagining briefly that he could feel warm lips pressing it once more. "Tell Jeffie she reminded me of my mother."

Kobe didn't answer for several seconds.

"I'll tell her that," he finally answered. Then he added, "If you don't make it out."

The sounds grew louder. Sammy could now distinguish the shrieks of different Thirteens. Thuds and bangs of doors being kicked open and desks being overturned echoed down the hall, foretelling their approaching doom. He thought for certain he would vomit. Any moment now the door would burst open. His fate would be decided. He wondered if his life would flash before his eyes as he died.

Don't be stupid.

The Thirteens were close. The urge to vomit had passed, but his stomach and legs felt like lead. His heart would surely burst out of his rib cage at any moment. He wondered if Kobe could hear his heart beating. Blind terror threatened to devour him whole.

Kobe whispered Sammy's name.

"Yeah?" he answered almost inaudibly.

"I'd be proud to die fighting next to you."

His words made Sammy feel alive again. He promised himself that no matter the cost, Kobe would get out of the building alive. The Thirteens were right outside the bathroom, their shadows blocked out what little light came in under the door. The door burst open. It slammed into the wall with a deafening BANG, revealing a group of Thirteens standing in the hallway.

Loud shrieks filled Sammy's ears. His field of vision was flooded with images of blood red eyes and horrific faces of varying degrees of mutilation. Sammy felt how badly they wanted to kill him, maim him . . . one of them even looked like she wanted to eat him.

Sammy and Kobe stood on cue, threw their hands out and blasted the huge pile of glass shards they had carefully piled on the desk. The Thirteens had no time to react.

Some of them shrieked warnings. Some just stood in awe of the spectacle flying at them like rain frozen in space. Glass went everywhere, embedding itself into the door, the wall, the ceiling, and most importantly, into the blast suits of the Thirteens. Sammy and Kobe blasted again, this time it was the Thirteens who moved, literally scattering onto the floor. The two Betas jumped over the desk and out into the hall, blasting past the Thirteens still trying to get up. Many of them were bleeding from glass shards still stuck in their chests, faces, arms, and in one case, the eyes. But even this wasn't enough to slow them.

They took up their fighting positions in the hall, each armed with one of Kobe's slivers, Sammy counted the enemy. *Fourteen total. Eleven wounded or with damaged blast suits. Very bad odds for us.*

Taking the battle into the hallway created a space constriction in Sammy and Kobe's favor. Their hope was that the narrowness of the corridor would limit the number of Thirteens that could attack at once. Then, if they had to give up ground, they could retreat toward the brick wall until support arrived.

The Thirteens swarmed onto Kobe and Sammy like angry hornets. Those who were the most damaged held back, trying to get shots on the Betas while the three with undamaged suits fought hand-to-hand. Sammy and Kobe fought well, standing their ground in combat, blasting those that got too close with weapons. The Thirteens' damaged suits could not handle the energy and they flew back each time, some of them badly injured from either the blasts or the impact into the walls.

It didn't take time for the Thirteens' strategy to evolve. The front three Thirteens stayed far away enough to avoid the Betas' slivers, but still absorbed most of the blasts with their suits. The two boys were getting tired, but the Thirteens seemed to get stronger. In sheer desperation, Sammy threw his sliver at the female Thirteen. She leaped into the air, but not high enough. The sliver sank deep into her thigh. Sammy blasted her backwards into another Thirteen who almost shot her in the back, but pulled his gun up just in time to miss her. Chunks of plaster rained down from the ceiling.

Only two blast suits left.

Then Kobe yelled in pain.

Sammy glanced back to see Kobe on the ground clutching his arm. A small chunk of Kobe's right bicep had been torn out from a well-aimed shot. He was putting pressure on the wound to stem the bleeding. The Thirteen who'd done the damage was a short man with scars carved into his face to make a strange pattern. Whipping a spare pistol out from his belt, he pointed it straight at Kobe's heart and pulled the trigger. With his left hand, Sammy shielded two shots from up the hall. With his right, he blasted at the gun. In mid-flight, the bullet was blasted off course, harmlessly striking the wall.

Quick as lightening, the man struck out at Sammy, landing a blow to his face. Sammy stepped back, momentarily stunned. Before he could recover, the man grabbed the fabric of his flight suit, his long claws digging through Sammy's uniform, into his chest, and headed butted him. Sammy brought his knee up, aiming for the groin. The man pushed his hips back and Sammy's knee hit air. Extending that leg out, he blast-jumped off his other foot, bringing his spiked toe into the man's crotch, ripping more than the blast suit. Still clinging to Sammy's suit, the Thirteen cried out in agony. Sammy tore his clothes from the man's clutched hands, leaving two holes in the chest of his garment.

With Kobe down one good arm, the battle quickly turned in favor of the Thirteens. They pressed their advantage, forcing Sammy and Kobe to give up ground in the hallway.

The battle raged on for close to fifteen minutes. Two stray shots had grazed Sammy: one cutting his leg, the other a slash across his rib. The leg wound was the worse of the two. The claw marks on his chest still oozed blood. All the wounds stung, but more disconcerting was his growing weariness which he fought just as hard as he fought the Thirteens. Running out of room, Kobe and Sammy turned the corner, making their final stand with the brick wall only twenty meters or so behind them.

Then . . .

KABOOM!

A tremendous shock wave shook the building. For half a moment, the entire battle stopped as everyone looked around, trying to determine where the explosion came from. No one had an answer. Sammy seized the chance to kick the last undamaged Thirteen in the chest, slashing him deeply with the toe spike. Then he turned to blast two more Thirteens back as Kobe did his best to help. Another shot hit Kobe, and he fell backwards from the blow. Sammy thought his friend might be dead until he saw Kobe half blast, half crawl to the corner of the hallway leaning back against the brick wall in a heap. Six Thirteens had either died or collapsed from a loss of blood. The remaining eight moved in closer for the kill.

Sammy didn't know what came over him in that moment, a sense of duty, a surge of hatred and fury, or a clearness of consciousness. Maybe a mixture of it all. Whatever it was—he saw again. Unlike times past, he did not see the way to win, he couldn't get them out of the factory, but he did see the perfect Sicilian defense.

For five solid minutes, he was nothing more than a blur of blocks and attacks. Never enough to push them back, just enough to keep them at bay. He jumped, dove, sliced, blasted, dodged, and shielded every time he needed to, keeping Kobe and himself alive for just a few minutes longer. Shots rang out in many directions, but Sammy was too absorbed in the fury of battle to allow them to hit him. The closest any bullets came was a third grazing shot that knocked the com off his head. He stopped caring how many Thirteens were dead, but he was pretty sure he got two more of them.

Inevitably, the exertion of the battle took its toll. It became increasingly difficult for Sammy to blast well. His eyes lost focus. His mind became sluggish. *I'm just a little tired that's all. If I just push through and get my second wind . . .* he thought, not realizing he was on something like his fourth wind. It took great willpower to force himself to keep fighting. He felt like he was holding a hurricane back with everything he had inside of himself.

Still, it was six on one. Miraculous as his fighting was, it was not enough. His body and brain had all but depleted his stores of energy. Random thoughts fired through his mind—strange thoughts—distancing his mind from the incredible movements of his body.

I think Jeffie liked Brickert all this time! Ever since I started letting her win Star Racers.

He dodged several rounds and shielded more away from Kobe.

Chicken cordon bleu would be oh so good with a creamy oatmeal sauce.

New sounds came from behind the Thirteens, but Sammy hardly noticed them.

Kawai probably wouldn't eat it. What would Al say about turkey?

A face appeared behind the Thirteens.

There he is. I can ask him.

But Sammy's raving mind did not grasp reality right away. *The Thirteens are turning around. Bunch of yellow chicken sandwiches! Why are they doing that?* he wondered as he fell to the ground in bone-drained exhaustion, shielding Kobe's body with his own and raising his arms to blast away projectiles that were no longer coming his way. Slowly, as his mind came back into focus, he saw that Al was indeed at the other end of the hall. So were Marie, Kaden, Gregor, and Li.

They've finally come to save us! That explosion was them blowing through the proximity mines!

One last surge of adrenaline boosted Sammy enough to make one final desperate move. He grabbed Kobe's sliver and threw it at one of the Thirteens. The man fell to the ground with a groan, impaling the sliver deeper inside of him. His hand cannon dropped alongside of him. Sammy picked it up and used the spikes on his shoe to slice the Thirteen's finger off. He clumsily pulled the trigger and shot a round of shrapnel into the wall.

Oops. I'm more tired than I realized!

He took more careful aim on the second shot and fired at the lean blond Thirteen who dropped in time to avoid getting hit. The Thirteen fixed his cold red eyes on Sammy's weakened state and smiled, displaying the blood smeared on his teeth and lips where the glass had cut him. Sammy sent a blast at the Thirteen's chest, but his target side-stepped it almost casually. *I am in deep, deep—*

Sammy aimed again, this time with the cannon and fired, but all he heard was a click. He threw the gun at the Thirteen and tried to scramble to his feet. It was like trying to pick up dead logs. As he stood, he backed into something cold and rough.

The brick wall.

The man said nothing. He stepped back three steps and pulled something from his belt. It blinked red. Both Sammy and the Thirteen gazed dully at the small object as it flashed the red light.

Sammy tried to remember where he had seen it. He knew he had used those before—*in simulations, yes*—but he could not put his finger on exactly what it was. The light blinked faster, and then he remembered.

A sticky!

The man hurled the sticky grenade at Sammy, who found it immensely difficult to gather the strength to shield himself. It took everything he had left in him. The sticky rebounded off the energy force of the blast, away from him and Kobe, and stuck on the ceiling not more than a meter away from Sammy's head. The light blinked very rapidly now. Sammy threw himself on top of Kobe and curled up on his back to use his feet and hands to maximize his shield.

A loud *BOOM* shook the floor and roared in Sammy's ears.

The explosion ripped into the ceiling and walls. The force of it shoved Sammy backwards, but nothing penetrated the shield he had produced using the last of his energy. From the force of the concussion wave, his head slammed hard into the floor. His ears rang like a high-pitched fire alarm. For several seconds, he saw nothing but stars. Then his vision cleared, leaving him with a pounding headache. He squinted through the pain, watching large chunks of ceiling and brick rain down around him.

One large crack in particular spread down the wall and onto the floor. Sammy heard a loud groaning noise like metal creaking under a heavy strain. A second crack traveled across the floor near him. Small chunks of the floor collapsed into a new hole the size of a basketball, tumbling down into a dark abyss.

Why is there a hole under the floor?

He didn't have time to think as the gap spread quickly toward him and Kobe. He checked to see if his friend was all right, but Kobe had lost consciousness. There was another groan of weight, this one even louder. As the damage spread, the largest chunks of the brick wall teetered dangerously.

"We've got to move, Kobe!" he yelled, shaking his friend.

Kobe gave no sign of waking. Sammy grabbed him under his arms, cursing his friend's weight, and heaved him away from the brick wall. Kobe collapsed back to the floor in a heap, now out of danger. Sammy was finally able to catch a glimpse of the battle raging on between his friends and the Thirteens just down the hall.

The blond Thirteen who had thrown the sticky bomb now lay on the floor, badly burned. Al and the others were still locked up with the few Thirteens standing. They seemed to be winning. His heart soared.

We're going to live, he thought. A feeling of tremendous relief flooded him. *I'm going home.*

Just as he thought this, he heard a loud crack.

The hole in the floor grew rapidly, the ground gave out beneath him, and he, too, fell into the hole. He looked up and saw the brick wall crashing down over the hole, sealing in darkness all around him as he fell down . . .

down . . .

    down . . .

        down . . .

            down . . .

18 | Falling

Al AND MARIE STOOD side by side blasting back bullets when an explosion rocked the hallway. A cloud of dust and smoke billowed toward them, obscuring the end of the passage and denying Al the chance to see if Kobe and Sammy had survived the detonation. Even his nightmares had never been this bad. How had things gone so horribly wrong?

The Thirteens had discovered their plans to bug the factory, they had blocked off their exits, and somehow the cruiser's long-range communications equipment had malfunctioned making it impossible to contact Command for help. It was the worst possible scenario.

Al asked himself again and again if he'd done the best he could, wondering how many more lives this failed mission would cost. Near the end of the hall, a burned and beaten blond Thirteen screeched out in a raspy, fading voice. The remaining Thirteens immediately began to retreat, running out the exit through a haze of smoke and dust where the brick wall had stood.

The shouts pushed thoughts of Martin and Cala away. Marie and Gregor dashed after the Thirteens. Li hobbled behind on his hurt foot. "Let them go!" Al called out.

They stopped.

"Where are Sammy and Kobe?" Gregor asked.

The dirty fog soon lifted, and Al's heart almost failed him. He didn't see either of them.

"Kobe!" Kaden yelled, seizing chunks of brick and heavy ceiling plaster. There, lying half-buried under the huge mound of rubble was a blood-and-muck covered body with familiar blond hair. Al and the others raced over to help lift the debris off Kobe. In little time, they had recovered Kobe's bleeding and bruised and probably broken body. Kaden rested his ear near his brother's mouth and listened.

"He's breathing," he announced with a relieved smile, though tears ran down his face.

Al felt some relief. "Let's find Sammy."

No sooner had they started digging through the mound of dirt then Gregor shouted to Al, "There's another bomb. We have to get out!"

"Get Sammy first," Al ordered.

"It's a class-C bomb, Al! It'll go off any second. We have to leave now or none of us go home alive."

Al froze, torn in half. He could not decide what to do. *I don't want to do this. Please, God, don't ask me to do this. He fought for me. I can't abandon him.*

Marie grabbed his arm and whispered urgently, "We have to go, Al. Now."

Al knew she was right, but he didn't respond. That way, at least, he would never have to say he gave the command to leave Sammy behind.

Marie led him out the same way the Thirteens had gone. Behind them, Gregor and Kaden carried Kobe. Li hobbled out last. The factory's dimness gave way to brilliant daylight. It surprised Al that it could be daytime with all the darkness inside of him.

Dead bodies of the Thirteens who had only just fled were strewn over the walkway and lawn. The cruiser's guns had mowed them down like a nasty bit of crabgrass. Once his team was safely out, Al turned to go back to get Sammy.

Another explosion went off. It seemed to rip the very air around him. Perhaps the whole earth was being torn asunder. Al was knocked down onto his back as a fireball spat out of the factory. He gasped for air, trying to regain his wind.

"Sammy!" he screamed through coughs and sputters. Smoke filled his lungs as he stared into the flames. Thick black fumes poured from where he had stood only seconds before.

"Al, please," Marie said in a quiet but strong voice, pulling at him, "we have to get out of here."

Al would not budge. "He was my responsibility."

"*Please.*"

He knelt on the grass, holding himself. He couldn't remember ever feeling so terrible before. Only a day ago, he'd considered himself to be the most capable Psion Beta ever produced from headquarters. "I've failed, Marie. I lost Martin and Sammy. Maybe Cala and Kobe."

"The sooner we get back, the sooner they can get medical treatment."

He knew she was right. *Save those who can be saved, cry later.* Steeling himself against his emotions, he got to his feet and ran with Marie to the cruiser. Gregor and Kaden were strapping in Kobe next to Cala. Bloody and beaten Cala.

"Get us out of here now," Al ordered. His voice broke, but he did not cry. He did not want to spend another second in this forsaken pit. The pilot took off before he had even strapped himself in.

⑥ ⑥ ⑥

Somehow, despite his crushing fatigue, Sammy managed to weakly blast one final time, cushioning his fall so the landing did not kill him. He hit the floor with a smack, pain shooting through his legs and arms. A weak scream came from his mouth but seemed disembodied to him. He didn't know what he was doing anymore. It took minutes before he realized he was lying down, he was so drained.

Bruised, bleeding, aching, exhausted, he rested his head on the stone floor. The coolness of it was blissful against his cheek, better than a pillow at the moment. For an unknown time, his mind floated freely along whatever absurd, random thoughts would carry him—in and out of sleep. Peaceful sleep in the perfect dark.

He lost track of time in the consuming absence of light. When he finally woke, he thought his head had been stuffed full of wet cotton balls that shifted around every time he moved. His body hurt from his toenails to his hair. He didn't get up or even try to move, but lay there serenely wondering why it was so quiet and dark. His unconcerned state ended when he remembered falling down a hole. He sat up quickly, ignoring the headache that hit him so powerfully it seemed his skull had been placed between an anvil and mallet.

I have to get back to the group.

"Al!" he shouted into his com. His voice sounded like an old saw digging into fresh wood. "I've fallen down a shaft or something. I don't know—it's too dark to see anything."

No answer.

"Al, do you hear me?" he asked. His voice started to sound more normal.

Instinctively he reached up for his com to adjust the earpiece, but only felt his ear.

My com! Where's my com?

He groped around blindly in the dark. With each empty reach, he became more frantic, almost clawing into the concrete floor. He suddenly felt terribly alone and afraid. The darkness seemed even heavier, more oppressive somehow, as the reality of his situation hit him.

I'm stranded! They've left me.

Blind, hot panic unlike anything he had ever known flooded his mind. The invisible mallet continued pounding until his head felt ready to split in two. The intense pain made his stomach lurch, and he vomited onto the floor. Blood rushed from his head leaving him light and woozy. He passed out.

⑥ ⑥ ⑥

Al leaned forward in the co-pilot's chair with an idea. Something he should have thought of much sooner. "What does Sammy's monitor show?" he asked the pilot just as they reached the shoreline of the Atlantic.

"Just a second. Let me call up the program," the pilot answered, punching buttons on the display before him. "Okay. What's his code?"

"Uh . . . zero-zero-nine."

A screen came to life. Two flat bars, one red, one green, streamed across in vivid brightness. No heart beat, no respiration. Al sank back into his chair and hoped the pilot would not be so tactless as to offer the interpretation aloud.

"I'm so sorry," was all he said to Al.

"Me, too," was what Al wanted to say, but his mouth was suddenly too heavy to move.

He unbuckled himself from the seat and went to the back of the cruiser to check on Cala. An orange goo covered her face and much of her upper body to slow bleeding and promote healing. Her monitor showed that her heart rate was slow but steady, her breathing still dangerously shallow. *It's a miracle she survived. A true miracle.*

She had been in very critical condition when Marie and Kaden found her in the blood-stained power room. They were all surprised that she was still alive after taking multiple shots to the neck and chest, and then left for dead by her assailants.

The Elite pilot, who had emergency medical training as all Elite must have, did the best patch-up job he could, and then hooked her up to an arti-blood bag. Martin had died long before help had arrived. Kaden had almost gone into shock from carrying Martin's mangled body back to the cruiser. The massive head trauma had left their friend utterly unrecognizable.

Al glanced around the ship at the remains of his team. Kobe hadn't regained consciousness. Kaden was watching over him closely, looking for any signs of instability. Gregor was either asleep or looking down at the ground, Al wasn't sure which. Li sat stone-faced and silent in his seat, his badly injured foot wrapped in bandages.

It was Marie who puzzled Al. She looked sad but calm. Occasionally she looked back at him, but he always averted his eyes. He could not bear to look at her right now. *What is she thinking? How is she so strong and I'm so weak?* Numbly, he sat down next to her and closed his eyes.

Marie. Sweet, beautiful Marie. The girl he would marry in less than a year if their plans worked out. He knew she was ready to comfort him whenever he showed even the slightest need. But he didn't want comfort. No, right now he wanted to scream in rage. He wanted to kill more Thirteens. He wanted to do evil things to them. That secret urge terrified him more than he wanted to admit to anyone, even himself. And since he could do none of these things, and sleep was the furthest thing from his exhausted mind, it would be a long and tortuous journey back to headquarters.

◐ ◐ ◐

Sammy woke up hours later. His first thought was, *What's that terrible smell?*

Then he remembered that he had thrown up. Then he remembered why. On cue, the same terror-laced hysteria he had felt earlier rose up inside his chest like a terrible dragon. This time he was more ready for it. He fought it back, telling himself over and over again that help would be coming, but another voice spoke inside his head, too.

They may not even know where you are.

Yes, they do, he told the voice. *I have a homing signal on my chest.*

His fingers brushed the spot where the beta symbol should have been and found it missing.

The second voice was quick to remind him: *It fell off during the fight. The Thirteen ripped it off you.*

His fingers again felt for it, touching only cold skin with dried blood crusted on. The panic grew stronger. He tasted the bitter flavor of his own blood in his mouth, and the nausea returned.

No com and no homing signal. I'll never be found!

He cried a little, but then began sucking in deep breaths to calm himself. He felt a little better. More deep breaths slowed the panic.

I've got to find something to do. I need light.

He reasoned if he could smell his way back to the vomit, it could be his point of reference. He took both his shoes off, and laid them at a ninety-degree angle near the pool of vomit to point himself around the room. With careful, short steps, he walked away from the vomit, hands outstretched. To keep his composure, he counted the number of steps he took.

Fifty-eight.

Fifty-nine.

Sixty.

Sixty-one.

His fingers hit something. A wall. Sixty-one steps to the wall. He put that important piece of information away, and started counting from one again, now following the wall.

⑤ ⑤ ⑤

When the cruiser was finally within distance to use its short-range communications, the pilot requested emergency medical staff to be waiting at the landing site. Minutes later, after receiving permission to land, the cruiser touched down on top of headquarters. A host of people were waiting for them.

As soon as the door opened, Al jumped out. "We need medical assistance!"

There were a few gasps and mutters of astonishment when he appeared in front of everyone. He had not even thought of what a shock it would be for them to see him with his suit bloodied, ripped, and filthy.

He quickly explained the details of Cala and Kobe's injuries to Doctor Rosmir and his staff as they carried her from the stealth cruiser into a waiting ambulance. Next, Kobe was carefully taken out, and finally Martin's body. It was not until after all this that Al noticed the crowd of people awaiting their return on the rooftop: government officials, Commander Wrobel, other Alphas, and finally his father, face paled and lined with worry. His father pushed through the crowd and grabbed his shoulders tightly.

"Are you okay?" he said, his voice shaking.

Al wanted to say: "Yes, I'm okay," but he couldn't. Everything came rushing out, and he nearly lost his composure. "No! Sir, I'm not okay. Nothing is okay right now. We lost Sammy and Martin!"

"What do you mean?" his father asked.

"They're dead and it's all my fault."

"Samuel and Martin are dead?" his father repeated. His grip slackened, but his face became stone.

Al nodded solemnly, tears forming in his eyes again. He recognized the face his father wore now. It was the one he put on to control himself, to show no emotion. But Al knew how much his father cared for Sammy.

"I'm so sorry, sir. I'm so sorry."

"This is not your fault, Albert. The best thing we can do right now is gather information. We need you to debrief us. We need to know everything that happened. Can you do that?"

Al nodded. His father put his hands back on Al's shoulders and pulled him close.

"Albert, this is not your fault."

"Yes, sir." Al said it, but he didn't believe it.

"Ho Chin?" his father called out to an Alpha nearby.

"Yes, Commander?" Ho Chin answered at attention.

"Please escort Albert to the meeting room on the fifth floor and then contact everyone else who should be there."

"Yes, sir." Ho Chin saluted Al's father and led Al downstairs.

Al walked through the roof entrance and down the long flight of stairs. The door opened up onto the fifth floor, and he saw someone with long blonde hair sitting on the floor in the hall. *Not Jeffie. Anyone but Jeffie right now.* He stopped moving, but the man, Ho Chin, nudged him forward, oblivious as to why Al wouldn't want see this particular girl at this particular time.

He tried avoiding her eyes, but could not help it. He saw in her eyes the same apprehension and terror as he'd seen in his father's. Of course everyone had feared the worst. They arrived home hours behind schedule with no word as to what had gone wrong.

Jeffie jumped up and ran toward him. "Al, what happened? Is everyone okay? Where's Sammy?"

Suddenly Sammy's death became even more real. Everyone at headquarters had known about Jeffie's crush on Sammy. Everyone but Sammy, at least. The irony of Sammy's naïveté had become a joke in the circle of the oldest Betas. And now Al had no idea what to say to her.

Jeffie stopped before she reached him, staring at his battle-worn state. He knew she could read his face. The truth was in large bold words all over him; even the way he stood, shouted:

"SAMMY IS DEAD!"

She shook her head slowly, and her lips mouthed the word "no" over and over again. Her neck flushed scarlet, and her eyes dripped the tears he wished he still had. "No!" She slumped to the floor. "NO! Al, Sammy is not dead! Please say he is not dead!"

Al wished he could explain to her how badly he wanted to pull Sammy out of a crushing pile of bricks, how his team had to run out of a building to save their lives, and how it had erupted into a fiery furnace the moment they escaped. But it didn't matter how desperately Al needed to justify his actions, he could not say anything. He knew he would choke on the words when they tried to come out of his mouth. He just wished he could make her pleas stop.

It was easy to let himself be steered into the room by Ho Chin. Her sounds followed him into the sim room. Ho Chin excused himself delicately and exited. When the door closed, cutting off Jeffie's pain-filled sobs, a great weight lifted off Al's shoulders. He had never been so helpless before, never in his whole life.

All too soon the door opened again, but Jeffie was not outside the room. It shamed him that he was glad she was gone. The room filled with people who were counting on him to tell them exactly what happened in Rio's death factory. He tried putting on the face his dad used—to cut himself off from emotions he wasn't ready to deal with—and he found that it helped to pull himself together.

Sammy pulled again, harder this time. CHUG! Chug! Chug. Chug. Cough. *Come on you stupid machine. Work for me.*

He kicked it hard.

"OW!" he yelled out. *No shoes on.* He grabbed a hold of the generator's power cord and took a deep breath.

Prime it, a voice said.

"What?" Sammy asked out loud.

The voice was in his head, but it sounded so real and familiar.

"You've got to prime it, kiddo," his dad said to him on a hot Saturday afternoon.

Samuel Senior stood on the back porch laughing at his son who wanted badly to mow the lawn. Normally Sammy's dad paid a guy to come to their house weekly to mow, trim, and weed, but Sammy wanted to do it just once because it looked fun.

He had even borrowed a little mower that actually ran on petrol. Their neighbor, a strange recluse named Mr. Nemosio, kept it as an antique, and Sammy wanted to try it out. "What's the point of having it if you never use it?" he'd asked, stumping the man.

"What do you mean 'prime it?'" young Sammy asked his father.

"There's a little button on the side of the engine. You press it a few times to prime the engine for starting up. Prime it."

Sammy pressed the button several times. Then grabbed the power cord and ripped it.

VRROOM! The engine roared, coming to life.

"Atta boy, Sammy. Make sure you take that back to Mr. Nemosio all cleaned up . . . and don't cut your toes off!"

Sammy let go of the generator's pull cord and felt around in the dark for a primer. Sure enough, not too far away his hand touched a large rubber button. He smiled to himself in the darkness. He mashed on it several times until he was sure the generator was good and primed. Then he felt his way back to the power cord and gave one more hard pull.

CHUG! Chug! Chug! Chug! Chug! Chug! Chug!

Lights flickered on, a few of them burst, and Sammy had to squint until his eyes adjusted to the blinding illumination. The large blue generator against the side wall came into view first. The room told its own story about its purpose and history: furniture scattered, ripped, and overturned; broken equipment strewn across the floor; blood stains one of the walls and the carpet. Someone here had found big trouble in a bad way. Two of the walls were lined with dusty shelves holding big plastic cylinders. He went to the shelf and opened one of the bins expecting to find more junk.

To his great delight, he found dried food and preserved water, most of it untouched. He remembered what Al had said in their first mission meeting: "CAG troops shut the factory down by force when they discovered it was also a secret operating facility for NWG resistance fighters."

In all likelihood, the room had been their storehouse. Food and water storage, broken equipment, an empty rack that looked like it was made for rifles . . . it made sense. When the CAG ransacked the place, they must have killed everyone present and searched everything, including the stuffing of the furniture.

He went through each of the food and water containers so he knew exactly how much he had. When he finished, he set about making the place fit for human use. He didn't know how long he'd be there, but luck favored the prepared, as his mom liked to say. How much luck he had left, he didn't want to find out.

⑤ ⑤ ⑤

Al did not sleep the first night back home. He kept replaying the debriefing over in his mind, the hours of discussion with Alphas and Command where and when each incident had happened. Despite everything that had gone wrong, the Panel still grilled him on his performance. Going over every excruciating detail had been wearisome and troubling. In the end, the Panel had made their decision about Al's leadership. Their words still echoed in his thoughts:

"After careful review of your leadership and decision-making throughout the entirety of the Rio Factory Mission, we have concluded that you, Albert Hayman, have surpassed all expectations, and we give you full recommendations for graduation into a Psion Alpha squadron."

Alphas and members of Command had come to him afterward, giving him resounding praise and accolade for his highly intuitive ability under the hottest of fires. But their words did not calm his storm of doubt. Nagging questions formed clouds in his mind. And the darkest of these remained the same: What happened to Sammy?

It wasn't enough knowing that Cala's condition was gradually improving, and that she would recover to at least some degree. Or that Kobe was already moved from serious condition to steady recovery. Martin was certainly dead, but he had to know about Sammy. Had he been alive when they left the building? And if so, whose fault was it? Whose hands bore Sammy's blood?

The need for answers drove sleep from his mind and fatigue from his exhausted body. Sleep wouldn't come, so he got out of his bed and slipped into a fresh jumpsuit.

He'd always liked the tranquility of headquarters at night. Over his nearly seven years here, he'd discovered the best cure for sleeplessness was more time in the sims. He'd been up enough during the wee hours of the day that he'd even gotten to know the names of all the ladies who cleaned the building top to bottom each weeknight. Tonight, though, the only sounds in the building belonged to him. He went to the fifth floor, to sim room one, and eye-scanned the door open. The white walls were ghostly pale in the dim lighting, but Al paid no attention to anything but the panel on the wall.

He touched the screen and it glowed with life:

Enter Command:

Al keyed in,

Beta Mission Logs

Please specify:

Rio Factory Mission Log

User Name:

Albert Hayman

Please verify with password and retinal scan:

MaLCovas

After the eye-scan, the panel began to separate millions of pieces of information into categories: Voice Recordings, Mission Checklists, Vitals, Tracking Signals, etc. Al began to realize just how much work it was going to be to cross reference hundreds of targeted pieces of data, and recreate the whole mission through voice feeds, time data, and vitals. *Weeks, maybe months.* His whole body let out a great yawn. Hot chocolate was his beverage of choice on late nights. He hurried downstairs to get it, and when he came back, he went to work.

🌀 🌀 🌀

Solitude and its accompanying loneliness had never been a problem for Sammy. He'd been lonely many times, particularly right after his parents' death, and had managed himself fairly well. But this was different. He had *no one* to talk to. So, on his fifth day alone, he started talking to himself. Little things at first, just to make noise, but after a week he was carrying out many of his thought processes verbally. That was as far as it went. When he got so lonely that it became a distraction, he sat down and thought about headquarters. He thought about Kawai's feathery hair, Brickert telling a funny joke, and he imagined getting the other half of his birthday present from Jeffie. That was his favorite memory, even though it hadn't happened yet.

"Someday it will, though. I just have to make sure of it."

From day one, he had set his mind to figuring out a way to make fire. He had no idea when the generator might decide to quit working or when he would be paid a surprise visit and need to kill the lights, so he wanted to have torches ready, just in case. Matches were not among his storage provisions, so he decided to build a small fire from scratch using the spare wood from the broken furniture. Trial and error eventually produced flames, but he quickly doused the hot coals since the fumes had nowhere to go.

Next he looked for a way out of the building. The storage bunker felt like a giant cage. He needed to get out so badly the urge often overwhelmed him. When those moments came, he took a few minutes to calm down, then set his mind to a specific task. His first idea was to build something so he could climb back out of the shaft he'd fallen down.

This idea eventually proved impossible. The opening to the shaft was too high to reach by blast-jumping alone, and he couldn't build anything sturdy to jump from because he had no tools. It seemed reasonable to believe the resistance group must have had a second entrance somewhere, an emergency exit perhaps, to enter and leave the compound.

For days he searched the walls and ceilings for some sign of a door, even a secret one. The room wasn't terribly large, a simple rectangle he estimated to be roughly twelve by sixteen meters. He poured over every brick, hunting for some kind of hint, but with no luck. When he wasn't searching for an escape, he was sleeping or exercising to keep his body in fighting condition.

His diet consisted of nothing but "gruel," as he called it: a soupy mixture of several dehydrated foods. It didn't taste too awful, and he knew how lucky he was to have anything at all, but after living off the wonders of the Robochef, he sorely missed a well-cooked meal.

"They could have at least hauled a stove down here so I could cook," he muttered to himself as he stirred more gruel with a large knife (he had no spoons and only small forks). "They hauled this honking huge generator in here! What's the point in putting it down here for nothing but lighting a few bulbs?"

The thought stuck in his mind for several minutes, and he mulled it over until it became even more puzzling. He had been running the generator almost non-stop for eight days. With almost a barrel of fuel in storage, and the generator using far less a day than he had initially feared, he was not in danger of running out of petrol anytime soon.

"Why would they haul something that big down here? Not just for the lights, right? If there was some kind of secret underground movement, they'd want computers. Radios or something to communicate secretly." He turned the question over some more. "And why would they make it so hard to find a way out?"

He tasted the gruel to see if he'd gotten the flavor mixture right. It tasted a little bland, so he added some salt. It helped a little, but his thoughts stayed on the generator.

"No. Not just for lights. How much power would it take to constantly run an interactive hologram? Would there be enough from a gas powered generator? And where would they hide the projector?" he asked himself. "That's got to be right! There's more to the bunker than just this one room. A hidden entrance, not a secret escape. Clever."

Using couch legs wrapped in cloth dipped in petrol, he made several torches. Then he turned off the generator and waited. It took almost half an hour before all the lights finally faded to black. The only illumination came from his torch. It cast a dancing light on the nearest bricks. Carefully, he walked around the perimeter of the room searching for a door, a gap in the wall. He ran his fingers along everything. It caught him by surprise when his fingers finally touched something that felt as smooth as steel.

It was the door, painted to look exactly like brick. Looking at it straight on, the door looked just like part of the wall. A masterful painting job. No doubt, when the power was on, the door could be perfectly concealed with an interactive hologram that looked and felt just like cold hard brick.

The door didn't have a knob but a grip built into the door to turn. It was pretty jammed, but after several minutes of hard work, he got it open.

He didn't know what to expect to find on the other side, but he certainly wasn't prepared for the stench that assaulted his nose.

"Ugh. Is that bird crap?" he asked himself.

He surveyed his surroundings by torchlight. The concealed room was much smaller than the main room, almost like an antechamber, and filled with two things: maps and birdcages. Sammy doubted map stores held as many maps as he saw here. The three dozen or so birdcages almost all held at least one bird skeleton.

He decided to investigate this room later. Right now he needed to get out of the building. He needed to see the sun or moon, or whatever was up in the big endless sky at this hour. Across the bird room was another door, not hidden, not painted, just a plain door. Its handle was badly rusted and its hinges protested in loud squeaks when he opened it.

A rich earthy smell greeted him. The concrete floor was gone, replaced by something spongier. Sammy pointed his torch downward and saw soil and moss. It wasn't in a room, but in a tunnel carved from the dirt and supported with wooden pillars. With torch in hand, he followed the path.

He could only estimate the distance he walked, but guessed it to be at least half a kilometer when the tunnel ended at a wooden staircase. The air still smelled no more hospitable than it had at the beginning of the tunnel, and that didn't seem to be a good sign. As the stairs climbed closer to the tunnel ceiling, his hair brushed against the hard dirt above him. He reached up and felt a trap door embedded in earth.

He gently pushed on the wooden trap door to see how easily it would give. He pushed harder. The trap door didn't budge.

"Can't you go a little easy on me?" Then, setting down the torch, he began to heave against the door, shoving it up with all his strength. He was so desperate to get out of this bunker that the aching in his shoulder didn't slow him down. Only centimeters away from freedom.

Eventually the door moved slightly, then a bit more. Giving it one last hard shove, he heard a loud rip as the door gave way to fresh air. Sammy breathed it in deeply. Dirt cascaded into the tunnel on his head as he opened the exit wider, looking up to see the twilight sky and grass blades peeking out over the edge.

Grass. There's grass planted above this thing, and I just tore a big hole in the yard. He stamped out his torch with his spiked shoes and climbed out of the tunnel.

Once he got his bearings, he realized he was on the lawn of a large chemical manufacturing plant across the road from the Rio factory. After smoothing the grass back as best he could over the doorway, and sticking the smoking torch into the ground several paces back from it as a marker, he crossed the street, headed for the factory.

Somewhere in the very back of his mind, he held a glimmer of hope that someone, whether friends or Alphas, were still there trying to find his body, ready to take him home. He had not even realized how badly he wanted someone, anyone, to be there until he crossed the square where he'd landed. The thought of seeing someone he knew brought moisture to his eyes.

"I'm coming," he whispered. "I'm coming right now."

The building was deserted as ever. Refusing to let himself cry, he navigated the wreckage of the factory slowly, taking it all in, not really knowing what he was looking for. Bullets and shrapnel littered the floor like junk food at a movie theater. Puddles of coagulated blood looked like spilled soda stains. But he saw no corpses.

In the basement, the hole he had fallen through was still buried beneath the huge pile of the charred brick and plaster that had caved down in the explosion. Much of the doorway and some of the hall had been blown out. Sammy wondered if that entire side of the building was safe. Out the exit he and Kobe should have escaped through, he saw the shells of more bullets, more blood stains on a concrete walkway, but still no bodies.

"They came and cleaned up," he told himself. "And they'll be back soon if they're going to use this place to make weapons. Can't stay much longer."

He wasn't ready to go back inside the bunker. He had a theory he wanted to test out. With his ample spare time, Sammy had devised several hypotheses to explain how Al's mission had gone so badly. His best idea was that the Thirteens had learned about Psion Command's pre-mission surveillance. Acting under the assumption that Psions would come back, the Thirteens made a few key changes to the factory and kept it under constant surveillance. This would have allowed them to dispatch a response team when someone spotted Al's team arrive.

That was his most optimistic theory.

His other guess was that someone, either on Al's team or higher up, had betrayed them. That person would have tipped off the CAG as to when they would be arriving, where they would be stationed, and what exits they would be using in case of an attack.

He felt compelled to at least try to see if the surveillance cameras in the factory would give any more information. The entrance Gregor and Li had used was still intact, allowing Sammy access into the left wing of the building. The path to the security room had been burned into his brain from hours of practices. Lots of equipment was scattered over the room.

On one wall was a large screen divided into over a dozen segments, each segment broadcasting live feed from the cameras still intact.

The hacker hardware Li and Gregor had used for the job was there, probably abandoned in their haste to leave when Al alerted them. Sammy knew enough about it to get it started, and then, through a mixture of memory and trial and error, figured out how to use it to hack the system and search the security archives.

It took him a couple of hours, but he finally found footage of the brick wall being constructed by two men in dirty work clothes smoking pipes. That had taken place only two weeks before Al's mission.

He went even further back into the records, trying several different cameras. He tried larger spaced areas like the lobby, the production areas, anything that would show the presence of Thirteens or Aegis in the building during the months just before Al's mission.

Nothing.

Either there truly was no footage or tracks had been hidden very well. Almost as an afterthought, he checked the camera watching the loading dock. It was easy to sift through the data; all the cameras were motion-activated. Most of the footage was of stray dogs or birds wandering through the zone. He sped through a scene of a car passing through the loading area, hit rewind so he could watch it again at normal speed.

A large, black sedan rolled past the dock and stopped almost right where Al's command station had been. Two Thirteens came out of the door near the mail slot, Sammy thought he recognized them from the factory, but wasn't quite sure. The rear car door nearest the Thirteens opened and they got in. As the car sped off, something caught Sammy's eye—something familiar. He rewound the scene again, slowing it down this time so he could watch the car closer.

His finger holding down the play button started going numb. A nasty feeling settled in his stomach. The car drove off again. Sammy rewound and played it again.

"Who is that?" he whispered. Then he played it again.

"NO!" he cried.

Still in disbelief, he played it back once more with the highest possible resolution.

"It can't be!" he shouted at the screen. "That can't be right!" The sickness in his stomach was as real as ever, but he couldn't tear his eyes away from the face of the man sitting in the front passenger seat.

The mission had been sabotaged from the beginning.

By Commander Wrobel.

How could Byron allow something like this to happen? Wasn't he supposed to be in charge of everything? How could all of this happen from someone so high up? He knew Wrobel, he'd talked to him, he'd laughed at his jokes. Wrobel had seemed like a genuinely good person. It didn't seem possible. It was just a horrible dream, and maybe when Sammy woke up it would all be a fading memory, and he could breathe a sigh of relief. But, no. It was real. And now, because of it, he was dead to everyone he knew. This thought struck him anew and with greater force than before.

They all think I'm dead. They're not coming back for me.

He had no distinct memory of returning to the bunker until the overpowering stench of bird droppings hit him for the second time, and the sickness in his gut became intolerable. He was not right in the head until the next morning after a fitful night of sleep. The singular thought of what he had seen replayed in his mind so much that his dreams seemed filled with smoky gray blurs resembling Wrobel's face and toppling brick walls.

He lay in his little "bed," not moving more than a few blinks and the occasional shift of weight, letting his mind process scenario after scenario. All of them looked as hopeless as the one before. The Thirteens could come back at any moment to clean up; maybe Wrobel would be with them, just to make sure Sammy was really dead. Once they lifted the brick wall upstairs, it would be over. He could see them repelling down the shaft armed and eager to finish him off. He, with no weapons and no allies, was a sitting duck.

But I can't just leave—where will I go?

A terrible weight settled over his chest, snuffing hope and happiness out of him as he imagined himself dying in a hundred different ways, each of them alone and helpless. That weight of despair grew heavier and heavier until Sammy could scarcely breathe. Even the room grew darker as though his eyes were dimming due to lack of oxygen to his brain.

Just as he was ready to abandon himself to what felt like destruction, the image of Jeffie bloomed in his mind. Her smile and her touch, but most of all, her love lifted the darkness from him. The crushing weight lightened until it disappeared. He sat up with a strange clarity in his mind. Ideas replaced despair, facts scattered away fear. His exodus would have to be smart—smart and speedy. Sammy made up his mind: he would leave as soon as he could. He would get home no matter what.

THE END

AFTERWORD

Thank you for purchasing *Psion Beta*, Fellow Bookworm, if I may call you that. Forgive me for leaving you with a cliffhanger ending. I chose this not to sell more copies of a sequel, but because the story of Sammy becoming a Psion Beta ends here. The story does continue, but is its own tale, and to continue it here would have made hefty reading for you, my friend. Sammy's next adventure, *Psion Gamma*, picks up almost right where we left him. It has also been published and hopefully you will enjoy it as much as you have enjoyed this.

It's quite an undertaking to self-publish a book. It requires a massive commitment of time and work, almost five years for this one book. If you enjoyed this novel, please tell your friends, family, or the person next to you on the airplane about it. I hope to be able to continue Sammy's adventure to the very end.

Thank you **again** for your support. Feel free to share with me your thoughts on Facebook by liking my Author Page, Amazon.com via consumer reviews, or you may contact me personally through www.jacobgowans.com. I will do my best to respond as soon as I can.

Once you have finished the *Psion* series, please check out a new series I have launched, *The Storyteller's Tale*. The first novel, *Flight from Blithmore*, is available on Amazon, Smashwords, and iBooks in electronic and paperback formats. I think you'll love it!

So farewell, Fellow Bookworm, and as my good friend always says … Long live Sammy!

WWW.JACOBGOWANS.COM

CPSIA information can be obtained at www.ICGtesting.com
Printed in the USA
LVOW10s2154200515

439322LV00001B/99/P